THE EXO PROJECT

THE EXO PROJECT

andrew deyoung

BOYDS MILLS PRESS
AN IMPRINT OF HIGHLIGHTS
Honesdale, Pennsylvania

For information about permission to reproduce selections from this book,
please contact permissions@highlights.com.

Boyds Mills Press
An Imprint of Highlights
815 Church Street
Honesdale, Pennsylvania 18431
Printed.in the United States of America

ISBN: 978-1-62979-610-9 (hc) • 978-1-62979-799-1 (e-book)

Library of Congress Control Number: 2016951174

First edition

10 9 8 7 6 5 4 3 2 1

Designed by Barbara Grzeslo
Production by Sue Cole
Text set in Joanna

For Sarah, who loved and supported me as I was
   writing this story;
and Maren, the baby girl who slept in the next
   room as I finished it, and who I hope will read
   it and enjoy it someday

PART 1

EARTH

1

matthew

The sun sizzled red in the sky as the front gate to the compound hissed open. Matthew squinted into the glare and checked his wrist meter. The temperature read 120 degrees Fahrenheit. Even with his radiation suit on he could feel sweat trickling down his neck, his skin beginning to burn under the solar radiation. Matthew gave a glance at the two others who were with him, his best friends Silas and Adam. Then, armored against the sun, they stepped out onto the cracked ground and began trudging toward the freeway.

Decades before, thousands of cars had streamed in and out of the city on this road, but now it was completely empty. The three boys gazed up at the fading billboards as they walked, signs advertising businesses that once catered to travelers: gas stations, restaurants, hotels. In the far distance, the towering skyscrapers of the city loomed on the horizon, the tips of the buildings wreathed in smog. Every few minutes, a transport train slid by on a track between the two lanes of the abandoned highway, windows tinted black against the sun.

Soon, panting, their skin burning, the boys found a station where they could catch the next train into the city.

At the station, a homeless man without a radiation suit was slumped over a bench.

"Give me your suit," he grunted, putting his hand on Silas's arm.

"No," Silas said, pulling away. "Get your own."

"Come on," said the man. "Just for a few minutes. I'll give it right back."

Sweat poured from the man's body and soaked through his yellowed shirt. His uncovered skin was beet-red and knotted through with black dabs of cancer. Matthew looked away, his stomach lurching with the sudden fear that the man would drop dead before their eyes.

At that moment, a transport train came sliding down the track toward them. It drew to a stop and the doors hissed open.

Silas stepped on first, then Matthew.

"Two for the Core," Silas said, then jerked his thumb over his shoulder. "I'm getting his fare."

"No," Matthew said. "Let me pay for myself."

Silas shook his head. "No way. You're not paying for anything tonight."

Matthew opened his mouth again to object, but Silas had already stripped back the sleeve of his radiation suit and passed his bare forearm below the scanner. His ident photo blinked on the screen, along with his account balance, showing a debt of more than 7,000 units. Matthew quickly glanced away and walked down the aisle, pretending not to have seen.

Silas took a seat next to Matthew as Adam paid his own fare. When it was the homeless man's turn, he held out his arm and the screen blinked red: a negative balance of nearly 100,000 units.

The driver shook his head.

"No," he said. "Too much debt. You can't ride."

The homeless man pleaded, his voice rising. "Please. Please, I can't go back out there. You don't understand. You have a suit. I have nothing!"

The driver stood and put one gloved hand on the homeless man's arm, tried to guide him off the transport.

"No, don't! I can find the money." His eyes darted around the compartment, his face pleading. "One of these boys can pay for me!"

Silas and Adam looked into their laps, but Matthew didn't look away.

The driver pushed at the homeless man harder, finally shoving him through the open doors. The homeless man's heel caught on a crumbled piece of concrete, and he stumbled backward onto the platform.

The transport jerked forward, and Matthew turned his eyes to the front of the transport, did his best to put it out of his mind. Tried not to think about whether the homeless man would still be there when they got back, in the exact same spot: dead, his skin baking to a cracked brown in the merciless sun.

At that moment, Matthew couldn't wait to ship off to space. To leave Earth behind. To get as far away as possible from this godforsaken, dying planet.

2

They called it the Exo Project.

It had been almost a year ago now that the announcement had come in over the web. Matthew had been sitting in his bedroom at the time, doing homework and wondering what to make for dinner for himself and his little sister, when his tablet buzzed with an incoming transmission.

Matthew glanced at it. A blue crest flickered onto the screen: the logo of OmniCore, the global Earth government. Matthew snatched the tablet from the desktop, his back going straight.

An official announcement. Everybody on the planet was probably watching it.

There was a silent moment—then the OmniCore logo faded from the screen, replaced by an image of the sun burning hot in the sky. The music in the background was ominous, threatening. Over the music came a man's voice.

"Earth is dying," the voice said, "burning up. Crops are failing, fresh water is becoming harder to find, and the future of the human race is at risk."

The camera panned down from the sun to a vast desert. Ant-like humans staggered across the dunes in radiation suits.

"But there's a new hope for humanity: the Exo Project."

The screen filled with images of serious-looking scientists hunched over lab tables, engineers drawing up 3-D blueprints with their fingertips in holographic computer environments, half-constructed spaceships in hangars, surrounded by scaffolding and showers of sparks.

"Exoplanets are worlds outside our solar system, and scientists have identified thousands of them that might sustain life. Now, with new innovations in cryogenics and lightspeed travel, these planets are within our reach, ready to be explored. There's just one thing missing: You."

Now the music swelled, and the next image that came on the screen was a close-up of a person's face: a young woman looking off-camera, hopeful and determined, the faintest trace of a smile on her lips. Slowly, the camera pulled back to reveal that she was marching across a flat expanse of concrete, carrying an OmniCore flag that flapped in the wind above her head. She wasn't alone. One by one, other people joined her, men and women of all ages, races, and ethnicities, smiling and nodding to each other as they came to march at her shoulder. Soon, the camera had pulled back far enough to reveal hundreds of people, maybe thousands, and the image panned around to reveal what they were marching toward: a spaceport with thousands of ships lined up on the tarmac.

"The Exo Project is seeking volunteers now. The future of the human race lies in your hands."

And with that, the announcement was over. The tablet screen

blinked back to the normal view. In the lower left-hand corner, Matthew saw that he had a new message. He tapped it open with his fingertip. It was a message from the Exo Project. It must have come through with the announcement. Matthew scrolled past a photograph of a young man gazing boldly toward the skies, past the banner commanding him to "Sign Up Now!", and squinted at the fine print at the bottom of the message.

Exo Project participants will be chosen by lottery, Matthew read. *The volunteers selected for participation will be cryogenically frozen for the lightspeed expedition. There is no means of return to Earth. Participants who find habitable planets will be refrozen until the first settlers arrive. Those who do not will take mission-termination pills.*

Matthew's skin felt cold. He wasn't certain what "mission-termination pills" referred to, but he had an idea.

The Exo Project was a suicide mission.

Then Matthew's eyes fell on the last line of the fine print.

The families of Exo Project participants will receive a reward of one million units.

Matthew's stomach dropped.

He had to volunteer. He had to put his name in the lottery.

So he did. And months later, Matthew learned that he'd been chosen randomly from millions of applicants to be part of the Exo Project.

He was going. He was leaving Earth, never to return.

3

At the Core, the three boys climbed off the transport under the shade of the tall buildings and made for the closest entrance. Past the doors, people coming from outside stowed their suits and immediately bought antiox treatments to offset the radiation they'd absorbed from the sun. The boys were low on units, though, so they walked past the antiox kiosk into the tangle of interconnected tunnels and skyways and made their way to the main promenade—a massive indoor thoroughfare of shops and restaurants. They went down to the lowest level and slipped into the darkest bar they could find.

Matthew and Adam sat in a booth out of the bartender's sight while Silas walked up to the bar and pitched his voice low to order three beers. He'd told Matthew about the scam on the transport on the way over—his cousin's friend's husband was a low-level hack at the public information office, and Silas had supposedly bartered a short-term change in the age on his ident.

The bartender wasn't buying it, though. From where he sat on the other side of the room, Matthew saw him shake his head, point at Silas, and begin to speak sharply. Silas's face turned red and he looked like he was about to pick a fight; Adam got up and tried to pull him away from the bar. Somewhere in all the arguing, Silas or Adam must have let slip that they were just trying to show their buddy a good time before he shipped off to space, and the bartender's face softened immediately.

"Well, hell," he said, his voice booming over the din of the bar. "Why didn't you say so? Get him over here!"

At the bartender's prodding the three sat at the bar while he poured them drinks on the house. After the first round, a man sitting at the other end of the bar ordered them another round of beers, then moved closer and slid into a stool right next to Matthew.

"Thanks for the drinks," Matthew said, grimacing at the bitter taste of the beer on his tongue.

"No problem," the man said. "You can pay me back by finding a new planet for us. For all of us. This one's had it."

The man looked at Matthew's face a moment under the glare of the lights just behind the bar. He squinted, cocked his head.

"Jesus Christ," he said. "You're just a boy. I thought the minimum age for the Project was seventeen. Are you even that old, son?"

Almost, thought Matthew.

Matthew was sixteen, but he'd be seventeen tomorrow—the same day he was scheduled to go into the freeze.

When Matthew had received his orders summoning him to report for cryostasis on his birthday, he wasn't sure whether to laugh or cry. He'd known about the Exo Project's age minimum, so he figured they wouldn't freeze him and launch him into space until he was seventeen—but he hadn't imagined they'd schedule his departure on his birthday. It was so soon. He thought he'd have more time to say good-bye.

On the other hand, he'd been the one to sign up for a suicide mission, hadn't he? If he was going to die, he might as well get on with it.

Besides, Matthew had never cared much about his birthday. At school, he had friends who made a big deal of their birthdays every year, threw huge parties with drinks and dancing and tons of gifts. But to Matthew, his birthday was just another day. In a way, getting frozen and being launched into space would make this his most memorable birthday ever.

Then Matthew looked at the postcard again. This time his eyes skipped past the departure date and fell on the destination they'd chosen for him.

Planet H-240, orbiting a star named Iota Draconis. One hundred light-years away. Even traveling at the speed of light in an Exo Project spaceship, it would take a century for Matthew to arrive at the planet. By the time he came out of the freeze, he'd still have only just turned seventeen. But Silas and Adam, his mother, his sister—everyone he'd ever known—would be dead.

Matthew blinked and shook his head.

Best not to think about it.

These thoughts flashed through Matthew's mind in the space of a moment; if the man had been paying attention, he'd have seen it in Matthew's face as a flinch, a microexpression of pain before returning to neutral.

What Matthew said was, "I'm old enough."

17

4

After Matthew, Silas, and Adam finished their beers, the man bought them a round of shots. Before Matthew could protest, a small glass of brown liquid was sitting in front of him on the bar. The man clapped him on the shoulder.

"Whiskey," he said. "Drink up, kid. Might be your last chance."

The whiskey tasted awful, burning as it sloshed down Matthew's throat to his stomach. He coughed, grimaced; the man laughed and bought him another, then cajoled him into drinking it down. As soon as the second shot hit Matthew's stomach, his head went fuzzy. The lights on the ceiling seemed to spin around his head like moons. His stomach lurched. Mumbling some words of apology, Matthew stood and ran out into the blinding lights of the promenade.

He staggered along the walkway, dimly aware of people clearing to the right and left as he passed. Finally he spotted a wastebin, lurched to his knees, and grabbed it with both hands as he heaved into it, the smell of his own retch wafting back up to his nose.

Still gripping the bin with pale knuckles, Matthew rested his forehead on the back of his hand and gasped. He closed his eyes and listened to the footsteps of passersby sound distantly around him as if echoing through layers of water.

The taste of bile coated Matthew's tongue. He lay sprawled in the promenade, his back propped against the wall and his arm still hooked over the edge of the wastebin in case his stomach heaved again. He took deep breaths, willing his gut to be still. Soon, his head cleared, and he opened his eyes to the harsh light. People glared at him and wrinkled their noses in disgust as they passed by.

Dripping with sweat and shame, Matthew dragged himself to his feet. He walked back toward the bar and stopped just outside, looking in the door. At the bar, Silas and Adam bellowed drunkenly at some joke the man was telling while he ordered yet another round of shots. They clinked their glasses together and threw their heads back in unison.

Matthew turned and walked away from the bar as fast as his feet would take him. He didn't know where he was going. All he knew was that he wanted to be somewhere, anywhere else.

Let Silas and Adam have their fun. His friends would be better off without him.

Matthew's stumbling feet took him nearer and nearer to the heart of the city, weaving through the network of indoor tunnels and windowed walkways. Gradually Matthew realized that he was walking to the cryocenter, the place where he would go to be frozen tomorrow.

The glass doors of the cryocenter opened with a hiss and

let Matthew into a massive, abandoned waiting room. The only person there was a bored-looking woman sitting behind a curved metallic desk.

Matthew walked to the desk and held out his arm for scanning. The woman frowned at her screen.

"You're not due until tomorrow. It really would be better to wait. Especially in your . . . state." She wrinkled her nose as she caught the scent of alcohol and bile on Matthew's breath. "Hangovers are never pleasant, but after a decade or two in the freeze, they're apocalyptic."

"I'm not here for that," Matthew said. "I'm here to see someone." He gave her the name.

The woman checked her computer, then stood. She led Matthew out of the reception room through a small metal door and into a long, fluorescent-lit corridor. The walls of the corridor were lined with white square compartments, each with a silver button set in the center. Each compartment was labelled with a name.

"You don't have to show me," Matthew said. "I've been here before."

The woman returned to the waiting room, and Matthew kept walking down the corridor. The compartments on his left were arranged alphabetically by last name; he kept going and going until he reached the Ts.

Tilson, Abigail.

Matthew stopped in front of the compartment and pressed the button. With a hiss and a burst of cold steam, the cryochamber came open and extended into the corridor in front of him. He looked down at the person lying inside.

A woman. His mother.

The indicator panels on her cryochamber blinked green and yellow. Matthew gazed at her face through glass and clear blue cryoliquid. It looked exactly as it had a year ago when he and his sister put her in the freeze—gently wrinkled, laugh lines fanning out from the corners of her eyes and mouth, thin lips, tufts of gray in the hair at her temples.

Here, laid out in front of him, was Matthew's reason for signing up for the Exo Project. Months before the Project had been announced, his mother had been diagnosed with cancer. It was everywhere; her body was riddled with it. The cure was simple. Just a short course of nanotreatments to get rid of the tumors. But the cure was also expensive: nearly one million units. They didn't have the money. So they put her in cryostasis instead, to halt the spread of the disease.

Then, when the Exo Project came along, Matthew knew it was the solution: The reward money for the families of chosen volunteers was almost exactly the amount needed for his mother's cancer treatments.

He could save his mother's life—by sacrificing his own.

"Hi, Mom," Matthew said now, his voice barely above a whisper. "How's it going in there?"

It was no use—the cryotechnicians had told him that she was unconscious and couldn't hear anything—but every time he visited his mother, he spoke to her frozen body all the same.

"Something's happening tomorrow, Mom," Matthew said. "Tomorrow I'm going into the freeze, like you. Then I'm going to get on a spaceship and be launched across the galaxy."

Matthew bowed his head, looked at his hands. He smiled.

"I know if you were awake right now, you'd probably be yelling at me for making such a dumb decision. Honestly, I wish you *were* awake to try to talk me out of it. Not that I'm changing my mind, it's just . . ."

Matthew's voice thickened, choked. He pressed his lips together and was silent a few breaths before going on.

"I just wish you were here, is all. I can't raise Sophie by myself. She's thirteen now, you believe that? A teenager. She *needs* you, Mom—that's why it has to be this way. I've tried my best to take care of her, but I don't know what I'm doing. I don't know how to raise a girl. She needs her mother."

Matthew put his hands on the cryochamber, felt the cold of the ice through the glass.

"Don't cry, okay?" he said, tears coming to his eyes now. "I know when you wake up and Sophie tells you what's going on that you're going to be upset, you're going to blame yourself—but don't, all right? This isn't your fault. None of it. This was my choice. It's not like there's much left to live for here on Earth anyway. Who knows? Maybe I'll find a habitable planet, then when everyone else comes, I can meet Sophie's great-grandkids or something."

He smiled.

"And if not . . ."

The smile left his face. He swallowed, cleared his throat.

"If not, I guess I'll see you on the other side."

Matthew straightened up, took his hands off the cryochamber. "Good-bye, Mom," he said. "I love you."

Matthew hit the button to send his mother back into the wall with a hiss. He turned and walked down the corridor, then through the waiting room and out into the hot, dark night.

5

Matthew got back home long after midnight. He and his sister Sophie lived in a massive compound owned by a company where employees and their families could live and work away from the harsh sun. Before going into cryostasis, Matthew's mother had worked for the company; Matthew himself had been enrolled in the company's employee training program until he was chosen for the Exo Project.

Matthew threaded his way through the corridors of the compound to their apartment. Inside, it was mostly dark except for a single yellow light coming from Sophie's bedroom. Matthew crept up to the door and peeked inside.

Sophie was asleep on top of her covers, and a reading light was on. Next to Sophie on the bed was a tablet screen.

Matthew crept to the bed and sat down. He picked up the tablet and turned it on to look at what Sophie had been reading before going to sleep.

A web article came to the screen; it was titled, "Will Any of the Exo Project Recruits Survive? Scientists Weigh In."

Matthew tapped at the screen to look at Sophie's search history. Her previous search queries included "dangers of space travel," "death in space," and "odds of exoplanets supporting life."

Next to him Sophie began to stir and talk in her sleep.

"No," she murmured. Then her voice got louder and louder, until she was almost shouting. "No, don't. Don't go. Come back!"

Sophie's body twisted back and forth on the bed, her arms jerking. Matthew leaned over her and tried to hold her still.

"Sophie," he said softly, then a little bit louder: "*Sophie.*"

Her eyes came half-open as she came out of the nightmare without completely waking. Her gaze touched glancingly on Matthew's face, then she gave a sigh and her eyes slid shut again.

"It's you," she mumbled dreamily. "But you were . . . you were dying."

"It was just a dream," Matthew whispered. He set a hand on the side of her head, brushed her bangs sideways with a sweep of his thumb. "I'm not dying. I'm here. I'm right here. Go back to sleep."

Sophie smacked her lips together and rolled onto her side, clasping both hands under her cheek and drawing her knees up toward her chest.

"But you're leaving me," she mumbled as she sank again into deep sleep, ". . . leaving me."

"Shhh," Matthew said, rubbing his hand in a small circle on her back. "We'll talk about it in the morning."

Matthew sat there a few moments, until he was sure that

Sophie was fully asleep, breathing heavily, and not bothered by another nightmare. Then he eased himself off of the bed, flipped the switch, and crept to the door. He went down the hallway and collapsed into his own bed.

. . .

The next morning, Matthew woke up to discover a small cake on the kitchen table, a gleaming squat cylinder of chocolate frosting with a single lit candle in the middle.

"Happy birthday, Matthew!" Sophie said. She was smiling but her eyes were wet and gleaming, and Matthew knew that she was already holding back tears.

"Wow," Matthew said, putting on a smile he didn't feel.

"All the ingredients are real," she said. "Nothing synthetic. I saved up for eggs, flour, cocoa. I hope you like it."

Matthew bit his lip. Since Earth's crops had started failing, real food was hard to come by. In the compound, they mostly lived on synthetic foods made in factories: fake vegetables, fake meat, and fake milk bought with the ration chits they were given every day. To get real ingredients like eggs and cocoa, Sophie would have to have been saving up her chits for weeks, skipping meals and going hungry. Suddenly, Matthew noticed how thin his sister had become, how perilously twig-like her wrists looked. He felt a pang in his stomach. How had he not noticed sooner? What kind of brother was he?

"Sophie, you shouldn't have done this," he said. "This is too much."

"But I wanted to," Sophie said. "This is the last birthday we'll ever celebrate together."

She went silent, her eyes growing glassy as she realized what she'd said.

"Well, thank you," Matthew said to cover up the silence. He gave her a peck on the cheek. "You're the best sister a guy could ask for."

Sophie smiled. "Go on, blow out the candle."

Matthew closed his eyes and snuffed the single candle.

"Did you make a wish?" Sophie asked once he'd opened his eyes. "Don't tell me what it is—then it won't come true."

He hadn't—he couldn't think of anything to wish for. Wishes required hope, and hope was something Matthew didn't have much of at the moment. But he couldn't say that, so instead he simply lied.

"I did. Don't worry, I won't tell."

Matthew wasn't particularly hungry—his stomach was a ball of jangling nerves—but he forced himself to eat a few bites anyway, then cajoled Sophie into eating the rest.

"It was delicious, Soph—really. Chocolate cake for breakfast. It's a perfect going-away present."

Then he glanced at the clock.

"You don't have to go yet, do you?" Sophie asked.

Matthew nodded. "I do."

He began to rise from the table, and before he'd stood up fully Sophie seized him in a hug that nearly caused him to lose his balance and fall back into the chair. She was pressed tight to his chest. After a moment, he sighed and set his chin against the crown of her head. Her body began to shake against his as she sobbed into the fabric of his shirt.

"Don't go," she pleaded. "Please, don't leave me."

"I have to, Soph," he said. "But don't worry—I asked Silas and Adam to take turns checking in on you until Mom gets out of the freeze. The money should come through soon, and then you can get her the treatments. It'll all be fine."

"It won't be fine, though," she cried. "Without you here it will never be fine."

"Hey, come on." Matthew pulled his head back and looked down at his sister.

She gazed up at him, eyes so huge and brown they nearly broke Matthew's heart.

"I know it seems bad now," he said. "But you'll get used to it—you will. Remember when Dad died? Remember how awful that was? But then it started to feel a little better, and a little better, until it was almost normal, not having him around. Until we could think of him and remember him and smile. That's what it'll be like for you. Someday you'll barely even think of me anymore—and when you do, you'll just smile, remembering your stupid big brother who flew off into space."

Sophie sniffled. "You think so?"

Matthew nodded. "I know so. But for right now you're going to have to be strong, okay? Not for me—for Mom. If you're sad about me when she wakes up, if you cry, then she'll cry too—she'll blame herself. But you can't let her do that. You need to tell her that it's not her fault. That this was my choice. Can you do that?"

28

Sophie nodded. She bit her lower lip, stepped back, and wiped her eyes.

"And give her a hug for me, would you?" Matthew asked. "Tell her I love her. I didn't say it enough, when she was around. I'd say it every day if I had the chance, if I could go back."

"I know," Sophie said. "Me too."

Matthew turned and left the kitchen, walked to the door where his radiation suit was hanging. He felt Sophie's eyes follow him, and he willed her not to start crying again. If she started up again, he didn't think he'd be able to leave. Didn't think he'd have the strength to do what needed to be done.

"Matthew," came her voice from behind him.

He cringed and turned to face her—but she wasn't crying. She stood in the doorway to the kitchen, fixing him from across the room with an intense, urgent look.

"I love you," she said.

He nodded, smiled. "I love you too, sis."

And then he left.

6

Matthew returned to the city, returned to the cryostation. As he approached the front desk, he searched inside himself for any trace of emotion—but there was nothing. He was empty. After saying good-bye to Sophie, he had nothing left. He felt completely numb.

He gave his name to the woman at the front desk—a different woman than the one who'd been there last night.

"There's a locker room that way," the woman said, nodding toward a corridor and sliding a piece of paper across the desk. "After you've changed, report to this room number."

Matthew walked down the hall and came into a room where a handful of men were changing out of their clothes and into identical blue suits. Matthew found his locker and opened it to see his cryosuit hanging inside.

A female voice hummed in the background, pre-recorded, piped in from the ceiling through speakers.

"Please disrobe completely before putting on your cryosuit. Remove all rings, necklaces, and watches. No foreign objects may be brought into the cryochamber."

Matthew stripped naked and quickly slipped into the suit. It was a little big, but a few seconds after he'd zipped it up the fabric began to contract. Matthew held out his arms and studied the suit as it melded to the contours of his body, sucking so tight against his limbs that it may as well have been a second skin.

Matthew glanced up and caught the gaze of another Exo Project participant—a man in his forties with stubble on his chin. The man grinned and shrugged.

"Wild, huh?" he said. "Can you believe this is really happening?"

Matthew nodded, but didn't say anything. He looked away. He didn't feel like talking to anyone. Soon he'd be in the freeze and he'd never see this man again. Why bother? He didn't want to spend his last moments on Earth making small talk with a stranger, pretending that what was happening to them was some weird lark, something they'd laugh about together someday.

Trying not to meet anyone else's gaze, Matthew slipped out of the locker room and back into the hallway. He glanced at his slip of paper and began picking his way through the corridors, trying to find the right door. Eventually he found it and opened the door to a small gray cube of a room. Inside, the other members of Matthew's mission sat waiting.

. . .

Each Exo Project team had three people. Matthew's team consisted of him, a boy his age named Sam, and a black woman in her sixties who'd introduced herself by her last name, Dunne.

Matthew had met them both a month earlier when they'd

reported for mission training. Their training had consisted of virtual reality simulations showing them how to operate their ship, what to do when they came out of the freeze at their destination, and what to do when they landed on the planet.

Each of them had a unique role in the mission, for which they'd received special training. Matthew was the communications officer, responsible for talking with Mission Control back home. For this task, he'd had to learn how to use a quantum transceiver, a device that communicated instantly over huge distances using the phenomenon of quantum entanglement.

Dunne was the science officer for the mission, responsible for taking readings on the planet's surface to determine if it was livable or not. It wasn't a difficult job—all she had to do was learn how to operate and read the sensor equipment—but in talking with her Matthew discovered that she did have a science background. In school, she'd nearly gotten a degree in particle physics before deciding that what she wanted to do with her life was help people. So she'd gone back and started over pre-med, then went to medical school to become a pediatrician. Dunne was more qualified than science officers for other teams were likely to be—more qualified, perhaps, than the mission needed her to be.

Dunne's expertise and professionalism put Matthew at ease. She took the training seriously. Watching her, talking with her, Matthew could almost make himself believe that their mission would be a success—that the likeliest outcome wasn't for them to die on the surface of the planet right after they landed.

If Dunne put Matthew at ease, though, Sam put him on edge.

Sam's black hair was pointy and unkempt, his cheeks and chin were perpetually rough with stubble, and he always seemed to be holding his body tense as a piece of wire wound tight, ready to spring or snap at any moment.

Sam was the mission's equipment specialist, responsible for keeping their equipment running properly. He didn't talk much during training—unless it was to badger the trainers about the way the mission had been designed. He seemed to regret signing up for the Exo Project in the first place. Matthew guessed that there were a lot of people like Sam: people who'd put their name in the lottery without thinking through the consequences, thinking that they'd never be selected.

. . .

Now, as Matthew came into the room, Sam and Dunne both raised their heads. Dunne stood and smiled at him, but Sam just grunted and returned his gaze to where it had been when Matthew walked in, staring at a corner of the floor.

Matthew met Dunne's eyes. "What's going on?" he asked. "I thought we'd go straight into the freeze when we got here."

"There's some kind of briefing," Dunne said. "We're just waiting here until they come get us to join all the other teams."

"A briefing?" Matthew said. "What more could they have to tell us? We've already been trained."

"I heard some people talking in the locker room when I was getting my cryosuit on," Sam said. "Sounds like they're bringing in some guy, some bigwig, from the Exo Project to give us a pep talk.

Get us pumped up before they send us out there to die."

Sam stood from his chair and walked toward Matthew. The look in his eyes was unnerving.

"What are you going to do?" Matthew asked. "You're going to say something to him, aren't you?"

Sam looked away. "None of your business," he said. "I can take care of myself."

"Look, Sam—I know you're scared. I'm scared too, but—"

Sam whirled around and put a finger in Matthew's face.

"I'm not scared!" he shouted. "Don't you dare say that I'm scared! But I'm not going to go quietly, either, okay? I'm not going to go like some dumb animal being led to the slaughterhouse. Not like you two."

At that moment, the door opened and a young woman in a uniform walked into the room.

"What's going on?" she said. "I heard yelling."

Dunne stepped forward. "Nothing," she said. "Are you here to take us to the briefing?"

The young woman gave Matthew and Sam a suspicious look.

"Yes," she said. "Come with me."

7

Dozens of other Exo Project participants were already in the briefing room, seated in chairs facing a lectern. Matthew surveyed the crowd. Most of the people were Dunne's age or older. Some were so old they looked close to dying already; one elderly woman pulled an oxygen tank on wheels behind her as she shuffled, hunched, to her seat.

The seats toward the back of the room were already taken, so Matthew, Sam, and Dunne sat down near the front. As soon as they settled into their seats, the door opened behind them and a hush came over the room. The young woman who had escorted them walked to the front of the room and spoke to the crowd.

"Good morning, everyone," she began. "Thank you all for being here on this historic day."

"Like we had a choice," Sam muttered.

"Today, Exo Project volunteers are preparing for their expeditions at cryostations just like this one, all across the planet. But we've got a special treat. OmniCore has been kind enough to send one of the masterminds of the Exo Project to speak to us."

The young woman beamed. "His name is Charles Keane, and I hope that you'll help me give him a warm welcome."

"Lucky us," Sam whispered, but the woman had already started to clap, and the crowd halfheartedly did the same as Keane—a man in a sleek OmniCore uniform—came in the room and walked to the front. Matthew put his hands together a few times until he realized the absurdity of what he was doing: clapping for the man who had most likely engineered his death. He let his hands drop to his sides and set his jaw.

"Thank you," Keane said when he reached the lectern. He was tall and thin, with dark hair, smooth features, and sleek, black-rimmed glasses. "Thank you for that warm welcome. And thank you to all of you for being part of this historic moment. The Exo Project is an amazing feat of innovation—it is the *peak* of human innovation, in fact, the most ambitious thing we have ever attempted as a species."

Keane stepped out from behind the lectern and began to wander the stage, gesturing with his hands.

"Just think of it! One thousand simultaneous expeditions across the galaxy, one thousand ships and crews traveling faster than the speed of light. Just imagine all the work, all the resources and meetings and late nights that have gone into every aspect of the mission: identifying potential Earthlike planets to explore, mapping a course through the stars to each one, and then of course engineering the technology that would get us there. But all this innovation, this triumph of science and technology and human cooperation on a massive scale, it would all be for nothing without one thing."

Keane paused, squared his feet and shoulders to the crowd, then laced his hands together and pointed with both forefingers.

"You," he said. "Gentlemen, ladies, you may not believe me, but I'm telling you the truth: At this moment, you are the most important part of the Exo Project. Without you, all this science, all this technology, all this innovation—it would all be useless."

At Matthew's side, he could sense Sam moving restlessly in his chair. Now, as soon as Keane paused, Sam burst to his feet.

"Yes?" Keane said, backing up slightly on the stage, balancing on his heels.

"If we're so valuable," Sam said, "then why haven't you come up with a way to get us back to Earth? You expect us all to die, don't you?"

Matthew gritted his teeth as Sam shouted at Keane.

Keane didn't respond with anger, though. His face became calm, almost expressionless as he prepared to answer Sam's question.

"Ah," he said. "I understand your concern. And I'm glad you asked the question. Really, I am. I'm glad because it gives me the opportunity to . . ." He churned a hand in the air as he searched for his next words. "To clear up some confusion, shall we say? To dispel some common misconceptions. Does that sound all right?"

Sam was silent. He sank slowly back into his chair. Keane nodded and lifted his head to the entire crowd.

"First of all, I don't want to lie to anyone here. It's true that there is no means of return to Earth once you're at your destination. This should have been perfectly clear to everyone who volunteered for the Exo Project."

Keane glanced briefly back at Sam with a reproach in his eyes.

"As to us expecting you to die," Keane continued. "This is simply not true. We'd prefer it if *no one* had to die as part of the Exo Project. But unfortunately there's simply no way around it. Deep space exploration is dangerous—even at light speed it takes decades to travel across the galaxy, and it's very difficult to turn around and come back to Earth over such a long distance. You—all of you gathered here today—were aware of these dangers, and yet you signed up anyway. Why?"

Keane paused for a moment, let the question hang in the air.

"Because you knew that the future of the human race was the most important thing. You knew that the lives of billions of people on planet Earth outweighed your own life."

Something strange came into Keane's voice then, a kind of euphoric tone, as if he were being carried away by his own speech. His eyes grew wide, and words came from his mouth quicker, in a passionate torrent.

"Earlier I spoke about the Exo Project as a feat of human innovation. But in light of this . . . this *question*"—here he waved dismissively at Sam, batting his concerns away like gnats—"I want to introduce another word to you. That word is *greatness*. The Exo Project is not just the height of human innovation—it's the height of human *greatness*. I truly believe that it will be the greatest thing we have ever accomplished as a species. And ladies and gentlemen, I submit to you that no work of human greatness has ever come without equally great human sacrifice."

At that, Matthew felt a chill. He knew that his participation in the Exo Project was a sacrifice, of course, but there was something in the way Keane said it that made the word sound different—sound *evil*.

"In Ancient Egypt, many thousands of slaves died in the desert constructing the Pyramids of Giza. The Romans built an empire that spanned the known world by forcing the people they conquered to serve them—and feeding those who refused to the lions. Millenia later, thousands more workers died of disease, of injury, and of exhaustion as they built railroads that spanned the continents, as they worked in factories and mines that created wealth for great men of history and built new, modern empires. And then, of course, hundreds of millions died in the wars of the twentieth and twenty-first centuries—but without these wars we wouldn't have made the innovations in aviation and rocket propulsion that let us take our first steps into space, or the advances in chemical technology, biological technology, and nanotechnology that today are used to create synthetic foods that feed the world and to cure illnesses that were once thought incurable."

Keane's head lifted to scan the audience, but Matthew could see that Keane wasn't looking *at* them—he was looking *through* them to some act of greatness that he wanted to achieve, that he wanted to be remembered for.

"I truly believe that the Exo Project will be humanity's greatest accomplishment yet—greater than the pyramids, greater than the Industrial Revolution, greater than all the scientific discoveries and technological advances of human history from the dawn of time until this present moment." Keane pointed a finger emphatically toward the ground he stood on. "And you, ladies and gentlemen—you are the sacrifice necessary to make that accomplishment a reality.

Yes, most of you will die—but it will be a quick death. At worst, you'll spend decades sleeping peacefully in cryostasis, then expire quickly, after taking the mission-termination pills. Compared to the sacrifice, the suffering, of the Egyptian slaves who died so their masters could achieve the greatness of the pyramids, your sacrifice, your suffering, will be small. But it will be remembered all the same."

Keane's eyes were frenzied. They burned with an ambition, a fire, that made Matthew want to lean back in his chair.

"Centuries from now," Keane said, "when future generations are living on the planet that one of you has found for us, they'll remember you and your sacrifice. They'll remember all of us. So go. Get out there. Find us a new home. Good luck, and Godspeed."

There was a sound of thunderous clapping from the back of the room. Matthew turned in his chair. At the back of the room stood dozens of OmniCore officers in matching uniforms. They were applauding Keane's speech loudly, faces shining with pride and inspiration.

But none of the Exo Project participants clapped, or smiled, or looked inspired. They simply gazed forward, their faces blank and emotionless.

Keane left the lectern and filed out of the room with the other OmniCore officers.

The woman who'd introduced Keane took the microphone once more.

"Now the freezing process will begin," she said. "You may wait here until your name is called."

A few minutes later a man in a lab coat came into the room

and read names off a handheld computer pad. Matthew was part of the first group.

He stood and followed the man with the others whose names had been chosen, feeling more than ever like a doomed person, a criminal being led to the gallows.

8

The man with the lab coat led them to a bright, sterile hallway and instructed them to each find a room. Matthew picked a door and went inside. An empty cryochamber sat waiting.

A white-coated cryotechnician walked in and instructed him to sit on the examining table. Matthew hoisted himself up. The technician checked his vitals.

"Everything seems normal," the tech said. "Though you're a little dehydrated."

Matthew cleared his throat. "I had a few drinks last night."

The tech chuckled. "Can't blame you there."

He prepared a syringe of clear red liquid.

"What's that?" Matthew asked.

"It prepares you for the freezing process. Changes the molecular makeup of your cells. Freezing live tissue isn't easy, you know. At low enough temperatures, the cells have the tendency to break down, sustain damage." He tapped the syringe with his forefinger. "This protects you. Helps your cells make it through the freezing process intact."

Without rolling up Matthew's sleeve, the technician injected the liquid into Matthew's arm. Afterward, Matthew studied the place where the liquid had entered his body, flexed and unflexed his hand.

"I don't feel any different."

"You're not supposed to. That's the point: your body functions exactly the same—only now we can freeze you."

He guided Matthew away from the examining table and led him to the cryochamber. Matthew lay down inside, and the technician began attaching biostat lines to his chest and arms.

"Okay. Now. What's going to happen is, I'm going to sedate you. Then I'm going to fill the pod with cryoliquid. It's a high-nutrient mix, that's what'll preserve you while you're in stasis. The suit will conduct the liquid directly to your skin and help you absorb nutrients."

"Will I feel anything?"

The tech's chin flattened and he shook his head. "Nah. Not after I sedate you. You won't dream, either. Next thing you know, you'll be up and orbiting at your destination. Got it?"

Matthew nodded. The technician disappeared for a moment, and Matthew squinted at the bright lights pointing down at him. When the technician returned, he was holding another syringe, and Matthew's heart took a leap in his chest.

Time was running out, Matthew's future disappearing into the point of that needle like water down a drain, light into a black hole. As soon as the syringe pierced his skin, it would be over. There'd be no turning back. He'd never see his mother or his sister, never hang out with Silas or Adam, never set foot on Earth again.

He needed more time.

"Wait!" he said.

"Sorry," the technician said, already squeezing the plunger to send the sedative surging into Matthew's arm.

Matthew's heart slowed, and the bright lights in the room began to fade. His eyes slid closed.

He fell into a blackness so deep it was as though he was swimming through oil. Then, slowly, he became aware of sensations—sights, sounds, smells, feelings. He sensed them through a long distance, as if he had a second body, a second skin, a second set of eyes and ears lying in the cryochamber.

Strange. Hadn't the technician just told him he shouldn't be able to feel anything?

Matthew heard a hissing sound as the chamber closed. Liquid streamed into the pod and began to lap at his fingers, his thighs, the sides of his head. Filling the pod, it streamed over Matthew's shut eyelids and pooled coolly in his nostrils.

Matthew heard a beeping sound and the liquid started growing colder around him, first gradually, then quickly. The cold pricked at his skin. Then it stabbed. He felt like screaming, like jerking his limbs and clawing his way out of the cryochamber, but his body wouldn't listen to him. The pain grew worse and worse—but at the moment when it became unbearable, it began to subside. The pain receded like a flashlight becoming dim in a vast dark tunnel, then shrunk to nothing.

He slept.

9

sophie

Sophie lay in her bedroom, gazing at the ceiling and thinking about Matthew. What was he doing at that moment? Was he okay? Was he in cryostasis already?

Sophie had been at the cryostation with Matthew when their mother had gone into the freeze, so she knew what the process looked like—knew the sight of the blue liquid filling the chamber with their mother's unconscious body inside, knew the sound of the heart rate monitor slowing as she entered a state of suspended animation. Matthew had put an arm around her as they watched, and she'd turned to cry into her brother's shirt.

"We'll get her out," Matthew had said then. "We'll find a way. I promise."

Now *he* was the one going into the freeze. Her big brother, who'd always taken care of her. He'd taken care of her when their father died and their mother was too grief-stricken to get out of bed for weeks, he'd taken care of her after their mother was diagnosed with cancer, and he'd taken care of her in the year since she'd gone into the freeze, been as good a parent to Sophie as the ones she'd had before they'd been taken away.

She knew Matthew thought he was taking care of her now, too, that his joining the Exo Project was the best thing for her—but Sophie couldn't help being angry. Matthew's leaving hurt more than their father's death had, more than their mother's cancer. It hurt more because he'd *chosen* it. Her parents had been taken away. But Matthew had *decided* to abandon her.

Still, when she'd woken early that morning to bake Matthew a birthday cake, she promised herself she wouldn't cry when her brother left, that she'd be strong for him. Of course she cried anyway, like a stupid baby. It was embarrassing. She'd managed to pull herself together at the last minute, to keep herself calm as they said their final good-byes. But then as soon as Matthew closed the door behind him, she'd broken down again, run to her room, and sobbed facedown on the bed until her pillow was wet with tears.

She lay that way for an hour until she'd cried every last tear and felt completely empty inside. Then she rolled onto her back and looked up at the ceiling.

"I have to stop this," she said aloud. She had to pull herself together. Matthew'd said she needed to be strong for their mother, and he was right. Matthew was gone—he was never coming back. The only thing left to do was get her mother out of the freeze, get her cured—then live. Live a life that made Matthew's sacrifice worthwhile.

At that moment, the doorbell rang out through the apartment. Sophie sat up.

It was probably Adam or Silas, coming to check on her.

46

Sophie got up and checked her face in the mirror. Her eyes were still a little puffy, but she didn't think Adam or Silas would notice. Boys never paid any attention to those things.

She walked to the door, opened it—then gave a start when it wasn't the familiar face of one of Matthew's friends that she saw, but an older man, one she didn't recognize. He wore a radiation suit, the helmet tucked under his arm as he stood in the hallway.

"Who are you?" Sophie asked. Her hand crept up to rest on her heart, which was beating fast in her chest.

"I'm with the Exo Project, miss. May I come in?"

Sophie nodded, stood aside to let him pass.

"Are you Sophie Tilson?" he asked.

"Yes, that's me."

"You have a brother named Matthew?"

Her heart fluttered. "Yes. What's happened? What's wrong?"

"Nothing. The freezing process went fine. Matthew's in good health, and he's being launched with the others to the departure site."

"So then why are you here?"

"Well, Matthew listed you as the person who should get his money. The reward money. Most of the Exo Project participants signed theirs over to someone staying behind."

Sophie breathed relief. "Yeah, that's right. Well, not exactly—the money's really for our mom, but she can't use it right now. She's in the freeze, see. That's why I'm getting it. She's sick, and I need it to get her—"

"Yes," the man said. "That's all fine. I'm just going to need to scan your ident to make everything official."

"Sure." Sophie peeled back her sleeve and offered the man her forearm.

What happened next went by in a rush, before she could react or even realize what was happening.

The man's hand clamped down on her arm in a vise grip that felt like it might crack her bones. Sophie gasped with the pain but didn't have time to cry out. The man yanked her closer and whirled her around—a violent dance that was almost graceful in its smoothness. His arm stole around her waist as he grasped her tightly to his body. Sophie could feel the man's breath flutter in her ear.

"I'm sorry," he whispered, his voice gravelly.

He plunged a syringe into the side of her neck. Sophie let out a soft squeak of protest when the needle pierced her skin, then slumped, her eyes slipping closed as blackness surrounded her.

PART 2

GLE'AH

10

kiva

Kiva went out from the village to watch the Great Mother set in a blaze of red on the horizon, then wait for the Three Sisters to blink on in the night sky. This was her tradition, her private ritual. She allowed no one to see her, no one to follow her as she slipped away from her father's hut on the edge of the village. As she came over the rise, a lip of rock separating the village from the surrounding plain, she paused to watch the wind ripple over the grass, a sudden tessellation of lines dancing in shifting patterns across the prairie before disappearing once more as the air went still. She walked down into the low, flat expanse, her fingers trailing in the purple and brown grasses, clutching at the tips. She lay down in her favorite spot, against the cleft swell of a small hillock, and waited.

Waited for the time that was neither night nor day. A thin cusp between the light and the darkness.

This was her favorite time—a secret she kept with herself. It was hers and hers alone.

As the Great Mother inched toward the horizon, Kiva felt the stirrings of something she couldn't quite name welling up inside her. It began in the back of her mind as a sort of itch, a tickle, the ghost of something she once knew but had long since forgotten. Then it—whatever it was—began to gain strength, like a light breeze growing to a mighty wind. Slowly, an image began to take shape in her mind: a blue orb, cloud-dappled, suspended in deep blackness.

And then, at the moment that the last red-rimmed sliver of sun fell below the curve of the planet Gle'ah, a sharp agony seized Kiva at the root of her torso. Her body convulsed with the force of the pain; her stomach and back clenched tight, and her heels ground deep into the grass.

Kiva's eyes clamped shut as, above, the Three Sisters—the moons of Gle'ah—began to glow in the darkening sky. In the far distance, Vale and Dalia, the Twins, had entered into the part of their orbit where they appeared to dance together, their two white orbs seeming to merge into a single elongated mass. Ao, the third moon of Gle'ah, passed by on a closer orbit, near enough to the planet that, had her eyes been open, Kiva could have traced the moon's path with her finger as it spun across the sky.

As it was, Kiva merely felt her hair float next to her ears in the pull of Ao's gravity as the moon passed overhead—and when the pale white sphere was directly above her, nearly lifting her entire body off the ground, the pain sharpened to an agonizing point in her chest as images fluoresced on her eyelids.

An explosion of light and fire.

A sea of stars elongating and whizzing past in the blackness.

A huge bird made of polished stone, coming through the clouds to land on the prairie.

And three dark silhouettes standing shoulder to shoulder on the horizon.

Then the moon spun on, releasing Kiva's body from its grip. The strands of her hair fell and pooled again on the ground. When Ao had disappeared over the horizon, the images on Kiva's eyelids faded, and the pain loosed its hold on her body. Her eyes snapped open, her lungs gasping for air. In the now-dark sky, the Twins went wobbly in her vision as tears brimmed at the edges of her eyes. She blinked away a single tear; it ran down her cheek and dripped in her ear.

Strangers

The word came to her unbidden.

They're coming.

11

Kiva pushed herself up and ran back to the village, the edges of the long grass-blades slicing at her feet. Her legs burned and her toes flexed in the grit as she hiked up the rise. At the top, she paused and placed her hands on her knees to catch her breath.

Her father's hut stood at the edge of the village. It was a squat structure made of mud and surrounded by a small, furrowed garden. Grath, Kiva's father, stood amidst the plants, working a hoe. Just outside the door, Quint, Kiva's younger sister, played in the dirt with two small figures carved from pieces of wood, chattering softly to herself as she made them talk to each other.

When Kiva approached, Quint lifted her head, her eyes wide and gleaming, and burst to her feet. She ran through the garden and threw her arms around Kiva's waist—and in spite of herself, a smile broke across Kiva's face. She bent her neck and planted a kiss on the top of Quint's head.

"Kiva!" Quint said, looking up at her older sister without letting go. "Where were you? Out on the prairie?"

Kiva nodded and laughed quietly to herself.

"Yes," she said, "you know I was."

Kiva knew that Quint adored her, practically worshiped her—the girl would follow her around everywhere, if she let her. Kiva still remembered the day Quint first came to them, the day their mother, Liana, and the Sisters brought the mewling, squawking baby to live in their hut. When Liana came through the door with Quint in her arms, Kiva had craned her neck to peer over the cloth wrappings at the girl's face. It was so smooth, the gray skin of the baby's forehead and cheeks almost shiny—and Kiva fell in love with her at once. The feeling was so strong and sudden that she felt she might fall over: this urgent, immediate need to protect Quint, to clasp her close and never let go.

Now, Quint unlaced her hands at Kiva's waist, stepped back, and frowned.

"What's wrong?" Quint asked. "You've been crying."

Kiva quickly wiped away the streaks her tears had left on her cheeks. At Quint's back, Grath stopped working, propped the hoe against the dirt and leaned both arms on it, listening.

Kiva met her father's eyes for a brief moment, then looked back to Quint and shook her head.

"It's nothing," Kiva said. "Nothing you should worry yourself about. Go on inside, okay? I'll come tuck you in soon."

Quint glanced at their father, then turned back to Kiva, her eyes narrowing with suspicion.

"Go on," Kiva said.

"Mind your sister," her father said.

Quint sighed. "Will you sing to me, too? And tell me a story?"

Kiva bowed her head. "If you want."

Satisfied, Quint grinned and scampered inside. Grath watched her go. After the girl had disappeared inside the hut, he turned to Kiva.

"All right," he said. "Now, what is it? What's happened?"

"I . . . I," Kiva stuttered. She didn't have the words to describe what had happened to her. Not yet.

"I saw something," she said finally.

Grath stood silent, waiting.

"People," Kiva said. "Dark shadows coming over the hill."

Grath's neck straightened. "Who? The Forsaken? What did they do to you?"

Kiva shook her head sharply. The Forsaken were men who used to live in the village; some had been banished for behaving violently, while others ran away because they were restless and craved the freedom of life outside the village. In the wilderness, they banded together and lived in an uneasy truce with Kiva's people—but even so, Grath had always told her to keep her distance from them. Sometimes when Kiva went beyond the edge of the village she could see the Forsaken lurking in the far distance, silhouettes against the sunset with weapons in hand. She was afraid of them. But it wasn't the Forsaken she'd seen—not this time.

This was something different.

"No," she said. "No. They weren't real. Or—they were real but they weren't . . . really there. They were in my head. In my mind."

Grath breathed out. His shoulders dropped and he unflexed his hands, returned to his work. There was a rasp of stone scraping against stone as the hoe cut into the soil and loosed dusty clods.

"A dream," he said, "You fell asleep."

"No," Kiva said, the word a knife that cut the evening air. "It was more than a dream."

She thought of the pain that had seized her gut and shot up through her spine. The memory of it lingered as a dull ache.

"A vision," she said.

Her father looked up again.

"Impossible," he said. "You must have imagined it. You're only thirteen seasons. Only the Sisters have visions. The Sisters and the Vagra."

"I know," Kiva said. "But this was a vision."

He considered that for a moment, then turned and walked toward the hut. Kiva fell in step behind him. He set the hoe against the wall, then nodded Kiva toward a spot on the ground.

Kiva sat down and waited for Grath to do the same. He clapped the dust off his hands, then eased himself to the dirt. He stretched out on his side and leaned on one elbow.

"Now," he said. "Tell me about this vision."

Kiva told him everything: the explosion of fire, the stars whizzing by like a handful of thrown pebbles, the bird bursting through the clouds to land on the plain, the three dark figures standing shoulder to shoulder against the horizon.

As she spoke, her father traced patterns in the dirt, his finger swooping as it drew broad curves and sharp angles. When she had finished, he sighed and drew his flat hand across the ground, wiping it smooth once more.

"We must take her to the Sisters," came a voice from the hut.

Kiva's head snapped up. It was Liana, standing framed in the doorway.

Grath leapt to his feet.

"Forgive me, Sister," he said, bowing his head. "If I had known you were here——"

"I didn't want to disturb your work," the woman said. "I came in without your noticing. I was waiting for you in bed. Then I grew tired of waiting."

"How long have you been listening?" Grath asked.

"Since Quint came inside and told me that the two of you were plotting something," Liana answered, smiling. "Long enough to know: the girl has had her first visitation from the Ancestors. She must come before the Sisters. She must tell her vision to the Vagra."

12

Kiva stood and bowed her head, looking at her bare feet as she waited for Liana to come from the door to fetch her. Kiva's father moved out of the way and walked to the hut.

Kiva felt the touch of her mother's hand on her shoulder.

"Come, child," Liana said. "There's nothing to be afraid of."

"Yes, Sister."

Liana's finger hooked underneath Kiva's chin and lifted her gaze to meet her own.

"Today is a happy day," Liana said, though she wasn't smiling. "You'll see."

"Yes, Sister."

Together they stepped past the furrows and began walking deeper into the village. Liana's hand was on Kiva's back, softly guiding her ahead. Kiva walked with her head hung.

The dirt under their feet was hard as stone, packed tight by the soles of many feet. As they went further into the village, the huts grew denser, each with its own garden outside. In the sky above, the Twins glowed and began to separate in their orbits, the two circles moving away from each other like a drop of water shattered by the wind. Though the Great Mother had long since set, the village had not yet gone to sleep. The shouts of children tussling reached Kiva's ears, and she lifted her head. The orange flicker of cookfires glowed in the doorways of some of the huts, smoke trailing through the holes in the roofs and curling into the air above the village. At one hut, a father and his children played in the dirt just outside the door; the children clamored to their feet and ran to the fence as Kiva and Liana passed, while their father stayed on the ground, a blade of grass wedged between his teeth. At another hut, a Sister was visiting her family; she raised a hand in greeting as Kiva and Liana passed, and Liana acknowledged the other woman with a bow of her head.

Halfway into the heart of the village, Kiva heard footsteps beside her. She lifted her head to see a boy named Po run up to her. Po was thirteen seasons just like Kiva, but he often seemed younger than that—he still acted like a little boy. Po was a pest, lurking close by when Kiva played with her friends, nipping at their heels. More than once they'd told him to go away or tried to lose him in the tangle of huts, but the village was small and sometimes they couldn't avoid him. Besides, Grath had often told Kiva that she should try to be nice to Po—his mother had died when he was just a baby, and he didn't have many friends in the village.

She sucked in a breath and tried to remind herself of this as Po drew up close to her elbow.

"What's going on, Kiva?" Po asked. "Where are you going?"

Kiva's teeth tightened. "I'm going to see the Vagra."

60

Po's mouth angled into a teasing smirk. "What did you do? Are you in trouble?"

Kiva didn't answer. Annoyance simmered in her veins.

Po danced around her, taunting. "Did you steal something? Hurt someone?"

From behind Kiva's shoulder came Liana's voice, scolding: "Enough. Get out of here, boy. This doesn't concern you."

Po halted and let Kiva and Liana walk on. But when Kiva glanced over her shoulder, she saw that he was still watching them. Watching her. Cheeks burning, she put her head forward and gazed at the ground just ahead of her feet.

Further on, Kiva and Liana came to a hut where two girls were leaning against the outer wall and whispering to each other. They were Kiva's friends, one named Rehal, the other Thruss. As Kiva drew near, their whispering rose to a chorus of giggles, and they raised their heads with wide smiles on their faces. Rehal waved.

Kiva looked up at Liana.

"These are your friends?" her mother asked.

Kiva nodded.

"Go on. Say good-bye to them."

Good-bye? A lump lodged in Kiva's throat, but she held back her tears.

Kiva went toward the hut, and Rehal and Thruss met her halfway.

"Did Po find you?" Rehal said. "He came by a little while ago. He was looking for you."

"Run, Kiva!" Thruss said, a smirk on her face. "That boy's in love with you. You'll have to go into hiding soon."

"Be nice," Rehal said, though she was grinning as well. "Po's harmless. I feel sorry for him."

"Kiva's the nice one," Thruss said. "She'd sooner be mated to that pest than tell him she can't stand him."

Rehal wrinkled her nose. "Well, no one's that nice."

The two girls burst out laughing. They stopped when they noticed that Kiva wasn't smiling.

"What's wrong?" Thruss asked. "I'm sorry—we were just teasing, Kiva. If you actually like Po—"

Kiva shook her head. "That's not it. It's something else." She leaned in, pitched her voice low so that Liana couldn't hear. "I had a vision. Liana's taking me to tell it to the Vagra. She says I have to say good-bye."

"Good-bye?" Rehal said, her eyebrows lifting. "Why?"

"You're going to join the Sisters," Thruss said.

Rehal's eyes grew wide and her jaw fell open. "The Ancestors spoke to you?"

"I don't know," Kiva said. "Maybe."

Kiva had often wondered when she would move from her father's hut to live with her mother and the rest of the Sisters in the center of the village—but whenever she asked Liana about it, her mother had been vague. When Kiva had asked what her first visitation from the Ancestors would feel like, how she'd know when it happened, Liana had simply said, "You'll know."

Now, Kiva wondered if what she'd experienced out on the plain at sunset—the pain coursing through her body, the images of things she didn't understand flashing past on the inside of her eyelids—was really what she'd been waiting for.

62

Rehal laughed and pulled Kiva close for a hug; then Thruss did the same.

"Why are you upset?" Thruss said. "You should be happy!"

Kiva shook her head, felt tears coming to her eyes. "It's too soon. I thought I'd have a little while longer. I want to stay here with you."

Girls usually went to join the Sisters from the ages of fifteen to eighteen; for a girl as young as Kiva to hear the voice of the Ancestors was rare.

"Oh, don't be sad," Thruss said. "We'll be joining you soon enough. Then we'll all be Sisters, together. And take mates, and have children of our own. Think of it!"

Thruss put on a happy face; Rehal nodded and smiled, too. But Kiva couldn't bring herself to smile. It was all so fast.

Rehal nodded behind Kiva's shoulder. "You should go," she said in a low voice. "Your mother's waiting. We'll talk soon, okay?"

Kiva nodded and went back to Liana's side. They walked on together, leaving Thruss and Rehal behind.

"Why did you tell me to say good-bye?" Kiva asked. "I'll see them again, won't I?"

"Of course you will," Liana said, without meeting Kiva's gaze. "But it won't be the same."

· · ·

Soon, Kiva and Liana came to the center of the village. They passed through an empty expanse where no huts had been built, a border of about one hundred paces between where the men and children lived and the Sisters' camp. The Sisters' huts were smaller, built to house and sleep only one person, and they had no gardens outside. Growing food to sustain the village was the men's job; once a week they brought the fruits of their labor to the Sisters as tribute, to be shared among the women and given to anyone in the village who couldn't grow enough to feed themselves.

As Kiva and Liana approached the Sisters' encampment, the pain Kiva had felt earlier crept back into her body, seized her in her chest and spread to her limbs. Tears leapt hot to her eyes, and she looked back at Liana.

Don't be afraid, Liana said.

But she didn't say it. Her lips hadn't moved. Yet Kiva heard the words nonetheless, felt them as she had felt the vision past the edge of the village.

Liana called out, spoke but did not speak, in a voice that was not a voice.

Sisters, rise! The Ancestors stir tonight. A new Sister has been chosen.

After a moment the answer came back, a chorus that echoed in Kiva's mind and vibrated in her body, so painful and deafening that it took her breath away and threatened to throw her to the ground:

Welcome, child.

Behind the voices of the Sisters, another voice, one that was both softer and more powerful: the Vagra.

Come, Kiva. I've been waiting.

13

Kiva and Liana stood just outside the encampment, Liana's hand resting warm on Kiva's shoulder. The Sisters' huts dotted the landscape, their placement haphazard, clumped closely together in some places, flung distant in others. Beyond, just visible over the roofs of the narrow huts, was a larger hut—round, made of mud.

The Vagra's hut. It was at the exact center of the village.

Slowly, the Sisters emerged from their huts and stood facing Kiva and Liana. No one moved for a long moment.

Then, a single figure stepped forward.

"Kiva," the figure said, walking closer, the moonlight falling across her cheeks.

Kiva blinked. She knew that voice, that face.

It was a girl her own age, thirteen: her name was Kyne, and she was Po's twin sister.

. . .

Kiva and Kyne had played together as children, but they had never been friends. Kyne was unpredictable, volatile—Kiva and her friends had been afraid of her. Even as a young girl, Kyne had ruled over the other children with her quick wit and sharp tongue. Warm and friendly one moment, she'd turn cruel the next, picking a victim seemingly at random and assailing her with biting insults until the girl ran, weeping, back to her hut.

Then, when Kiva and Kyne were eleven seasons old, Kyne had disappeared one day. When they asked Po where she'd gone, he told them that she'd left their hut in the middle of the night and hadn't come back. He didn't know why. A week later, Kyne reappeared, walking through the village with a group of Sisters. Kiva and her friends dared each other to talk to Kyne and find out what happened, but in the end the only one with the courage to approach Kyne had been Kiva.

She'd felt the eyes of the Sisters on her as she walked up to Kyne.

"Kyne," she'd begun, suddenly too timid to ask Kyne outright what had happened to her. "Do you . . . do you want to play with us?"

Kyne had turned up her nose at that.

"I don't have time to play," she said. "I'm one of the Sisters now."

Rumors in the village confirmed that what Kyne claimed was true. She'd seen a vision and was now the youngest girl to ever join the leaders of the Vagri in the center of the village. Some whispered that Kyne was going to be the next Vagra, as soon as the current Vagra died—and by the way Kyne carried herself through the village, her back straight and her nose lifted in the air, Kiva could tell that she believed it.

. . .

Now, looking at her, Kiva could see that Kyne hadn't changed. She had the same sharp nose and cheekbones, the same thin mouth pulled into a perpetual sneer. The same black eyes, which now fixed Kiva with a poisonous look.

"What are you doing here?" Kyne asked.

"She's had a vision," Liana said. "The Ancestors have spoken to her."

"We'll see about that," Kyne said, looking at Kiva, sizing her up.

Kiva's stomach burbled with an instant rage that she could barely understand. She didn't know why she was suddenly so angry. All she knew was that she wanted to wipe that smug look off Kyne's face.

Kyne smirked. "You're sure it was a vision? Maybe you just fell and hit your head. I'd hate to see you embarrass yourself in front of all the Sisters. In front of the Vagra."

"It was real," Kiva said. "It was a vision."

Kyne stepped closer and spoke so near to Kiva's face that she could feel the warmth of Kyne's breath on her cheeks. "Prove it," she said. "Tell me about this vision."

At Kiva's back, Liana cut in. "She doesn't have to explain herself to you. We came here to see the Vagra."

Kyne directed her smirk at Liana. "But I'll be Vagra soon enough."

Liana made a noncommittal motion with her shoulders, as if she didn't quite believe that Kyne would be Vagra but didn't care enough to argue, either.

"Perhaps," she said. "But you're not Vagra yet, are you?"

Kyne's gaze turned back to Kiva with a look of hauteur merging into anger, and Kiva understood at once that Kyne felt threatened by her—that the presence of another girl her own age among the Sisters would be a challenge to the status she'd gained among them. She could see all this in Kyne's eyes, but it was more than that: she could *feel* it as well, could hear it in echoes from Kyne's mind.

Enough! came a booming voice from the center of the camp—though whether it was a real voice or the sound of one of the Sisters' thoughts, Kiva couldn't be sure.

The chatter stopped and the Sisters turned to face the spot from which the voice had come.

Seeing the old woman standing there, Kiva felt certain that the booming shout couldn't have come from her. She was too small, too stooped to make such a sound. She stood outside the door to the mud hut in the center of the village.

The Vagra.

"Liana is right, Kyne," the Vagra said. "I'm not dead yet—so stop acting as though I am, as though the Ancestors have already named you to replace me."

The Vagra's lips moved with the words, but it was clear that it was not her voice alone that made the sounds Kiva was hearing—the sound echoed on two registers: the small, cracked voice of an old woman, and the reverberating boom of the woman's thoughts, beamed to all of the Sisters over the air through the power of her mind.

Kyne bowed her head, her face paling. "I'm sorry, Vagra, I merely thought—"

"Enough," the Vagra interrupted. "Bring the girl to me."

14

Kiva didn't move at first. Liana nodded her forward, to where the Vagra stood waiting.

"Go on," Liana said. "There's nothing to be afraid of."

Kiva obeyed. She walked ahead, toward the Vagra's hut, as Liana lingered behind. Kyne moved aside, and the rest of the Sisters parted to let Kiva pass.

When she came close to the Vagra's hut, the old woman held out her hand. It was wrinkled, warped, knotted.

"Come here, child."

Slowly, her steps halting, Kiva walked forward and took the Vagra's hand. The skin was loose and soft.

"Now you must wait," the Vagra said to the Sisters. "I'll tell you of my decision soon enough."

And with that, the two—old woman and teenage girl—turned and walked into the circular hut.

Kiva walked inside and blinked as her eyes adjusted to the darkness. The hut was sparsely furnished, practically empty. By the door was a bench made from blades of dried prairie grass lashed in a webbed pattern to a rough wooden frame; on the opposite side of the room was a cot of similar construction. In the center of the room, a hole in the roof let in the light of the Twins above.

The Vagra moved to the center of the room, the moonlight glistening on her hair. She crouched near a shallow pit filled with ashes and charred branches. From a small basket she took pieces of wood and placed them in the pit, propped one against the other. With a rock and flint she lit some kindling, then knelt and blew the small flames into a roaring blaze. Some of the smoke billowed up through the hole in the roof, but more of it stayed in the hut and filled the close space with a thick gray haze. Kiva coughed.

The Vagra stood and extended a hand.

"Come here."

With halting steps Kiva walked to the center of the room, toward the old woman's outstretched arm. When she reached the radius of the Vagra's grip, the older woman grabbed her by the shoulders. Kiva nearly tripped as the old woman's arms pulled her closer to the fire. Kiva's feet came dangerously close to the glowing embers, and the heat of the flames stung the bare skin of her calf. She sucked in a breath, but the Vagra paid no mind.

When the Vagra had Kiva where she wanted her, she reached into the basket once more and brought out a cut sheaf of grasses. The Vagra knelt and brushed the sheaf over Kiva's body, flicking her wrist as the dry blades scratched lightly across Kiva's shoulders, arms, and chest.

Then the old woman picked up a shallow clay bowl and a dull knife with a dark wooden handle. She set the bowl on the ground before her, then crumpled the sheaf of grasses she'd touched Kiva with in her hands, grinding it to dust in the bowl. She gripped the handle of the knife in one hand, the blade in the other. Kiva flinched as the Vagra drew near.

"Give me your hand," she said.

"Why?"

The Vagra sighed impatiently. "The faster you cooperate, the faster it will be over."

Kiva slowly extended a quivering hand. The Vagra seized it out of the air and yanked it toward herself. She put the blade against Kiva's palm and drew the sharp edge across it. Kiva hissed and bit her lip against the pain.

The old woman shaped Kiva's hand into a fist above the bowl. Blood, black and shiny in the dim hut, dripped from between her fingers and pooled in the dust. The Vagra hunched over, mixed the blood and dust into a dark paste with two fingers, then threw some of the paste into the fire.

The flames hissed, roared, pouring even more smoke into the room, then died down again. The fire had changed color—still red at the lapping tips of the flames, at their root the tongues of fire had turned from yellow to pale green.

Kiva trembled, her breaths coming shallow but her heart pounding in her chest. She looked from the fire to the Vagra, who'd begun wiping the bloody paste from her hands with a damp, dirty cloth. Then she took a clean cloth and tied it around the cut on Kiva's hand.

"Go," she said, nodding toward the bench at the door. "Bring it here." She pointed to the spot next to the fire.

Kiva walked to the door, lifted the bench, and hefted it to the place where the Vagra pointed.

The old woman lowered herself onto the bench.

"Sit," she commanded, and Kiva sank to her knees in the dirt.

The Vagra closed her eyes and took a deep breath through her nose.

"Now, tell me about this vision."

Kiva told her what she had seen.

The old woman's eyes remained closed. She breathed slowly in and out. Then, finally, she spoke.

"What you saw was no dream."

"So Liana was right," Kiva said. "I'm to be one of the Sisters."

The old woman's eyes came open and she shook her head.

"No, child," she said. "Not one of the Sisters. The Ancestors have chosen you to replace me. You will be the new Vagra."

PART 3

PREMONITIONS

15

matthew

On the day Matthew had gone into cryostasis the technician told him that he wouldn't feel anything, that going into the freeze would be painless, and that he wouldn't dream—that he'd experience the light-years in cryostasis as lost time.

The technician had lied.

Matthew may have been frozen in cryostasis, but his mind was awake—awake and dreaming. While his body slept, images and memories of Earth, of his family, of his past, drifted through his mind like movies he had no choice but to watch, playing on a never-ending loop.

. . .

Matthew squinted into the sunlight. Wisps of cloud curled their fingers across the sky, broke, and reformed on the wind. At the edges of his vision, black birds perched on the bare fingers of the trees, squawking tentatively into the bright day, their voices confused and afraid.

"Is it brighter than usual?" Matthew's mother asked. "Maybe they're right. Maybe we shouldn't be out here."

"It's fine. A little sun never hurt anyone," Matthew's father said.

Matthew looked down from the blinding white sky and met his father's eyes. They all sat together on a blanket in the backyard of their old house, the one they lived in before everything went bad and they had to move into the compound at the edge of the city. His father looked back at Matthew and nodded, as though Matthew had asked him a question.

"We're fine. Everything's fine. Go on, eat your sandwich."

Matthew took a bite, even though he wasn't hungry. His father had made his turkey sandwich the wrong way, put mayonnaise on it instead of butter, added mustard, which Matthew didn't like at all, and hadn't cut off the crusts, as his mother always did. But Matthew knew not to complain. He'd sensed something forced in the way his father had come home from work with a wild smile plastered on his face and announced, his voice buoyant and just a little too loud, that they were going to have a picnic.

Matthew chewed, swallowed, and looked at his mother, who was taking small, nervous bites of her own sandwich. She saw him looking and smiled thinly.

"It's fine," she said. "We're fine."

But then Matthew's father stood up and strode to where Sophie, only two years old, was playing in the dirt, and Matthew saw for the first time as he walked away the redness on the back of his neck.

"Mom, why—," he began, meaning to ask why his father's skin had turned so red, but something in his mother's eyes told him to stop. "Why is the grass so brown?" he asked instead.

"I don't know, honey," his mother said. "I guess we just haven't watered it in so long. What with the rationing and all."

Matthew finished his sandwich while his father crouched and scooped up Sophie by the armpits, threw her squealing into the air and caught her again. He spun her around in a circle, laughing his wild laugh.

Then he collapsed into the dirt, Sophie still cradled in his arms.

Matthew's mother gasped and ran to his father, put her hands lightly on his body just underneath his neck, patted him to feel for a pulse. She ignored Sophie, who'd had the wind knocked out of her when she fell to the ground and was taking a series of shuddering breaths, preparing to scream. Matthew walked to his sister and touched her shoulder, and at once Sophie cut the air with a wail.

"Dale," his mother said, still ignoring both of them. "Dale, wake up!"

Matthew began to cry along with Sophie.

His mother's eyes snapped up. "Stop crying," she said. "You have to help me move him. You have to help me get him inside."

. . .

There was a hole in Matthew's memory between the backyard and the house—even in cryosleep, his mind couldn't recall how he and his mother managed to get both his father and Sophie back inside. The next thing he remembered was sitting on the couch, his sister's warm body pressed up next to his. All cried out, Sophie was now whimpering quietly. Across the room, the TV was on—

their mother had turned it on and put them in front of it to keep them quiet while she attended to their father in the next room. But in her rush, she hadn't taken the time to find a show Matthew and Sophie might like to watch, so it was the news on the screen, talking heads speaking sentences the two children were too young to understand.

"... reporting that the self-replicating nanites created to combat the effects of global warming backfired instead, eating through the atmosphere's delicate ozone layer ..."

From the hallway came the sound of water running. Their mother drawing their father a cold bath.

"Goddammit, Dale, what the hell were you thinking?" Their mother was trying to whisper, but in her anger her hiss was loud enough for Matthew to hear in the living room.

"Just got a little lightheaded," their father mumbled, awake now. "It's nothing. Nothing to be worried about."

"... a deadly convergence of rapid global heating and an alarming spike in levels of solar radiation ..."

"We're moving," their mother said. "That's it. We're moving."

"What, to one of those . . . those compounds? You honestly think we can afford to buy our way into one of those?"

Sophie squeezed up closer to Matthew. The place on Matthew's body where she pressed against him was hot and sweaty, but he put his arm around his sister and pulled her tight anyway.

"I've heard of some where you can pay by working," their mother said. "Corporate-owned."

". . . Government sources advising people to stay inside unless absolutely necessary ..."

80

"Those places are traps," their father said. "Sign one of those contracts and they own you for life. It's modern-day slavery."

"You'd rather keep working construction? You'd rather work outside? You'll die, Dale."

"I won't," their father said.

Under Matthew's arm, Sophie turned from the TV. Matthew looked down and met her gaze. Her eyes so big, so brown.

"Daddy okay?" Sophie asked.

"... the death of all life on planet Earth ..."

Matthew felt himself beginning to cry again but fought the tears back, tried to be strong for his little sister.

"He'll be fine," Matthew said. "We're fine. Everything's fine."

. . .

But everything wasn't fine. Their father did die, one of the first victims of a new disease that would come to be known as "sun poisoning." It was an affliction suffered by those who spent long hours outside, before radiation suits became commonplace. Their bodies unable to handle the extreme heat and solar radiation, victims of sun poisoning simply dropped dead—severely burned, dehydrated, organs failing.

And Matthew's mother did, in spite of her husband's objections, sign a contract with a company called Cheminex, a manufacturer of industrial solvents. The contract allowed her, Sophie, and Matthew to live in a company-owned compound at the edge of the city that was equal parts factory, apartment building, and shopping mall. Inside was a school for Matthew and Sophie, walking trails, stores, and indoor parks with fake grass where people threw balls for their dogs to fetch and pretended that everything was normal.

The only price for all this was that their mother had to work ten hours every day with toxic chemicals—and that Matthew and Sophie had to do their best to pretend they didn't smell the chemicals on her when she came home at the end of the day and made them dinner.

.   .   .

Now Matthew's dreaming skipped ahead in time, to the day that their mother revealed to them that she had cancer. She and Sophie sat together on the couch—Sophie crying, their mother sitting silent, rubbing his sister's back in a small circle—while Matthew paced the room thinking, *Not again, not again, not this again.*

"It's those chemicals," Matthew said finally. "Those goddamn chemicals you work with every day."

"Watch your language," his mother said. "And besides, it's not the chemicals. The bosses told me it's not. My work is perfectly safe. This is just something that happens."

"Cancer isn't just *something that happens,*" Matthew said.

"Well, getting angry about it won't help," their mother said.

Matthew ignored her. "What we need is a plan. Time. If we can't afford the treatments then maybe we can just slow the cancer down while we save up our money."

"And how do you propose doing that?" their mother asked.

"I don't know," Matthew said. "Maybe . . ."

.   .   .

Another jump, and now Matthew was sitting in an examining room, holding his mother's thin hand. He looked down at the hand and thought about how dry and cold and frail it felt, wondering if it would shatter to pieces in his if he squeezed it too hard. Sophie on the other side, propping their mother up, sniffling.

The technician on the other side of the room, busying himself at a metal table, then turning, holding a syringe aloft, tapping at the shaft with his latexed fingernail. The cryochamber waiting behind him.

Matthew squeezed his mother's hand.

"We'll get you out," he said. "I promise. I don't know how yet, but we'll get you out."

. . .

All the while, as these memories played through Matthew's mind in a never-ending loop, his body lay in a cryochamber, sleeping beneath layers of blue ice. To either side, two more cryochambers lay horizontal, like coffins in a crypt—Dunne and Sam sleeping inside and dreaming their own dreams, perhaps, of the lives they'd left behind on Earth.

And meanwhile, just beyond the thin membrane of the hull, stars and nebulae and clouds of luminous space dust flew by in a blur as the ship's lightspeed drive propelled them across the galaxy and toward their destination.

16

kiva

With straightened fingers Kiva eased aside one half of the split cloth that hung in the doorway of the Vagra's hut and peered outside. The Sisters had gathered, the oldest of the women sitting cross-legged in front, with the younger women and girls behind them, standing on tiptoes and straining to see. One exception was Kyne, who sat in the front of the crowd with the older women and stared straight toward the door, where Kiva was standing.

Kiva drew in her breath sharply and stepped back into the darkness of the hut. Had Kyne seen her?

Kiva shook her head and forced herself to laugh. It shouldn't have mattered whether Kyne had seen her or not—it wasn't like she was hiding in the Vagra's hut. The old woman's hut was where Kiva had lived for the past four seasons, ever since her vision past the edge of the village. Everyone knew that she and the old woman were inside; the Sisters were waiting for them, after all. Besides, wasn't she next in line to lead the village? Why should she care what Kyne saw, what she thought?

Kiva turned to face the Vagra, who sat on the cot in the middle of the room. The old woman was hunched over, barely able to sit straight, but her eyes were alert, looking at Kiva expectantly.

"Have they gathered?" she asked in a quavering voice.

Kiva nodded. "They have, Vagra. Are you ready?"

The Vagra nodded and held out her hand. Kiva crossed the room to take it, then helped the old woman stand. She wobbled on her feet. Fearful she might fall, Kiva quickly propped her shoulder up under the Vagra's armpit and looped her own arm around the Vagra's back.

The Vagra glanced at Kiva as they made their way slowly to the door.

"I should be making you lead these meetings," she said. "I'm too frail for this."

Kiva's stomach fluttered at the thought of facing the Sisters all alone. She shook her head.

"But you're still the Vagra," she said. "As long as you're alive, the Sisters look to you to lead them."

The old woman chuckled.

"Don't worry, child. I won't be alive much longer. You'll get your chance soon enough."

Kiva sighed and put her eyes forward.

That's not what I'm worried about.

The thought came to Kiva's mind before she could think to suppress it. She held her breath as she waited for the Vagra to say something. But they walked a few more steps, and still the Vagra kept her tongue.

Kiva let her breath out.

The Vagra's powers had been diminishing along with her

health. It seemed that the old woman could no longer hear what Kiva was thinking—not consistently, anyway. This was in part a comfort, since it meant that the Vagra no longer surprised Kiva by picking up on something she hadn't even realized that she'd been thinking. But it was also a source of worry—a constant reminder that the Vagra's days as the leader of the village were numbered, and that Kiva would soon be forced to take her place as the new Vagra.

Hang on just a little bit longer, Vagra, Kiva thought, confident now that the old woman wouldn't hear her. *I'm not ready yet.*

Eventually Kiva and the Vagra reached the door. The chatter of the Sisters quieted when they walked through the door into the light of day. Under a heavy silence in which Kiva felt the Sisters' eyes on her, she helped the Vagra take a seat on the ground, then knelt in the dirt a couple paces behind her.

"Sisters," the Vagra said. "We gather today in the presence of the Ancestors."

"*The Ancestors are the ones who have gone before, the ones who have passed on,*" the Sisters replied. Kiva chanted with them, thoughts and voices moving together in unison. "*They went to a place both beyond and within this place. They walk alongside us. They bind us to one another. They heal us. And they speak to us. They show us things we must see.*"

The monthly Sisters' council meeting had begun.

. . .

First came a report on the crop yields from the men's gardens in the village. An older Sister named Mira had been placed in charge of the village's food supply; she reported that this month's yield was higher than expected, and the Vagri now had more food than they needed.

"Commend the men on their hard work," the Vagra said. "Tell them to take a week's rest from working in their gardens." A knowing smile came across the old woman's face. "And perhaps, Sisters, this would be a good time to visit your men in their huts. For such a bountiful yield they deserve to be . . . *rewarded*."

A murmur of laughter rippled across the crowd; in the back, the younger Sisters, the ones who hadn't been mated yet, tittered.

Next was a time for the blessing of new babies before they went to live with their fathers in the village, or the welcoming of girls who'd had their first visitation by the Ancestors and were ready to join the Sisters in the center of the village. Often, the Vagra simply skipped over this part of the meeting—there weren't always new babies to bless, or new Sisters to welcome. Today there were no babies ("Another reason for you to visit your men, Sisters," the Vagra said with a wry smile, to more laughter), but there were two new Sisters: Thruss and Rehal.

Kiva caught their eyes as they were brought forward and the two girls grinned nervously.

"Come here, Sisters," the Vagra said. "Don't be afraid."

Over the past two weeks, both Thruss and Rehal had been brought separately by their mothers to the Vagra's hut. Kiva had looked on as the Vagra performed the blood ceremony on them, mixing the thick fluid of their veins with the dust of dead Gle'an grass and throwing the mixture into the fire to see the flames change color. For both girls, the ceremony had confirmed it: the Ancestors were with them.

Now, Kiva listened as her old friends described their first visitation from the Ancestors to the gathered Sisters. Kiva had done the same thing at the first council meeting she'd attended, describing her vision of the Strangers to the silent crowd. Neither Thruss nor Rehal had anything quite so interesting to recount: both had merely caught small snatches of someone else's thoughts, nothing more. Even among the Sisters, visions were rare—only the women who were strongest with the Ancestors received them.

Not that Kiva had been seeing many visions lately.

She sighed and tried to put it out of her mind.

After Thruss and Rehal had been welcomed by the Vagra, they returned to the crowd of Sisters.

Then, the main part of the monthly council meeting began: a time when the Sisters could bring their requests, disagreements, and grievances to the Vagra for resolution. This was where Kiva's power to hear the thoughts of anyone in the village was most useful. Since living with the Vagra, Kiva had learned how to block the flood of thoughts coming into her mind at every moment and pick out only one voice at a time. She and the Vagra spoke often about what Kiva heard—thoughts of disagreements and resentments between the Sisters, problems among the men, children misbehaving. Usually she and the Vagra were able to guess at the problems that existed in the village and devise a solution long before one of the Sisters brought it before them at a meeting.

Not always, though. Some of the Sisters, and even some of the men, were harder to read than others, seeming to keep their thoughts and feelings so deep inside them that not even Kiva could hear them. One such person was Kyne, who rose now from her seated position at the front of the crowd and cleared her throat to speak.

"Vagra," Kyne said. "Kiva. Sisters. I want to speak today about the Strangers. About Kiva's vision."

A cluster of nerves fluttered up from the pit of Kiva's stomach. Her vision. When she'd told it to the Sisters at her first council meeting, a hush had come over the crowd and many of the women lifted their hands to their mouths in fear. Moments later, the women burst out speaking all at once, in a panic. The Vagra had calmed them by reassuring them that the Ancestors would tell Kiva more when the time came. That silenced the Sisters' voices, but it didn't silence their fears, didn't stop them from rising at later council meetings to ask questions about the Strangers: what they wanted, whether they meant the Vagri harm, when they might come—questions Kiva didn't know the answers to.

"So speak," the Vagra said now. "What about the Strangers?"

"It's been four seasons since Kiva foresaw their coming, Vagra. And still no preparations have been made. No precautions taken."

The Vagra bowed her head in silent acknowledgment of Kyne's complaint.

"That's true," the old woman said. "We await instruction from the Ancestors. We know that the Strangers are coming—that much was clear from Kiva's vision. But we don't know who they are. We don't know why they're coming to this place. And we don't know whether they're a threat to us."

Kiva felt her face grow hot. The Vagra's words were an

acknowledgment of Kiva's failure—that's not how the old woman meant them, but that's how the Sisters would take them. Echoes from their minds flooded into Kiva's brain, confirming her fears.

But how?

How could Kiva not know more about the Strangers by now?

Aren't the Ancestors with her?

Maybe the Vagra was wrong. Maybe Kiva's not the one we've been waiting for.

"I understand, Vagra," Kyne said. "But we can't wait any longer. The Strangers could be here any day now. And if they are a threat . . ."

Kyne trailed off, leaving the rest of the sentence unspoken, to be finished by each of the Sisters in their minds:

. . . they could destroy us all.

"We must go to the Forsaken," Kyne said. "They've helped the Vagri fight off enemies before. They have weapons. They can protect us."

"I see," the Vagra said. She put a finger to her lips and thought for a few moments. "And who would we send to the Forsaken? What would we say?"

Kyne stood up straight, thrust her chest out proudly. "I will go to them," she said. "I will ask them to send some of their men to the village, to stand guard in case the Strangers come."

The Vagra shook her head. "No. I will not allow it."

"But Vagra—"

"Enough," the Vagra said, a hand lifted in the air to silence Kyne. "Most of you are too young to remember the last time the Vagri had to enlist the help of the Forsaken to fight off an enemy.

I am not. Sisters, making contact with the Forsaken is no simple matter. It should not be taken lightly. Asking the Forsaken to come here to fight for us is easy. Making them return to the wilderness after the fight is over is not."

"The Forsaken are only men, men who used to live in our village," Kyne said. "We can control them. They'll listen to us, just like our own men listen to us—because they know we have the wisdom of the Ancestors on our side."

"No," the Vagra said, shaking her head. "A man with a weapon cannot be controlled. A whole group of them even less so. Anyone who says they believe otherwise is either a liar or a fool."

Kyne colored.

"It's true the Forsaken are men who used to live among us," the Vagra continued. "But remember why they left, Sisters: because they could not live in this village in peace, as we do. Something happens to the men when they join the Forsaken, when they take up weapons. They become wild, violent—they live to fight, to kill. The Forsaken are an energy that cannot be contained, cannot be controlled. As long as that energy is directed outward, the Forsaken serve us by driving our enemies away. But beware of turning that energy inward, toward this village. If the Forsaken come here, they may serve us for a time. But what happens then? What happens after they've driven the Strangers away, after they start to get restless? What happens if they begin to turn their attention to us and lust after our power over the Vagri? No. I won't allow it. We're a peaceful people, Sisters—we have been ever since the days when First Mother heard the voice of the Ancestors, calling her to begin a new kind of tribe, one that doesn't live by killing. I'm not going to risk changing that by bringing weapons into this village, simply because you're afraid."

Kyne's blush deepened, but by the way the Vagra's head swiveled from side to side as she spoke, Kiva knew that the old woman's scolding wasn't meant for Kyne alone—she meant for all the Sisters to hear her warning about the Forsaken.

"But what about the Strangers?" Kyne demanded. "If we won't ask the Forsaken to protect us, then what will we do?"

There were nods and murmurs in the crowd.

"You leave that to Kiva and me," the Vagra said. "The Ancestors will tell us what we must do soon enough."

There was a long moment of silence. Kiva could tell by the looks on the faces of the Sisters—especially Kyne—that though the Vagra's words had put an end to the debate for now, the Sisters still weren't satisfied. Their fears, their doubts, their dissatisfaction with Kiva: all these were things that would rear their heads again and again and again.

"Anything else?" the Vagra asked.

The silence stretched out.

"Very well," the Vagra said. "The meeting is over. Return to your huts, Sisters."

17

After Kiva helped the Vagra back into the hut, the old woman turned toward her, eyes blazing with sudden urgency.

"You should have spoken up in the meeting," she said. "The Sisters won't respect you if you're always so timid."

Kiva bit her lower lip, chastened. "But it's not my time yet. You're Vagra still."

"That's true," the Vagra said as she lowered herself carefully to sit on the cot, the wood creaking as the stretched fabric strained to hold the old woman's weight. "But you will be Vagra after I'm gone. You need to start acting like it now. Being Vagra isn't just about communing with the Ancestors. You actually have to lead."

Kiva's eyes stung. She blinked, willed herself not to cry under the Vagra's scolding.

"I know I should have said something to put Kyne in her place," she said. "But I didn't know what to say. She's right. I don't know what to do about the Strangers. No more than I knew four seasons ago. The Ancestors show me the same vision every time: the blinding flash of light, the stone bird flying between the stars, the three figures on the horizon. That's it. I don't know. Maybe . . ." She trailed off, shook her head. "Maybe Kyne is right. Maybe we *should* go to the Forsaken for protection."

"No," the Vagra said, her voice firm. "We can't. Not unless you're sure."

"Sure of what?" Kiva asked.

"Sure that letting the Strangers come would be worse."

Kiva studied the Vagra's face closely. The old woman had taught her much—taught her how to push away the constant din of the Vagri's thoughts in her mind and listen to one voice at a time, taught her how to lead, when the time came—but Kiva couldn't shake the sense that there were things she still kept secret. Things the Vagra would rather take to her grave than talk about. Things Kiva needed to know.

"What happened?" she asked, finally. "The last time you went to the Forsaken for help."

The Vagra shook her head. "It didn't end well."

"I need to know," Kiva said. "If I'm going to lead the Vagri, then I need to know *everything*."

The Vagra was silent for a few moments. Then she sighed. A hardness in her seemed to break as she let out her breath.

"Sit," she said, nodding at the ground in front of her.

Kiva lowered herself to the ground, crossed her legs beneath her, and looked up at the Vagra's face.

"How much do you already know?" the Vagra asked.

Kiva hesitated to admit what she'd heard. The hatred of violence was so deeply ingrained in the village that the Sisters forbade the children from even telling stories that featured it.

"Come, child," the Vagra said. "Don't play dumb. I'm no fool. I know the men still talk about it, late at night when their women aren't around."

The Vagra was right. Kiva'd heard the tale as a girl from Grath, when Liana was away in the Sisters' camp.

"Marauders came and captured the village," Kiva said. "They tried to kill you so they could rule the village in your place. But you escaped. Went to the Forsaken. Together, you came back and took the village back from the marauders. The leader of the Forsaken died in battle, but there was a boy—a brave boy named Xendr Chathe, who killed many enemy fighters. He became the new leader of the Forsaken, and led them into the prairie to get rid of our enemies as far as the foot of the mountains."

The Vagra nodded. "That's right, as far as it goes—but it's only half the story."

The old woman's eyes drifted up toward the ceiling of the hut. A silence drew out, but Kiva didn't prod the Vagra to go on. She sensed that the old woman was only trying to decide where to begin.

"It was almost fifty seasons ago," she said. "I was a younger woman then—around the age your mother is now. We hadn't seen a single enemy in all the time I'd been Vagra. I thought that maybe they'd decided to leave us alone. But I was wrong. They were only gathering their strength. When they came for us, it was with greater numbers than ever before. I can still see them thundering into the village, killing the men and children. The blood of my people running black in the lanes between the huts."

The Vagra closed her eyes, seemed to hold her breath. She shook her head and gave a shudder.

"I didn't stay to see what they'd do with me—I ran. I escaped into the prairie and went to the meeting place with the Forsaken. I lit a fire and waited for them to arrive. The leader of the Forsaken in those days was a man named Tevek. A bad man, it turned out—though I didn't know it at the time. Or maybe I did know it but simply didn't have any other choice than to ask for his help. Anyway, Tevek gathered his men and we rode back to the village. The Forsaken killed most of the marauders and drove the rest away into the prairie. I thought that would be the end of it. But it wasn't."

"What happened?" Kiva asked.

"Tevek didn't want to go back to the wilderness. He wanted what the marauders wanted. He wanted to rule the village. He wanted to make the Vagri his slaves—to make the Sisters follow him instead of me, and to force the men and children to work for him."

A sick feeling clenched at Kiva's gut. "*Slaves*," she said. The word tasted foul on her tongue—it was unfamiliar, though she could guess at its meaning. "I don't understand. How could Tevek take power away from the Vagra? How could he force a man to work who doesn't want to?"

"This is what I've been trying to tell you," the Vagra said. "The Forsaken may be from us, but they're different than us. Something happens to a man when he picks up a weapon—he begins to see the world as something that can belong to him, if he wants it. He begins to see the world as a thing to be taken by force."

Kiva shuddered. "So what did you do?"

The Vagra hesitated before going on. Kiva's pulse quickened—she sensed that the Vagra was coming to the part of the story that she'd wanted to keep secret, the part of the story that she wanted to die with her.

"Xendr Chathe," she said. "He was only a boy at the time, younger even than you are now—fourteen, maybe fifteen. But he'd distinguished himself in the battle against the marauders, killed twice as many of them as some of the most experienced Forsaken warriors. Stories of his bravery spread throughout the village, and I could tell that the Forsaken admired him. The boy warrior. As soon as I learned of Tevek's plans to take over the village and rule it as his own, I met secretly with Xendr. We struck a deal—if I could get rid of Tevek and make Xendr the new leader of the Forsaken, he'd take his men away from the village and never come back unless I summoned him."

"Get rid of Tevek? What do you mean?" Kiva asked, a droplet of unease falling into her stomach and spreading out like ice.

The Vagra gave Kiva a grim look. "I've never told anyone about this. No one in the village can ever know. You have to promise."

"Of course," Kiva said, giving the assurance the Vagra needed to continue with her story—even though she wasn't sure she wanted to hear what the old woman would say next.

"Tevek wanted to be mated to me," she said. "That was to be the first step in his plan to take over the village—a symbol to the Vagri and the Forsaken that he was now the ruler of the village, that I'd given all my power to him. That night, after my secret meeting with Xendr Chathe, I pretended to agree to Tevek's demand. I took him into my hut. Then, as soon as he followed me through the door, I whirled around and put a dagger in his chest."

Kiva sucked in a breath. Covering her mouth in shock, she looked around the hut. It had happened here. In this very room. Her eyes followed the Vagra's to a table that sat next to the cot, with a dagger sitting on top. It was the blade that the old woman used to conduct blood ceremonies on girls who'd heard the voice of the Ancestors. Was it the same one she'd used to kill Tevek? Kiva didn't know, and she wasn't about to ask.

"But what did you do with the body?" Kiva asked, still not meeting the Vagra's eyes. "What did you tell the Sisters?"

"I told them that he'd simply dropped dead while we'd been talking," she said. "I said that he must have been injured in the battle and didn't tell anybody. And they believed it. No one suspected me of killing him myself. No one knew. Except Xendr Chathe."

"But he left," Kiva said. "He held up his part of the deal."

The Vagra nodded solemnly. "Yes, he did. The next morning I called a ceremony with all the Sisters, all the Vagri, all the Forsaken. We gave Tevek a hero's funeral—put his body on a pyre and burned it. Then, in front of everyone, I honored Xendr Chathe for his bravery in battle. Afterward, Xendr gave a speech to the Forsaken. He called them to follow him into the plains, where they'd continue pursuing the marauders until all the enemies of the Vagri had been wiped off the face of Gle'ah. He whipped them into a frenzy, promised they'd all be heroes, that they wouldn't stop until each of them, every Forsaken warrior, had a thousand kills to his name. Then he left the village and they marched out after him, shouting and whooping and waving their weapons in the air all the way. And that was that. Life in the village went on as it had before. No one ever knew what I did. No one ever knew how close they were to being enslaved by Tevek."

"And the Forsaken?" Kiva asked. "What have they been doing all this time?"

"The Forsaken spent the next forty seasons following Xendr Chathe deeper and deeper into the plains, looking for new enemies to fight, new people to kill." The Vagra closed her eyes again, drew a long breath through her nostrils. "I saw it in my visions, sometimes. The people they slaughtered. The violence that was the price of peace in this village. And every time he and his men returned from one of their murderous excursions, I held my breath. Wondered if this would be the time that Xendr would grow tired of our deal. If he'd come back to this village, wanting what his predecessor wanted. But he never did."

The Vagra let her eyes come open. She blinked. Her eyes seemed to clear. She fixed Kiva with a hard gaze.

"For fifty seasons Xendr Chathe has kept his part of the bargain. He's kept the Forsaken's attention focused outward, away from this village. But if you bring them into this village, I'm not sure how long that will last. Xendr is an old man now—not as old as me, but still, he may have grown tired of living in the wilderness. That's why you have to be sure before you go to him for help. Sure that letting the Strangers come will be worse than bringing the Forsaken back into the village."

Kiva stood and paced across the room. The dilemma the Vagra was giving to her seemed to be an impossible one. If she went to the Forsaken for protection, they might take over the village and destroy the Vagri's way of life; if she didn't, they might be destroyed by the Strangers. And if she did nothing . . .

At the far end of the hut Kiva turned back to face the Vagra once more.

"I need more time," she said.

But the old woman shook her head.

"More time is the one thing you don't have," she said. "You saw what happened in the council meeting. The Sisters are growing restless. They're beginning to doubt your leadership. If you don't come up with a plan to deal with the Strangers, and soon, they'll find someone else to lead them. Someone like . . ."

The old woman trailed off. She didn't have to say the name. Kiva knew who the Vagra meant.

Kiva walked to the door and peered through the slit in the doorhang. The Sisters still lingered outside, milling about and murmuring to each other. Kiva's eyes darted back and forth until she found the person she was looking for, who was at that moment smiling a good-bye at the woman she'd been talking to and turning to walk to her hut.

Kyne.

Kyne's face darkened as she walked away from the Sisters, and Kiva's heart thrummed deep in her chest.

Someone like Kyne.

18

kyne

Kyne seethed as she walked back to her hut from the Sisters' council meeting. A darkness spread inside her like night bleeding black across the evening sky. It began in her chest and curled its inky tentacles into her brain, her stomach, her limbs, all the way to the tips of her fingers and toes.

She'd felt this darkness before. As a girl, she'd felt it whenever she overheard one of the fathers gossiping about her in sorrowful tones, whenever she saw one of the other children give her a furtive look of pity, or fascination, or disgust. Anything that reminded her of the way she feared the Vagri saw her—as the girl who had no mother, the girl who'd killed her mother—made the darkness inside her grow.

Kyne couldn't remember a single moment of her life when she'd been without this darkness. It had been with her ever since the day her mother had died after giving birth to her and her twin brother, Po. Sometimes the darkness grew so large it seemed to be bigger than her entire body; other times it shrank to the size of a small dot just underneath her breastbone—but no matter its size, the darkness was always there.

There was only one thing to do when the darkness got big enough that it took over every part of her: lash out at whoever was unfortunate enough to be nearby. The darkness inside Kyne isolated her; she knew this, but she didn't care. In the moment, all that mattered was making others hurt the way she hurt. And she proved to be skilled at hurting others with her words, at spotting the one thing that made her target vulnerable: a limp, a scar, a stutter, a family embarrassment. Whatever it was, Kyne would pick at it and pick at it until her victim broke down into tears and the other children looked at Kyne no longer with pity, but with fear—fear that if they weren't careful, they'd be next.

It felt good, lashing out. But the good feeling never lasted long.

Now, as Kyne ducked to step inside her small hut in the Sisters' camp, she looked around the close room and felt her rage grow from a simmer to a boil. Kyne usually found her living quarters cozy, but now the smallness of the space was simply a reminder of where she didn't live: the Vagra's hut in the center of the village. It was a reminder that the Ancestors hadn't chosen her.

A roar of fury rose up inside her chest, but she didn't want to let it loose for fear that one of the other Sisters would hear. Instead, Kyne's eyes fell on a lamp sitting by her bedside, a lit wick angled out of a clay pot filled with oil. She crossed the room to the lamp in a single step and extinguished the flame between her thumb and forefinger. In the brief moment before the flame was smothered, she felt a small but sharp pain on her fingertips and thought of her humiliation at the council meeting—*the Vagra called me a fool,* Kyne thought, *she said I was afraid, and in front of everyone, all the Sisters.* Then, the wick snuffed, she cupped her palm on the side of the clay basin and flung it across the room. It shattered in an explosion of clay shards and splashing oil.

Kyne stood for a moment facing the place where the lamp had struck the wall, her hands curled into fists at her sides. She felt better, a little. But not enough. The darkness was still there, roiling just underneath her skin.

"Kyne?" came a voice behind her.

"What?" Kyne snapped as she whirled around to face the doorway.

It was Thruss and Rehal, Kiva's friends. Kyne had played with all three of them when they were girls, but they'd never been her friends. Kiva, Thruss, and Rehal had never *wanted* to play with Kyne—she knew this. But they had tolerated Kyne's presence because they were afraid of her.

There was fear in their eyes now, too, but Kyne sensed it wasn't her they were afraid of this time. At least, not just her.

"Well?" Kyne demanded. "Go on, don't just stand there. What is it?"

"We're sorry, Sister," Thruss said.

Kyne's anger began to dissolve. It pleased her to hear Thruss address her with respect, as "Sister" rather than "Kyne." She felt a smile creep to her lips, but she quickly suppressed it. Let Thruss and Rehal squirm a while longer.

"We wanted to ask you about what happened at the council meeting. We didn't understand everything that was said."

Kyne sniffed. Why had Thruss and Rehal come to Kyne with their questions rather than to Kiva? Maybe now they were more afraid of Kiva than they'd ever been of Kyne.

"Sit," Kyne said, nodding toward two wooden footstools. Thruss and Rehal sat, but Kyne kept her feet, towering over the other two girls. "What is it you want to know?"

Rehal cleared her throat.

"The Strangers," she said. "You and the Vagra kept talking about someone called the Strangers."

Kiva nodded. "The Strangers are . . . creatures, beings—no one knows—that Kiva saw in her first vision. The one she had four seasons ago, the one that put her next in line to be Vagra after the old woman is dead. Kiva told us about the vision at the first council meeting she attended, just like you had to tell us about your visitation from the Ancestors."

"But why doesn't anyone in the village know about this?" Rehal asked. "The men, the children? Why wasn't anyone told?"

"The Sisters often talk about things that they don't share with the men and children," Kyne said. "You'll have to get used to it. The things we discuss in council—you can't tell your father, your brothers. Not even your mate, if the day ever comes when you decide to take one."

"These Strangers," Thruss said, leaning forward. "Kiva knows they're coming, but she doesn't know why, or whether they're a threat. But you think they are. And that's why you want to go to the Forsaken."

"Yes," Kyne said. "But the Vagra doesn't approve. As you saw."

104

"But you're right, aren't you?" Thruss said. "Kiva and the Vagra, they don't have a better plan, do they?"

"Thruss, don't," Rehal said, her voice soft but pleading. "Kiva's our friend. If she thinks that there's a better way—"

"But we don't know *what* she thinks," Thruss said. "She didn't even talk during the meeting. And she's *not* our friend anymore. We've barely seen her since she was named to be Vagra."

Kyne watched Rehal and Thruss with a growing sense of amazement, not quite believing what she was hearing. If Kiva's own friends doubted her, what must the rest of the Sisters think? When the girls turned their gazes back to Kyne, she felt dizzy.

The girls' faces tugged at something in Kyne—something deep in her mind, something she'd buried there long ago, on the day she'd first come to the Sisters' camp. She'd been young when she'd first heard the voice of the Ancestors: eleven seasons, the youngest girl to ever receive a vision from the beings who watched over and guided the Vagri. As she'd marched to the Vagra's hut to undergo the blood ritual, she'd felt the Sisters' eyes on her and heard in her mind the whisper of their thoughts.

Look at her.

So young.

The Ancestors must have a plan for her.

Perhaps she'll be our next Vagra.

In that moment, Kyne had felt something grow from nothing inside her, larger and more insistent than the darkness had ever been: ambition, the dream of being the leader of the village, of seeing the faces of the Vagri looking toward her not with pity or fear—but with admiration, expectation, and deference. The way people look at a leader.

The way Thruss and Rehal were looking at her now.

Kyne had buried her ambition deep inside her on the day that Kiva, not Kyne, had been named the next Vagra—but now Kyne felt it growing again, coming to the surface. With effort, she pushed it back down, put the thought behind the barrier she'd built for herself in her mind.

Not here. Not where Kiva could hear her thoughts.

"Maybe . . . maybe Kiva needs our help," Thruss said. "Maybe she *wants* to go to the Forsaken but she can't because she's scared of them, or scared of the Vagra. Maybe *we* need to—"

"Stop," Kyne said. "The first thing you need to do is stop talking, right now. Don't even *think* what you were about to say, not here. It's not safe. Kiva could be listening."

Thruss's eyes widened; Rehal's too.

"She can hear *everything* we're thinking?" Rehal asked.

"Not everything," Kyne said. "All at once, the voices of the men, children, and the Sisters are too much for her—Kiva can only understand our thoughts by letting in one voice at a time. Still, she could be listening to any one of us. You have to learn how to guard your thoughts, Sisters."

"But then how—," Thruss began. Kyne cut her off by lifting her flattened palm into the air.

"Not here," she said. "I can teach you. Until then we can't talk about this unless we're outside the village, safely away from the reach of Kiva's powers."

Thruss nodded. Rehal looked nervous, hesitant about what was happening, but she didn't protest.

"And what about the Forsaken?" Thruss asked.

Kyne turned away. She didn't agree with the Vagra's hesitance to go to the Forsaken for protection against the Strangers, but the old woman had been right about one thing: making contact with the Forsaken would be no simple task. What Kyne needed was a man, someone who could be sent to live with the Forsaken as one of them but who would also be loyal to her and report back on what the Forsaken wanted, how they could be controlled.

Or not a man—a *boy*, maybe, someone unattached, with no hut or mate or children of his own.

Kyne smiled to herself.

"You leave the Forsaken to me. I have a plan."

19

kiva

That evening, Kiva felt the Vagra's eyes on her when she slipped out of the hut. Cheeks burning, she looped her hair behind her ears with a dart of her fingers and then left her hands there by her cheeks, hiding her face from the old woman's disapproving stare as she ducked through the doorway. Kiva knew that she should be staying in tonight, meditating in the darkness with her eyes closed and reaching up to the Ancestors with her mind, summoning them to give her another vision of the Strangers.

But she couldn't. Not tonight. After her humiliation at the Sisters' council meeting that afternoon, Kiva didn't think she could face another night of struggling to hear the voice of the Ancestors, a night of getting more and more frustrated as no new vision came, a night of failing again, and again, and again.

No. Tonight Kiva wanted to take a break, to go somewhere as far away from the Sisters' camp as possible and try to forget everything: the Strangers, the Forsaken, the Vagra, Kyne. Tonight, Kiva wanted to be with her family.

Outside the Vagra's hut Kiva paused, lifted her gaze. Her heels raised up as she balanced for a moment on the balls of her feet, craning her neck. From here she could see the entire Sisters' camp, the entire village, all the way to the lip of the rise. Beyond, the Great Mother loomed on the horizon. She'd have to hurry if she wanted to be at Grath and Quint's hut by sundown.

Kiva put her head down and began walking. Shadows lengthened in the Sisters' camp, darkness rising up from the ground like a creeping mist. Most of the Sisters were either in their own huts or visiting their men and children in the main village. Only a few women stood in the doorways of their huts and gave Kiva unsmiling nods as she passed. Kiva could have listened to their minds, could have known what they were thinking as she walked by—whether they supported her or thought that the Vagra had made a mistake when she named Kiva next in line to lead— but she didn't want to know. Not tonight, not when she was trying to forget her troubles rather than linger on them. She pushed their thoughts away and kept on into the village.

The main village was even emptier than the Sisters' camp had been. Kiva had been back into the village a handful of times since she'd gone to live with the Sisters, sometimes to visit Grath and Quint, but more often on business that the Vagra was too weak to do herself—visiting the sick, checking on how new babies were doing with their fathers, communicating the Vagra's decisions and decrees to men who'd had their mates bring petitions before the Sisters' council. Every time she set foot in the main village, she'd found it mostly empty.

The people—her people—were afraid of her. Though the men and children treated her kindly whenever she visited one of their homes, something had changed in the way they looked at her. A fissure had opened up between Kiva and the Vagri; they gazed at her as if from across a gulf. They respected her, even admired her, but they feared her, too. When she spoke with them, she wanted them to treat her as the girl she'd been, the girl they'd known. All they could think about, though, was the person she would become, the mighty Vagra.

Can she hear my thoughts right now? they'd think. *I don't like it. I wish she'd leave. I wish she'd just go back to her hut and leave me alone.*

That's why she never saw anyone when she walked through the village, Kiva knew—because the Vagri didn't want to be around her. Whenever they saw her coming they retreated to their huts to avoid having their thoughts heard by the next Vagra.

As Kiva passed one hut after another, she wished she could call out to the people she knew were hiding inside. She wanted to tell them that hiding was pointless—she could hear their minds chattering through the walls of their homes, if she wanted to. She had no interest in eavesdropping on their thoughts tonight, anyway. She wanted to be alone in her own mind for a change.

But she said nothing. Only walked on in silence.

Walking this way, Kiva didn't hear Po come up until she heard the scratch of his footsteps directly behind her.

"Where are you going?" he asked.

"Nowhere," Kiva said. "I'm just going to visit Grath and Quint."

"Do you need company?"

Kiva shook her head. "No. I want to be alone right now."

"Why?"

"That's none of your concern."

Po strode around behind her, from her right ear to her left. Kiva had to resist the urge to rear up on him, to clench her hands and shove him in the chest with both fists—tall and strong though he was. But pushing Po away wasn't something she should have to do. Wasn't she one of the Sisters now? In line to become the next leader of the village? Why couldn't he do as she said?

Po jumped around her, loped on his long legs until he stood in front of her, walking backwards and looking at her with a leering grin.

"Don't you ever get tired?" he asked.

"Yes. Tired of you."

His smile dimmed. "No. Tired of being so cold. So distant. Of never letting anybody in."

Kiva brushed him aside and walked on faster. The light in the sky was dimming, and the first of the stars were beginning to come out. Kiva didn't have time for this. She wanted to get to Grath's hut before sundown.

"I'm going to get my own hut soon, you know," Po said, still keeping pace at Kiva's heels. "My father said I could. We're going to start building it tomorrow. My own hut, my own garden. And someday, when I'm older, one of the Sisters . . ." Po trailed off. "I'll have my own mate, I mean. My own family."

Kiva stopped walking. She closed her eyes and let out a long breath. She sensed what Po was thinking. She'd sensed it a long time, in fact, even before the Ancestors had given her the power to read the thoughts of others—sensed Po's growing interest in her. She'd never encouraged Po to think that they could ever be together, but she knew that he wanted it all the same. But the thing that Po hoped for could never be, not only because Kiva could never think of him as anything other than the annoying boy who never left her alone when they were kids, but because the Vagra wasn't allowed to take a mate.

She needed to tell Po the truth right now—and make sure he understood. She opened her eyes and looked at him.

"Look, Po," she said, unable to hide the note of pity that crept into her voice. "I'm flattered, I really am, but I don't think that's going to happen. I can't—"

"Don't," Po interrupted, his face crumbling for a moment before going smooth, resolving into an empty grin. "That's not what I meant. That's not what I meant at all. Why would you assume I was talking about you? That's pretty conceited. You think that just because you're going to be Vagra that everything's about you now? You, you, you."

Kiva breathed out angrily, for an exasperated moment unable to find any words. She'd tried to be kind to Po, tried to be honest, and this was how he repaid her?

"I'm sorry, Po," she said finally. "I—"

"I get it," he cut in, lifting a hand in the air as he half-turned. "I'm leaving, all right? Go on. Be alone, if that's what you want so much. It doesn't matter to me."

Then he turned and walked away—but not before tossing one last taunt over his shoulder.

"Be alone your entire life, for all I care."

20

po

Po's cheeks burned as he made his way through the village, putting distance between himself and Kiva. His breath came hard and labored, even though he was walking slowly. A restless energy buzzed in his limbs, vibrated its way to the end of his arm. He felt like moving, lashing out at something, hurting it, destroying it. He lifted a hand to cover his eyes for a few steps, then let it fall back to his side as a fist.

Soon, he came to the hut he shared with his father. He paused at the edge of the garden and glanced at a lone post, the remnants of a fence that had fallen into disrepair. Somewhere from the depths of his mind Kiva's words came back to him—*I'm flattered, I really am, but I don't think that's going to happen*—and suddenly, without quite knowing why, he kicked at the post with his bare foot, then kicked it again, and again, each blow aching in the arch of his sole, until the post had uprooted and was lying loose on the ground.

"What's wrong?"

Po snapped his head up. From the black shadows near the hut, Kyne walked out into the light and came to the fence.

"Nothing," Po said to his twin sister. "It's nothing."

Kyne glanced at the ground. "The post says otherwise."

"Just leave it," Po said, not quite knowing whether he was talking about the post or something else he wanted his sister to leave alone.

"Oh, come on."

Kyne reached forward as if to grab him by the shoulder. Po jerked away and took a step back.

"Don't touch me," he said.

"It's Kiva, isn't it? You like her."

Po's teeth tightened. "This has nothing to do with Kiva."

"Po, don't lie to me. I *saw* you together."

Heat rose up around Po's neck. "You were spying on us?"

"You were arguing in the middle of the village. I didn't need to spy." Kyne's voice softened. "I'm not making fun of you, Po. I'm your sister. Just tell me the truth."

Po's shoulders slumped, and a breath he didn't know he'd been holding came out of him in a rush. He looked at the ground, then back up at his sister's face. He squinted, studying her.

Po knew Kyne better than anyone in the village, but at the same time, it often seemed like there was no one Po knew *worse*, no one who was more of a mystery to him. Their father always said that Kyne looked like their mother, who'd died giving birth to them— and when Po was a boy he'd often looked at his sister's face when she was sleeping, studying its contours and wondering about the mother neither of them had ever known.

But as they'd grown, his sister became mysterious to him in a completely different way, and he began studying her face for a different reason entirely: to guess at what might lie just beneath the surface, to speculate about what she was thinking, what she might do next.

His sister wasn't *actually* cruel by nature, Po knew. As children, neither of them had many friends in the village, so they'd spent most of their time together: playing together, talking together, quarreling together. When Po felt sad or lonely, Kyne was always there for him.

But there was another side to Kyne. A dangerous side. She liked to be in control. And reducing one of the other girls in the village to tears, or yelling at a boy or even one of the fathers until he went quiet, feeling small—it was one way she could control others, wield power over them.

She wielded power over Po, too. Since he had no mother, the custom of the village said that his older sister would be his guardian and authority until he came of age, got his own hut and garden. Kyne was only older than him by ten minutes, but it still counted: she could tell him what to do, if she wanted to.

It was a power she hadn't used much when they were kids, except as a joke. But things had changed since Kyne had left him to live with the Sisters in the middle of the village. He barely saw her anymore, and when he did, things between them weren't the same. Now more than ever, there seemed to be two Kynes: his twin sister, his best and closest friend in the world—and a cruel, angry person whose mood could turn black in the space of a moment.

Now, Po looked at the expression on Kyne's face and thought: *This is the good Kyne. This is my sister. I can trust her.*

"Come on," Kyne said. "Just tell me."

Po nodded. "Fine. I do, okay? I like Kiva. You happy now?"

He had half-expected Kyne to laugh, but there was no trace of mockery on his sister's face. She smiled.

"So," she said. "Was that so hard?"

Po sighed and shook his head. "No," he said. "It doesn't matter, though. She doesn't like me. Not like that, anyway."

"Are you sure about that?" Kyne asked.

"Yes. She told me."

Kyne made a sound in the back of her throat.

Po tried to meet his sister's eyes. "What is it?"

Kyne turned again to face him. "Did you know that the Vagra can't be mated?"

Po's heart thrummed; he could feel his pulse in the tips of his fingers.

"You mean . . ." Po's mind scrambled. "Kiva can't take a mate or have children?"

"That's right. The idea is, a Vagra should be too busy taking care of the whole tribe to bother with a family of her own. The *Vagri* are her only family."

Po thought back again to Kiva's words to him.

Look, Po.

I'm flattered, I really am, but I don't think that's going to happen.

I can't—

Po had cut her off after that, embarrassed and simply wanting the moment to end—but what had Kiva been about to say? What if she'd been about to tell him that she *wanted* to be with him, but couldn't because she was next in line to be Vagra?

Of course. That had to be it. Kiva seemed so sad, so burdened, when he'd come up behind her. She didn't want to be Vagra. That was what had been wrong with her; that was why she hadn't wanted to talk to Po.

"What if . . . ," Po began, then trailed off, afraid to speak the thought aloud in front of Kyne.

"What if Kiva weren't Vagra? What if we could find someone else to lead in her place? Is that what you were about to say?"

"Yes," Po said.

"I've been thinking about the same thing," Kyne said. "She's not right for it. Kiva—she's too timid, too weak. Some kind of . . . of trouble is coming, and Kiva's not ready for it. She can't lead the village."

"But didn't the Ancestors choose her?" Po asked, "What can we do?"

Kyne looked back at Po. "I have a plan. I think it could work. But I need your help."

"Anything. What is it?"

Kyne's mouth curled at one corner. "The Forsaken," she said.

Her eyes were dark. Po's blood chilled as he realized he had guessed wrong.

This wasn't his sister. This was the other Kyne. The bad Kyne.

Po took a step back. "No," he said. "No, not that. Please. I don't want to. I want to stay here, in the village. Please don't send me to them."

"It's only for a while," Kyne said. "The Forsaken are the key—the key to taking power from Kiva, the key to fighting back whatever trouble is coming for us. I need someone among them. Someone I can trust."

Panic began to spread over the surface of Po's skin, itching like a rash. That morning, when his father had suggested that it might be time for him to build his own hut, plant his own garden, Po had felt the future begin to open up before him. Now it was closing again, narrowing to a single path he didn't want to take.

"Isn't there another way?" Po asked.

"You want Kiva, don't you?" Kyne asked. "It will only be for a month or so. Maybe two. Just until I can get the Sisters and the Forsaken on my side. Then, as soon as I'm Vagra, you can come back to the village, and live the rest of your life with Kiva."

"But won't she be angry?"

Kyne shook her head. "I don't even think she *wants* to be Vagra. She might be mad at first, but when everything's done and I'm Vagra, Kiva will be grateful to you. To both of us. I promise."

Po breathed out. Resignation flooded his body like a physical force, sapping him of the will to resist Kyne.

"When?"

Kyne's eyes flashed. Her face was feverish.

"Tonight," Kyne answered. "You have to leave tonight."

21

kiva

At last Kiva reached her father's hut at the edge of the village. She ducked through the door and paused just inside, letting her eyes adjust to the dimness.

"Kiva!" Quint shouted from somewhere in the dark, and suddenly Kiva felt herself tackled in a hug, staggering back toward the door as her little sister's arms squeezed tight around her waist.

Kiva laughed.

"Oof! You're getting too big to run at me like that."

Kiva ruffled the younger girl's hair, planted a kiss on the crown of her head. Four seasons old when Kiva had her vision and left to live in the Sisters' camp, Quint was eight now. Kiva didn't have time to visit very often, and every time she did she felt a confusing surge of bitterness and love as she saw how much her sister had grown while she wasn't looking.

"Quint," came another voice from the other side of the hut, a woman's. Kiva looked up.

It was Liana. She'd been at the Sisters' meeting that evening, looking on from the side of the crowd. Seeing her face now, Kiva felt everything she'd been trying to forget flood back into her mind: the Strangers, the Forsaken, the Vagra, Kyne.

"Remember what we talked about?" Liana said to Quint. "You have to treat your sister with respect. Soon enough, she won't just be your sister anymore. She'll be the Vagra, in charge of the whole village."

The pressure of Quint's arms around Kiva's waist eased. She let go of Kiva and stepped back. All the brightness had gone from the girl's face. Now, she looked at Kiva with a trace of fear, as a child might look at a complete stranger. Kiva bit her lip.

"It's fine," Kiva said. "She's not doing any harm. Really."

There was a beat of silence. Grath knelt in the middle of the room over a pot set on some glowing embers; he watched Liana and Kiva but didn't say anything.

"What brings you all the way to the edge of the village?" Liana asked at last. "Are you on business from the Vagra?"

Kiva shook her head. "No. Just visiting."

Liana nodded. "Grath is making sweetroot stew. You're welcome to some."

"Thank you," Kiva said. "Are you staying here tonight?"

"I am," Liana said.

"You can stay too, if you want," Grath said, rising from the fire and wiping his hands on a cloth. "We've kept your old bed the same."

"No," Liana said, looking first at Grath, then back at Kiva. "I'm sure she can't stay."

Kiva bristled, her body tightening. Liana probably thought Kiva was shirking her duty by coming here tonight—she should've been trying to summon the Ancestors to tell her more about the Strangers, not coming to the outskirts of the village for a visit.

"She's right," Kiva said, trying her best not to let her disappointment show in her voice. "I can't stay. But thank you for the offer. A bowl of stew, then I'll be on my way."

Liana nodded and turned away, walked with Quint to the wall and sat on the ground. Grath turned back to the pot, threw the cloth over his shoulder and gave the stew another stir. And Kiva, in the silence, wandered away, back to the door.

She peered outside. The doorway pointed away from the village and toward the rise. Beyond was the plain. Kiva hadn't set foot on it since the day of her first vision.

She sensed movement behind her and glanced backward to see Grath approach. Just behind her shoulder, he stopped.

"When you were a girl," he began, his voice low so Liana and Quint couldn't hear, "you used to love going out there to the plain. Do you remember? Every night at sundown, I'd look around and suddenly you'd be gone."

"I remember," Kiva said, looking out toward the horizon. She felt an ache in her chest.

"You know, the stew won't be ready for a while," Grath said.

Kiva looked back. Grath was smiling.

"Go," Grath said. "The village will still be here when you get back."

Kiva turned back to the door. The sky was streaked with color; if she hurried, she could get to the plain in time to see the Great Mother dip below the horizon. She smiled and gave Grath one more glance. Then she put her eyes forward and darted through the door to the foot of the hill, feeling as though she was fleeing, escaping.

Kiva ran up the rise as quickly as her legs would take her. The muscles in her thighs burned but she still felt lighter with each step, felt the cares of the village dropping off her one by one, until it seemed that when she reached the top of the rise she'd fly into the air and float away into the sky.

Coming down on the other side, Kiva's heels jarred against the ground, digging into the dirt and sliding down the hill at each footfall. She was deliberately careless with her steps, allowing herself to wobble on her feet. A few times she grabbed at the prairie grass rising up around her for balance, but the stalks gave her no purchase and she tumbled harmlessly to the bottom of the hill.

As she sprang to her feet, Kiva felt herself laughing. So this was what it was like to be alone. She'd practically forgotten, after spending the past four seasons trapped in the center of the village amidst a cacophonous storm of thoughts and feelings coming at her from every angle. But here on the prairie there were no huts, no people, no thoughts grappling for space in her head. Here, the only thing that grabbed at her were the grasses that bent in the wind, grazing her calves as she passed into the plain. Here, Kiva could be free—for a little while at least.

Kiva came into the broad expanse of the plain. She hoisted her dress to her knees, the fabric pooling in her hands like sand, and dashed to the hillock that had been her favorite spot. She threw herself down and bent an elbow, casting her wrist across her forehead. Peering from beneath her thumb, she glanced at the soft glow of the Great Mother receding on the horizon and squinted until the blotch of red went blurry.

Kiva's eyes shut, and she listened to the sound of silence in her head. She felt herself drifting, hovering on the edge of sleep.

And it was then, as Kiva balanced on the cusp between two worlds, between wakefulness and sleep, that another vision came over her.

The vision happened much as before. It began just as the Great Mother set, with a blinding pain that gripped Kiva at the base of her torso and shot up through her spine. Lying sideways, her body convulsed, her back and legs arched in a near-semicircle, before inverting and folding her over in the other direction, head to knees.

As before, Ao passed overhead just as the vision seized her, the moon's gravity lifting Kiva's hair into the air as if she were floating underwater. Kiva spread her arms and let them be pulled into Ao's distant grip.

The burst of light and fire.

The stone bird winging its way between pinprick stars that elongated like raindrops in the wind.

The three dark figures standing silhouetted against the horizon—and one of them stepping forward into the light. His face became visible.

A boy. Skin pale, eyes blue.

"Who are you?" Kiva demanded. "What do you want? Why are you coming to Gle'ah?"

The boy said nothing.

Then the vision ended as Ao passed out of reach and dropped Kiva back to the ground, her hands splayed in the dirt.

As before, Kiva came gasping back to her senses with a word on her tongue. The first time, in the vision she'd had when she was thirteen, the word had been *Strangers*.

This time, the word was *Matthew*.

She spoke it aloud, setting her fingers lightly on her lips to feel them form the strange, foreign sounds. The boy's name? Perhaps.

Kiva pushed herself to her feet and walked back to the village, her eyes on her feet. She reflected on what she'd seen.

The vision had been exactly the same as before, with only one difference: she had seen the boy—had seen *Matthew*—even as the other Strangers remained black silhouettes, shrouded by darkness. For some reason, the Ancestors wanted her to see his face, to know his name.

But why?

22

matthew

Over the span of a century Matthew traveled and dreamed, dreamed and traveled—and in the dim space between dreams he often wondered how far he'd come, how close he was to his destination.

Matthew didn't know for certain. Sometimes, it seemed as though he'd been dreaming, waiting to be awoken, forever, for centuries, millennia. And other times, it felt as though he'd gone to sleep only seconds before. That he'd wake up on the other end to find that one hundred light-years had passed by in the blink of an eye.

. . .

Then, one day, Matthew dreamed a different kind of dream—a dream of things he'd never seen, of a foreign planet that had no place in his memories.

The dream began in a haze, a cloud of luminous, white space dust. Then the planet—an orb mottled in shades of pink and orange—emerged from the haze and grew bigger and bigger until the orb blotted out everything else.

He passed through another haze as his consciousness entered the planet's orbit, descended into its upper atmosphere. Then yet another clearing, the dissipation of the haze and his first vision of the planet's gently undulating surface, the rounded, swelling hills like waves, like a sea of bodies sleeping one next to the other.

Closer, he saw that the waves on the planet's surface had their own waves, a pattern within a pattern: a sea of grasses that rippled with the wind.

The colors were strange: below, the grasses were painted in vivid shades of purple and burgundy; above, the sky was pinkish orange from one horizon to the next. Embedded in the sky was a glowing orb: a sun, creeping across the sky.

The dream sped up as if on a video loop; the sun rushed across the sky and knelt to touch the land. Then the vision slowed again as the sun hit the horizon and began to dim, to turn a bright red that blended with the distant grasses. The sky exploded with shades of purple and red, mirroring the planet's surface, until he couldn't be sure which expanse was land and which was sky.

And then Matthew's feet were on the ground, pressing through the prairie as the grasses bent against his knees. He came over a hill, and saw her.

A girl. She lay in the cleft place beneath a small hillock, her eyes closed, a ragged, sleeveless cloth dress covering her from her shoulders to her knees. Her skin was gray. Her hair lay pooled around her head, black but reflecting a rainbow of colors in its strands.

She was beautiful. And she was in pain.

The girl's eyes snapped open. She sat up, propped her hand behind her, and looked at him.

"Who are you?" the girl demanded. "What do you want?"

"Don't be afraid," Matthew said, reaching out a hand to calm her. "I'm not going to hurt you."

.   .   .

At that moment, a shock of electricity coursed white-hot through Matthew's body. The girl disappeared as Matthew's eyes snapped open. He sat bolt upright and gasped. At once, the real world flooded in around him, overwhelming his senses. He was sitting in an open cryochamber, his legs submerged beneath several thawed inches of the blue liquid he'd been sleeping in for the past hundred years. To either side of him sat Sam and Dunne taking choking gulps of the air, trying to find their breath just like he was. And above their heads, through a small circular window, a planet loomed.

Matthew was awake. He had arrived.

23

kiva

Kiva woke from her vision with a gasp, the world flooding back in through her eyes, ears, and nostrils. She lifted herself from the ground, propped one hand in the dirt behind her, and put the other on her heaving chest.

Kiva was, once again, on the plain, lying in the grass just beyond the border of the village. Three weeks had come and gone since her last vision, the one in which the Ancestors had shown her the boy—had shown her *Matthew*, she reminded herself. After that vision, she'd realized that the best way to learn more about the Strangers must be to leave the village, escape to a quiet place where the thoughts of the Vagri didn't crowd in her head, and wait for the Ancestors to speak. And so that was exactly what she'd done. Every morning when the Great Mother rose she left the Vagra's hut, went out past the edge of the rise, lay down just beneath the hillock, and waited. She returned to the village in the evening only to sleep, long after darkness fell.

She'd done this every night; every night it had failed—but

not this night. The Ancestors had given her another vision of the Strangers. As before, the vision began the same, then ended with one new detail. First was the explosion of light and fire—a burst of power, she'd come to assume, launching the Strangers toward Gle'ah. Then came the image of the stone bird flying between the stars. Next she saw the bird landing on the prairie, and the three Strangers standing side by side against the horizon, and the detail that her last vision had added: one of the Strangers stepping forward, a boy. Matthew.

To this, her new vision had added yet one more thing: Matthew had spoken to her.

Don't be afraid, he'd said. *I'm not going to hurt you.*

This was what Kiva had been waiting for: proof that the Strangers weren't a threat to the Vagri. They had nothing to fear. The Strangers weren't going to hurt them.

Kiva got up and made her way back to the village. She walked quickly, eager to share what she'd learned with the Vagra. The old woman's health had been getting worse and worse. She mostly stayed in her cot, and was increasingly hard to rouse from sleep. Kiva feared that she'd be dead soon. Still, if the Vagra could summon the strength to call one more meeting—a meeting in which Kiva could tell the Sisters what she'd learned about the Strangers—it might be all that Kiva needed. Just one meeting for Kiva to put the Sisters' fears to rest, demonstrate her ability to communicate with the Ancestors, and prove that she was fit to lead—all before the Vagra died and passed power to her.

Kiva walked a little faster.

It was afternoon, and the village was still bustling with people. Kiva felt the eyes of the Vagri on her as she passed, but she didn't pay them any mind. She had to talk to the Vagra.

Kiva parted the cloth hanging in the doorway and walked into the darkness of the hut. A dank, stale smell hung in the air. Kiva blinked, gave her eyes a moment to adjust, then walked to the cot. The Vagra was lying atop it, completely still.

Kiva knelt next to the cot.

"Vagra," she said softly. "Vagra, wake up. I have to talk to you."

The old woman didn't move. Kiva reached toward her shoulder to give it a jostle. As soon as her hand touched the Vagra's body she snatched it back, leapt to her feet, and staggered away. She looked at her palm, then back at the Vagra.

The Vagra's body was completely cold. Even through the cloths that covered her Kiva could feel that all the warmth had gone from her body.

Panic flooded Kiva's veins as she realized that she was alone in the hut—that the person she was looking at was no longer a person at all, but a lump of dead flesh. Kiva fell to her knees next to the cot again and clawed at the old woman's body frantically, pulling at her blankets and clothes.

"Vagra!" she shouted. "Vagra, please. Not yet. I can't do this without you."

But it was no use. The old woman was gone.

Feeling a sudden revulsion at the dead body, Kiva scrambled backward from the cot on her heels and hands. She kept moving until her shoulders hit the wall of the hut. Breathing hard, she sat against the wall with wide eyes and a pounding heart.

The walls seemed to be closing in. Kiva was trapped. The old woman was no longer the Vagra. Kiva was the leader of the village now.

How long Kiva sat that way she couldn't be sure. But in time her heart slowed, her breathing calmed.

She knew what she had to do next. There was no escaping it.

Kiva pushed herself to her feet. Looking purposefully away from the Vagra's dead body, she let her eyes focus on a place in the air in front of her as she gathered herself. She brushed her hands down the front of her dress, smoothing out the wrinkles. Ran her fingers once through her hair. Then walked to the door.

Outside the hut, she scanned the landscape until she spotted a Sister walking nearby.

"Thruss!" she called.

Thruss paused, raised her head, met Kiva's eyes. She walked over.

"Yes?"

"I need to call a meeting of the Sisters' council. Can you spread the word?"

Thruss nodded.

"Good," Kiva said. "We'll meet in an hour."

.   .   .

Kiva paced inside the hut as the Sisters gathered outside, all the while trying not to let her gaze pass over the Vagra's dead body. Only when she was sure that all the women had come did she allow herself to look toward the cot where the old woman lay. She looked so lonesome lying there in the middle of the empty hut, so fragile. Kiva felt a twinge of regret as she realized that the old woman had died alone—that she'd slipped away while Kiva had been out on the plain, listening for the voice of the Ancestors.

Kiva crossed the room to the cot. Knelt by the old woman's side. Put her hand on the Vagra's chest.

"I'm sorry, Vagra," she said. "I wish I could've been here for you. You've taught me so much. How to hear the voices of the Vagri. How to listen to the Ancestors. How to lead. I wish you could be with me now."

Her hand still lying on the Vagra's chest, she looked up through the hole in the roof. Day was fading, the deep colors of evening beginning to bleed across the sky. Kiva closed her eyes.

"I don't know if you're up there with the Ancestors or not. But if you are, help me now. Guide me. I can't do this without you."

Kiva pushed out a breath and stood up. She walked to the door. The Sisters went quiet as she came outside.

"Sisters," she said, trying her best to make her voice firm and unwavering, "the old woman has passed on. She goes to be with the Ancestors. I am your Vagra now."

A buzz fluttered up into the air from the crowd. The Sisters turned from Kiva and began talking and gesturing to each other, their faces full of confusion and unease. Kiva put her arms up to silence the Sisters and shouted louder.

"Sisters, please! I know you have many questions—and there will be time for those later. Tonight we must prepare the old woman's body for burial."

But by then the noise of the crowd had risen so high that Kiva could scarcely hear her own voice. Nobody was listening to her. Most of the Sisters seemed to be turning their attention away from Kiva toward a certain part of the crowd. The crowd thinned, moved, knotted in a different place off to Kiva's left, like scavengers flocking to a corpse. She craned her neck to see who the Sisters had gathered round.

It was Kyne.

Kyne was silent in the middle of the chattering mob, motioning for them to calm themselves. Her mouth moved, and though Kiva couldn't hear Kyne over the voices of the rest of the Sisters, she could clearly understand the words from the shape Kyne's mouth made as she spoke them: "Not here."

In the back of Kiva's mind, the thoughts of the Sisters roared like wind rustling through the grasses of the prairie. She opened her mind to listen to their thoughts, one at a time.

Dead.

The Vagra's dead.

Our leader. Gone.

But Kiva's not ready.

She can't lead.

Too weak.

Can't protect us.

Can't protect us from the Strangers.

Kyne.

It has to be Kyne.

She has a plan. She'll use the Forsaken. She'll command them to kill the Strangers.

Kyne must be our Vagra.

Kiva's stomach sank as she realized what was happening.

She'd learned what she needed to know about the Strangers—but too late. While she'd been spending her days out on the prairie listening for the voice of the Ancestors, she'd run out of time.

The Sisters were on Kyne's side now.

24

matthew

After Matthew woke he spent what seemed like an eternity learning to breathe again. His lungs ached. Each gasp felt like a stab in the chest—he'd have screamed at the pain, but that would have required more breath, and more breath was the one thing he didn't have. Clamping a hand on the side of his cryochamber, he gasped over and over again, willing his lungs to thaw and let the oxygen he gulped from the air into his bloodstream.

After his fifth or sixth gulp of air, his mind began to clear, and he became aware enough of his body to realize that it wasn't just his lungs that hurt. Every part of him was filled with a pain worse than he'd ever felt, an ache so deep and so sharp it felt as though his cells were torturing him.

Wincing, hissing air through his teeth, he swung his legs over the side of his cryochamber. Hands on knees, he panted, gazing miserably at the floor. Then a wave of nausea overtook him, his abdominal muscles clenched tight around his empty stomach, and he heaved a few small drops of bile onto the floor.

After the pain subsided, he lifted his head to look at how his shipmates were doing. Dunne looked even worse than he did—her face was dazed and stricken, a dribble of clear vomit smeared down her chin. Sam's face was gray and sunken, but he was smiling a crooked grin.

"Goddamn hangovers," he said. "Am I right?"

Matthew didn't laugh.

"Our bodies are in shock from the unfreezing process," Dunne said.

"Like I said, a hundred-year hangover," Sam said. "Hair of the dog is the only thing for it."

Matthew shook his head. "No way," he croaked. "You want a drink at a time like this?"

"Why not?" Sam said. "I snuck a flask into my personals." He rummaged in the cabinet at his cryochamber's head, then came out with a glinting aluminum flask. He unscrewed the top and took a long pull. "If I'm going to die down there, no way in hell I'm doing it sober."

Watching Sam, Matthew remembered how sick he'd been after a night of drinking with Silas and Adam, and another wave of nausea rose up in his throat. He choked it back.

Silas and Adam. It seemed like only yesterday that he'd been with them. And yet it was a century ago. Matthew felt with a dizzy wave the vastness of space just outside the ship's hull, the huge emptiness that lay between him and the tiny corner of the universe he knew as home. He thought of his mother, of Sophie. All of them—his friends, his family, everyone he'd ever known—were dead. The realization hit him like a punch to the gut, and all at once he felt breathless again. He closed his eyes and hoped that his mother's cancer had been cured, that Sophie had lived a long life, that Silas and Adam had married and had children and grandchildren.

Dunne coughed, bringing Matthew out of his thoughts. "What we need is food."

Matthew climbed out of his cryochamber and put his feet on the ground. Their bodies still covered in slimy cryoliquid, the three of them stumbled from the stasis room into a narrow corridor. At a window Matthew paused and glanced outside at the planet below. The orb was covered in a pinkish-orange haze, and here and there where the haze was thin enough he could see to the surface: rust red, the color of dried blood.

The sight of the planet stirred something in him, but he didn't know what. Ghostly afterimages lingered in the back of his mind, airy and insubstantial as mist; Matthew couldn't be sure what the images were of or if they were even there at all. Had he been dreaming before he'd been woken up? He thought so, but he couldn't remember. He gazed at the planet a moment more, then gave his head a little shake and turned away from the window.

It was probably nothing. Just his imagination.

Matthew turned down the corridor and hurried to catch up with Dunne and Sam as they came into the body of the ship.

The ship was called the *Corvus*, and though this was technically the first time Matthew had ever set foot in it, he'd learned its layout and how to work its systems in virtual reality simulations during training. Dunne and Sam, who'd been through the same training, walked confidently ahead of Matthew. Together the three of them walked past the airlock, the room through which they'd later pass onto the planet's surface. The airlock also housed a speeder, a hovering vehicle designed to carry one or two people, which they could use to explore the planet.

They passed a laboratory, a small sleeping quarters, and the ship's control room, then found their way to a room with the ship's food supplies and a small metal table. As Matthew and Sam sat at the table, Dunne prepared them a meal: a synthetic sludge packed with proteins and carbohydrates, which was supposed to help their bodies recover from the freeze. The stuff was gray and tasteless, but Matthew devoured it anyway, hunched over his bowl as he shoveled it into his mouth.

"Jesus. You'd think it was your last meal or something," Sam said.

Matthew lifted his head from his bowl but couldn't think of a retort. It probably *was* his last meal. Matthew looked past Sam and glanced once more out the windows of the control room to the thick atmosphere of the planet below, and nearly threw up all over again at the cold certainty that washed over him and brought a sweat to his forehead.

He was going to die here.

25

kyne

It's time, my daughter.

Kyne walked slowly through the dark hills, feeling the stiff blades of grass bend beneath her feet, her way lit by the three moons of Gle'ah. She looked up into the sky and closed her eyes for a moment, let her face be bathed in silver moonlight.

Time for you to take your rightful place among your people.

The words rippled through her mind with every step—the only words her mother had ever spoken to her. She'd spoken them to Kyne in a vision, her first visitation from the Ancestors when she was eleven seasons old.

The vision had been simple, but powerful—the most significant moment of Kyne's life. She'd been lying in bed, trying and failing to sleep, when the vision came to her. A figure walked up and knelt at her bedside. She looked, saw that it wasn't her father—the figure was, rather, a beautiful woman who looked at Kyne tenderly. Kyne knew immediately that it must be her mother.

"Mama," she'd said in the vision, absurdly, as if her mother had never died, "I can't sleep."

Her mother smiled, teeth flashing white in the darkness. The smile was like a warm flower that bloomed in Kyne's chest and spread across her whole body, opening up parts of her she'd never realized were closed.

"It's all right, my girl," her mother had said. "You've spent enough time wasting away in darkness. It's time, my daughter. Time for you to take your rightful place among your people."

Now, Kyne opened up her eyes once more and looked to the horizon.

What *was* her rightful place? Her mother hadn't said. At the time, Kyne had believed what the other Sisters had said of her—that a girl who heard the voice of the Ancestors so young *must* be destined to be Vagra. Then Kiva came along, and Kyne didn't know anymore. But now, it seemed again like leading her people might be Kyne's destiny, after all. Perhaps this was what the Ancestors were preparing her for all along. Maybe everything, her whole miserable life—her mother's death, her awful childhood, and her uncertain status among the Sisters—had always been leading to this: Kyne seizing power from Kiva, and saving her people from the Strangers.

Maybe.

Kyne trudged on through the prairie, thinking of the events of the past three weeks.

It had been surprisingly easy to divide the loyalty of the Sisters, to bring them under her sway. Kyne was still shocked by how easy it had been. She'd known that there were some in the village who thought the Vagra had made a mistake in choosing Kiva to be her successor, when it had been Kyne who was the youngest girl to ever hear the voice of the Ancestors, Kyne who had a plan to deal with the Strangers.

But Kyne still hadn't expected them to be so eager to join her secret rebellion. She'd thought that most of the Sisters would be hesitant to support her plan of defying Kiva and the Vagra by going directly to the Forsaken for protection against the Strangers. What she found instead, every time she snuck into one of the women's huts to tell her about it, was that their eyes lit up with conspiratorial glee. They were just as uncertain about Kiva's leadership as Kyne was.

Kyne couldn't have done it without Kiva, though. That was the most delicious part of the whole thing—that Kiva's actions were undermining her authority more than anything Kyne could have done on her own. The night Kyne talked with Thruss and Rehal and laid the foundations for her plan to grab power, Kiva began disappearing from the village. No one knew why she slipped away into the plains for hours at a time, but Kiva's absence helped Kyne's rebellion in two ways: it gave Kyne the opportunity to talk about her plans with the Sisters freely, without fear of having her thoughts overheard by Kiva, and it added to the Sisters' belief that Kiva wasn't ready to lead. The rumor was that Kiva left every day because she was afraid. Kyne didn't know if that was true— she suspected that Kiva was trying to get to a quiet place to hear the voice of the Ancestors more clearly. But she wasn't about to contradict the rumor.

There was only one problem: Kyne wasn't very strong with the

Ancestors. She could only occasionally hear the thoughts of others and hadn't had a single vision since that first night when she was eleven. It was her deepest secret, one she couldn't allow herself to think of when she was in the village and the other Sisters could hear her. Everyone thought that she was specially blessed by the Ancestors. But she wasn't.

When I'm Vagra, though, she thought. *When I'm Vagra—then the Ancestors will come back to me. They're waiting for me to prove myself.*

Just then, Kyne came to her destination: a large rock the size of one of the huts in the village. She put a hand on it, let her fingers trail against the rough stone as she circled around to the far side. There beneath the rock was a deep hollow, a stony pit cut out of the smooth sameness of the prairie.

The rock and the pit marked the border between the Vagri's land and the wilderness where the Forsaken roamed. Vagri children were warned never to pass it, and the Forsaken, for their part, had agreed to stay on their side. The pit, however, was an in-between place—a place for the leaders of the Vagri and the Forsaken to meet together when there was something for them to discuss. The last time the pit was used as a meeting place was fifty seasons ago. Tales of violence were discouraged in the village, so nobody talked much about what had happened, but occasionally the men would whisper the story to each other over cookfires: an army of marauders, a secret meeting between the Vagra and the Forsaken, and a daring Forsaken boy named Xendr Chathe who drove the enemy from the village and then pursued them all the way to the foot of the mountains.

Now, as Kyne picked her way down into the pit, steadying herself here and there with a hand on the rocks, she wondered if future generations of Vagri would tell stories about her. If what happened here tonight would one day be the stuff of legend.

At the bottom, Po waited next to a bonfire. The flames glinted in his eyes and in the pointed tip of his spear, which he held propped on the ground next to him. As Kyne came closer to her brother, she saw a long gash sliced across one cheek, from his ear to his chin.

"What happened to you?" she asked.

"It's nothing," Po said. He made a show of glancing past Kyne's shoulder. "Where are the rest of the Sisters?"

"They'll be here. Kiva is holding the death ceremony for the Vagra in the village. They'll come after that's done and Kiva's gone to bed."

Po lifted an eyebrow. "You skipped out on the death ceremony? Won't Kiva notice you're gone?"

Kyne sneered. "Let her notice. I don't care anymore. She can't stop what's happening."

Kyne let her gaze wander around the pit. "Where's Xendr Chathe?" she asked. Kyne wanted him there to demonstrate to the Sisters that she could get the leader of the Forsaken on her side.

"He's not here," Po said. "He won't see you. He doesn't want to get involved."

Kyne looked daggers at her brother. "No Xendr? Remember our agreement, Po—if you help me, then maybe I'll let you come back to the village once I'm Vagra. But if you can't get me what I need . . ." Kyne trailed off, leaving the threat unspoken, implicit.

Po licked his lips. "Xendr's waiting. Biding his time, to see which way the Sisters go. If you get their support, then he'll join you. I know he will. Besides, I convinced him to give you permission to use this place for your meeting, didn't I? Kiva will never find you way out here."

Kyne looked away. Her brother *had* done well to find her a place where she and the Sisters who were loyal to her could talk openly of rebellion, far from the reach of Kiva's telepathic mind. But Kyne couldn't allow herself to show appreciation. She needed to keep Po on his toes, keep him working, keep him scrambling and desperate to please her. Po had done much for her since she sent him away to the Forsaken. But he needed to do so much more.

"I also brought you something," Po said.

Po reached into a leather pouch hanging around his waist and came out with a bit of something Kyne couldn't quite make out. She moved closer to him and strained to see what he was holding in the orange glow of the firelight. He reached out his hand. It was a substance she'd never seen before, a delicate interwoven clump of tiny white strands that stuck to Kyne's fingers when Po handed it to her.

"They call it *maiora*," Po said. "You're supposed to eat it."

She put the maiora on her tongue. It melted at once. Then, after a few moments, a strange tingling sensation spread across her body, and foreign images stabbed their way into her mind.

A bird made of stone, flung across the stars.

Three dark figures stepping out onto the grass.

Death and blood. Vagri bodies slumped on the wet ground, stacked atop each other like firewood as the village burned.

Kyne came to with a gasp and found that she'd fallen to her knees during the vision.

The images were familiar. Kiva's vision. The one she'd told to the Sisters seasons ago, when she'd been named the next Vagra.

But then Kyne shook her head. No—this vision was different. Kiva's vision hadn't shown dead Vagri, hadn't shown the village burning to the ground. Could this be a vision of what the Strangers would do to the Vagri if they weren't stopped?

Kyne looked at her hands and saw remnants of the maiora, tiny strings of it still sticking to her fingertips. She lifted her fingers to her mouth and licked them off, hungry for more, desperate for one more image from the vision.

None came. Still, the maiora hummed in her veins as she took her feet once more. Her body felt like a glowing ember, her senses heightened to everything around her—every sound, every rustling of the wind.

"How long does it last?" she asked.

"Not long," Po said. "A few minutes."

Kyne looked at her brother and pushed a long, quivering breath out through her nose.

"I need more," she said.

"I don't have any more," Po said. "But I can get some."

Kyne nodded. "Good."

She turned her head. Her perception still heightened for the moment by the maiora, she felt something. Women. Coming this way.

The Sisters.

"Quiet!" she hissed at Po, though he hadn't been speaking. "They're coming."

She turned her body toward the place where they would come down into the pit. She wanted to be completely calm and collected when they first saw her. She wanted to look like a leader.

She wanted to look like the Vagra.

26

kiva

Every death contains within it the seeds of a rebirth. Every end is a beginning.

These were the words of the Vagri death ritual, the words Kiva had spoken over the Vagra's body before two men from the village laid her in a grave and covered her body with dirt.

Now, Kiva sat in her hut and wondered about the words she'd said. The Vagra's death *would* be a beginning—that much was certain. But the beginning of what?

She closed her eyes and listened to the voices again—the thoughts of the Sisters buzzing in her ears like a swarm of gnats.

Tonight.

Kyne said to meet her tonight.

The stone pit on the edge of the Forsaken's land.

It's almost time.

I'm afraid. It's no small thing Kyne's asking of us.

What about Kiva? Does she know? Can she hear me right now?

Kiva's eyes slid back open. The silver light of the moons spilled through the hole in the roof, lighting up her eyelashes and gilding the edges of her vision.

Every thought echoed powerfully in her mind. She might have heard these voices earlier—the voices of rebellion—if she hadn't been spending so much time on the prairie, trying to summon the Ancestors to reveal more about the Strangers. But no matter. She was listening now.

It was time for Kiva to do something. It was time for her to take a stand.

Kiva pushed herself to her feet and tiptoed to the door of the Vagra's hut. She pulled aside the split cloth hanging in the doorway and peered out into the night.

Outside, the Sisters were on the move, slipping from their huts, steam from their breath puffing in front of their mouths in the cool night air. Then—quickly, silently—they began to move off together.

Kiva guessed that there must be at least twenty of them, maybe as many as thirty, nearly a third of the Sisters. Thirty women who'd listened to Kyne. Thirty women who were ready to turn against Kiva.

She crept from her hut and followed the Sisters through the village at a safe distance, careful to remain hidden, careful to conceal her thoughts. Near the edge of the village she paused, crouching behind a half-crumbled fence, as the Sisters filed one-by-one over the rise and into the prairie beyond.

Kiva tensed her muscles and sprang after them, hiked up the rise and pursued the Sisters into the plain. She chased them for what seemed like hours, keeping far enough away that she wouldn't be spotted but close enough that the band of women didn't disappear over the horizon. Staying low to the ground, she'd run ahead, then dive behind the grass at the crest of the next hill and lift her head to peer over it.

Kiva pushed against the ground, lifting her chest like a coiled snake. Through swaying blades of grass, Kiva spotted them: a distant line of figures receding into dots. The Sisters were making their way toward an outcropping of rock. Walking in a long line, they snaked their way toward the rock and then disappeared behind it.

Kiva stood and made to run after them—but then something stopped her.

There was a rustling in the grasses some dozen paces behind her.

Kiva's heart beat faster, a feeling of alarm flooding her veins.

"Who's there?" she said, unable to hide the fear in her voice. She looked at the spot the rustling had come from and advanced toward it, her hands clenched into fists at her sides. "I know you're there. Come out!"

The grasses swayed, parted—and then Quint came forward, head hanging.

"Quint!" Kiva breathed out a relieved laugh.

"I'm sorry, Vagra," Quint said. "I didn't mean to scare you. It's just—it was the Sisters. They woke me when they were passing by our hut. Then I saw you, and I followed you to see where you were going."

Kiva flinched at hearing her sister address her so formally, calling her *Vagra*. She felt an ache deep in her chest.

"Come here," Kiva said. "Please."

Quint trudged forward, head still down.

"Look at me," Kiva said, hunching down to look at her sister eye to eye.

Quint's gaze tilted up to meet Kiva's. There was fear in her eyes—the fear of a child about to be scolded, punished.

"You don't have to apologize," Kiva said. "And you don't have to call me *Vagra*."

The fear began to melt from Quint's face. She shook her head. "But Liana said—"

"I know what she said. I was there. But she was wrong. Yes, things have changed. I've changed, you've changed. But there are some things that will never change."

Kiva's voice grew thick. She felt the weight of what she was saying press against her chest. The back of her throat began to ache, but she forced herself to keep talking.

"I'll always be your sister—that will never change. To you, I'll always be Kiva. Okay?"

"Okay."

Kiva glanced at the rock where the Sisters had gone, then back to Quint. It was too dangerous to send Quint back to the village alone. Kiva didn't want her sister getting lost and running into one of the Forsaken warriors alone.

"Look, I don't have time to bring you back to the village," she said. "I need to see what those Sisters are up to. If I let you come with me, do you think you can stay out of sight?"

Quint smiled and nodded. Kiva put a hand on the little girl's shoulder and they ran toward the rock. When they got close, they slowed, hunched down, and crept to the edge of the pit.

27

matthew

After they'd eaten, Dunne, Sam, and Matthew took turns showering the cryoliquid off their bodies and changing into new suits. Matthew was just walking back into the control room in fresh clothes when he heard a sound of electronic squawking and buzzing. Soon the buzzing clarified into the sound of a woman's voice.

"*Corvus.* Come in, *Corvus.* Do you copy?"

The quantum transceiver. Matthew moved toward the control room, then grabbed the transceiver and clicked the button on the side. Sam and Dunne moved close to hear.

"Copy, Control. This is *Corvus.*"

"Who am I talking to, *Corvus*?" The voice sounded like that of a young woman not so much older, Matthew guessed, than he was.

"This is Matthew Tilson. And who's this?"

"My name is Alison Nagita, transmitting from Exo Project Mission Control." A pause, then Alison continued. "What's your status? We got a reading from your transceiver that the *Corvus* is in orbit around H-240. Is that right?"

"It is, Mission Control."

"And the rest of the crew came out of the freeze all right?"

Matthew winced. "A little shaken up still. But we're all alive."

"Good. We're going to need you to get into your suits, prepare to initiate the entry sequence."

Matthew glanced back at the table. Dunne's face was stricken, ashen.

"I thought they'd give us some time," she said, gazing at the table and speaking quietly, as if to herself. "I thought we'd have more time."

Sam snorted. "Why? We're going to die down there; may as well get on with it."

He looked up at Matthew and nodded. Matthew nodded back and pushed the button on the transceiver.

"Roger that, Control. Preparing for descent now."

. . .

Matthew gritted his teeth as the Corvus rattled and pitched, jostling him in his seat. Displays and buttons lit up in different colors reflected on the visor of his helmet like spots swimming before his eyes. Past the glare, a mist washed over the cockpit window as the ship sank deeper into the planet's atmosphere.

There was a stomach-churning moment of free fall as the ship hit a pocket of warm air, then a bone-rattling crash as the Corvus regained stability once more. Matthew let out a breath and glanced toward Dunne and Sam, strapped in next to him. Their arms were clamped down at their sides, their helmets facing straight forward.

Matthew looked back at the window just in time to see the

planet come into focus below. The land was flat as far as he could see, with low, gentle swells rising up one after the other like desert dunes. As the ship sank lower, he saw movement atop the dunes, grasses dancing this way and that.

Matthew's breath fled his throat and buried itself in his chest.

The feeling he'd had when he first looked down at the planet from the ship returned, stronger than before. Matthew knew this place. He didn't remember how, but he knew it nonetheless. The sight of the planet's surface lodged like a splinter in his brain. It was an itch he couldn't reach, a piece of grit that wouldn't blink out of his eye.

The horizon rose up, squeezing out the dark night sky. The ship bucked and jostled as it made contact with the ground, then sank down slowly as the landing gear settled in place and gently let the ship down. The thrusters fired one last time, and in the control room the blinking displays went dark one by one.

A hand on his shoulder shook him out of his reverie. He looked to the side, to Dunne strapped into the next seat over.

"We made it," she said, but there was no pleasure, no relief, in her voice or her face.

Matthew nodded and returned his eyes to the window.

The Corvus had landed.

28

kiva

Kiva peered down to the bottom of the stone pit. Kyne stood next to a bonfire, her face lit by dancing flames. Arrayed before her were the Sisters, standing on their feet and craning their necks to see to the front of the crowd.

Next to Kyne was Po. He was dressed like a Forsaken warrior and held a weapon in his hand—a long stick with a sharpened rock at one end. Kiva gave a soft gasp when she saw him. She'd heard the rumors that Po had joined the Forsaken, but she'd scarcely believed it was true until this moment. Why would Po have gone to the Forsaken? It didn't make sense. The last time they'd spoken, he'd been so excited about getting a hut and a garden of his own. Kiva had also rejected him that night, told him that they could never be together—but that was no reason to do something as rash as running away from the village and starting an entirely new life with the Forsaken.

Kyne was silent for a long moment, looking back and forth between the Sisters' faces.

Finally, she spoke.

"Sisters. You took a risk by coming here tonight. I thank you for it."

The silence stretched out, with only the crackle of the burning wood to break the hush.

"I called you here tonight for one reason: Kiva, the girl who is to be our new Vagra, is weak."

A murmur now, rippling through the crowd.

"But we don't need her. Sisters, I believe the Vagra made a mistake in choosing Kiva to succeed her. The Ancestors speak to me, too. I have heard their voice—and if you follow me, I'll be a better leader for the Vagri than Kiva ever could be."

Kiva scanned the crowd for faces she recognized—her heart sank when she saw that Thruss and Rehal were there. How could her own friends have been sucked in by Kyne's lies? How could they believe what she said about Kiva?

A voice rose up from the crowd. "You're wrong, Kyne."

The crowd parted as the women turned to face the one who'd spoken.

"Is that . . . ?" Quint said, but didn't finish her question.

"It is," Kiva said, smiling.

Liana. Their mother. Kiva's friends might betray her, but at least she could always depend on her mother to support her. It had taken bravery for Liana to come tonight, to speak against Kyne in a crowd full of her supporters.

Liana stepped through the crowd until she and Kyne were face-to-face.

"This is blasphemy," Liana said. "The *Ancestors* choose the Vagra, not you—and certainly not anyone else who's come to hear your lies." Liana turned around and faced the rest of the women. "Sisters, you should be ashamed of yourselves! My daughter was chosen by the Ancestors. They speak to her, and her alone."

"Do they?" Kyne asked. "The Ancestors have many ways of speaking. All of us, all of the Sisters, have heard their voice. All of us have heard the thoughts of others echoing in our minds. And many of us have seen visions."

Liana nodded. "Yes. But none so strong as the Vagra."

"No?" Kyne let this question hang in the air. "Sisters, you know me. You know that I first heard the voice of the Ancestors when I was only eleven seasons old. They speak to me still. And they show me things. Things that the Vagra has kept hidden from us all." She paused and added: "If Kiva even *is* the real Vagra."

"But why? Why would the Ancestors choose you, when they've always spoken through the Vagra?" Liana demanded.

Kyne paused before answering, until Kiva could sense that the entire crowd was hanging on her silence, desperate for her to speak again.

"The Strangers," Kyne said. "Kiva first saw them in a vision four seasons ago—but she still hasn't told us why they're coming here, to Gle'ah. But I know why. Sisters, I'm telling you the truth: the Strangers are a threat. They bring death with them."

A fearful buzz rippled across the gathered crowd.

"I saw it in a vision from the Ancestors," Kyne said. "When the Strangers get here, they'll kill us all, burn our village to the ground."

The fear in the crowd rose to a near panic. Kiva could feel the desperate terror bleeding from each of the Sisters—in this state, they'd believe anything Kyne told them.

"Kiva is too weak to deal with the Strangers," Kyne shouted over the din. "That is why the Ancestors speak to me. Why they've chosen me—" Kyne paused and pounded at the flat of her chest with her fist "—to lead the Vagri against this threat."

Kiva sank down and turned away from the pit, putting her back against the cool of the rock. She closed her eyes and listened to the wild chattering of the crowd, bubbling up from the pit behind her and cascading over her shoulder.

The Sisters—so uncertain, so fearful. It wasn't their fault they'd been taken in by Kyne's lies. They were afraid. They needed a leader. They needed their Vagra.

They needed Kiva.

She had to speak. And she had to do it quickly, before she could change her mind.

In a single fluid movement, Kiva pushed herself from the ground and whirled around to face the pit as she came to her feet.

"Kyne!" she called out with both her voice and her mind, so that her shout boomed in her hearers' ears on two frequencies. "What is the meaning of this?"

Below, Kyne's head snapped up, and the gathered Sisters turned as one to look at her standing at the top of the pit. There was fear in their eyes. But it was no longer the Strangers they were afraid of.

They were afraid of Kiva. Even Kyne had been shocked into silence.

The crowd was completely quiet as Kiva made her way down into the pit. When she reached the bottom, the Sisters parted to let her pass through to Kyne.

Kyne held herself straight and proud, but Kiva could tell that her presence had unsettled her.

"Kiva," she said, a slight quaver in her voice. "I didn't expect—"

"Save your breath, Kyne," Kiva said. "I heard everything."

Inside, Kiva felt as though every part of her was shaking. Could the Sisters see how afraid she was? She felt as though she was performing—pretending to be confident, to be a leader, to be the Vagra. But judging by the faces of the Sisters, and of Kyne, they believed the performance.

Kiva turned from Kyne to face the crowd.

"Sisters, I'm disappointed in you," she said, looking directly at Thruss and Rehal. They hung their heads. "Kyne cares nothing for you, for the Vagri, for the Ancestors. All she wants is power. Can't you see that?"

She turned back to Kyne.

"And you. I don't know what your plan to overthrow me was, but I'm guessing it had something to do with him." Kiva nodded toward Po, who'd been standing silent the whole time, his spear propped on the ground. "You wanted to make an alliance with the Forsaken to get rid of me by force, is that it?"

"We'll need the Forsaken," Kyne said. "We'll need them to deal with the Strangers, when they come."

"No, we won't," Kiva said to Kyne, then turned back to the crowd once more.

"Sisters, Kyne is lying. The Strangers aren't a threat to us. Just today, before I discovered the Vagra dead, the Ancestors gave me another vision. In my vision, one of the Strangers spoke to me. He told me not to be afraid. He told me that he wasn't going to hurt me."

Kyne moved in front of Kiva. "But what about my vision?" she demanded. "I saw the village destroyed, every one of the Vagri dead. How do you explain that?"

The crowd was silent as Kiva stared at Kyne, trying to figure out if she was lying or not. She reached into Kyne's mind with her own, but as usual Kyne's thoughts were shielded from her. All but the echo of a single word.

... *maiora* ...

Kiva blinked, shook her head.

"Making an alliance with the Forsaken won't help. Their weapons are just as much a threat to us as the Strangers are. How do you know that what you saw wasn't a warning from the Ancestors—a vision of what will happen if we bring the Forsaken into our village?"

The crowd erupted once more into chatter.

At that moment, a blinding pain stabbed a jagged line through Kiva's brain. Her vision went dim. The noise of the crowd receded until it seemed as though Kiva was hearing it from a long distance.

Kiva lifted a hand to her temple. She wobbled on her feet. Stumbled.

And above, in the blackness, a speck of light moved untethered from the constellation of stars and arced a burning line across the sky.

Kiva teetered, listed to one side, then fell. The Sisters gasped and crowded around her.

"Kiva!" came Quint's voice from the top of the pit. She ran around the edge of the pit and bounded down the steep grade.

"Let me through!" Quint shouted as she pushed through the sea of bodies.

Finally, she made it to where Kiva lay on the ground, her body convulsing with the force of whatever had taken hold of her. The Sisters backed away as Quint went to her knees beside her sister. She clutched Kiva's face with both hands.

"Kiva," Quint whispered, her voice catching.

Kiva's body stopped shaking and her eyelids slowly slid open. Her eyes were strangely vacant, gleaming with the light of the bonfire. Her chest heaved. She looked up at Quint, but gave no sign of recognition.

And when she spoke, it was with a strange, low voice that seemed to emanate from somewhere so deep in her chest it may as well have been vibrating up from under the ground.

"They're here."

PART 4

CONTACT

29

matthew

"We're stepping out, Mission Control."

"Copy, Corvus. Keep us posted."

Matthew, Dunne, and Sam stood in the airlock, waiting as the clean air of the *Corvus* leaked out of the room and the air of planet H-240 came hissing in, along with whatever noxious gases it might contain. The room looked no different through the visor of his suit as the air of one world replaced the air of another—it was odd, thought Matthew, how the things that could kill you were so often invisible.

Best not to think about it.

A light that had been flashing red turned green and the door slowly opened. It hinged down, creating a ramp from the ship to the ground.

Dunne and Sam stepped out of the ship into the moonlight, but Matthew hung back. Sam turned.

"Come on," he said, waving an arm.

Matthew looked at his feet as he tripped down the ramp, stared at them through his visor as if they were something disconnected from his body—which, at the moment, they seemed to be. At the bottom, the ramp rested on the ground of the planet. Matthew glanced up at Dunne and Sam. Sam gazed off in the other direction, toward the horizon, while Dunne stood closer to Matthew, staring into the display screen of her sensor as she turned in a slow circle.

"Status, Corvus."

Matthew pressed a button on the outside of his suit to patch the radio communicator in his helmet into the quantum transceiver feed. "Give us a minute, Control," he said.

He felt dizzy—as though he had run out of breathable air and was about to fall over. He took in a sharp breath, but it seemed as if the oxygen wasn't absorbing into his bloodstream or reaching his brain. His vision went sharp, and he suddenly felt as though he was going to topple over where he stood.

"Calm down, Matthew." Sam had come back nearer to the ship and was staring into Matthew's face from a few paces away. "Breathe. You don't want to die before we're actually *supposed* to, do you?"

Matthew took a deep, slow breath and laughed, even though it wasn't really funny. He leaned over and put his hands on his knees, blinking as his vision came back into focus.

"You okay?" Dunne asked.

"He'll be fine, doc. Just a little nerves, is all."

"It's just so weird," Matthew said. "It's weird, right?"

Sam and Dunne assented in silence—it *was* weird. They were on another planet, billions of miles from where they had started. Yet for all that, the landscape felt so similar to Earth, and that was the most dizzyingly strange thing of all: the fact that this place that was totally alien to Matthew could also be so strikingly, eerily familiar. Like any other place he'd ever been, this planet had land and sky, rocks, hills, and—strangest of all, stretching out in every direction as far as he could see—grass.

"Grass," Matthew said aloud now, reduced to monosyllables.

"Yes," Dunne said. She ran her hand over the top of it, letting the tips of the blades scratch at her glove. "Prairie grass."

"Does that mean this place will support life?" Matthew asked. "If grass can grow here, we might be able to survive too, right?"

Dunne squinted and looked again at her handheld sensor. "I don't know. A lot of organisms can survive in environments where humans would die almost immediately. At the bottom of the ocean, for instance—it's a vibrant ecosystem, but if you put a human down there, they'd die within thirty seconds because of extreme water pressure and cold."

"Cut to the chase, Doc," Sam said. "You're the science officer, right? Well, give us some science here. Are we going to die or what?"

Dunne poked at the display of her handheld sensor array, looking at one reading after another. "There's oxygen in the air. More than on Earth, actually. Nitrogen. A bit more CO_2 than I'd like to see, but it's survivable."

"Any poisonous gases?" Matthew asked.

Dunne shook her head without looking up. "Not that I can see. Though it wouldn't take much to kill us, if there's something small the sensor isn't picking up." She tapped again at the display. "Temperature is mild. About 65 degrees Fahrenheit. Fifty percent humidity. Gravity very close to Earth's—I'm reading about 94 percent."

"What about water?" Matthew asked. "If there're plants, they must be getting water from somewhere, right?"

"I'm reading significant groundwater below the surface," Dunne said.

"Is it fresh? Drinkable?"

Dunne squinted at the screen. "I can't tell. But it doesn't matter. We could dig wells, purify it if it's undrinkable. All that matters is it's there."

Matthew's mind raced.

Breathable air. Temperate climate. Water.

"You mean to tell me that this place is actually . . ." Matthew trailed off, as if saying the rest aloud—*actually habitable?*—would jinx it somehow.

Dunne looked up from the sensor screen, her lips parted.

"I think so," she said. There was a laugh in her voice. "I think we might be able to survive here."

"So . . . is it safe to take off our helmets?"

Dunne nodded. "If these readings are correct."

They stood looking at each other for a few moments, not moving. It was still so hard to believe that they were safe. Matthew had been prepared to find a harsh landscape that would kill them. He'd never expected the planet they landed on to be one that might support life.

"Aw, hell," Sam said, his voice gruff. "I'll do it."

He reached up and snapped his helmet off. He lifted it up over his head, then lowered it to his waist, breathing heavy through his nose.

"Well?" Matthew asked.

Sam made a gagging sound, his face contorted, and he fell to the ground in a convulsion.

Dunne and Matthew rushed toward him. Matthew's heart was racing.

Then Sam rolled over laughing, a smile on his face.

"You should have seen your faces," he said. "It's fine, all right? The air's fine. You can take off your helmets. You're not going to die."

Matthew looked at Dunne, grinning in spite of himself. He reached up to remove his helmet. The air rushed cool to fill his nostrils.

The three of them took off their outer suits, twisting and snapping them away bit by bit as if shedding an exoskeleton. They'd just set the last pieces of their suits on the floor when Dunne's handheld began buzzing.

"What's that?" Sam asked.

Dunne looked at the screen. Her face fell, went gray. She looked as though she was going to be sick.

"Another reading," she said. "The sensor just picked it up."

"Picked *what* up?" Matthew asked.

"Radiation," Dunne said. "Lots of it. More than there was on Earth when we left."

Matthew looked into the sky. "But it's night. How can there be radiation?"

"It's not solar radiation that I'm picking up. The readings are coming from the ground. If I didn't know better, I'd say . . ." She trailed off.

"You'd say what?" Sam demanded.

"I'd say that the planet itself is radioactive."

30

"What do you mean?" Sam asked. "We're just going to bake down here? Burn up and die, just like we would've on Earth?"

Dunne didn't say anything.

"But what about the grass? How can it survive on a planet with such high radiation?" Matthew asked.

"It must have evolved a way to survive in the environment," Dunne said. "Like I said, organisms can thrive in all sorts of hostile ecosystems."

"Just not us."

"Right." Dunne sounded defeated. "Not us."

"How long do you think we can survive?"

Dunne shrugged. "Twenty-four hours, max. Maybe less."

"Christ, a whole day? Is it going to hurt?"

Dunne shook her head. "We can use the suicide pills. As soon as we notice the effects of the radiation and confirm that we won't survive, we can go back in the ship and take the pills."

Matthew felt sick to his stomach. They'd been so close. The

planet seemed to have everything they needed to keep them alive. They were going to survive.

But it was just another false hope. He was going to die after all.

"How long is this going to take?" Sam asked.

"About an hour before we feel the effects of the radiation," Dunne said. "Maybe less."

The transceiver, clipped to Matthew's waist, crackled.

"Status, *Corvus*."

Matthew told Control what was happening.

"Roger, *Corvus*. I'm sorry to hear that."

"Yeah," Matthew said, his voice hoarse as he spoke into the transceiver. "Us too."

"Look, Matthew," Alison began, then paused. There seemed to be real regret, real sadness, in her voice. "This is going to sound callous, given what you're going through over there, but I have to ask. Before you take the pills. You need to send confirmation of the radiation. We need to be sure that H-240 isn't habitable. You understand, don't you?"

Matthew nodded, then clicked the button on the side of the transceiver again. "I do. We'll let you know."

.   .   .

Matthew, Dunne, and Sam wandered through the prairie as they waited for the effects of the radiation to take hold. Their paths diverged and crossed at random as they circled around the ship, not walking together but careful not to let each other or the *Corvus* out of their sight and get lost in the unmarked expanse of grass.

Matthew paused at the top of a small hill and looked up. Above him, two birdlike creatures flitted about in the air. Their bodies were black, but where the light caught them their fine feathers glistened white.

It was night where they had landed, but the light of a sunrise was beginning to warm the horizon. Two moons were still visible in the weakening darkness, dancing together in the sky and then gradually parting. On the far horizon, a larger orb rose and moved so quickly across the sky that Matthew could have traced its path with his finger. As it came overhead, Matthew's aimless steps brought him close to Dunne again, and as the moon peaked over their heads, Matthew watched Dunne's gray-flecked hair lift up into the air and float like tentacles in water. He felt a lightness wash over his own body; his arms lifted up at his sides without his telling them to. Then the moon passed on and the weight returned to his limbs.

"Wow," he said.

"Yeah," Dunne said. "At first it was only the two moons I saw, but I guess that makes three. Looks like that one orbits so close that it affects the planet's gravitational pull. They might even be in a binary orbit."

Matthew watched the moon until it set on the far horizon, then looked back to Dunne. "Shouldn't we be feeling something by now? Burns? Radiation sickness?"

Dunne nodded. "Yes. We should be feeling the effects of the radiation."

"But I'm not. Are you?"

"No."

They angled their steps back toward the ship, walking faster now, and in lockstep. Sam walked to meet them.

"Maybe the radiation isn't high enough. Maybe it's too low for us to feel the effects," Matthew said.

"That would be bad too. If the radiation was low enough, we wouldn't be able to feel it in the moment, but it would still kill us over the long haul. Cancer. Birth defects. Mutation." Dunne shook her head. "But even so, that can't be right. The handheld told me that the radiation was higher than it is on Earth. We should be feeling some pain right now, even if it's only small, like a low-grade sunburn."

They got closer to the ship. "What's going on?" Sam asked.

Dunne ignored him and went straight for the open airlock, where she'd left her handheld.

"Could it be malfunctioning?" Matthew asked. "Maybe your readings were wrong."

"What's malfunctioning? What are you two talking about?"

Dunne stabbed at the handheld with her index finger. "I suppose it's possible. But it was right about everything else. The breathable air, the temperature."

Matthew touched the transceiver clipped to his collar. "Control, this is Corvus."

"Go ahead, Corvus. What's your status?"

"We're wondering about the odds of a malfunction in the handheld sensor array."

A beat of silence as Alison checked with her superiors.

"We haven't seen any occurrences of that, Corvus, but anything's possible. What's going on over there?"

"What is it?" Sam asked, his voice low as though to hide his words from the people back on Earth. "We might be safe after all?"

Dunne sighed. "Maybe."

"What do you mean, maybe? You sound disappointed. We're still alive, we're not burning up like you said we would. Crack a smile or something, doc."

"I just don't trust it."

"Corvus, we need your status. What's going on over there?"

"So what do we do now?" Matthew asked.

"Maybe nothing," Sam said. "Maybe this is the one. The planet we were sent here to find. I mean, there was always a chance, right? A chance that we'd actually be the ones?"

"Corvus, talk to us. Is H-240 a positive planetary match? Is that what you're telling us?"

"We have to wait," Dunne said. "The readings might be wrong. But they might be right. There might be radiation here. We don't know."

"How can we be sure?" Matthew asked. "Do we wait for five, ten years until one of us gets cancer?

"Ten years?" Sam gaped. "You've got to be kidding me. What the hell kind of plan is that?"

"Corvus, don't leave us hanging over here. Tell us something."

"Jesus Christ," Sam grunted. "Would you shut her up? I can't hear myself think."

Matthew snatched the transceiver from his collar and flung

it toward the ship, where it whizzed through the open door and clattered down on the floor of the airlock. He turned to Dunne. "So what do we do? What's the plan?"

"Tests," she said. "Soil samples. And grass. Blood and tissue from the two of you. I need to see whether or not the radiation is manifesting at a cellular level. Then we'll know for sure. Then we'll know if this is a planet where the human race can survive."

"How long will that take?" Matthew asked.

Dunne squinted at the ground. "Not long," she said finally. "Just a few hours for the tests."

Matthew breathed out sharply and nodded.

"All right, let's do it. When do we get started?"

31

kiva

A pinkish orb embedded in a sea of black—their world, Gle'ah, seen from a far distance.

The bird made of metal, stone, and fire, blazing through the atmosphere and coming down through the air to kneel on the grassland.

A door opening in the bird's side and three suited figures coming out, their faces obscured by gleaming shells that surrounded their heads.

One of the figures removing his shell, his face coming into view.

The boy. The boy from her dream. Matthew. His eyes cast about, this way and that, then fell on her.

His eyes were blue. They darted off to the side, and when they came back to Kiva they were filled with panic.

"Look out!" Matthew shouted, and Kiva looked away to see one of the other figures pointing a smooth gray stick with an opening at one end toward where she stood.

The stick roared, and the vision ended in a blaze of strange white light.

. . .

When Kiva opened her eyes, she saw Quint's face hovering above hers, the girl's features distorted by fear and her cheeks mottled with tears. Behind her stood the Sisters, silent at last as they craned to see if Kiva was all right.

"Kiva!" Quint said. "Are you awake? Is that really you?"

Kiva let out a final gasp as the last of the blinding pain left her body. The relief that flooded over her as the vision receded was a physical sensation, a coolness that spread like a gulp of water from her belly to her fingertips. She panted, filling her lungs with air, pulled herself up to an elbow, then answered Quint.

"Of course it's me. What kind of question is that?"

She tried to smile, to turn the whole thing into a joke, but Quint's frown deepened.

"You spoke," she said. "You opened your eyes and spoke to me. But you didn't sound like yourself."

Kiva bent her head toward Quint and pitched her voice low. "What did I say?"

"You said, 'They're here.'"

Kiva winced, hoping that no one else had heard—but when she looked over Quint's shoulder to the faces of the Sisters, she knew at once that they had, that those who'd crowded closest to her and Quint during the vision had heard the entranced thing that she'd said and quickly spread it through the crowd to those who stood on tiptoes at the back. Voices buzzed low on the air as the Sisters whispered to each other.

"Vagra, what should we do?" a voice called from somewhere in the middle of the crowd.

Kiva closed her eyes and let out a long sigh. She'd managed to keep the Sisters' doubts about her leadership at bay—by confronting Kyne, she'd convinced them that she had what it took to be Vagra, and with her vision she'd demonstrated that the Ancestors truly did communicate through her. But now that she'd convinced them, she'd have to lead them. Over and over again, she'd have to prove that she was worthy to lead the Vagri—every day, every hour, every minute, for the rest of her life.

Kiva lifted herself to her feet by degrees, moving slowly to give herself time to think of her next move. Still uncertain of her body, she first tested the strength of one leg, then the other, as she drew herself to her full height. As she stood the Sisters backed away slowly. Only Quint stayed by her side.

Kiva scanned the crowd, looking for someone.

"Liana," she said when she'd found her.

Liana stepped forward and bowed her head. "Yes, Vagra."

Kiva gritted her teeth at the formal way Liana spoke to her— her own mother, forced to bow and genuflect, to pretend that they meant nothing more to each other than a Vagra did to one of her subjects.

"You're still loyal to me, is that right? You came here tonight to oppose this little rebellion?"

Liana nodded. "I did, Vagra. I am."

"Then I want you to lead these women back to the village."

"What about the Strangers?" Liana asked.

"Leave the Strangers to me," Kiva said, speaking loudly so that everyone could hear her. She turned to the rest of the crowd. "Remember your responsibilities, Sisters, the roles to which the Ancestors have called each of you. The men and children look to you for wisdom, for guidance. What if they wake in the morning and wonder where you've gone? Enough of this fighting. You must return."

The Sisters were silent. Some hung their heads. Others flexed their jaws, gave each other sidelong glances. The meaning of their expressions wasn't clear, but Kiva could sense that not all of the Sisters were taking kindly to her show of authority.

She'd have to deal with them later, though. There were more pressing matters for her to see to.

"Thruss? Rehal?" she called as the Sisters trudged out of the pit.

The two girls turned and walked to Kiva.

"Forgive us, Kiva," Rehal said when she'd come close.

Kiva gave her a sharp look. Rehal and Thruss had been her friends, once—but seeing their faces among the crowd of women supporting Kyne was a betrayal she wouldn't soon forget.

"Vagra, I mean," Rehal said, chastened. "Please, Vagra, we were only afraid."

Thruss nodded. "We don't support Kyne. We only wanted to hear what she would say."

Kiva lifted a hand. "Enough," she said. "You want to make it up to me? Stand with me now. Come with me to meet the Strangers."

Both girls were silent. There was fear in their eyes. But they nodded.

"What about me?" came a voice at Kiva's waist.

She looked down. Quint.

"I thought you'd gone," Kiva said, crouching to her sister's level. "You should go with the women. I want you back in the village, safe in your bed."

But Quint shook her head. "I want to come with you."

"Maybe I can help, too," came another voice.

Kiva lifted her head. It was Po. He'd come forward from where he'd been standing by the bonfire, his weapon still propped on the ground.

"You," Kiva said, rising to her full height once more.

She advanced toward Po with her finger outstretched and jabbed him in the chest. "You're part of this, too. You left the village to join the Forsaken because you were mad at me, is that it? And now you're siding with Kyne, trying to turn the Forsaken and the Sisters against me."

"It wasn't my choice," Po said, his face going pale. "Kyne made me do it. I didn't want to leave the village—but she's my sister. What was I supposed to do? I have to obey her."

Kiva looked long at Po. She had a feeling that he wasn't telling her the whole truth. But her anger began to dissipate all the same. All at once, she noticed the long gash that ran down Po's cheek from his temple to his chin.

She reached out to touch his face. "What happened here?"

Po jerked his head back, stepped away. "It's nothing," he said. "Just an accident."

"Some accident," Kiva said.

Po looked at her but didn't say anything. They waited a long beat.

"All right," she said at last. "So none of this was your choice. You never supported Kyne. You were just doing what you were told. Fine. I believe you. But what about the rest of the Forsaken? What about Xendr Chathe? Where does he stand in all of this?"

Po flinched. "Xendr knew what Kyne was doing."

Kiva blinked once, twice. She clenched her fists at her sides. "Let me guess: he wanted to see how things would play out. See which way the Sisters would go, who they'd support, then throw his support behind the winner. Is that it?"

Po nodded. "Yes. But only to know whose side he should take if what Kyne was saying was real—if there really were Strangers coming, and if you weren't ready to lead the Vagri against them."

"Oh, is that all?" Kiva let a sharp breath out through clenched teeth. "How comforting."

"Don't be angry." Po took a step closer and reached for Kiva's shoulder. Kiva stepped back. Po let his arm fall back to his side.

"Okay," he said. "I understand. But anyway, it's over now. After what happened tonight, there can be no question. The Strangers are real. You're ready to lead. And Kyne's rebellion is over."

"I'm not so sure about the last part," Kiva said. "But the rest is true."

"So let me help," Po said. "Let us help. Let me go and gather the Forsaken. We can kill the Strangers before they even get close enough to the village to threaten it."

Kiva shook her head. "No."

"No?" Po looked surprised and confused. "But why? Kiva, don't be foolish, these Strangers—"

"Foolish?" Kiva cut in. "Remember who you're talking to, Po."

Po stopped himself, breathed out. "I'm sorry, Vagra, I just meant—"

Kiva waved his apology away, her anger fading. "I know what you meant. I'm sorry, too."

180

"So? Will you let us help you or not?"

"Let me think for a moment."

Kiva turned and walked a few steps away from Po, away from Rehal, Thruss, and Quint. She felt their eyes following her, the wish flashing through each of their minds that she would see reason and allow them to go to the Strangers with the Forsaken at their side, weapons in hand. She felt their fear—their fear of the Strangers, their fear for themselves.

But she still didn't want to use the Forsaken. After what the Vagra had told her about the last time the Forsaken had protected the village, she didn't trust them. She didn't even think she needed them—the Strangers didn't mean them any harm.

And yet, there was a seed of doubt in her mind. Her most recent vision—the one she'd seen just moments before—had shown one of the Strangers holding what must have been a weapon, with fire leaping from the end of it.

Maybe it was a good thing that Po had joined the Forsaken, after all. With him among the Forsaken, she might be able to control them—the same way the old Vagra had controlled Xendr Chathe fifty seasons ago.

"Fine," Kiva said at last. "You can come with us. But don't summon all of the Forsaken. I want you and only two more. One for each of the Strangers."

"There are only three of them?" Po asked.

"Yes," Kiva said. "That's what my visions show."

She looked at Po, Thruss, Rehal, and Quint, something forming in her mind as her eyes wandered across their inquisitive faces. She mentally added two Forsaken men to their numbers.

"What?" Quint asked. "What is it?"

"Nothing," Kiva said. "I'm just—I'm thinking."

"Thinking about what?" Thruss asked.

"A plan," Kiva said. "I think I've got a plan."

32

matthew

After Dunne had taken blood and tissue samples from Matthew and Sam, she returned to the ship to do her tests.

Matthew and Sam went back out into the hills to explore. Before they left, Sam paused in the airlock and knelt near a metal chest bolted to the floor.

"What are you doing?" Matthew asked.

Sam didn't look up. "Precautions," he said.

He snapped open the latches and lifted the lid, then reached inside and took out something long and sleek and gray. He lifted the object. An ion shotgun.

A cold rush passed over Matthew's body, and a sick feeling grew in his stomach.

"What's that for?" he asked.

"Dunne's got her tests. You've got the transceiver to communicate with Control. This is what I'm here for."

Sam moved sideways and slipped past Matthew, stepping out onto the grass.

"But why would we need guns?" Matthew asked. "Why would they even send those along with us?"

Sam walked out a few paces, the ion shotgun cradled in his hands. He stopped and scanned the horizon as if searching for a target.

"Did you hear me?"

"I heard you," Sam said, his voice impatient. "And I don't know why. Maybe they figured that if we did find a planet that could support life, there might actually be something living there already. Something we need to protect ourselves from."

Sam turned his head and glanced at Matthew out of the corner of his eye. "Well? Are you coming or not?"

Matthew stepped out of the airlock and followed Sam. They moved into the hills and made their way across the prairie, Sam pressing forward as if he expected to find something to shoot over the top of each new rise, Matthew lagging behind, struggling to keep pace as he waded through the tall grasses. Though the grass covered every inch of the ground, the planet felt desertlike to Matthew. There was a barrenness to the landscape, to the way the small swells rose up with regularity in every direction, sameness as far as the eye could see. At the top of each hill, Matthew expected to see something new as he staggered up after Sam: a tree, a rock formation, something.

But every time, all he saw were more hills. More grass.

Until.

Sam paused at the top of an uncommonly tall hill. Matthew made his way up behind, his feet rustling the grasses around him.

Without looking back, Sam jerked a hand into the air and pulled it into a fist. Matthew stopped.

"What is it?"

Sam glared back and held a finger to his lips.

"Get down," he whispered fiercely, sinking to his knees as Matthew followed suit. Then Sam waved him forward.

Matthew crawled on his elbows until he was almost even with Sam.

"There," Sam said, and pointed the way with an incline of his head.

Matthew looked. In the far distance, some three or four hills away: something. Something different. Something that was not the barren sameness of the undulating grasses.

Two specks. Moving.

Sam crouched down lower and raised a pair of binoculars to his eyes. After a few seconds, he handed the binoculars to Matthew. Matthew looked.

The image swam liquid before Matthew's eyes as the binoculars adjusted, blinked into focus. Then he could see them.

Figures. Creatures. Beings.

He wasn't sure what to call them.

They almost looked . . .

Matthew took his eyes away from the viewfinder. "Are those—?"

"Yeah," Sam said.

Matthew looked through the binoculars again. The figures had come closer—now they were unmistakable. Living organisms.

Humanoid. Wearing clothes. Two children, a boy and a girl. They held hands, walking slowly, picking their way through the sharp blades of grass with bare feet. The girl was slightly taller than the boy. Matthew thought with a flash of Sophie—perhaps this girl and boy were sister and brother. Their mouths moved. They were talking to each other.

Matthew's breath came fast. "But that's . . ."

He wanted to say *impossible*, but he cut himself short. He had flown across the galaxy in cryogenic stasis, in a ship that could travel at the speed of light, and now he was exploring an alien planet.

Nothing was impossible.

"Come on," Sam said in a low growl. He darted forward, keeping low to the ground. The binoculars clutched in one sweaty hand, Matthew followed.

Together they slipped down into a low place between two hills. The two beings, the two *children*—whatever they were—slid out of sight. In the hollow, Sam paused, raised his hand to signal Matthew to stop. Matthew raised his head. He tilted his ear to the wind.

He heard the sound of laughter, wafting over the hills like torn bits of paper blowing on the wind. The sound grew louder and more whole. It sounded like music, like the tinkling of chimes. For a moment, Matthew closed his eyes and simply listened.

When he opened his eyes, the children had come around the base of the hill and were visible once more. They stood at a distance, but even without the binoculars held to his eyes Matthew could see clearly now that they were exactly like humans in every way but one: the color of their skin, which was a gray so deep it bled into hues of purple and blue, like bodies recently dead. But they were alive.

Alive and—by the looks on their faces—startled, shocked, afraid.

"My God," Matthew muttered to himself. He held his breath.

The boy shrank back a pace into the tall grasses, while the girl moved forward and to one side, stepping between them and the boy. Her hair was long and jet black; her eyes were glassy with fear, but her jaw was set hard.

Sam rose up from his crouch, the ion shotgun clutched at his side. Something in Matthew's chest jerked.

"Sam?" Matthew asked.

Sam didn't say anything. With one hand he whipped the shotgun up to his chest, brought the other across his body to cradle the stock. He held the butt tight against his shoulder and gazed down the barrel at the boy and girl. They were still, frozen like deer at the foot of the far hill.

Matthew felt himself rising.

"Sam, no!"

Matthew rushed forward without thinking and threw himself at the muzzle of the shotgun, arms outstretched. His hands closed over the barrel just as the deafening report of the gun reached his ears. He lost his balance and went sprawling, but he'd done what he needed to: Sam's shot went wide. A white orb screamed out of the gun and hit a patch of ground ten yards away from the children. Stunned at the sound of the blast and the charred circle where the ionized energy had burned the grass to ash, the children turned and fled.

Sam lifted the shotgun to his shoulder once more, but he was too late.

They were gone.

Matthew pushed himself to his feet and grabbed once again at the muzzle of the shotgun. He tried to wrest it from Sam's hands, but Sam tightened his grip and yanked it back.

"You don't want to do that." Sam didn't say anything more, but his eyes contained a threat.

Matthew didn't care.

"What the hell was that?" he demanded.

Something flashed across Sam's eyes. Embarrassment? Guilt?

"I saw a threat," Sam said. "I took care of it. That's what I'm here for."

"A threat? Those were *kids*, Sam. They weren't a threat to anybody."

Sam's jaw clenched. He looked at Matthew for a long moment, then glanced away.

"You saw what you saw. I saw what I saw."

Matthew grabbed Sam's shoulder and spun him around so they faced each other. "And what did you see, huh? What was so dangerous that you needed to pull out a gun?"

Sam dropped the gun to the ground and shoved Matthew away with the flats of both hands—hard.

"You touch me again, I'll—"

"Tell me," Matthew demanded. "What did you see? I want to know *exactly* what you thought you were doing."

Sam paused, backed off a step, ran a hand over his mouth to his chin.

"Look, they were—they were just things, okay? Animals."

"Animals my ass. They were kids."

"Look, you can call them what you want, but the fact is we're on another planet, we don't know what the hell they are. Those things may have looked and sounded like humans, but all we know for sure is that they were alien creatures. I treated them with caution because that was the logical thing to do. The doc would've said the same thing if she were here."

Matthew looked off to the side and shook his head slowly, letting out a sharp, angry breath.

"Well, either way, they're gone now. And regardless of what Dunne would've said, if there's real humanoid life on this planet, we're going to need our science officer with us to check it out."

Sam nodded and strolled back to where the ion shotgun lay in the grass. Matthew darted around him and plucked it from the ground.

"Don't even think about it, asshole," Sam said.

Sam grabbed at the stock and shot Matthew a warning look. Matthew looked back into his eyes and saw immediately that he wouldn't back down. Sam was bigger than he was, stronger. He could overpower him. He could take the gun. He could even kill Matthew, if he wanted to. Who would stop him?

"I need it," Sam kept on. "You say those things were kids—fine. That means there are grown-ups too, right? And maybe they have weapons."

"Yeah, and because of you the kids are probably telling them that we're hostile, that we tried to kill them on sight."

Sam winced. "I know. I screwed up. But you can trust me. Okay?"

Matthew loosed his grip and let Sam take the gun.

"All right. But no more mistakes."

Sam nodded, and together they made their way back to the Corvus.

33

kiva

Kiva waited for Po to fetch two Forsaken men and bring them to the pit. After they came, they all began to walk to the place where Kiva sensed the Strangers had landed. As they began to walk, morning broke around them, the light of the Great Mother warming the edge of the horizon.

Kiva stopped, lifted a flat hand to signal her followers to stop too. She closed her eyes. She sensed that the Strangers had landed somewhere to the south and east of the village; getting there from the pit, which was due north, had brought them close to the village, to the grassland just beyond its border. Kiva opened her eyes again and looked to her left, saw the rise jutting into the air some thousand paces away.

They still had a long way to go, but Kiva sensed something right where they stood. Some disturbance.

"What is it, Vagra?" Rehal asked. "Are we close?"

Kiva shook her head. "Someone's coming. They're afraid."

"The Strangers?" Thruss asked, unable to hide the fear in her voice.

But it wasn't the Strangers. At that moment, two Vagri children came over the nearest hill, panting as they ran through the waist-high grasses, their faces streaked with tears. They stopped and cowered when they saw Kiva and the people with her.

Kiva walked to them, a hand held out.

"Don't be afraid," she said to the children, a boy and a girl. "Tell me what's happened."

Their eyes were glassy, looking past Kiva, and their breaths were panicked gasps. They were in shock. Whatever they'd seen, it hadn't just scared them—it had terrified them.

Kiva turned to the older child, the girl, and hooked her finger under her chin, tilted her head up softly.

"Look at me," Kiva said, then waited for the girl's eyes to focus, her breath to slow. "You're safe now, okay?"

The girl turned to the little boy and touched him on the shoulder. He raised his eyes to his sister, then looked at Kiva. Kiva gave him what she hoped was a reassuring smile.

"What are your names?" Kiva asked.

The girl nudged her younger brother.

"Ferrin," he said.

"And you?"

"Edela," the girl said.

"Those are nice names," Kiva said.

The children angled their eyes toward the ground.

"Now," Kiva said, "tell me what happened."

The girl spoke.

"We snuck off in the morning, before the Great Mother rose. We were out in the prairie, just walking."

"How far? Which way?" Kiva asked.

"To the west," Edela said, waving off in the distance, "maybe three or four lengths beyond the edge of the village. The Great Mother had come up, and we were about to turn back. That's when we saw them."

Kiva's body went tight. "Who?"

"I don't know. Creatures I've never seen before. They walked on two legs, like us, but there was something different about them. Something strange."

"I want you to be sure. Try hard to remember. It wasn't just one of the Forsaken that you saw?"

The girl shook her head. "No, Vagra. I'm sure of it. They wore strange clothes, blue coverings that clung tight to their bodies. And their skin was the wrong color; it was pink, like the color of the sky, but paler."

"How many?"

"Two."

Kiva nodded. "Good. What else?"

The girl squinted. "One of them carried something. I don't know what it was. It looked like a stick. But fire leapt from the end of it."

"He tried to hurt you?"

The girl nodded. "Yes. He pointed the stick at us and a bright light came toward us. But it missed us—it hit the ground and burned up the grass."

Kiva sucked in a breath. It was all so much like her vision, the one that had come over her at the pit.

"Children, may I . . ." She hesitated. "I need to touch you to search your minds. I need to see exactly what you saw. May I do that? It won't hurt, I promise."

The boy looked to the girl. The girl met Kiva's gaze and nodded. "Yes," she said.

Kiva reached out her hands and placed them dead center on the children's chests, palms flat. She closed her eyes.

In a flash, she was inside their minds, seeing what they had seen out on the grasslands.

The sight of the Strangers as they came over the hill.

The boy from her dream—the same one, the one with the deep blue eyes.

Matthew.

Another boy standing and leveling his weapon, fire leaping from the end of it.

The children ducked and turned away, lifting their heads only when they saw the flaming orb of white light hit the ground and vaporize the grass just next to them.

They looked up to see the two figures struggling in the distance, Matthew grabbing at the weapon.

Kiva came out of the vision with a shallow gasp. For a moment the world pitched and she put a hand on her chest to steady herself.

"Thank you," she said to the children after she'd found her balance. She stood. "Go home to be with your father; he's probably worried about you. Stay in your hut today. Everything is going to be fine."

Kiva rose and watched the children as they walked toward the village, then turned to Thruss, Rehal, Quint, Po, and the two Forsaken men. They'd heard everything.

Thruss's face had gone pale.

"Po was right," she said. "We have to kill them."

Kiva shook her head. "No."

"But Vagra, you heard—"

"I heard exactly what you heard," Kiva said. "But I also saw something—something that none of you have seen. I saw exactly what those children saw. I saw one of the Strangers fight the one who attacked them. I've seen it in my visions as well. We have an ally among them. The Ancestors have shown me this."

"So what do we do?" Po asked.

"We stick with the plan," Kiva said. "Come on, let's go."

34

matthew

Matthew and Sam stood in the airlock, waiting as the contaminated air was sucked out of the compartment and replaced, once again, with the safe air of the *Corvus*.

"I'm exhausted," Sam said, holding his arms out to let jets of warm steam clean the radiation from his clothes. "How long were we out there?"

Matthew glanced at the display over the doorway. "A couple hours."

The light over their heads turned green once the radiation had been eliminated.

Sam yawned and ground the heel of his hand into his eye as they stepped out of the airlock into the controlled environment of the ship.

"You'd think after a hundred years asleep I wouldn't be tired, but damned if I'm not beat. I'm going to catch some shut-eye. What about you?"

Matthew shook his head. "I'm going to find Dunne."

Matthew found Dunne in the laboratory, sitting hunched over

a tablet at a long metal table. She raised her head when he walked into the room.

"Find anything?" Matthew asked.

"I found plenty," she said. "Now if I could only figure out what it means."

Dunne put the tablet on the table, then pushed it across toward Matthew. Matthew looked at the screen and saw a pattern of shapes and colors that he recognized as cells, laid together like bricks.

"What am I looking at?" he asked.

"That's you," Dunne said. "Well, your tissue sample, anyway. Notice anything?"

Matthew looked closely, absently reaching one hand across his body and massaging the place on his side from which Dunne had taken the sample hours earlier.

"No," he said finally.

"Exactly. Nothing. No radiation damage." She reached across the table and swiped a finger across the display. The image zoomed tight into a single cell. "At the cellular level, the mitochondrial level—even when I looked right at the cell nucleus, at the DNA. No damage. No mutations."

"Nothing."

Dunne nodded. "Exactly, nothing."

Matthew looked up. "But that's good, right? That's normal?"

"Not exactly. Even without the high level of radiation, I'd have expected to see *something*—some level of damage to the DNA or the cells just from regular wear and tear. I'd at least expect to see some endogenous damage from normal metabolic—"

Matthew lifted his hands off the table, held them in the air in a gesture of surrender. "I'm going to have to stop you right there. You're saying that some damage to my DNA is—"

"Normal, yes. Just by eating food and processing the nutrients, your body creates some by-products that cause damage on the cellular level. There are natural biological processes to repair this damage, but still, a normal tissue sample will have some percentage of the cells that aren't shipshape. Even when radiation isn't a factor."

"And you didn't even see that?"

Dunne shook her head. "No, not even a little bit."

"So what does it mean?" he asked.

"That's what I kept knocking my head against. Then I had an idea: why not re-subject the tissues to the outside radiation? The air inside the *Corvus* is decontaminated. I thought it wouldn't matter, that whatever radiation we'd all absorbed outside would be enough to see what was going on in the samples, but obviously I was wrong about that. So I put your tissue sample in the containment chamber and filled the chamber with the irradiated air from outside."

Dunne spun her chair away from the table, toward the containment chamber. Matthew came around and joined her at the control panel. The containment chamber was a compartment about the size and shape of a coffin in the center of the lab surrounded in plate glass. From the top of the chamber, a narrow tube ran to the ceiling and a discharge in the outer hull. Inside the chamber was a small-rimmed plastic dish containing Matthew's tissue sample.

"Look at the display," Dunne instructed, and tilted her head toward the control panel.

Matthew looked at the screen and saw the familiar view of biological cells squeezed up next to each other.

Dunne pushed both arms into a pair of rubber gloves that came up to her elbows and allowed her to reach inside the containment chamber. She adjusted the placement of the dish; on the screen, the arrangement of cells wobbled, then came into focus again.

"Watch that one," she said, extracting her arms and moving back to the control panel. She tapped the screen. "That one in the middle."

She turned a knob, and as she did the picture zoomed in even further, until only the single cell was visible. Matthew watched for a few seconds, then glanced at Dunne.

"What am I looking for?" he asked.

"Just watch," Dunne said, not taking her eyes off the display. "It comes and goes in a split second. You'll miss it if you're not looking carefully."

Matthew looked back at the screen. For a few long moments, nothing happened. No change, no movement.

Then, something happened—so subtle that at first Matthew thought it was a trick of his eyes.

At the edge of the screen, the cell was breaking down. The membrane tearing open.

And then, just as abruptly as the cell broke open, it zipped shut again in a flash.

It was all so fast that at the end of it Matthew wondered if he had imagined the whole thing, if it was just a glitch in the display.

He looked to Dunne. "What did I just see?"

"It's fast, right? At first I thought I was seeing things too. But then it kept happening. I recorded it, slowed it down, and sure enough . . ." Her fingers flicked over the panel, then she pointed back at the screen. "There."

In slow motion, one microscopic frame at a time, the cell burst open and then, just as quickly, closed up again.

"But what's happening?"

"The biological cells are breaking down, just like we'd expect them to under high radiation. They're literally cooking. Popping open."

"And then repairing themselves."

"Right! But not repairing themselves, exactly—that's impossible. The body just doesn't have the resources to do that, to regenerate cells that quickly."

"What, then?"

Dunne shook her head, reached a hand up to her face and ran the fingers idly over her cheek as she thought. "That's what I don't know. Yet. But one thing's for sure. The radiation on this planet is enough to kill us by itself. But there's something else in the environment. Something that's keeping us alive. I'll find it. I just need more time."

"We might not have that much time," Matthew said.

Dunne raised an eyebrow. "Why's that?"

"We're not alone. There's something else here. Someone else."

Dunne's mouth dropped open.

35

For a few seconds, Dunne was unable to speak. Then she put a hand to her chest and felt behind her with the other, grasping in the air for a chair. Fearing that she was going to faint, Matthew helped her get settled in a tall metal stool.

"I want you to tell me everything," Dunne said.

"We saw them maybe five miles away, to the northeast."

"How many?" Dunne asked.

"Two of them. Children."

"Children," Dunne said to herself in a kind of marveled whisper. "They were humanoid, then? Like us, basically?"

Matthew nodded. "Yes. Two arms, two legs."

"What else?"

"I don't know. We didn't get very close."

"Why not?" Dunne asked.

Matthew cringed. "Sam. He . . . he had a gun, from the airlock, and I guess he must have panicked or something, because—"

A horrified look came over Dunne's face. "He didn't."

"He did."

"Did he hurt them? Kill them?"

Matthew shook his head. "No. He missed. They ran away."

Dunne set an elbow on the table and put her hand over her mouth. Her breath came sharp but shallow from her chest, streaming through her splayed fingers. She gazed off to the side, staring with glassy eyes at a spot on the wall.

"Were they wearing clothes?" she asked, turning toward him again with renewed urgency. "Were they talking to each other? Did they have tools of any kind?"

"No tools that I could see," Matthew said. "But they were wearing clothes, and it looked like they were talking to each other until they saw us. Why? Is that important?"

"Of course it's important! It changes everything! Clothes and language—that's not just life. The grass outside, that's life. But what you're describing is more than that. What you're describing is culture. And culture means sentience, consciousness. It means that we might be the first people in the history of the human race to make contact with intelligent life on another planet. You understand that?"

"Does this mean that the planet might be habitable after all?"

Dunne shook her head. "Not necessarily. Not for us, anyway. I still don't understand what effect this place has on humans. Those kids you saw out there—if that's really what you saw—their species has had millions of years to evolve in this environment. Things that wouldn't bother them might kill us over time."

"So what do we do now?"

Dunne's back slowly pulled straight and she rested her hands on her legs. Her eyes still had a far-off look, but the shock had worn off her face. The expression she wore now was one of determination.

"We have to find them," she said. "The creatures you saw. We have to make contact. We have to study them. If I can understand their biology, then maybe I can figure out what's going on *there*." She nodded her head back toward the containment chamber with Matthew's tissue sample inside, toward the screen where the recording of his cells tearing open and regenerating ran on a continuous loop.

"Okay," Matthew said. "Let's do it."

Dunne nodded and stood up. "Where's Sam?"

"I'm right here," came a gruff voice from the corridor.

Matthew's head snapped around. Sam stepped into the room.

"You startled me," Matthew said. "I thought you were getting some shut-eye."

Sam leaned against the doorframe, crossed his arms over his chest, and shrugged. "Couldn't sleep."

"Were you listening to us long?" Matthew asked.

"Long enough," Sam said.

"Then you know that we're going to go find those creatures you and Matthew saw," Dunne said.

"You won't have to go far," Sam said. "That's why I was coming to find you."

"What do you mean?" Matthew asked.

"I mean they're here."

. . .

There were three of them, standing some hundred paces beyond the door to the airlock, far enough away that Matthew couldn't quite make out their features. They were female, each wearing a dull-colored knee-length dress. A wind whipped up, and the grass swished around their knees, whipped their hair sideways.

Matthew stepped away from the window to give Dunne a chance to look.

"Women," she said, then squinted. "Girls, by the look of it, though it's hard to tell from this distance. Hardly the scouting party that I'd expect."

Sam knelt and opened the chest of guns. He took out the shotgun he'd had before, then glanced up to Matthew.

"Want one?"

"No," Matthew said, "and you don't need one either. There's no reason to go out there with guns. Not after what happened last time. It's just three girls. They don't have any weapons. They're not a threat."

"You don't know that," Sam said. "We haven't really made contact yet. You don't know what they're capable of."

Dunne stepped back from the window and addressed Matthew.

"I agree with Sam," she said. "They look familiar, like something we recognize and interpret as safe and unthreatening. But we don't know anything about them. For all we know they might breathe fire or shoot death rays from their eyes."

Matthew scoffed.

"I'm exaggerating to make a point," Dunne said. "What I'm saying is, we need to be cautious. There's no reason we shouldn't take precautions against danger when we make first contact."

"There is if he can't keep his finger off the trigger!" Matthew said, his voice rising.

Sam stood, gun in hand. "I'll be more careful this time."

Matthew shook his head. "No. This time, we're doing it my way."

Dunne's brow knotted. "What do you suggest?"

"I'll go out there. Alone. You two can hang back if you're so afraid of them. Watch from the doorway to see how it goes. If they attack me, then you can come out with guns blazing."

Dunne raked a hand through her hair, then rubbed at the back of her neck as she considered. "It's a risk."

"Yes, but it's my risk," Matthew said. "And it's a risk worth taking. We've seen five of them so far—the two kids, now these three. There are bound to be more of them out there. Hundreds, thousands. Millions, even. You want to kill every one of them? The three of us, against the whole planet?"

Dunne was silent for a moment, then nodded. "Okay. Let's do it. But one change."

"What?"

She looked him square in the eyes. "I'm coming with you."

36

po

Blades of grass scratched at Po's face. He lifted his head and chest from the ground and peered over the swell of the hill. Below, the Sisters stood in a tight knot—Thruss, Rehal, and Kiva. Their lips moved, but Po was too far away to make out what they were saying, couldn't even hear their voices as a murmur carried on the wind.

Off to the left, some distance away from where Kiva and her friends clumped on the grass, stood what looked to Po like a huge bird made of gleaming black stone. Kiva said it carried the Strangers in its belly.

"Nothing's happening," Quint said, crouched a few paces behind Po.

"I can see that," Po muttered.

"Then get back down," Quint said. "Wait for the signal."

Po lowered himself back to the ground and looked to his right and left, where the other Forsaken men lay on the ground as well, poised to react to Kiva's signal as it was relayed to Quint. Kiva had told them what to look for before she'd gone down with Thruss and Rehal: when she understood the situation, understood whether the Strangers meant them harm or not, she'd raise her arm in the air. Then, if she dropped it back to her side, that meant all was safe; raising a single finger meant that Po should fire a harmless warning shot; and a clenched fist meant that the Forsaken should use their weapons to kill every last one of the Strangers.

Po rolled onto his side, reached over his shoulder to take an arrow from the quiver on his back, then eyed the point of the arrowhead as he notched the fletched end in the taut string of his bow.

"Hold on," Quint said suddenly.

"What is it?" Po glanced back.

Quint was craning her neck from her crouch, eyes narrowed as she tried to get a better look.

"Something's happening," Quint said.

kiva

A low-pitched whirring sound sliced through the air, a thrum of mechanical parts moving and scraping against each other. Part of the bird's black shell was peeling away from its body and lowering on a hinge toward the ground. Kiva's pulse quickened. She could feel the fear of Thruss and Rehal rising, and she reached out to grab each of her friends by the hand. She looked first to Thruss, then to Rehal, forcing a smile she was pleased to see each girl return.

She closed her eyes and reached out with her mind into the empty space where the Ancestors dwelled, hoping for some final echo to confirm that she was doing the right thing. She saw and heard nothing—but she felt a sense of peace wash over her, a feeling of resignation, a feeling that whatever happened next was unstoppable and had been ordained long ago, a feeling that was almost hopeful as it came from the Ancestors and coursed through her body.

Kiva let out a slow breath and opened her eyes. She nodded to herself, nodded at the wisdom of the feeling that had come to her from the Ancestors. Then she spoke.

"Don't be afraid, Sisters," she said. "Whatever happens next, we are in the care of the Ancestors. Whatever happens next, we must let it come and meet it without fear."

The door touched the ground as she finished speaking, and the loud thrum ceased.

There came a silence in which nothing could be heard but the breeze whispering in Kiva's ears.

Then a figure stepped into the opening in the bird's side.

The light of the Great Mother didn't reach the figure where it stood. Its face was shrouded in darkness.

For a moment, nothing moved. Even the wind, the grasses were still.

Then the figure stepped forward, and the breath left Kiva's body as she saw the broad shoulders and long, lanky limbs, the dark hair, the smooth cheeks, and the blue eyes of a boy—the same boy she'd seen in her visions.

"Matthew," she said aloud.

37

matthew

Matthew stepped from the airlock onto the planet as if into a dream. His feet and limbs felt heavy, slow-moving, as though he were pulling them through water.

It was the girl who made each step seem like such an effort— the one who stood in the center, grasping the hands of the girls on either side. She watched him, unblinking, as he came down the ramp to put his feet on the grass. Matthew felt pinned back by her eyes; walking deeper into her gaze felt like walking into a stiff wind. Her presence seemed to thicken the air around him, heighten everything—the lines of the horizon, the swell of the hills, the weak, red light of the sun, the blades of grass: each felt sharper, somehow hyperreal.

And the sound she'd made. Was it his name that she'd said?

Matthew shook his head.

Impossible.

He wanted to look away, but for some reason he couldn't break the girl's gaze. Looking into her eyes, the feeling he'd had when he first looked out on the planet—the feeling of familiarity, of déjà vu, of a dim dream-memory lodged like a grain of sand somewhere deep in his mind—this feeling returned. But stronger.

His feet firmly planted on the ground at the end of the ramp, Matthew walked forward a few steps more, then stopped.

For a long moment nobody moved or spoke. Matthew licked his lips. His fingers fluttered at his sides. The girl went on looking straight at him, as if waiting for him to make the first move, and the feeling that washed over Matthew next was one, absurdly, of embarrassment.

What was the right thing to say at a time like this—when meeting an alien race for the first time? The only thing Matthew could think of was the line he'd heard in movies, *Greetings, we come in peace*, but as soon as it came to his mind Matthew dismissed it as silly, far too clichéd and familiar for a moment as powerfully strange as this one.

The girl rescued him by speaking first.

"Who are you?" she asked. "Why have you come here?"

"We . . . ," Matthew began, his voice cracking on the word. He cleared his throat and went on. "We call ourselves *humans*. We come from far away. From a different planet."

Matthew waved an arm in the air, toward the stars.

Matthew heard a rustling behind him and glanced halfway back to see Dunne move into his peripheral vision. She moved up just behind his shoulder and spoke into his ear.

"You can understand them?" she asked.

"I . . . I don't know," Matthew stammered. "Yes. Can't you?"

He glanced back at the girl, realizing for the first time that though he'd perceived and understood the words she had spoken to him, the language she spoke wasn't his own. Matthew had heard her words as a meaningless babble, but somewhere between his ears and his brain the alien language had mysteriously blossomed into sense.

What the hell is going on here?

One of the other girls leaned over the shoulder of the girl who'd spoken and said something in a low voice. Matthew dimly heard the same meaningless babble, and this time he could make no sense of the sounds. The first girl, the leader, nodded as she listened to what the other girl was saying in her ear.

Then she spoke to Matthew once more, the words again beginning in his ears as nonsense and ending in his mind as meaning: "We want to know if you mean us harm. If you came to kill us."

"No," Matthew said.

"Then why did you attack our children?"

"That was a mistake. A miscommunication. We were . . ." Matthew paused, struggling to explain. "We were scared. Surprised. One of us attacked without thinking. It won't happen again."

The girl dropped her gaze to the ground for a moment, then raised it again, and Matthew was surprised anew by how deep and piercing her brown eyes were. On top of everything—on top of the powerful strangeness of this moment and his inexplicable ability to understand her words—the girl was beautiful, almost unbearably so. Matthew felt strange in her presence, exposed. Across the space that separated them, he became intensely aware of her body, of the lithe but unbendable way she held herself—and in his awareness of her, he became aware of himself as well, of his body as an awkward and clumsy thing, of the pervasive *wrongness* of his being in that place, the alien air rushing in and out of his chest.

We shouldn't be here, he thought to himself. *This isn't our place. It's theirs. Hers.*

"How do we know you're telling the truth?" the girl asked. "How do we know you won't attack again?"

Matthew splayed out his palms in a gesture of helpless empty-handedness. "You'll just have to trust us. You'll have to trust me."

The girl's lips curled into an angry smile. "I'd like to. But it's difficult. How can I trust what you say, when the one who attacked our children is hiding with a weapon?"

38

kiva

Matthew exchanged some whispered words with the darker-skinned woman standing behind him. Then he shouted back toward the stone bird where Kiva had sensed another Stranger hiding. After a few moments, a figure came out: another boy, taller and broader than Matthew but with the same pale skin. He crept out cautiously, one step at a time.

He held a weapon, the fire-breathing stick Kiva had seen in her vision.

Matthew and the woman began to yell at the boy. Kiva couldn't understand the woman's words, but Matthew's echoed loudly in her ears.

"Sam, put it down!"

The boy grunted something back and moved slowly forward. The weapon was cradled in his arms, one end propped against his shoulder, the other searching the landscape for a target.

"Vagra," said a fearful voice. It was Thruss.

Kiva raised her arm.

po

Shouts echoed through the air. The words were in an alien language, but even without knowing their meaning, Po could hear the tone of fear and anger.

His fingers clenched around the place where he'd notched the arrow in his bow.

"What's happening?" he demanded.

Quint squinted, peering over the low rise of the hill, her lips pulled into a thin line.

"There's a third. Another boy. He has a weapon. Kiva's about to give the signal."

"Which one?" Po demanded. "Which signal?"

Quint shook her head. "Wait. Just wait."

The shouting got louder. Po recognized Kiva's voice, though he couldn't hear what she was saying. He imagined that the next sound he heard would be of Kiva wailing as she died. Still lying on the ground, he began to pull back the bow, the notched arrow wedged tightly between his two knuckles.

He looked to the two Forsaken men at his side.

"Follow my lead," he said. "Don't attack until I do."

"What are you doing?" Quint asked over the sound of more shouting. "She hasn't given the signal yet."

Po pushed himself to a crouch, then rose to his feet, his legs unbending beneath him as he raised his taut bow, the arrow's fletching brushing against his cheek, his eyes finding at once the boy whose own weapon was tracking across the hill to aim toward where Po stood.

matthew

"Sam, put it down! Don't be a fool!"

Matthew had turned completely away from the three girls and was moving toward Sam, his arm outstretched as if approaching a spooked animal.

"Not on your life," Sam growled.

"This isn't making things better," Dunne said, her voice firm but not shouting. "Matthew had found a way to communicate. We were getting somewhere."

"Oh, really?" Sam shouted, his voice dripping with sarcasm. "What did they say?"

Matthew lowered his voice, tried to speak calmly. "They understand that the thing with the kids was just a mistake. A misunderstanding. They want to trust us. But first you'll have to put the gun down."

"Yeah? And what if it's a trap?" Sam's eyes darted back and forth, scanning the empty hilltops.

The voice of the girl, pitched to a shout, echoed foreign again in Matthew's ears and exploded into meaning in his mind.

"You have to control him!" she yelled. "If he doesn't put down his weapon, I can't protect you!"

"Sam, it's not a trap!" Matthew shouted. "There's no one there!"

But at that moment, Sam's gun stopped, moved up to aim at a single spot on the horizon. Matthew glanced up and saw a figure rising over the swell of the hill. His arms were raised and he appeared to have something in his hands.

"Sam, don't," Matthew growled, but he knew that his words were of no use anymore.

His feet began to move.

The gun yelped, and a ball of ionized energy screamed out of the barrel. Sam's aim, again, was wide, and the energy hurtled harmlessly over the figure's head.

Moments after Sam fired, Matthew ran at him and rammed him with his shoulder. Sam staggered but kept his feet.

Matthew's hands closed around the hot metal of the gun, and he clenched them tight. Sam's eyes, inches from Matthew's own, flashed with fury. He grunted as he tried to wrest the gun back from Matthew's grip. Matthew felt Sam's breath hot and foul against his face.

Then, suddenly, Matthew felt a small, sharp twinge of pain low in his rib cage. He opened his mouth to gasp but found that he couldn't draw a breath. The pain bloomed red, spreading fire through his torso. Across the gun barrel, Sam's eyes fluttered down and grew wide.

Matthew looked down.

There was an arrow buried in his chest.

39

kiva

It all happened so quickly that later, back in the safety of her hut, it would seem to Kiva that she'd seen it twice: once as it really happened, and then a second time in the brief quiet that followed as she played it back more slowly in her mind, subdividing the blur into a sequence of events that could be analyzed and understood, one following the other in a chain of action and reaction.

Po rising over the hillside. The boy with the weapon aiming and letting loose a white orb of light over Po's shoulder. Matthew running to wrest the weapon from the boy's hands, just in time to place himself in the path of the whizzing arrow Po had loosed from his bow.

For a moment afterward everything was still, and in that brief space Kiva wondered if perhaps time had stopped, and that now they were all frozen on the cusp before everything fell apart. There was comfort in the thought—in the notion that they could stay here forever, looking over the edge but never going over.

Then Rehal let loose a piercing scream, and the illusion was broken.

Matthew spun to the ground, still gripping the weapon tight in his hands. It slipped loose from the other boy's fingers and went arcing through the air, the gleaming metal glistening in the Great Mother's red light before it landed in the grass.

At the top of the hill, the two Forsaken men rose up beside Po and came thundering down, spears in hand. Po came over the swell a few steps behind them, notching another arrow in his bow as his feet moved down the incline.

"Stop!" Kiva yelled. "Don't hurt them!"

Po and the Forsaken drew up at the bottom of the hill, their steps faltering to a stop. They stood only a few paces from the boy who'd shot at Po. They brandished their weapons at him, Po training his bow at the boy's chest, but they didn't attack.

From where she stood, Kiva could see the boy's head angle toward the spot where the weapon had gone into the grass.

"Get the weapon!" Kiva shouted, coming forward.

The boy made a move for it, but the Forsaken leapt forward with their spears and the boy stepped back, his arms raised. Quint, who'd come down the hill after Po, went for the weapon and picked it up.

The dark-skinned woman rushed toward where Matthew lay on the ground and sank to her knees next to his body. Kiva and the Sisters converged on the spot.

Matthew's face was pale, but he was still alive. The woman spoke some words to him, her voice low, and Matthew muttered back something Kiva couldn't hear.

Kiva turned to Po.

"What happened?" she demanded.

"I, I thought—," he stammered. "The signal."

"I didn't give the signal," Kiva said. She looked to Quint.

The girl shook her head. "It wasn't me. He got up and shot the arrow before I said anything."

"But all the shouting," Po said. "I heard the shouting and thought you were in danger."

On the ground, the woman spoke softly to Matthew as she wrapped her fingers around the arrow's shaft. Matthew shook his head, pleading, trying to lift his shoulders off the ground—but the woman held him down with the other hand as she yanked the arrow out of his chest.

Kiva winced as Matthew's screams pierced the air.

"I'm sorry, Vagra," Po said. "Forgive me."

Kiva shook her head. "What's done is done. Now we have to deal with the consequences."

On the ground, blood was pouring from Matthew's wound. The woman ripped the sleeve off her shirt to stanch the bleeding.

Thruss stepped forward. "We should kill them."

Kiva looked up at Thruss. "What did you say?"

"It's like you said. What's done is done. The boy is going to die anyway. We should just kill them all and be done with it."

Kiva's gaze wandered. She looked at Matthew's face. It was growing pale. His eyes were glassy, and his lips moved without making a sound.

Kiva thought back to her visions of the Strangers, her visions of Matthew. Everything the Ancestors had shown her had come true.

But she'd never foreseen this.

This was the moment she'd been waiting for, preparing for. Waiting and preparing—for what? To let Matthew die? To kill the Strangers and be done with it, as Thruss said?

Kiva shook her head.

"No," she said.

"But Vagra . . . ," came Po's voice at her side.

"No," she said, more firmly now. "We have to save him."

40

matthew

"Stay with me, Matthew."

Dunne's face had doubled into twin seas of eyes, of noses, of mouths. The two faces floated in the air like binary stars, orbited each other, then floated back together and merged.

Her face was kind. Dunne was kind. She reminded Matthew of his mother.

His mother.

It was a fine thought. A fine last thought—the memory of his mother.

Matthew smiled. He sighed. His body felt distant. The pain was there, but he didn't mind it anymore. His eyes slid slowly closed.

"No!" Dunne shouted.

Matthew felt her hand cup his chin and shake his head. He felt a jangling deep in his skull.

"Keep your eyes open," she demanded. "Whatever you do, don't close your eyes."

"But I'm so tired," Matthew said. His words came out slow and slurred, as if he were drunk.

Dunne nodded. "I know. But you can't. I need to go in the ship for my medical supplies, okay? You're going to be all right. I just need you to hold this while I'm gone." She grabbed his hands and moved them up to the cloth on his chest.

Matthew shook his head. "They won't let you. They won't let you go."

"They will. Just let them try and stop me."

Before Dunne could leave, another floating face entered Matthew's vision. It was the girl—the beautiful girl, the girl whose alien words he could somehow understand.

Matthew's smile grew larger.

"You," he said. "It's you."

"I'm sorry that Po shot you," she said. "But we're going to help you."

"What did she say?" Dunne asked.

"They're going to help," Matthew said.

Dunne shook her head. "No. I'm not going to let them touch you."

"It's fine," Matthew said. "I trust them. I trust her."

The girl continued. "I need a bowl."

"In our ship," Matthew said. "Can she go inside?"

"Yes," the girl said. "Only if you promise that she won't come out with another weapon."

"You can send one of your men with her," Matthew suggested.

"No." The girl shook her head. "I trust you."

Matthew told Dunne what the girl needed. Dunne still looked suspicious. The girl knelt beside Matthew and moved closer to his body, her hands inching toward the place where Dunne still held the torn cloth tight against Matthew's wound. She looked to Dunne and nodded for her to take her hands away.

Dunne hesitated a few moments more, then withdrew her hands and let the girl place hers tight against Matthew's chest. Then she left.

The girl's eyes were fixed on the place where her hands held the cloth against Matthew's wound, but Matthew kept his eyes on her face. He no longer felt like closing them.

"Do you have names?" he asked.

"What?" the girl asked.

"Names," he said. "Do you call yourselves anything?"

"We are called the Vagri. That is the name of our people."

Matthew shook his head. "No, I mean *your* name. What do you call *yourself?*"

The girl seemed to laugh. "Kiva."

"It's a pleasure to meet you, Kiva. That's what we say on my planet when we meet another person. *It's a pleasure to meet you.*" He gulped and took a breath. "And my name's Matthew."

The girl nodded. "I know."

She smiled a strange smile—there seemed to be some hidden meaning in it. But before Matthew could ask her what she meant, how she knew his name, she said, "It's a pleasure to meet you, Matthew."

Now it was Matthew's turn to laugh. His laugh quickly turned into a wince when the shaking in his chest jarred loose the pain and the sensations of his body came thundering back.

"Don't talk anymore," Kiva said, concern shrouding her eyes. "It will be over soon."

Dunne came back with a shallow metal bowl in her hands. Kiva nodded to a place on the ground next to Matthew's shoulder. Dunne set the bowl down.

Kiva called another of the girls over.

"I need grass," she said. "One long blade. A dead one, almost completely dry."

The girl nodded and went in search of what Kiva wanted. She came back soon after and handed a long, browned blade of grass to Kiva. Kiva took it and, holding it over the bowl, rubbed it to dust between her hands. Then she called the boy named Po—the one who'd put an arrow into Matthew.

"Your knife," she said. "I know you have one."

Po crouched, reached inside the sheath of woven grass binding his feet and pulled out a small dagger hidden inside. He handed it to Kiva.

"What's going on?" Dunne moved to stop Kiva.

"Hold her back," Kiva said, and the two girls moved toward Dunne. They held her by the shoulders as Kiva hunched over Matthew's pale body.

Holding her hands over the metal bowl, Kiva put the knife against her palm and wrapped her fingers around it, then yanked it out of her clenched hand as if from a sheath. Balling the empty hand into a fist, she squeezed her blood into the bowl. It came out dark gray, almost black, the color of melted lead. With two fingers, she smeared the blood into the dusted grass, making a wet paste.

"I need to get a better look at the wound," she said.

Matthew nodded and pulled away the cloth that had crusted against his skin. He drew a hissing breath through his teeth as the air touched the wound. He felt the warm trickle of fresh blood running down his side.

"Don't look," Kiva said.

"I won't."

There was the sound of tearing cloth as she ripped his shirt open. Then Kiva daubed her fingers in the mingled blood and grass at the bottom of the bowl.

"This will hurt," she said.

"Wait, what?" Matthew said, lifting his head from the ground.

But it was too late.

Kiva daubed her bloody fingers on Matthew's wound.

It was as if she had put acid on his skin. He closed his eyes and let out a scream. Pain gripped his chest like a claw, taking root and growing, spreading from the wound to his whole torso, then his whole body—his legs, his arms, his head. The pain flowed up his neck and into his head, and for a moment he thought his skull might explode from the force of the agony that filled it.

Through the pain, he felt Kiva put a hand on his bare shoulder to steady him. Her other hand slipped gently into his.

"Hold on to me," came her voice. "It will get worse before it gets better."

Matthew responded with an even louder groan, and his hand clenched tight around hers.

In the midst of the pain, images began flashing across the inside of his eyelids.

A wasteland—a parched, cracked desert, baking under a scorched sky.

Lightning splitting the sky, arcing jagged to the ground from the dusty clouds.

Below, humans staggering back and forth, some crying out for water—others for death.

The end of humanity, of everything he'd ever known.

And then he was brought from the desert to the stars—where he stood on the landing bay of a space station and watched through the opening as electrical storms raged on the Earth below.

"You have to choose," came a voice beside him, and in the vision Matthew turned to see his mother and Sophie standing next to him.

They met his eyes, and a chill passed through him when he saw their skin—it was blue, cold, and dead. Ice crystals glistened on their cheeks like stars.

"You have to choose," Sophie said, repeating what their mother had said seconds earlier.

Matthew shook his head. "But I don't know how."

Neither Sophie nor his mother said anything. They turned away from Earth and looked into the landing bay. Matthew followed their gazes to see massive ships hulking in the still darkness—and somehow he knew that these ships were waiting for him.

Waiting for his word on the transceiver to launch into space and bring what remained of humanity to this planet.

Matthew's hand clamped tighter around Kiva's. The muscles in his back seized, and his body lifted off the ground, became a bridge rooted to the dirt only by his heels and the back of his head. Kiva moved closer to him, her free arm clenching his body tighter to her own.

"Shhhh," she said, though he wasn't making any sound. "Shhh."

Slowly, his muscles unclenched and he sank back to the ground.

His eyes opened. He gasped once, then panted as he found his breath again. His chest heaved.

"What the hell was that?" Matthew asked as the last of the pain left his body. Kiva's face hovered above his.

"I think it worked," Kiva said. "I've never tried it until now, but I think . . . I think you're healed."

Matthew's brow knotted. He propped himself up on his elbows and looked from Kiva to Dunne, who stood just a few paces back, the other girls still pressing against her shoulders and holding her where she stood.

Dunne stared at Matthew with a stunned look on her face.

"My God," she said. "I can't believe it."

Matthew propped himself up further and turned his eyes to his own body, to the place where the arrow had entered his chest. Kiva moved away and knelt in the grass, sitting back on her heels to watch him.

His hand wandered down to the spot. He felt with his fingertips at the place where Kiva had smeared her blood. At first he prodded gingerly, then pressed down on the wound with all his might, testing for pain. He didn't find any.

He glanced up at Kiva for a long moment but didn't say anything. Then he looked back down to the spot and began rubbing furiously at it. The caked grass and dried blood crumbled away.

Underneath, the skin was smooth and new. The wound was gone. There wasn't even a scar.

Matthew was completely healed.

"How?" he asked. His head snapped up. "Who *are* you?"

Kiva rocked back, shifting her weight from her knees to the balls of her feet, and looked down, shielding her eyes as she slowly brushed the dust from the skirt of her dress.

After a moment, she stood up and offered Matthew a hand. He took it and she helped him to his feet.

"I'll show you," she said.

41

kiva

Kiva walked away from Matthew and huddled with Po, Thruss, Rehal, and Quint.

"We're going to take them to the village," she said.

"Are you sure that's a good idea?" Thruss asked.

Kiva hesitated. She wasn't sure if it was a good idea or not. But something made her want to do it all the same. She couldn't explain why. Maybe it was that after everything that had happened—Po putting an arrow in Matthew's chest, and Kiva healing him—she thought bringing the Strangers to their village might be the gesture of trust needed to begin making peace.

"There will be no danger to the Vagri," she assured them. "Po, I want you and your men to come with us to keep an eye on them. Especially that one."

She nodded toward the Stranger who'd had the weapon.

"If he tries anything," Kiva said, "you have my permission to kill him."

Po nodded. Kiva turned and walked to Matthew, who was talking with the woman.

"I'd like to go back inside the ship before we leave," Matthew said.

Ship. That must be what they call the bird that brought them to Gle'ah.

"I want to change out of these bloody clothes, and Dunne needs a few things. One of your men can come with us if you want."

Kiva shook her head. "No, it's fine. I trust the two of you. But he needs to stay out here, where we can keep an eye on him."

She nodded toward the other boy, still standing with his hands raised at the end of one of the Forsaken's spears. Quint still had his weapon.

"That's Sam," Matthew said. "And I understand. But that little girl . . ."

"My sister," Kiva said. "Quint."

"Well, you should tell her to be careful with that gun. She could hurt herself."

Gun, thought Kiva.

Matthew and the woman—*Dunne,* he'd called her—went into the ship. They came back out a few minutes later, Matthew wearing a new blue suit, one not torn or stained with his blood, and Dunne carrying a smooth, rectangular object in her hand.

"Don't worry," Matthew said when he saw Kiva looking at the object. "It's just a bioscanner. It can't hurt anyone."

Kiva nodded her assent, though she didn't understand the word he'd used.

"All right, let's go. I'll lead the way." She glanced at Matthew. "Matthew, will you walk with me?"

. . .

They tramped silently through the grass for a long stretch. Kiva used the time to read everyone's thoughts. Thruss and Rehal were on edge, still afraid of the Strangers and nervous about what would happen when they got to the village; Po and the Forsaken were alert, ready to attack the Strangers at the first sign of provocation; and Quint—well, Quint seemed to think this was all a great adventure.

Kiva couldn't read the minds of the Strangers quite as clearly. From the one Matthew called *Dunne* she sensed excitement and curiosity at what she might find once Kiva led them to the village. The boy who'd attacked them—Matthew called him *Sam*—was a mystery. When Kiva reached into his mind with hers, all she found was a yawning absence, a dark void that made her shiver every time she looked at his face.

But Matthew's thoughts she could read clearly—so clearly it was almost as though he was speaking aloud as he walked at Kiva's side.

How did she do that?

Kiva glanced sideways. Matthew was feeling gingerly at the spot on his ribs where Po had shot him—where Kiva had daubed her blood to heal him.

"I didn't do it," Kiva said. "The Ancestors did."

Matthew looked at her. "What's that?"

"You were wondering how I healed you," Kiva said. "But I didn't. The Ancestors did."

"The Ancestors?" Matthew said. He blinked and gave his head

a little shake. "But I didn't say anything."

"I heard your thoughts," Kiva said. "That's another thing the Ancestors do."

"Are they the ones helping us communicate with each other?" Matthew asked.

"I think so."

"So they healed me, they let you read other people's thoughts, and they're allowing us to communicate with each other even though we don't speak the same language. But how?"

Kiva looked forward. "They just are. In our village, the Ancestors come to girls and speak to them, show them visions, or allow them to hear the minds of others. After that, the girls join the women as the leaders of our people. The Sisters."

"The Sisters," Matthew repeated. "And you're one of the Sisters, then?"

Kiva shook her head. "No. Not just one of the Sisters. The Ancestors are stronger with some than with others—and they're stronger with me than with anyone in my village. I am the Vagra."

"So the Sisters lead the village, but you're the leader of the Sisters. The Vagra. Is that right?"

Kiva nodded.

Matthew retreated into his own thoughts, and Kiva let him be. They walked in silence once more. Soon, they came to the place just outside the village where Kiva always went to listen for the voice of the Ancestors. This was where she'd first seen her vision of the Strangers, where she'd first seen Matthew's face.

Kiva slowed.

"Matthew," she said.

He turned to her.

"Do you remember this place?" she asked.

He looked around. Kiva held her breath as his eyes passed over the hillock where, just a day ago, he'd come upon her from within a shared vision. But his eyes only grazed the spot, and when his gaze came back to her his face wore a befuddled look.

"I don't think so," he said. "I've never been here before. Why should I remember it?"

Kiva opened her mouth without making a sound. Her cheeks burned.

Maybe there was no connection between her and Matthew after all. Maybe it was all in her head.

"Nothing," she said, and walked on ahead of Matthew. "It's nothing."

Matthew's footsteps rustled in the grass as he ran to catch up with her.

"Wait," he said. "I'm sorry. I offended you, somehow. I don't know, maybe—"

He broke off speaking, but Kiva heard the echo of his thoughts coming from behind her.

But there is something familiar about this place, isn't there? About Kiva. I do feel like I've been here before, like I've met her—but that's impossible, isn't it?

Kiva held her breath when she heard this thought. She longed to speak to Matthew about this feeling of familiarity, to ask him what he did and didn't know about this place, about her—but they weren't alone, and they were drawing close to the village.

Kiva's questions would have to wait.

When they reached the top of the rise and the huts came into view, Kiva knew immediately that news of the Strangers had spread throughout the village. Morning had broken hours ago, and normally the village would be full of men working in their gardens, children chasing each other through the narrow lanes between huts—but instead, everything was empty. The Sisters, coming back from the pit, must have spread news of Kiva's vision as they came into the village. And Edela and Ferrin must have told even more of the Vagri that one of the Strangers had attacked them. Kiva sensed the fear rising from the huts like smoke. She could practically smell it.

"Thruss, Rehal," Kiva called. They came to her.

"Yes, Vagra?" they said together.

Kiva moved a few steps ahead of Matthew and bowed her head, spoke low so he couldn't hear.

"Go to the Sisters' camp," she said. "Tell them we're coming. Tell them I've brought the Strangers here so we can learn about each other and make peace. Make sure they know the Strangers have no weapons, and that we have Forsaken here to keep them from hurting anyone. Can you do that?"

Both nodded, and Rehal began to walk away.

Thruss stayed behind. "Should I tell them about what happened out there?"

"You leave that to me," Kiva said. "The Sisters don't need to know everything right now. Only those things that are helpful. You understand?"

Thruss bowed her head. "Yes, Vagra," she said, then followed Rehal to the Sisters' camp.

"What about me?" Quint asked.

Kiva knelt to a crouch and spoke to her sister at eye level. "You're the most important of all. I need you to stay with us. If people see you with the Strangers, they'll know that there's nothing to be afraid of."

"But I *am* afraid of them," Quint admitted in a small voice.

Kiva bent her head closer to Quint's ear and pitched her voice at a conspiratorial whisper. "I know. So am I, a little."

The girl's eyes widened. "You are?"

"Yes. I'm afraid of a lot of things. Of the Strangers. Of the Forsaken. Sometimes even of the Sisters."

"Of the Sisters? Why?"

"I'm afraid that they won't think I'm a good leader. But I try to be brave. And that's what I want you to do. Do you think that you can be brave right now?"

Quint nodded solemnly. "Yes. I can."

"Good girl," Kiva said. She squeezed Quint's arm and stood, then moved to speak to Po. She put her mouth close to his ear and spoke so that Quint couldn't hear her.

"Keep close," she said. "I want one of you guarding each of them. No mistakes."

"Yes, Vagra," Po said.

"Let them go where they want, and see whatever they want to see." She glanced at Sam, who was surveying the village with black, expressionless eyes—then looked back to Po. "But if they try to hurt anyone, kill them."

42

matthew

Matthew cast his gaze over the village. It was surrounded on all sides by the ridge they were perched on. The circular depression the village was set in looked like a crater. The village itself was laid out in circles, too. From the high vantage point on the ridge, the village was reminiscent of a target: a broad outer ring of some one hundred squat mud huts giving way to an empty space, and then a smaller circle of huts in the center.

"I don't like this," Sam muttered behind Matthew's shoulder.

Matthew turned to face him.

"Yeah, well, I don't care what you think," Matthew said, louder than he intended. "The last time you *didn't like* something, you almost got me killed, remember? It's only because of her that I'm alive."

Matthew looked toward Kiva, who was moving down the hill into the village and talking in whispers with the other two girls.

"But we're unarmed," Sam said. "We can't defend ourselves. They could kill us."

"They could have killed us already," Dunne said. "But they didn't."

"She's right," Matthew said. "We'll be fine. As long as you don't act like an asshole and do something stupid again."

Sam's eyes burned, but he didn't have a retort.

"What were the two of you talking about?" Dunne asked. "You and—what's her name?"

"Kiva," Matthew said. "She was telling me about how their society works. They're called the Vagri. The village is led by the women—the Sisters, Kiva called them."

"Interesting," Dunne said. "A matriarchal society. It explains some things. I'd wondered why these men would be obeying the commands of a girl."

"She's not just any girl," Matthew said. "She's the leader of the village. They call her the Vagra."

"So, a council of women leading the village. And a young girl as, what? Some kind of spiritual leader?"

Matthew nodded. "That's right. She talked about someone called the Ancestors. I think the Ancestors are their gods. Kiva said the Ancestors show her things, that they help her read other people's thoughts. She said they're the ones who made it so we can understand each other. And that they healed me."

Dunne made a noise in her throat. "Telepathy, supernatural healing rituals. I'd call it baseless superstition, except I saw her heal you with her blood. That much seems undeniable."

"And Kiva and I can communicate with each other," Matthew added.

Dunne nodded. "Yes."

Matthew looked down the hill. The two girls had gone, and now Kiva stood waiting with her sister, the boy who'd put the arrow in his chest, and the two armed men.

"They're waiting," Matthew said. "Sam, if you're so scared, you can head back to the ship. I'm going into the village."

He walked down the hill. Dunne came after him, and after a moment, so did Sam.

"Welcome to our village," Kiva said. "I know we've gotten off to a bad start."

Matthew suppressed a chuckle. Sam had shot at two kids, and Matthew had nearly been killed by an arrow. *Bad start* was putting it mildly.

"But that's behind us now," Kiva said. "Now you'll learn about us. We'll learn about you. That way, our people can grow to respect one another, and we can live in peace."

Matthew nodded. "Yes," he said. "Good. That's exactly what we want. We didn't come here to fight. We came here to learn."

Kiva's eyes glanced over Matthew's shoulder, and he turned to follow her gaze. She was looking at the bioscanner in Dunne's hand.

"That . . . that thing," Kiva said.

"A bioscanner. It's a . . ." Matthew stopped. How to explain? "It's technology—a machine that allows us to look inside the body and see how it works."

"You want to use it to look inside our bodies?" Kiva said.

"That's the idea."

"And you're sure it won't hurt us?"

"I'm positive. You can trust me."

Kiva took a step closer. "I'd better be the first one. To show my people there's nothing to be afraid of."

Matthew looked around. "But there's still no one here."

"Oh, they're here," Kiva said. "They're hiding in their huts, but they're here. And they're watching."

Matthew explained to Dunne what Kiva wanted to do. Dunne went to Kiva and held the bioscanner up to her body. The men with spears moved closer, but Kiva waved them back.

"It's fine," she said. Then she spoke louder, nearly at a shout: "There's nothing to be afraid of! The Strangers are merely here to learn! Please, come out of your huts!"

She glanced at Dunne and nodded. Dunne pressed a button on the bioscanner, and a horizontal line of light shot out from the end of it and scanned Kiva from head to toe. Dunne looked at the display, gave Kiva a look that wordlessly communicated thanks, and then stepped back.

Then they looked at the huts and waited. Soon, a man appeared in one of the doorways and walked slowly into the day. As soon as he'd left the hut, two children scampered out behind him, ran to a distance of some twenty paces away, and then stared at Matthew, Dunne, and Sam with their fingers hooked on their lower lips. Matthew looked at Dunne and smiled.

It was working.

Soon another man appeared, a baby slung on his hip; and another, an old man, walking with a cane.

Dunne walked toward them with her bioscanner and got to work.

.   .   .

Dunne scanned one Vagri person after another, gathering data about their biology.

"They're anatomically similar to us," Dunne told Matthew. "A few small differences, but their bodies and organs seem to work in the same way as ours."

After she scanned them, Dunne asked questions, Matthew and Kiva translating. They quickly discovered the basic facts about life in the Vagri village.

The outer huts were where the men and children lived. The outer village also had huts for bathing, for storing food, and multiple wells to supply the villagers with water. The men raised crops for the village in small gardens outside each of their huts, containing a few species of greens, a pungent onion-like plant, and a sugary tuber that reminded Matthew of sweet potatoes. The men also took care of the children, and one of the men—the one who'd come out with a baby on his hip—showed them how to squeeze sweet milk from the tuber into an infant's mouth.

The only thing the men didn't do, it seemed, was lead—that was a role for the women.

"Where do the Sisters live?" Matthew asked Kiva.

"In the center of the village," she said. "I'll show you."

They began a slow trek to the middle of the village, winding their way between the huts. Kiva and Matthew led the way. Matthew glanced back to look at Dunne and Sam, at the armed men flanking them. He had someone guarding him, too—the same boy who'd put the arrow in his chest. He didn't mind the escort—he understood why Kiva would want her people to see that she was protecting them—but he was getting more and more nervous about Sam. Sam's agitation hadn't decreased at all since they'd come into the village; if anything, he was looking jumpier and more afraid than ever. If Sam tried anything—made a grab for his gun or for the man's spear—they'd all be dead in a matter of moments.

"You're anxious," Kiva said. "About that boy. Sam. You're afraid he might do something foolish."

Matthew gave her a sideways glance.

"You forget—I can read your mind."

"Of course," Matthew said.

He'd have to be more careful around Kiva—it was impossible to hide anything from her.

They strolled for a few moments in silence.

"How old are you?" Matthew asked.

"Seventeen seasons."

"Seasons. How long is that?"

"A season is three hundred and eighty days," Kiva said.

"That's not too different from our year," Matthew said. "That's how we measure time where I come from."

"And how old are you?" Kiva asked. "How many years?"

"Six—no, seventeen," Matthew said, correcting himself. He grimaced as he remembered that he'd turned a year older the moment he came out of the freeze. It was his birthday. "We're the same age, basically. You're so young to be leading this entire village."

"Am I?" Kiva asked. "I could say the same about you. Aren't you a little young to be flying through the stars to different worlds?"

Matthew sniffed a laugh. "I suppose I am."

"Anyway, my age doesn't matter. The Ancestors choose our leaders. They are the ones who chose me to be the Vagra."

"Is that what I should call you? Vagra?"

"No," she said. "You don't have to call me Vagra. That's what my people call me. But you can keep calling me Kiva."

Kiva looked at him and smiled. Matthew felt a warmth spread through his chest. She was beautiful when she smiled. She was always beautiful, actually—but when she smiled, the skin at the corners of her eyes crinkled and her eyes seemed to sparkle. Matthew realized, suddenly, that she could probably sense him thinking these things—and for a moment the thought of her beauty shriveled inside him, shrunk to the back of his mind.

But no. He didn't care if she could hear his thoughts. Let her hear. She should know that she was beautiful.

"Good," Matthew said, and returned her smile. "It's a pretty name. Kiva."

Kiva dropped her gaze, showing Matthew her profile. Her fingers trembling, she tucked a strand of hair behind her ears. Her smile grew wider.

A thrill surged through Matthew's body.

43

kiva

Warmth rushed to Kiva's cheeks. She angled away from Matthew so he couldn't see her blush.

The interest she sensed from him wasn't something new to her, of course. She'd felt the same thing from the young men of the village for many seasons now—felt the way their eyes wandered toward her as she walked through the village, felt their mingled desire and resentment as they wondered what it would be like if she might someday come to visit their hut in the night and slip into their bed. At moments like these, she thanked the Ancestors that the Sisters had control over who they mated with—and that the Vagra, who couldn't be mated, didn't have to worry about such things.

But there was something different this time. Something different about Matthew's interest.

Or, perhaps, Kiva reflected, the difference was not in him, but in her. Her mind shifted from her perception of Matthew's thoughts—*God, she's beautiful*—and luxuriated for a few moments in her own awareness of Matthew's body ambling slowly through the village beside her. She'd never been so aware of a boy before, so cognizant of his physical presence. Kiva raised her head and stole a glance at him. He wore a new, untorn shirt, but she still remembered the feeling of ripping through the old one with her hands, still remembered the sight of his bare chest exposed to the air.

Now his skin was covered again, but there was a place between his neck and the line of his collarbone. A curved place. Kiva hadn't noticed it before—other boys had it too, she was sure. But on Matthew it was different, somehow. On Matthew, it reminded her of the place outside the village, the nestled hillock just past the rise where she'd had her first vision of the Strangers. On Matthew, it looked like a place she'd like to rest her head to breathe him in deeply. On Matthew, it looked like a place she wanted to live.

Matthew walked tight by her side. Their hands and the tops of their arms brushed together, so lightly that Kiva couldn't be sure whether it was an accident, or which one of them was making it happen if it wasn't. She could have reached out to Matthew's mind to find out, but she decided not to—and she didn't pull away, either. Instead, she briefly closed her eyes and leaned closer to Matthew, let herself luxuriate in the moment.

Matthew's voice broke through her reverie.

"So, why are the Sisters in charge of the village? And why do they have to live in a separate camp?"

"The shape of our village mirrors the shape of life on Gle'ah."

"Gle'ah," Matthew repeated. "That's what you call this planet?"

Kiva nodded and went on. "On this world, all things revolve around the Great Mother, the sun—just as the life of this village revolves around me, the Vagra. The Great Mother holds us, keeps us in her grip. The Three Sisters—Vale and Dalia and Ao. Perhaps you saw them in the night."

"Your moons."

"Yes. The Three Sisters stay near to the Great Mother, just as I have the Sisters around me, helping me. Further out live the men and the children, who work the land to bring food to us all."

Matthew squinted. "But why?"

Kiva shrugged. "Because it has always been that way. The Ancestors have decreed it to be that way. They have chosen the Vagra and the Sisters to think on the higher things, the things of the sun and the moons and the stars. And the Ancestors have chosen the men to occupy themselves with the lower things—with the dirt and the plants and the raising of our children."

"And fighting," Matthew offered.

"No," Kiva said, a firmness taking hold in her voice. "We are a peaceful people."

"But these men—," Matthew began, gesturing at Po and the two other Forsaken men.

"They are not of us," Kiva said. "They are Forsaken from our village. It's only when the Vagri are under threat that we go to them for protection."

"Under threat," Matthew repeated, frowning. "You mean us."

Kiva nodded. "Yes. I foresaw your coming four seasons ago, in a vision. I thought you might be a threat. Most people in the village still do. But hopefully after today you can start proving to us that we have nothing to fear from you."

Matthew didn't say anything. They went on walking.

In the lazy, shapeless space between the two encampments, it could have been easy to forget that they were standing in the middle of a village. Kiva's steps slowed and she dropped her gaze to look at the dusty ground only a few paces out ahead of her. For a moment, she wondered what it might be like if they were really just on a stroll together, what it might be like if she was not the Vagra but just another girl; if he was not a Stranger but just another boy. What it might be like to reach out and take hold of his hand and take him with her to her hut, the place where she lived and slept.

It was a pleasant daydream—but she couldn't indulge it for long. As they came closer to the Sisters' settlement, she felt voices begin to jostle in her mind and crowd out her own thoughts. Anxiety began to gnaw at her stomach. She lifted her head and saw, just beyond the first row of huts, Thruss and Rehal trying to speak over a chattering crowd, faces flushed with the difficulty of trying to get the Sisters to listen to them.

She took a deep breath.

"Wait here," she said to Matthew.

Kiva stepped forward and replaced Thruss and Rehal at the head of the crowd.

"Sisters, please!" she shouted. They quieted at once, but their faces were still flushed with fear and anger. "I understand your concern, but I swear to you—by the power of the Ancestors in my veins—that there's nothing to be afraid of. I've spoken with one of the Strangers—the Ancestors allow us to understand each other. The Strangers won't harm us. We have much to learn about each other, though, and that's why I've brought them here. If we learn about each other instead of trying to kill each other, maybe we can live together in peace. Perhaps then we will no longer be so strange to each other—them to us, and us to them. Perhaps then the Strangers may become our friends."

Kiva let this statement hang in the air. In the crowd, there were scattered mutters—some of dissatisfaction, some of begrudging agreement.

"Please, Sisters, go about your business as if they weren't here," Kiva said. "Return to your huts. Visit your friends, or your men and children in the main village. Whatever you do, let the Strangers pass in peace. The Forsaken are here to protect us with their weapons. But I'm confident that won't be necessary."

She glanced at Po, then at Sam, and hoped that she was right.

44

matthew

Once again, Matthew hung back while Kiva moved forward to talk to the gathered crowd.

Kiva's voice boomed as she spoke to them, but Matthew couldn't hear what she was saying. He was distracted by something else.

He closed his eyes and held his breath.

"What is it?" came Dunne's voice. "Are you okay?"

The pain that he'd felt by the ship, the blinding pain surging through his veins after Kiva had daubed her blood on his wound, had returned. It had grown as they walked nearer to the center of the village—and now it was practically unbearable.

As pain gripped Matthew's body, voices crowded in his skull. He felt as though he were standing in the middle of a crowded room where everyone was speaking at once, in a language he couldn't understand.

Matthew shook his head.

"It's nothing," he said.

Slowly, like a wave breaking on the shore and receding back

into the ocean, the pain and the voices subsided.

Matthew opened his eyes and forced himself to breathe.

Panting, he looked into the cluster of small huts to find that the women had largely dispersed while his eyes were closed. Now, they mulled about in groups of two or three, speaking to each other in hushed voices.

Kiva walked toward Matthew, Dunne, and Sam. "Please come in," she said. "This is the Sisters' camp. This is where the women live—the leaders of the Vagri."

Matthew and Dunne moved into the camp. Once again, Dunne ranged back and forth, looking for women who'd allow her to use her bioscanner on them. Matthew cast a glance over his shoulder and saw that Sam was frozen by the edge of the Sisters' camp. His face had a peculiar expression on it—Matthew wasn't certain if it was anger, fear, or some combination that kept him from moving forward.

Odd. What was there to be afraid of?

Matthew put Sam out of his mind and turned to Kiva. "Is everything all right? The women didn't seem very happy to see us."

"The Sisters don't think it's right for you to be here. They're angry with me for letting you in and showing you our ways. We've never had an outsider come this far into our village."

Matthew glanced off to the side at a group of three women who were whispering to each other by the door of one of the huts. As he and Kiva passed, they stopped their whispering and stared at him and Kiva with dark expressions.

"They wish that you had just killed us," Matthew said, thinking of the tone of the voices he'd heard in his head.

"Yes," Kiva said. "Some of them do. How did you know?"

Matthew squinted. "I don't know. Somehow I just . . ." He looked down, splayed his fingers wide at his sides. "I don't know."

"You can still feel them inside you, then."

"Feel who?"

"The Ancestors."

Matthew shrugged. "I don't know. What do they feel like?"

"Pain," Kiva said. "You'll feel them in a pain that courses through your veins."

Matthew laughed bitterly. "Then yes. If feeling the Ancestors means feeling pain, I can still *feel the Ancestors*. You feel this all the time, then? How can you bear it?"

"I've gotten used to it. When I had my first vision, the pain was impossible. But I've learned how to control the Ancestors, how not to be overwhelmed by them."

Matthew was about to ask her how, but then Dunne walked up to him, her face knotted with confusion.

"Dunne," Matthew said, trying to blink away the throbbing pain in his temples. "Hey, what's wrong with Sam? He's still hanging back all the way at the edge of the camp, and I don't know—"

"Forget him," Dunne said. "I've got a more pressing question. I need you to ask how they reproduce."

Matthew blinked and shook his head. "Wait, what? Please don't make me ask that. You said that they're the same as us, right? Didn't you say that?"

Dunne nodded. "I did. The men are, anyway. Same sex organs, same kind of genetic material for reproduction."

"But the women are different?"

"Not exactly. Basically, everything's the same. But with one crucial difference. None of the women I've scanned—ten or twelve of them by now—have any genetic material to contribute to reproduction. I mean no ovaries. No eggs. Nothing for the male of the species to fertilize."

"You mean . . ."

"I mean they're barren," Dunne said. "Every last one of them."

45

kiva

Outwardly, Kiva was calm, almost emotionless. But on the inside, a hundred questions buzzed in her mind, bouncing back and forth in her skull. She was so preoccupied she barely noticed that Matthew and Dunne had begun to speak excitedly to each other, their voices rising and their hands beginning to move in the air.

The Ancestors. They are still inside Matthew. He can hear their voice—like the Sisters. Like me.

Kiva's mind scrambled to understand what was going on.

The Ancestors favor Matthew—a Stranger, a boy. What does it mean?

It might not mean anything, of course. Kiva was the one who had put the Ancestors inside Matthew's body—when she'd spilled her blood to heal him, they'd entered his veins, gone inside to do their work on him. It wasn't unheard of for the Vagra to perform the healing ritual on a man. The Vagra before her had done it—when one of the huts in the village had collapsed and Orloph, Rehal's father, was injured and near death. Then the Vagra had taken him to her hut and allowed the Ancestors to enter his body and heal it. He walked back into the village the next day, whole. That night, there'd been a celebration in the village. Kiva had been nine seasons old when all this happened—and she still remembered it well.

But she didn't remember that Orloph had begun to hear the voice of the Ancestors. He hadn't taken on the powers of the Sisters and the Vagra. The Ancestors had gone inside Orloph's body to heal him, but they didn't stay to give him visions. They didn't allow him to hear the thoughts of others.

The men were lesser creatures, concerned with the lower things: caring for the children, building huts for the Vagri to live in, growing food for the Vagri to eat. Kiva had heard this over and over as a child—from Grath, from Liana, from the other adults in the village, and finally, from the lips of the Vagra herself.

But now . . .

She left the thought unfinished as she looked to Matthew once more. There was something different about him. Even before she'd healed him, she'd seen him in her visions. More than seen him— she'd *shared* a vision with him. His consciousness had been inside hers—in the dream where he'd come over the hill to find her lying in the grass. He couldn't seem to remember this dream, but Kiva had a feeling it would come back to him soon.

First the vision, the dream they'd dreamed together—and now this. What were the Ancestors trying to tell her?

She had to be sure.

Matthew broke off from his conversation with Dunne and moved toward Kiva, breaking through her racing thoughts. His cheeks were red, and Kiva quickly recalled the color of the blood on his chest when she'd ripped his shirt open back on the plain.

He was blushing.

Matthew cleared his throat. "We want to know . . . ," he began, then broke off and muttered to himself, "God, this is embarrassing."

"What is it?"

"We want to know how you reproduce," Matthew said. "How you make babies."

Now it was Kiva's turn to blush, her gray skin turning a deeper shade as her black blood rushed hotly to her cheeks. But she answered without hesitating.

"Our women mate with our men," she said. "They visit their huts at night, after the men have finished their daily work. Sometimes they come back with a baby growing inside them."

"And after the children are born, then what?"

"Then we bring the child to the men. The men care for the children until they come of age. Until the boys are ready to build their own huts and grow food for the village. And until the girls have their first visitation by the Ancestors."

Matthew relayed everything back to Dunne. Sam stood off to the side, listening to what Matthew said with his lips pursed.

After Matthew had finished, Dunne spoke back to him. Matthew nodded and turned back to Kiva.

"The women and the men—do they get married? Do they have families?"

Kiva squinted. "I don't understand."

"Do your people choose one person to be with and have children with?"

Kiva nodded. "I see. Usually the women choose one man and stay with that one for most of their lives. But they don't have to. Some of the women have more than one man that they mate with.

Sometimes two or more women share the same man. It's all up to the women—they choose who they want."

Matthew was silent a moment.

"What about you?" he asked. "Have you chosen a mate yet?"

Kiva dropped her gaze. Her hair fell across her face. "The Vagra doesn't take a mate," she said.

"Why?"

"Haven't you learned by now? Because the Ancestors have chosen it to be that way. As Vagra, my allegiance can be to no one man, to no one child. I am the mother to all the Vagri—to all the Sisters, to all the men and children."

Matthew waited a few seconds before relaying Kiva's responses back to Dunne. In those short moments, he seemed to retreat inside himself. Kiva couldn't quite make out his thoughts, but the look on his face was unmistakable.

It was a look of disappointment. Of sadness.

Whether Matthew's sadness was for himself or for her, Kiva couldn't tell.

46

Before long, the Great Mother began sinking low on the horizon.

"It's getting late," Matthew said to Kiva. "We need to start walking back to our ship if we want to be there by sundown."

Kiva nodded.

But Matthew didn't go. He lingered nearby.

"What is it?" Kiva asked.

"The gun. We need it back. Our weapons could corrupt your people. We don't want that."

"I understand," Kiva said. "But we'd rather be corrupted by your weapons than be killed by them. You haven't shown yourselves to be very trustworthy with them."

"I know," Matthew said. "And I'm sorry. But I promise you that things are different now. If you allow us to take the gun, I'll lock it up and we won't use it again. We know now that we don't need it. You're a peaceful people. We can be peaceful too."

Kiva considered for a moment, then went to speak with the men. She got the gun, returned to Matthew, and put it in his hands.

"Be careful," she said as she let it out of her grasp.

"Thank you," Matthew said. He turned to go.

"Matthew," came Kiva's voice from behind him.

He stopped and looked back over his shoulder.

"You'll come again tomorrow?"

Matthew blinked. "If you want me to."

"I do," Kiva said. "There are things I need to discuss with you. You've asked many questions today. But I have my own questions to ask of you."

Matthew agreed and began moving away.

"Matthew," Kiva called out to him once more.

He turned.

"When you come," she said, "come alone."

As the Strangers left the village, Kiva moved to intercept the Forsaken. She put a hand on one of the men's shoulders, and he stopped and turned to look at her.

"Let them go," she said.

"But the weapon," he said, watching the Strangers as they moved into the outer village.

Kiva shook her head. "Let them go," she repeated. "We don't have anything to fear from them. Not anymore."

The men nodded. Their bodies relaxed. Their grips loosened around their spears.

"Where's Po?" Kiva asked after a moment.

The men glanced at each other, shrugged, then looked back to Kiva.

"Don't know," one of them said. "I was keeping my attention on the woman, the one Po told me to watch, and—"

"It's all right," Kiva said. "Go back to Xendr Chathe. Tell him

257

that I'm pleased with your help, but that it isn't needed anymore. Tell him the Strangers are no longer a threat to us."

Both men nodded. "Thank you, Vagra," each muttered in turn. And then they were gone.

Kiva turned to see Quint, Thruss, and Rehal standing nearby. The three had wandered around while the Strangers explored, Quint straying but never going too far from Kiva as Rehal and Thruss ranged farther to observe the reactions of the Sisters to the Strangers' presence.

Quint ran forward and wrapped her arms around Kiva's waist. As Kiva felt her sister's arms squeezing her, something seemed to unwind in her chest, a tightness that she hadn't even realized was there until now.

She opened her eyes and looked down. Quint, without letting go of Kiva's waist, looked up at her, eyes wide.

"Thank you," Kiva said.

"For what?"

Kiva shook her head. "I don't know. For being here, I guess. It helped, having you nearby. It made me feel less alone. I don't think I could've made it through this day without you."

Quint smiled a smile so wide and radiant that it made Kiva dizzy. She took a deep breath before continuing.

"It's getting late. You should go back to Grath."

Quint nodded, then left for the outer village, giving Kiva one last hug before she went.

Thruss and Rehal moved close, and Kiva greeted them with a grim look. They made a tight circle and spoke in low voices.

"Okay, tell me," Kiva said. "What are the Sisters saying?"

"They're quiet, mostly," Thruss said after a moment of heavy silence.

Kiva looked to Rehal. "How about you?"

Rehal shrugged. "It went as well as it could have, I suppose. Those who did come out of their huts were mostly curious. A few of them were angry. They asked me what you were thinking, bringing outsiders into the camp."

"They reacted well to the woman," Thruss said. "Some of them even allowed her to touch them, to take their blood. Those who did bragged to the others that they had touched a Stranger, as if it was something to be proud of. They told the others that there was nothing to fear."

"Yes, the woman helped," Rehal agreed. "But they kept their distance from the two others. That boy who kept to the edge of the encampment. And the other one. Your boy."

Kiva blinked. Her heart thudded. "My boy? Is that what they're saying about him?"

Rehal flinched and bowed her head. "I'm sorry, Vagra. I didn't mean anything by it. It's just, the way you were with him . . ."

"That's enough," Kiva said. She didn't want to hear any more.

But it was too late. She could already hear everything. The thoughts of Thruss and Rehal, the thoughts of the Sisters as they began to retreat to their huts for the night or go to their men in the village.

The way she talked to that boy. The way she walked so closely to him, practically touching.

If I didn't know better . . . If I didn't know better I'd think . . .

No. It can't be. She wouldn't. Not the Vagra.

But the way she looked at him.

It's not right.

Kiva pushed the voices away.

"What about Po?" she asked. "Did you see where he went?"

"No, Vagra," Rehal said. "I was too busy with the Sisters."

Thruss, her lips pressed tight together, made a noise in the back of her throat.

"What is it?" Kiva asked. "Tell me."

"It's probably nothing."

"I'll be the judge of that."

Thruss hesitated a moment more, then said, "He was speaking to Kyne. I saw that much. Kyne pulled him away by the arm and then whispered in his ear. I didn't see him leave, though."

Kiva held stock still for a moment, then nodded slowly.

"Thank you," she said. "Thank you both. You've been a help to me today." She paused and forced a smile. "To your people. To the Vagri. I'm grateful to you."

Thruss and Rehal nodded, accepting Kiva's gratitude, and left.

Kiva watched them go, then made for the other side of the camp. She walked faster and faster with every step. Soon she was running, her dress swishing around her thighs.

She slowed when she came upon Kyne's hut. Her steps halted just outside the door. She lifted her hand and pulled aside the cloth hanging in the doorway.

There was a small cot covered with rumpled blankets and a low table beside it. An oil lamp, the wick blackened and extinguished.

Kiva came back outside and wandered around the hut, looking

this way and that as if she expected to see Po and Kyne somewhere nearby.

But no. They were gone.

Kiva let out a sigh and hung her head, and as she did she spotted something on the ground nearby. She moved to examine it more closely.

It was an arrow. She crouched by it, her toes nearly touching the grass fletching, but she didn't pick it up. Her eyes followed the line of the shaft toward the arrowhead, covered in the dried, rusty red of blood. Stranger blood.

Matthew's blood.

Kiva lifted her head, following the arrow's line toward where it pointed on the horizon. It pointed toward the rock outcropping and the stone pit at the edge of the Vagri's land.

It pointed to where the Forsaken lived.

47

po

"It's disgusting," Kyne grumbled as they walked through the grass beyond the village. "It's not right."

Po was silent.

"Kiva should have killed them when she had the chance," Kyne muttered. "She should have had you and the Forsaken murder them where they stood. Instead she brings them to the village? To the Sisters' camp?" She shook her head as a guttural sound rose up from the back of her throat.

Kyne was talking to herself, but Po couldn't stop himself from speaking up.

"The Vagra, you mean," he said.

Kyne wheeled around and looked at him with rage in her eyes.

"You called her Kiva," Po said, his voice more timid now. "But she's the Vagra now. She can do as she pleases."

Kyne turned away and kept on walking. "She's no Vagra of mine. Not after what she did. Endangering the village like that. Now the Sisters must see I was right about her."

Po was silent. He hadn't told her about what happened at the Strangers' ship. If Kyne knew that he had nearly killed one of the Strangers, but that Kiva stopped him and performed a healing ritual over him—well, it could only make matters worse.

"And the way she was looking at him. At that *creature*." Kyne shook her head. "It makes me sick to think about it."

As much as he hated to admit it, there was a sick feeling in the pit of Po's stomach, as well—but it wasn't disgust he was feeling. It was something else. Anger, perhaps. Po had seen what Kyne saw, what everyone saw—the way that Kiva and the Stranger looked at each other, how close together they walked, the way their hands brushed together. Po felt certain that Kiva, the Vagra, wasn't capable of what Kyne was suggesting. Still, it was painful for him to watch, and when he'd followed the Stranger around the Sisters' village as Kiva had commanded him to, he'd begun to feel as though he was invisible.

So, when he'd felt Kyne's hand on his elbow, pulling him away to her hut, he'd gone willingly.

.   .   .

"You have to take me," she'd said in the hut. "You have to take me to see Xendr Chathe."

Po squinted and shook his head. "No. I don't have to do anything you say. I answer to Xendr now. And he's loyal to the Vagra."

"Really?" Kyne asked, her lip curling into a sneer. "And what will he say when he learns that his precious Vagra has used his men not to kill the Strangers, but to bring them into the village? The Vagra isn't the only one who has visions, you know. I see things as well. When you gave me the maiora at the pit, I saw a vision of the Strangers bringing death to the Vagri."

"So that was real?" Po said. "I thought you were making that up to get the Sisters on your side."

Kyne gave Po a poisonous look. "It was real. And it's still coming for us. What Kiva's doing is only making it worse. Xendr needs to hear about it. We can still prevent it from happening."

Finally, Po had agreed to bring her—but not before leaving a sign for Kiva, an arrow placed on the ground, the chiseled, blood-stained head pointing in the direction that Kyne was forcing him to take her. Pointing in the direction of the Forsaken camp.

. . .

Now, as they crested the last hill and came in view of the Forsaken camp, Kyne drew in a sharp breath.

The camp itself was not much to look at. Nestled into a low place on the grasslands, it was dominated on its far end by a single hut, where Xendr Chathe lived. Closer to where Po and Kyne stood were dozens of small tents made of woven grass. This was where the Forsaken slept, one to a tent. To someone who'd heard stories about the Forsaken camp her entire life, like Kyne, the sight must have been a disappointment.

No, if Kyne was gasping at her first sight of where the Forsaken lived, Po guessed it wasn't the camp itself that shocked her. It was the chaos that reigned there.

Just beyond the tents, a group of Forsaken clustered in a circle, roaring at the top of their lungs.

"What are they doing?" Kyne asked.

"Watching a sparring match. The Forsaken haven't been in any battles for the past ten seasons. So they fight to keep their skills up."

As they came close, the mob parted and two men came bursting out. Po and Kyne leapt back as the two men flew past them, one staggering back on his heels, the other lunging forward with fists clenched. The staggering man had a knife in one hand; when he'd regained his footing he made a wild swipe in the air. But the other man ducked, then struck his opponent's wrist with the flat of his hand. The knife fell into the grass. Then, the man who'd knocked the knife away continued his attack, knocking his opponent down with a kick to the chest. He dove on top of him and punched him in the head with his fists, over and over again until the crowd rushed in and pulled him away.

Po and Kyne walked on as some of the men dragged the loser's limp body away and tried to sit him up, slap him back to consciousness.

"Have you ever done that?" Kyne asked. She looked at his face. "Is that what happened to your cheek?"

She reached toward the gash on Po's face, but he jerked his head back and looked away. The gash had been given to him on his first night—all new Forsaken were required to win a fight before they'd be let in the camp. His first fight had lasted only ten seconds, and the man who'd subdued him—a huge beast of a warrior with scars notched all the way up and down his arms—had marked Po's face with a dagger to celebrate his win. That night, Po slept alone on the plain, shivering and crying and wishing that he could go back to the village.

But he didn't. The next day he returned to the Forsaken camp and fought again—only this time, he kept running away from his opponent until the man got exhausted and showed Po his back. Then Po dove on him, wrapped his arms around the man's neck, and squeezed until he fell down, unconscious. Po was ashamed to have won in such a cowardly way. But when he pulled himself off the ground, his opponent still lying limp beneath him, the Forsaken men all slapped his back and congratulated him—and Po, in spite of himself, had smiled, pride blooming in his chest and making his whole body feel bigger.

"I've done it before," Po said now. "Everyone in the camp has to."

They moved past the crowd watching the sparring matches and into the Forsaken camp—and here they came upon another strange scene. Men were clustered around a rectangular structure that had purple-gray smoke pouring through the door and a hole in the roof. From time to time, they'd reach for a pipe, smoke it lazily, then set it down again, propping their elbows on the ground. Nearly half the camp seemed to be there.

"What's going on here?" Kyne asked.

Po sighed and answered with a single word: "Maiora." He didn't offer any other explanation.

Xendr Chathe had been the one to discover maiora on a scouting party. But he couldn't have anticipated how the substance, a downy, sticky white webbing that brought powerful hallucinations when ingested or smoked, would spread through the Forsaken camp like wildfire. The maiora now had enthusiasts, fanatics. The rectangular building on the edge of the camp was a maiora den; the building was usually so full that those who couldn't fit inside clustered outside the door and smoked their pipes on mats set under the sky. The camp was now evenly split between those who thought the maiora should be forbidden— that it would make the Forsaken weak and vulnerable to attack— and those who thought that it was a link to a higher consciousness, to the Ancestors, that it could give each of them the power of the Sisters and the Vagra.

Kyne followed Po as he cut a path between the tents that steered wide of the maiora den. He stopped at the door to Xendr Chathe's hut.

"Wait here," he said in a low voice. "I'll tell you when you can come in."

Kyne's eyes flashed. "But—"

"Just wait," Po insisted. "In the village, the Sisters are in charge—but things are different here. There hasn't been a girl in the camp for . . . well, for a long time. You can't just walk into Xendr Chathe's hut like it's nothing. *Wait here.* I'll tell you when to come in."

Po waited for Kyne to nod her assent, then lifted the veil over the door and walked inside to speak with the leader of the Forsaken.

48

Xendr Chathe's hut was vast, larger than any other building Po had ever been in. Standing at one end of the hut, he couldn't see to the far wall. The space was lit here and there by the orange glow of small lamps that barely pierced the darkness. The far side of the dwelling was shrouded in blackness. Squinting, Po could only just make out the hulking shape of a body slumped in a chair.

"Xendr," Po said into the darkness, his voice thin and timid.

The shape moved, lifted itself from the chair. Xendr was facing away; all Po could see was a robe hanging from the man's broad shoulders and covering his massive back.

"What is it?" Xendr asked without turning, his voice rasping like a handful of stones scratching one against the other.

"I'm sorry to disturb you, Xendr, I—"

"What is it?" Xendr bellowed impatiently.

"It's . . . it's one of the Sisters. One of the women from the village. She's asked for an audience with you."

Xendr Chathe turned and moved forward from the darkness

into the dim light. He stepped gingerly, with the trace of a limp—the walk of an aging warrior who no longer fully trusted his creaky bones. But his robe hung open, and underneath, his bare chest was still thickly muscled from many seasons of ranging and scouting through the hills, of raiding foreign villages and doing battle with the enemies of the Vagri.

At least, those were the stories. In the time Po had been with the Forsaken, there hadn't been a single battle or raid. Rumors in the camp held that Xendr had killed every last one of their enemies, or that they'd fled so far from the plains that no one would see them for another hundred seasons. The Forsaken were a society of warriors—but for a long time now, longer than most of the younger Forsaken could remember, there'd been no one in the barren landscape for them to go to war against.

"Who is it?" Xendr asked. "Your sister? I told you I didn't want to see her."

"She insisted."

Xendr grunted his irritation. "It's been a long time since we've had a woman in the camp."

"I know," Po said. "If you want me to tell her to leave—"

"Xendr, if I may . . ."

Po wheeled around to find Kyne standing behind him.

"I told you to wait outside," Po said.

"I know," Kyne said. "But I heard you through the curtain. I can speak for myself. I don't need you or anyone else to announce me, to beg permission from the great Xendr Chathe." Her voice dripped with sarcasm.

Po moved toward Kyne, expecting Xendr to ask him to forcibly remove her from his presence, but to his surprise Xendr simply laughed.

"She's got a lot of nerve, your sister!" Xendr boomed. "I like that. Go ahead, then—speak! Let's hear what you have to say."

Kyne hesitated. "I'd prefer to speak with you alone."

Xendr moved forward until he was only a few paces away from Kyne. The look he fixed her with was hard and unblinking. "Whatever you want to say, you can say it in front of both of us. I don't keep secrets from my men."

Kyne was silent for a few moments.

"I come to you with an offer of alliance," she said at last.

Xendr grunted. "Alliance. What are you talking about?"

"An alliance between you and me. Between the Forsaken and the Sisters of the village."

Xendr was quiet. He walked back to his chair, flipped it around so it was facing Kyne, then fell into it heavily, slouched to one side, his legs splayed out on the ground in front of him.

"And why would I want this . . . *alliance?* The Sisters answer to the Vagra, not to you."

"Things are changing. The arrival of the Strangers—"

Xendr scoffed. "*The Strangers.* Everyone keeps talking about these Strangers. Why is everyone so afraid of them? We've protected the Vagri from threats in the past. We'll do it again."

"Then you haven't heard," Kyne said. "You haven't heard that the Vagra forbade your men from hurting the Strangers. That she brought them into the village. Into the Sisters' camp."

Xendr's face froze and he sat up in his chair. "No," he said. "That I hadn't heard."

"Then you also haven't heard that the Vagra seems to be . . ." Kyne paused. "Distracted. By one of the Strangers. A boy."

Po's heart beat faster. Anger boiled in his stomach.

"Distracted," Xendr said. "What do you mean?"

"Her loyalties are divided," Kyne answered. "She's incapable of leading the Vagri."

Xendr leaned back in his chair again. "And you would have me do . . . what? The Vagra has been chosen by the Ancestors. You may think that doesn't mean anything to me, but it does. I grew up in the village, the same as you did. I still remember the words my father taught me: *The Ancestors are the ones who have gone before. Those who have passed on. They went to a place both beyond and within this place. They walk alongside us. They bind us to one another. They heal us. And they speak to us.* Going against the Vagra is severing our only true link with the Ancestors."

"Kiva is not the true Vagra," Kyne said. "I heard the Ancestors before her, when I was only eleven seasons old. And now you have the maiora. I've tried it for myself, and when I did I saw a vision of death and blood in the village—a warning of what the Strangers are capable of. The maiora is the only link to the Ancestors we need. Help me. We can take control of the village and rule together. You and me. You and your men, you don't have to be Forsaken any longer. We can live together, all of us, one people, under our joint rule, yours and mine."

Xendr heaved himself from his chair, grunting, and wandered

away into the darkness at the back of the hut.

"You've given me a lot to consider," he said. "May I have some time to think about your offer?"

"There's not much time," Kyne said. "The Strangers are already here. They could be preparing to kill us as we speak."

"Even so, rebellion against the Vagra is no small thing. I need time. A day or two. Please," Xendr said.

Kyne pursed her lips and, after a moment, nodded.

"Very good," Xendr said, then extended his arm toward the door. "Now, if you'll give us a moment, I need to speak with Po. One of my men can bring you back to your village."

"I don't want an escort," Kyne said. "I can return to the village on my own."

Kyne went to the door. After she'd gone, Xendr moved close to Po and spoke in a low voice.

"What do you think?" he asked.

Po pressed his lips together and let out a slow breath through his nostrils. He didn't know what to say. Kyne was simply carrying out her plan, the one she'd told Po about weeks ago. That was why he had come to join the Forsaken in the first place—to help his sister be Vagra so that one day he could be with Kiva. His hand drifted up to the scar on his cheek as he thought about how much he'd done to put Kyne's plan into motion, how much he'd sacrificed.

And yet, now that the time had come, it didn't feel right. Kyne had told him that Kiva would be grateful to them for taking the burden of being Vagra away from her—but she hadn't seemed grateful when she'd confronted them at the pit. He'd begun to realize that Kyne had been lying to him, manipulating him.

"I don't know," Po said finally. "I don't like it, though. Kyne's my sister, but I still don't trust her."

Xendr nodded slowly and looked off to the side. "Neither do I. Still, what she offers is tempting. I fought my whole life to protect that village. But our enemies are gone, and I'm an old man now. I'm tired. To return to the village, to have a hut, a garden, a woman—I can't pretend I haven't thought about it, sometimes."

Po had been thinking about a life in the village, too—the life he'd left behind when he followed Kyne's command to leave. Some nights, it was all he could think about.

"So you're going to do it? You'll take Kyne's alliance?"

Xendr shook his head. "It's not that simple. I made a promise."

Po squinted. "What kind of promise?"

"To the old Vagra. She helped me, once, when I was a younger man—younger even than you. She helped me become leader of the Forsaken. In exchange, I made an oath to stay away from the village for as long as I lived. But she's dead now, and if what Kyne says about this new Vagra is true, if she really is distracted by this Stranger, this boy . . ." Xendr trailed off and then raised his head, met Po's eyes. "I didn't fight my whole life so that a new Vagra could destroy everything I fought to protect."

Heat rose to Po's cheeks. His body clenched. An image of Kiva and Matthew walking together, hands touching and heads angled inward, came to Po's mind—he pushed it away and gave his head a hard shake.

"No. Kyne's wrong. I didn't agree with the Vagra bringing the Strangers to the village. But she would never betray her people. Not for these . . . these creatures. No. I don't believe it."

Po had spoken louder than he meant to, and Xendr looked at him with surprise. Then he gave a nod, a signal that he wouldn't pursue the subject any further if Po didn't want to talk about it.

"One thing Kyne offers that appeals to me is a way to control the maiora," Xendr said. "I wish I'd never discovered it. It's taken over the camp, but I still don't know what it is. I don't know if it's good or bad."

"The Vagra," Po said. "She can help us. She can tell us whether the maiora is of the Ancestors or not."

"You know her, yes? She's a . . . a friend of yours?"

Po hesitated. "We knew each other as children," he said.

Xendr nodded. "Go to her. Tell her about the maiora. Tell her that we need her help."

"And what should I tell Kyne?"

Xendr looked at the ground and put a finger to his lips as he thought. "Don't tell her anything. Not yet. Not until we see what the Vagra can do for us. We'll remain loyal to her for now, but Kyne may be right—the Vagra may not be the right person to lead. It may be time for a change."

"How will we know?"

Xendr didn't answer right away. He turned and walked to the wall of the hut, where various weapons—a spear, a bow and arrows, and a sword—were leaning against the wall. With a sudden motion of his arms, he threw his robe to the ground. His broad shoulders and sinewy back glistened in the lamplight. In the dimness, Po could just make out the scars notched up and down both of Xendr's arms—self-inflicted wounds, according to the rumors in the camp, one cut for each of Xendr's kills in battle. He reached down and picked up a sword.

"Just keep an eye on her," Xendr said, turning the sword back and forth in his hands to examine the blade. "Watch the new Vagra closely. If she makes a mistake—one wrong step—I want to know about it."

49

matthew

"It's disgusting," Sam muttered as they plodded back to the *Corvus*. "It's not right."

"What are you saying?" Matthew asked.

Sam shook his head. "Nothing. It's nothing."

"No, I'm really interested," Matthew said, anger rising in his chest. "I mean, you haven't said a word for hours—not since you nearly *got me killed* by firing off that goddamn gun of yours at the wrong time. You've been acting weird all day. And now you finally speak up and tell me that it's nothing? No. I want to know what your deal is. What's so disgusting? What's not right? Tell me."

Sam walked in silence a few paces, angling his face away. Finally, with a sharp intake of breath, he turned back to Matthew and spoke.

"Fine, you want to know what's disgusting? It's the way they live, whatever *they* are. It's wrong, it . . . it's unnatural. It makes me sick to my stomach." Sam's lip curled and he swallowed, as if he were really choking back vomit rising at the back of his throat. "The way their women stalk around at night, going from one man's bed to another like it's no big deal. It's nauseating. They treat their men like slaves—slaves for sex, for taking care of their children and growing food. And what do they do? Sit around in the center of that village like they're the rulers of everything."

"So, we should kill them all? Use your guns to kill them one by one?" Matthew shook the ion shotgun in Sam's face, clutching it single-handed by the stock.

Sam pushed Matthew's hand away. "Get away from me. I know what I saw. I know what's right and what's wrong. I'm not blinded like you are."

"Blinded. What are you talking about?"

Sam sneered. "You know exactly what I'm talking about. That girl, that little witch of yours. She's got you under some kind of a spell. I saw how you were sniffing around her. Everyone did. It's disgusting—even they think it's disgusting. You stay with your own kind."

"Stay with my own kind? Can you even hear yourself right now?"

"Would both of you just shut the hell up?" Dunne snapped.

Sam and Matthew, stunned at Dunne's sudden outburst, turned to look at her. She walked on without paying any attention to them.

"We've still got at least an hour's walk ahead of us," Dunne said, half to herself. "We haven't eaten or slept in hours. So why don't you both just keep your mouths shut and save your energy for walking?"

"But he said—," Matthew began, until Dunne cut him off with a flat hand in the air.

"I heard what he said. I'm too old—and too damn tired. If

you want to fight, you can keep it to yourselves. Stay out here and wrestle, for all I care. Me, I'm going to the ship to get some food and some sleep."

Dunne kept walking and didn't look back. Matthew knew that she'd go on whether he and Sam followed her or not.

He fell in step behind her. After a moment, so did Sam.

They walked the rest of the way in complete silence.

. . .

By the time they reached the Corvus night had fallen, the sky gone black. A broad swath of stars was painted across the sky, and the two distant moons of Gle'ah glowed side by side. Once, in the distance, Matthew could see the nearer moon pass overhead, its path far enough away that he could see, but not feel, the effect of its gravitation—the grasses near the horizon, glistening white in the moonlight, rising up as the orb passed, like tiny hairs raised to the soft touch of fingertips.

Matthew smiled and thought—not for the first time—that if they could figure out what was going on in this place, if the radiation or the Vagri didn't kill them first, that he wouldn't mind living out the rest of his days on Gle'ah.

At the Corvus, Matthew knelt to put away the gun in the metal chest as Sam made his way toward his berth.

"Lock it," Dunne said when Sam had gone. "And give me the key."

Matthew locked the chest and, still perched on his haunches, turned to put the key in Dunne's fingers. She turned and went a few steps outside the ship, cocked her arm, and threw it away.

Matthew could hear the rasp of the key sliding into the grass somewhere distant.

"There," Dunne said. She clapped her hands together, brushing the palms back and forth.

Matthew rose and prepared to leave the airlock with Dunne, but he was stopped by a small sound.

Static. White noise. And beneath that—the thin sound of a young woman's voice.

Matthew reached his hand into a small crevice between the gun locker and the airlock wall. His fingers fumbled for a few seconds, then found the transceiver. Of course—he'd thrown it into the airlock hours ago, frustrated with Control's constant badgering. It must have fallen behind the gun locker. He'd completely forgotten about it.

"Corvus. Corvus, do you copy? This is Mission Control. Corvus, are you there?"

Matthew clicked the button on the side of the transceiver and spoke into the microphone.

"I'm here, Control."

"Is that you, Matthew? We thought we'd lost you. We thought you were dead."

"It's me, Alison. We're alive and well."

"What's going on over there?"

Matthew pressed down on the button again and drew in a breath to speak, but stopped short when he saw Dunne. She was shaking her head fiercely and drawing the flat of her hand across her neck. When she'd caught his eye, she silently mouthed the word *no*.

Matthew took his finger off the button.

"What is it?"

"What are you going to tell them?" Dunne whispered.

Matthew shrugged. "I don't know. The truth?"

"Don't. Not everything. Not yet."

"Why?"

"You know your history, Matthew? As a species, we don't have such a great track record when we encounter beings that aren't like us."

Matthew thought about that, then nodded slowly. "So what do you want me to tell them?"

"Stall. Tell them about the radiation. Tell them I still have more tests to run. Just don't tell them about the Vagri, the village—any of that."

The transceiver buzzed. "Waiting on your response, Corvus. Do you have good news for us?"

Matthew cleared his throat and spoke once more into the microphone. "Don't break out the champagne just yet, Control. We need a bit more time on this end . . ."

50

alison

". . . just a few more days to figure out what's going on over here," Matthew's voice buzzed on the transceiver.

Alison Nagita pressed the red button in front of her and leaned into the microphone.

"Roger that, Corvus. Take your time. We'll check back in soon."

"Thanks, Control. Corvus out."

The transceiver crackled and went dark. Alison sat back from the microphone and let her eyes wander from the quantum transceiver to the other displays in front of her—readout screens showing the levels of oxygen and CO_2 in the air, reserve energy, food and water supplies, and a map showing the trajectory of their orbit. Higher in her line of sight was a video screen of the view outside; it showed the surface of planet Earth sliding by silently below as the *Ark 1* space station—the station where she lived and worked—orbited above. At the moment, though, Earth's surface wasn't actually visible—the ground was covered by a massive dust cloud, flashing here and there with lightning.

The view would be the same on the other side of the planet,

Alison knew—no matter what part of Earth *Ark 1* orbited over, no matter where the camera was pointed, all the video screen ever showed was dust and electrical storms in every direction. Conditions on the planet had continued to worsen in the century since the Exo Project participants had gone into the freeze and been launched across the galaxy. Battered by extreme heat and solar radiation, Earth had become a desert from pole to pole. Winds whipped across the continents, picking up dust clouds that reached into the middle of the oceans, and the static in the air from the blowing sand created dry electrical storms the size of massive hurricanes.

Alison stared at the screen and wondered, once again, if anyone was alive down there.

If her family was alive—her mother, father, and younger brothers.

Over her shoulder, someone cleared their throat, and Alison swiveled in her chair to face the control room. It was arranged in tiered rows of workstations much like hers, and on a normal day there would be techs at each chair, speaking softly into headsets as they monitored the space station's life-support systems.

But today was not a normal day. By order of the OmniCore leadership board, the room had been cleared, the techs replaced with a retinue of senior leaders, mostly men. Alison sat in the lowest tier, the men arrayed behind and above her, staring down at her intently. She recognized some of them—men who'd scarcely noticed her or acknowledged her existence as she passed them in the hallway between her sleeping quarters and the control room every morning.

There was one man, though, whom she didn't recognize—a

man in the back of the room, sitting in the top tier in a chair with a view of the entire control room. Everyone in the room turned to this man and waited for him to speak.

Alison hadn't seen him before, but she'd heard the whispers. Rumor had it that he was the legendary Charles Keane, the powerful and brilliant OmniCore officer who'd masterminded the Exo Project one hundred years ago. He was in his forties when the exoplanet expeditions had been launched, and should have been long dead by now—but he'd gone into the freeze with the rest of the Exo Project participants, with instructions to wake him if any of the expeditions found a habitable world. So far, the *Corvus* was the only ship that had landed on a planet that might be habitable, the only crew who hadn't had to take the suicide pills. OmniCore had taken an active interest in what was happening on the surface of planet H-240 in the Iota Draconis system one hundred light-years away.

"What's your name, miss?" Keane asked.

"My name's Alison, sir. Alison Nagita."

"Ms. Nagita," Keane said, nodding toward her with a smile as he sat forward in his chair. "Tell me about yourself."

Alison's eyes narrowed. "Sir?"

"I like to know something about the people I work with," Keane said.

"What do you want to know?"

"How did you come to enlist in OmniCore? You seem a bit . . . young."

"I'm seventeen, sir," Alison said. "I applied through the internship program."

"Ah," Keane said. "A trainee. And you've been with us . . . ?"

"For a year," Alison said. "Ever since . . ."

She trailed off and swallowed. Keane nodded.

"I know," Keane said. "I've been briefed."

Alison let out a breath. If Keane had been briefed, then what he knew was that it had been just under a year ago when the storms began, when what was left of the OmniCore government fled to the skies and the rest of humanity went underground, seeking shelter with the only world powers that could still protect them: corporations. The world's largest corporations had been secretly preparing for the complete collapse of civilization for years, and when it finally happened, they were ready—ready to survive, and ready to help others survive, too. For a price.

Communications with the underground compounds on the surface were spotty at best, and Alison—who'd been living on the space station for only a couple of weeks when things fell apart on Earth—still didn't know if her family was alive or not, if they'd managed to pay their way into one of the corporate compounds or if they'd died with billions of others when the planet's food supply finally gave out, when the last of the fresh water finally dried up.

"May I ask why you enlisted with OmniCore?" Keane asked.

"I wanted to go to space, sir," Alison said. "I wanted to help find a new place for humanity to live. Earth is—well, you know what's happening on Earth. And my family . . ."

Alison's voice stopped. She couldn't go on. She dropped her gaze to her lap.

"I understand. They're on the surface?"

"Yes, sir," Alison croaked. "If we find a planet, I want to find them and—"

"*When* we find a planet, Ms. Nagita," Keane cut in, lifting a finger in the air. "*When*, not if. And when it happens, mark my words—we'll find your family, and together you'll be among the first to settle there. You have my word on that."

Alison smiled, squinting slightly as she studied Keane's face, his inscrutable brown eyes behind his black-rimmed glasses, and wondered if he was telling the truth. She hoped so.

"Now then," Keane said. "You've been the one to speak to the crew of the *Corvus*, yes?"

Alison nodded, glad to be moving on to another topic. "Yes, that's right."

"And what is your assessment of what's going on down there?"

Alison pondered for a moment. "It sounds promising, sir. The radiation levels they're reading are troubling. But it's still the first exoplanet expedition that hasn't died in the first—"

"Yes, I know," Keane interrupted with a wave of his hand. "As I said—I've been briefed. But what about this young man you've been speaking to, this . . ."

"Matthew Tilson, sir," Alison offered.

"Yes. Matthew. What's your opinion of him?"

"Meaning, sir?"

"Meaning, is he trustworthy? Are his assessments of the situation solid? Is he telling us what we need to know to determine if this planet is habitable?"

"He didn't communicate with us for a while, sir. There was a space of about eighteen hours where the comm just went dark. But when I've spoken with him, he seems to be forthcoming. I think they're doing the best they can out there."

"I see," Keane said. He lifted himself from his chair and strode forward, standing on the edge of the top tier, the tips of his shoes right up against the edge as he towered over everyone else—the other men and, at the bottom of the room, Alison.

"You're right about one thing, Ms. Nagita," Keane said. "It's a promising situation out there. H-240 may be the planet we've been waiting for. But you're also wrong about one thing."

"And what's that, sir?"

Keane tilted his head down at her. "That boy is lying."

"But why? Why would he lie? And how can you tell?"

Keane shrugged. "It's a hunch. Nothing more. But I've learned to trust my hunches over the years. They've never led me wrong. As for why he's lying, though—that, I can only guess."

"So what do we do about it?" Alison asked. "They're light-years away. We can't control what they do or what they tell us."

Keane lifted a finger in the air. "That's where you're wrong."

Alison squinted. "How, then?"

"It's called leverage, Ms. Nagita," Keane said.

His mouth stretched into a grin that revealed a row of perfectly straight, perfectly white teeth.

"You didn't think I'd send them halfway across the galaxy without *leverage*, did you?"

PART 5

THE VOICE OF THE ANCESTORS

51

kiva

Kiva woke the next morning when it was still dark outside, yanked from deep sleep by the dim sense of a foreign presence at the edge of her hut—someone who didn't belong there.

She sat up in her cot and looked to the door. Her skin tingled.

"Who's there?" Kiva called out.

The cloth parted and Po's face appeared in the doorway.

"Po," Kiva said. "What are you doing here?"

"Forgive me, Vagra," he said, hanging back. "I didn't mean to frighten you."

"You didn't," Kiva said, though he had. "I mean, it's all right. What is it?"

Po hesitated. "May I come in?"

Kiva nodded, setting her blanket aside and swinging her legs over the side of the cot. "Yes, of course."

Po walked inside but didn't come far into the hut. He lingered a few steps past the door. Kiva went to the center of the room and put some dry logs on the glowing embers from the fire of the night before and banked them into flame. She turned back to Po, seeing now that he was unarmed—he'd come without his spear or his bow and arrows.

"Now," she said. "Tell me what this is all about."

Po nodded, then grimaced, his hands fidgeting as they hung at his sides.

"I honestly don't know where to begin," he said.

Kiva's eyes narrowed. "What is it?"

Po sighed. "Something's happened. In the Forsaken camp."

Kiva waited for Po to go on.

"Have you heard of maiora?"

Kiva tensed. That word. She'd heard it before, in an echo from Kyne's mind during their confrontation at the pit. "What is it?" Kiva asked.

"It's a . . . I don't know what to call it. It's a food, a special kind of food that changes the person who eats it. Xendr Chathe found it on a scouting mission."

"What does it do?"

"It gives visions to whoever eats it. Or hallucinations, I don't know. Nobody knows what it does, not really." Po, his head angled down and away, glanced at Kiva out of the corner of his eye. "Some say it gives the person who uses it the power of the Ancestors."

Kiva was silent for a long moment. A substance that gave people the power of the Ancestors. Her power. If what Po was saying was true, it would change everything. She just didn't know how. Would it be good or bad for everyone—women and men, Vagri and Forsaken—to have the power of the Vagra any time they wanted it? Would such a substance bind her people even closer together? Or tear them apart?

290

"Who knows about it?" Kiva asked finally. "About the—what do you call it?"

"*Maiora*. All the Forsaken know about it. It's taken over the village." Po paused. "And Kyne. She knows too."

Kiva began to understand. She took a step closer to Po.

"Po, where did you disappear to yesterday?" she asked.

Po's face was stricken.

"I'm sorry, Vagra."

"It's okay," Kiva said. "You don't have to apologize. Just tell me what happened."

"She made me take her to Xendr Chathe. Kyne. She wants to lead the Forsaken against you. She offered to unite the villages, and to rule together with Xendr."

Kiva's heart pounded. "And what did he say to that?"

Po shook his head. "He said no. He's loyal to you. He won't join Kyne's rebellion. But he needs your help. He needs to know what the maiora is. Whether it's good or bad."

Kiva nodded slowly. "How can I help?"

"Just come with me," Po pleaded. "Come to the Forsaken camp. Now, before Kyne wakes up and senses that I'm here. See the maiora for yourself. Then ask the Ancestors for guidance."

Kiva's gaze drifted and she turned her back to Po, thinking. Matthew's face flashed before her eyes. Yesterday evening, she'd told him to come to the village in the morning—and she'd told him to come alone. She couldn't go with Po. Not now.

"I can't leave the village," she said, still facing away from Po. "I have things to attend to here."

"What things?"

"That's none of your concern."

"Then what shall I tell Xendr?"

Kiva turned around as an idea sprung to her mind. "Go to the Strangers."

Po's eyes narrowed to slits. "The Strangers? Why?"

"The woman. Dunne. She knows things. She can use her machines. She'll help you."

Po breathed heavily, color rising to his cheeks, his head shaking almost imperceptibly. Kiva set a hand on his shoulder and watched as his eyes cleared, the agitation passing from his body.

"Tell Xendr Chathe that I am glad to have his loyalty," she said. "And yours. I mean it, Po."

Po held her gaze for a long moment, then nodded and turned to leave.

"You'll let me know what happens?" Kiva asked. "With Dunne and the maiora?"

Po simply nodded and kept moving toward the door, but for some reason Kiva didn't feel ready to let him leave.

"Po," she called out.

He paused with his hand on the doorhang, and Kiva suddenly realized that she didn't know why she'd stopped him from going. For a moment, she struggled to find what it was she wanted to say.

"Po, when this is over . . . ," she began.

In the space between them, she felt something grow, some strong feeling emanating from the Forsaken boy standing before her: hope mingled with desire, both emotions shot through with fear—fear that his hopes would be dashed, that his desire would never be satisfied.

Kiva closed her eyes, inwardly cursing her own stupidity. She could never be what Po wanted. She was the Vagra—even if she wanted to, she could never be mated to Po. But even so, she felt a pain in him that she wanted to heal, a deep wrongness that she wanted to set right.

She and Po had never been friends. But that didn't mean he didn't deserve a chance at happiness.

"I'm just sorry, okay?" she said, opening her eyes again. "I'm sorry that Kyne drove you out of the village, and I'm sorry that I was too distracted with my visions of the Strangers to stop her."

"It's all right," Po said. "I'm fine. I really am."

Kiva shook her head. "No. It's not all right. When this is all over, I want you to come back to the village. Build a hut and plant a garden. Find a mate. Have babies. Have a life."

Po's cheeks colored, but he didn't say anything. He simply bowed his head and left the hut. Kiva went to the door and pulled back the doorhang—and as she stood watching him walk through the village toward the Forsaken camp, the sky beginning to lighten above him, she couldn't shake the feeling that she'd done something wrong, even if she didn't know what. That in trying to make things right with Po, she'd made them worse instead.

After a while, she went back to her hut. She lay down, webbed her fingers behind her head. Looked at the circular hole in the ceiling. And waited for dawn.

Waited for Matthew.

52

matthew

Matthew's sleep that night was fitful, filled with uncertain dreams that fled into the dark, forgetful depths of his mind the moment he awoke. Blinking, he looked around the sleeping quarters of the *Corvus* and found that he was alone.

Sam and Dunne weren't in their berths.

Matthew rubbed a hand over his eyes and got up to search the ship. First he went to the airlock, where he found the door wide open. He craned his neck outside and looked around, but the landscape was empty. In the airlock, he knelt to check the gun locker. It was still locked tight. The speeder was still in the airlock as well.

Matthew pressed a button to close the airlock and then went to the lab. As he'd expected, Dunne was there, hunched over a handheld display. She lifted her head as he walked into the room.

"Working already?" Matthew asked. "How long have you been at it?"

"Couple hours," Dunne said, dropping the handheld to run

her hands over her eyes. "I couldn't sleep. Too many questions."

Matthew nodded. "What about Sam? Where did he go?"

"He's gone? He was still asleep when I got up."

"I can't find him anywhere. The airlock was wide open."

Dunne's expression grew worried, the lines on her forehead and at the corners of her eyes deepening. "Did you check the guns? The speeder?"

Matthew nodded. "The guns are still locked up. Wherever Sam is, he's unarmed. The speeder's still here too."

"Good."

"Yes, but where is he?"

Dunne shrugged. "To be perfectly honest, I don't care. If we're lucky, he'll do something stupid and get himself killed out there. Good riddance. We'd be better off without him."

Matthew flinched to hear the harshness of Dunne's words, but he didn't disagree with her. He found Sam's moods puzzling, and a little frightening. When he'd first met him, Sam had simply seemed boorish, loud and full of bluster, but the way he'd turned sullen and broody when they encountered the Vagri perplexed Matthew— and the things he'd said the night before as they walked back to the ship made Matthew begin to think that Sam was slightly unhinged.

"What's wrong with him, you think?" Matthew asked. "With Sam, I mean."

"He's afraid, that's all," Dunne said, looking Matthew square in the eyes and speaking as if the answer were obvious. "He's afraid, and his fear makes him angry. There's nothing difficult to understand about Sam. He's the kind of person who thinks his hatreds are holy, that his prejudices are written into the DNA of the universe. He despises what he doesn't understand. And he'd destroy it if he got the chance."

As Dunne spoke, Matthew's heart beat faster and his veins thrummed with the thrill of hearing someone say something that was so obviously true and right—of articulating something that he'd felt but couldn't, until then, put into words.

Of course. Sam hated the Vagri because he didn't understand them. Because he was afraid of them. Their gray skin, their society where women, not men, were in control, where sex and family and authority were so different than they were on the Earth they'd left behind—it was foreign and strange, and unnerving to Sam. To all of them, really. But only Sam thought, somehow, that his fear made him righteous, and that the Vagri's strangeness made them evil.

"Is that what he's doing, then? Trying to come up with a way to destroy the Vagri?" Matthew asked.

"My guess is that he's moping somewhere, licking his wounds, feeding on his own anger." Dunne's focus wandered and she shook her head with disgust. "He's powerless here. Those men with their spears and their arrows could put him down in seconds if they had to. It's not him we have to worry about. It's Earth. If this ends up being a planet where we can live, there are plenty more people like Sam who will flood to this place. Thousands, millions of them. What do you think happens to the Vagri then?"

Matthew took a deep, slow breath, Kiva's face flashing before his eyes. She was powerful—the most powerful person in her village. Matthew had seen what she could do; he'd felt her power surging through his veins, so strong he felt as though it might tear him apart from the inside out. But she was vulnerable, too. Settlers from Earth wouldn't hesitate to destroy her and the society she led if the Vagri came between them and what they wanted.

"So what do we do?" he asked.

Dunne shook her head. "I don't know. We just need time. This is the human race's first contact with sentient creatures from another planet. This is history. We have the opportunity to get things right this time. Maybe we can live in peace with the Vagri, if we understand them first. That's what I'm working on today— analyzing these blood and tissue samples that I took yesterday."

Matthew nodded. "I'm going back to the village. Kiva asked me to come."

"Do you need company?"

Matthew shook his head. "No. She told me to come alone."

Dunne squinted. "Be careful. Try not to get shot this time."

Matthew chuckled and left Dunne to her work in the laboratory, making his way toward the airlock.

Making his way toward Kiva.

53

kiva

Long before Matthew's footsteps scratched at the dirt just outside her door, Kiva felt him coming, followed his progress in her mind and looked out through his eyes as he strode across the plains of Gle'ah. She could feel what he was feeling so clearly that the closer he came, the less certain she was if the anxious feeling in her stomach was really hers, or his, or something that belonged to both of them at the same time. The feeling grew stronger with each step Matthew took across the prairie. She'd felt the feelings of others many times, of course, and heard their thoughts echo in her skull, but this was different, more intense—it felt as though Kiva was wearing Matthew's body as a second skin. The sensation was at once delirious and painful, like a fever her body hadn't yet mustered the strength to sweat out.

While Matthew walked through the prairie, Kiva paced her hut, but when he climbed the rise and came within sight of the village, she willed her body to be still. She sat on the ground and crossed her legs beneath her. She closed her eyes and breathed slowly through her nose.

She didn't want to look nervous when Matthew came through the door. She wanted to look cool and calm. She wanted to look like the Vagra.

But then, when Matthew's steps drew up just outside the hut and she felt him hesitate at the door, her eyes snapped open and she said too quickly and too loudly, "Come in!"

The cloth hanging in the doorway moved to the side, and Matthew stepped into the hut. He lingered for a moment at the edge of the room.

Kiva breathed a sigh of relief. She felt a smile curl the corners of her mouth. Now that Matthew was here all the discomfort fled from her body, and she found herself wondering what she'd been so worried about. In spite of everything—in spite of the fact that the Vagri and the Strangers were still suspicious of one another—she felt a comfort in Matthew's presence. It was something about the softness in his eyes and the gentle curve of his mouth. Something about his broad shoulders and his long, lanky arms. Something about the way his flesh and blood called out to hers across the electrified space between them.

There was no explaining it. But there was also no denying it.

Matthew cleared his throat and seemed to be trying to find something to say.

"Come here," Kiva said. "Sit next to me."

Matthew walked forward and lowered himself to the ground. Rather than sitting cross-legged like Kiva, he sat with his legs stretched out, his arm draped over one bent knee. Kiva smiled at his feigned nonchalance.

"Do you know why I asked you here today?" she asked.

Matthew squinted. "I think so."

"Why?" Kiva asked, testing him. She waited as he searched his mind for an answer.

"Because you want to know why we came to your planet."

Kiva smiled and closed her eyes for a brief moment as she assented with a nod. "Among other things. But let's start there. Why *are* you here, on Gle'ah?"

Matthew drew a long breath through his nostrils before he spoke. "We were sent by our own planet. By our own people. Sent to find a new place to live."

Kiva was silent, waiting for Matthew to continue. His gaze left hers and dropped to the ground. A cloudy, far-off look came across his face. He picked at the dirt with a finger.

"My planet, it's—it's completely ruined. What's worse, we're the ones who ruined it."

"How?" Kiva asked. "How can you ruin an entire planet?"

"We just . . . used it up. The water and fuel are almost gone. Crops are failing. And everything's burning up. Cancers from solar radiation and chemicals eat away at everyone's bodies." Matthew shrugged and looked back up at Kiva with a dark look on his face. "That was how it was when I left, anyway. But that was many years ago. Things could be even worse now. My people could be nearly extinct."

"What is your planet called?" Kiva asked.

"Earth."

"Earth," Kiva said to herself, the word feeling strange on her tongue. "So, your people can't survive on this . . . Earth. Is that it?"

Matthew nodded, a look of embarrassment passing across his face—as if Earth was a place he was ashamed to be from.

"And now that you've found Gle'ah, you've got a choice, don't you? You can tell your people to come to this place. Or you can let them die on Earth—the place that you destroyed."

"Yes," Matthew said. His voice was tentative, and he glanced at Kiva cautiously out of the corner of his eye. "What are you asking me?"

"I'm asking what will happen if your people follow you here and make this planet their own? What will happen to the Vagri?"

Matthew looked away. "I don't know."

Kiva craned her neck down, trying to make Matthew meet her eyes. "But you suspect."

"Yes."

"And what do you suspect?"

Matthew shook his head. "It wouldn't be good for you. For the Vagri. For this planet. My people . . ." Matthew trailed off and paused for a moment. Then he raised his head and met Kiva's gaze again at last. His face held no expression, and he spoke his next words so plainly that Kiva knew they must be true.

"Everything we touch, we destroy."

54

matthew

After Matthew told Kiva the truth about his mission and about what would happen if the people of Earth came to colonize Gle'ah, she seemed to disappear inside herself.

Then she walked to the side of the room and crouched to pick up sticks of firewood from a pile at the wall. The firewood stacked in her arms, she walked back to the center of the room and let it clatter down atop a mound of gray ashes surrounded by rocks.

"What are you doing?" Matthew asked, his back straightening.

"There's a question you want to ask me," Kiva said as she picked up two rocks from just beside the fire pit and began to strike them together. Sparks fell into the kindling, the dry wood lit quickly, and Kiva went to her knees to blow the embers into flame.

"I don't understand," Matthew said.

"But you do," Kiva said, pausing to look back at him. "You do understand. You just haven't learned how to trust what's inside you."

Matthew swallowed. Kiva's words felt like they were cutting at him, stabbing him. They felt like an arrowhead plunging deep into his chest. Suddenly, thoughts that Matthew hadn't allowed himself to entertain, questions he hadn't allowed himself to ask, began to bubble to the surface. His face grew serious and he returned his gaze to the ground, where he found that he'd been absentmindedly picking a deep hole in the dirt with his finger.

"What's happening to me?" he asked finally, his voice thin in the still air.

Kiva cocked her head as the fire began to roar beside her, filling the hut with smoke.

"You tell me," she said.

Matthew shrugged. "I just feel . . . strange."

"Since the healing," Kiva offered. "After I healed you with my blood."

Matthew nodded. "Yes. Before that, too, but even more after. It's like . . . like I can *sense* things. Echoes. Echoes from all over, all at once—from Sam, from Dunne. From you."

"You're hearing the thoughts of others."

Matthew closed his eyes and shook his head, a pained look flashing across his face. "What I hear I don't understand. But I'm *feeling* them."

"It hurts."

Matthew's eyes opened. He nodded.

Kiva bowed her head. "What you are experiencing is the same thing I went through when the Ancestors first visited me. When I was chosen to be the next Vagra."

Kiva's face was barely visible through the growing haze. Matthew drew shallow breaths, trying not to cough.

"How old were you?" he asked.

"I was thirteen seasons old."

"Thirteen! God, you were so young."

"When I had my first vision, the woman who was Vagra at the time performed a ceremony over me to tell if the Ancestors truly favored me or if I was only imagining that they were speaking to me. I want to perform this same ceremony on you now."

Matthew touched his cheek with the tingling fingertips of one hand as he wondered what this ceremony might involve. The last time Kiva had performed a ceremony over him, she'd kept him from dying—but it had also hurt like hell.

"Fine," he said at last. "Sure, great, let's do it."

Kiva nodded, stood, and advanced toward him through the smoke. She held a sheaf of dead grasses in one hand.

"Don't be nervous," she said. "Please stand."

Matthew pulled himself to his feet and stood tall, pulling his shoulders back toward his spine.

Kiva brushed the sheaf of grasses against Matthew's chest, shoulders, and back, flicking her wrist as she circled behind him and came around the other side. Then she knelt and crumbled the grass to dust into a shallow clay bowl. When she stood again and faced Matthew, she had a dagger in her right hand.

"This will hurt a little," she said. "But only a little."

Matthew swallowed, nodded. "Okay."

"Give me your hand."

Matthew hesitated for a short moment before stretching out his hand. Kiva cradled it with her empty hand, then pressed the dagger against his palm with the other. She jerked the point across his hand in a quick, straight line. Matthew hissed as the knife split his skin open and drew blood.

"Now make a fist," Kiva said.

Matthew did as he was told and closed his hand. Kiva caught his blood in the bowl. Then she put two fingers into the bowl and daubed the mingled blood and grass into a paste. She turned back to the fire and threw some of the paste into the flames. They sparked, leapt higher, and turned green at the root.

"Well?" Matthew asked.

"It's as I suspected," Kiva said. "The Ancestors are with you. They favor you. They are quickening in your blood and giving you the second sight. That's never happened before."

"What's never happened before?" Matthew cradled his hand. The cut on his palm throbbed with every heartbeat.

Kiva turned to face him once more. "The Ancestors have never seen fit to quicken in the blood of a boy. Much less an outsider, like you."

"Why is it happening, then? Why is it happening to *me*?"

Kiva shook her head. "I don't know. The Ancestors obviously want you for something. They have some business with you."

Kiva walked to the wall again and came back to Matthew with two cloths—one wet, one dry. With the wet cloth, she washed Matthew's cut hand, then tied the dry one around the gash.

As Kiva dressed Matthew's wound, a troubling thought bubbled up in his mind.

When Kiva had first healed him on the plain, daubing her thickened blood on his arrow wound, unbearable pain had coursed through his body—and in the midst of the pain, strange images had flashed across his eyelids. He'd dismissed them at the time as a hallucination—he'd lost a lot of blood and was close to dying, after all. But now he wondered if they might be more significant. If they might be a vision from the Ancestors.

He tried to remember what he'd seen.

There'd been a wasteland, a desert. Earth? Perhaps.

He'd also seen a space station orbiting Earth. He'd been inside it. There, he stood in a landing bay full of ships, spaceships waiting to fly to Gle'ah as soon as he told Exo Project Mission Control that it was safe.

And—oh God—his mother and sister.

Could they . . . no. No. It was impossible. It had been far too long for them to be—

Matthew blinked.

"The Ancestors," he said, then paused. He gulped.

Kiva looked up into his eyes. "Yes?"

"Yesterday, you said they show you things, right?"

Kiva nodded. "*They show us things we must see,*" she recited. "Visions."

"Right. And these visions. They're, what? The past? The future?"

"Things that have been, things that will be," Kiva said. "Also things that *might* be—if you don't stop them from happening." She narrowed her eyes. "Why? What have the Ancestors shown you?"

Matthew shook his head and pulled his hand away. The smooth warmth of Kiva's fingertips against his skin as she dressed his wound was pleasurable—but at the moment, he didn't want to be distracted by her touch. He needed to think.

Could his mother and Sophie still be alive? Were they in danger?

"I don't know," he said, turning his back to Kiva. "I just don't know."

55

kiva

Matthew walked a few steps away from Kiva, drifting into his own thoughts. Kiva withdrew her power from him, giving him some privacy in his own mind. She turned back to the fire, which still burned green at the roots: the sign of the Ancestors' strong presence in Matthew's blood.

She glanced at Matthew, still facing away from her, and fell to wondering about him. From the beginning, Matthew had appeared in her visions of the Strangers—the Ancestors wanted her to know that there was something important about him. Now, the Ancestors were emphasizing that importance by favoring him with their power, by giving him visions that no Vagri man had ever experienced. Clearly, Matthew had some part to play in what was to come.

And yet.

Was Matthew really on her side? Wasn't he still a Stranger? He'd admitted that his people would destroy the Vagri if they came to live on Gle'ah—but when the time came to make a decision, would Matthew side with her people, or with his?

Kiva had to be sure. She had to be certain that he was on her side. And if he wasn't, then she had to convince him.

"Let's get out of here," Kiva said suddenly.

Matthew turned. "What?"

"Come with me. I want to show you something."

He nodded. For a moment they just stood there, looking at each other, each waiting for the other to move. Then, Kiva seized Matthew's hand in hers and pulled him toward the door. Outside, she quickly dropped his hand, fearful to let the Sisters see them touching. But as she led Matthew through the encampment, the feeling of Matthew's hand in hers lingered in her mind, the warmth and weight of it, the feeling of his fingers laced together with hers.

She smiled down at the ground, her cheeks burning, wondering what was coming over her.

At her heels, Matthew said nothing. They walked on in silence.

Their steps slowed as they reached the main village and they meandered their way to the border. Kiva hiked up the rise, Matthew close behind her.

"Where are we going?" Matthew asked.

"Stop here," Kiva said when they'd reached the top.

Matthew stood, perched on the lip of rock that separated the village from the plain. "This is what you wanted to show me? But I've already seen it. We stood at this exact spot yesterday, when we first came to the village."

"Just look," she said, grabbing him by the shoulders and turning his body until he faced the village once more. "*Really* look. And while you do, I'm going to tell you a story."

"A story?" Matthew's lips curved into a teasing smile.

Kiva ignored him. "My father told me this story when I was a little girl," she said. "I must've begged him to tell it a thousand times. It's about the beginning of the Vagri, and about where the Ancestors came from."

Matthew grew silent. He drew a long breath through his lips. His gaze sharpened.

"In the beginning of time," Kiva began, "when Gle'ah was first created, everything was engulfed in Chaos, and Death floated in the air. People lived during those times, but they didn't yet understand how to work together and survive. Everyone was alone, and when people came upon each other on the plain, they were so afraid that they fought and killed each other on sight.

"But in that time there also lived a man and a woman who came together and lived in peace with each other, and each cared for the other. He was First Father; she was First Mother—though her womb was barren because of the Death that hung in the air."

Kiva closed her eyes as she remembered what came next, the words she'd heard countless times as a girl coming back to her lips now as if the story were speaking through her.

"One day, First Mother said to First Father, 'Come, let us make a family, a tribe like this world has never seen: a people who live together in peace and harmony rather than Chaos.'

"But First Father replied, 'How can we do this, since your womb is barren? Let's go to this cave instead, where we can lie down together and wait to die—for we are no match for the Chaos that covers Gle'ah, or the Death that floats in the air.'

"But First Mother refused. 'No,' she said, then cast her eyes into the sky, and pointed, and said, 'Look.'"

Kiva paused and remembered the way Grath always told this part of the story—his voice hushed, a whisper so soft that Kiva would have to lean forward to hear. He'd point with his finger toward the roof of the hut, the firelight throwing his shadow on the wall, and Kiva would look up as if the thing he was pointing at were real, as if she could see it if she looked hard enough.

"And in the sky, a star came down and blazed through the air to land at the spot where you are standing."

She pointed down at the village below, at the massive, cratered depression that the Vagri huts sat in, the lip of rock encircling it on every side. She studied Matthew's face. His mouth had come open a crack.

"First Mother said, 'We must go together to the place where that star struck Gle'ah.'

"But First Father was afraid, and he refused.

"So First Mother went on alone—and when she came to the place where the white light had fallen to Gle'ah, healing entered her body and wiped away the Death, and her womb was no longer barren, and her mind was suddenly full of voices.

"The voices said, 'We are the Ancestors. We have come here to give you hope, to make you into a people who live in the midst of Death, and who will wipe the Chaos away from the face of Gle'ah.'

"First Mother returned to First Father and brought him to that place, and when he came his body was full of healing as well—but because he was afraid and had doubted, the Ancestors chose not to speak to him as they had spoken to First Mother.

"Together, First Mother and First Father lived in the place where the star had struck Gle'ah, surrounded at all times by the

Ancestors, who protected them, and healed them, and gave them many children. And these children became the Vagri. And when First Mother grew old and was near to death, she picked from among her daughters one who heard the voices of the Ancestors more clearly than the others—and she chose this girl to be a mother to all her children, a Vagra to care for the Vagri and keep them from falling once more into Chaos."

Kiva let out a long breath and said nothing for a moment to let the story sink in, to give it space to grow and deepen in Matthew's mind. She hadn't told it as well as Grath always did, perhaps—but she'd told it, and she'd done her best.

"And that," she said now, "is the story of how the Ancestors and the Vagri came to be."

Matthew turned to face her. "Is it true?" he asked. "Did it really happen that way?"

Kiva shrugged. "It's a story. It doesn't have to be true to be true."

As she spoke them, the words sounded like nonsense—but Matthew nodded as though she'd said something profound and looked back out over the village. Kiva moved closer to him and stood by his side.

"I told you this story because—"

"I know why you told me," Matthew said.

Kiva glanced at him, surprised. "You do?"

Matthew nodded. "You wanted me to know that your people came from chaos. That you made a way of life for yourself in the middle of death. And that you've got a responsibility to protect that way of life." He glanced at her out of the corner of his eye. "Right?"

"Yes," Kiva said. "I suppose that's right."

"And I get it," Matthew said, turning his body to face her fully. "I really do. But it's not that simple."

"Why? Why isn't it simple? Why can't it be?"

"Because," Matthew said. "I have a responsibility too. I have a mission. The Vagri are *your* people, but the people back on Earth, they're *my* people—even if they've screwed everything up. And if I don't do something, they'll all die."

Kiva didn't say anything. She just looked at Matthew for a long moment, then turned back to face the village where she'd lived her entire life.

The village. It looked so small. When she was a girl, it had seemed big, but she could see now that it wasn't. It was small. Tiny. Cowering underneath the vastness of the sky, surrounded on all sides by prairie that stretched to the horizon. The huts made of mud and grass, the people made of flesh and blood and bone. A single breath could blow it all away—everything she'd ever known.

Matthew stood so close that the hairs on her arm stood up. And yet, at the same time, he seemed a million miles away—and the space between them seemed impenetrable, absolute.

"I think you should go now," Kiva said. She wouldn't meet his eyes, wouldn't look at him. She couldn't.

"Okay," he said. "I understand. I'll go."

"Good," Kiva said, and began walking down the rise back into the village.

"Do you want me to come back tomorrow?" Matthew called down after her. There was a hoping, pleading tone in his voice.

"I don't know," Kiva said, loud enough for him to hear over his shoulder, then again, quieter, just for herself, "I don't know."

56

matthew

Matthew stood at the top of the rise and watched Kiva recede into the village. Then he turned and walked into the prairie.

As he walked, Matthew felt ashamed and angry with himself in a way he couldn't quite place—it had something to do with his mission, something to do with Kiva, and something to do with the way she went cold when he told her about his responsibility to the humans back on Earth.

He didn't want to think about it. So he walked a little faster, moved as quickly as he could without running.

Halfway between the village and the *Corvus*, Matthew looked up at the crest of the next hill and saw a figure standing silhouetted against the sunset.

"Sam?"

The figure turned and walked down the other side of the hill. Matthew broke into a run, his legs burning as he climbed the swell.

But when he reached the top of the hill, Sam was gone. Nothing but waving grass in every direction.

Matthew shook his head. He felt as thought he'd wandered into a dream. Was he starting to see things?

Back at the Corvus, Matthew found Dunne still in the laboratory, hunched over her handheld display.

"Hey, has Sam come back?" Matthew asked. "I thought I saw him out on the—"

Dunne's head snapped up, and Matthew stopped talking. Her eyes were wide, bloodshot, frenzied with excitement.

"What is it?" Matthew asked.

"Look at this," Dunne said. She set the handheld on the table and pushed it across.

Matthew looked. The display swarmed with tiny black dots against a white background.

"What am I looking at?"

"Kiva's blood sample," Dunne said.

Matthew arched an eyebrow. "And these dots are what? Blood cells?"

Dunne shook her head. "This is several orders of magnitude larger than the cellular level. This view is magnified to the molecular level."

Dunne paused, then reached over and tapped at the display with her index finger.

"Those aren't blood cells," she said. "Those are the Ancestors."

Matthew grabbed the handheld and stared more closely at the screen, at the little black dots that swam in Kiva's blood sample. Suddenly, he became very aware of the blood coursing through his own veins, of his heart beating in his chest. Whatever he was looking at, it was something that now swam in *his* bloodstream as well.

"What are they?" he asked.

"Some type of nanite. You know what those are?"

Matthew shook his head. "Not really."

"Nanites are basically machines," Dunne said. "But they're not like regular machines. They're built at an extremely small scale, just a few nanometers in width, and designed to do work at a molecular level."

Matthew held up his hands. "Wait. *Machines, built, designed.* You mean that someone actually *made* these things?"

"I don't know. You saw as well as I did that the Vagri haven't progressed nearly far enough to develop sophisticated technology—much less nanotechnology. They didn't make the Ancestors. But at the same time, there's no way these things could have evolved naturally. The way they behave, what they *do* . . ."

"What *do* they do?" Matthew asked.

"I'll show you," Dunne said. She reached across the table for the handheld display, tapped at the screen. Then she set the display back on the table so Matthew could see it.

"Remember that?"

Matthew looked at the screen. It was the video that Dunne had shown him a day ago of one of his biological cells, bursting open from the radiation in the air and then miraculously repairing itself.

Matthew nodded. "Yes. I remember."

"Well, the answer was right in front of us all along. We just weren't looking closely enough." She tapped at the screen, and the view zoomed in by several orders of magnitude until Matthew could begin to see the individual molecules of his cell wall.

"I've slowed it down so you can see what's going on," Dunne said. "Watch closely."

Matthew watched as his cell burst open once more, sending clumps of molecules flying.

Then the Ancestors appeared—vibrating black dots swarming through the white toward the broken biological material. The Ancestors grabbed hold of the clumps of molecules and, so quickly that Matthew could barely keep up, put everything back together again.

"Holy shit," Matthew muttered, and looked up at Dunne. "So the Ancestors are what's keeping us alive in this environment. They're the ones keeping us from dying in the radiation."

Dunne nodded. "They're everywhere. Flying around in the air. In our lungs, in our cells. In our bloodstream. They're like a virus."

"Except that they don't make us sick."

"No. They keep us alive. And there's more. They're communicating."

Matthew shook his head and laughed, a single bark of amused astonishment. "Of course they are."

"Watch this." She reached forward and tapped the screen on the handheld once more.

The display went dark, but by squinting Matthew could see hundreds of tiny, flashing points of light, starting in one corner and spreading across the screen in a wave.

"What am I looking at?"

"This is Kiva's blood sample at the maximum magnification I

316

can manage, in a completely dark chamber. You can see the light?"

Matthew nodded. "Where's it coming from?"

"Well, this is pretty speculative—we don't have any quantum sensors—but I think what we're seeing is a photon energy transfer between the nanites. Between the Ancestors. One of them releases a small burst of light energy, the next absorbs it and releases another burst in response, and so on."

"So, these waves of light," Matthew said. "That's the Ancestors communicating?"

"Yeah, I think so. Even some nanites made by Earth scientists are designed to communicate with each other. The ones that cure cancer, for instance. When they find a tumor, they release an amino acid that basically signals to the rest of them, 'Hey, come over here!'"

"So, the Ancestors must work the same way," Matthew offered. "They find something that needs to be fixed—like a busted cell or my injury from that arrow—and they communicate to get it healed."

Dunne squinted and shook her head. "No. Well, yes, I suppose. But I think it's more than that. It's more than healing. I mean, look at Kiva—she's a *telepath*. She can communicate with you, somehow. She can hear people's thoughts. So maybe the Ancestors are using this photon energy transfer to beam other people's brain waves through the air, directly into her mind."

"But why only the women?" Matthew asked. "If the Ancestors are everywhere, why do they bring visions to the women, but not to the men?"

"That's the most fascinating part of all," Dunne said, smiling, her eyes sparkling. "The body scans I took. Remember how I told you that all the women were barren? No ovaries?"

Matthew nodded.

"Well, the women don't need ovaries because their bodies are crawling with Ancestors. In their blood, their lungs, their brains. And yes, in their uteruses." She tilted her head down at Matthew. "You see what I'm saying?"

Matthew's mouth dropped open. "The Ancestors are making their babies."

Dunne nodded. "Yes. The Ancestors literally take the genetic material from the male and use it to construct an embryo from the molecular level on up, one cell at a time. No need for an egg. But as a result, the women have higher concentrations of the Ancestors in their bodies than the men. The men have enough to keep them healthy in this high-radiation environment, but not much more than that."

"And the women end up being telepaths . . . what? As a side effect?"

Dunne shrugged. "Something like that, I guess. Kiva said that girls join the Sisters after they are visited by the Ancestors. It's a rite of passage, something they have to experience as part of becoming an adult. Their first vision must be a sign that they've become biologically capable of bearing children."

Matthew was silent for a moment. He stared at the handheld screen, at the waves of light passing back and forth across the display as the Ancestors passed messages in some kind of primitive language. A pain twinged just beneath his skin, and Matthew put his hand to his chest, to the place where Kiva's blood had entered his body. The constellation of quantum blinks on the screen was happening inside him, too.

"There's still one question, though," Dunne said, and Matthew lifted his head.

"What's that?"

Dunne nodded toward him, her eyes never leaving his. "You," she said.

Matthew swallowed. "What do you mean?"

"Your blood and tissue samples show a higher concentration of the Ancestors than either mine or Sam's. Higher than those of the Vagri men and children. And that's *before* Kiva gave you her blood. I'm guessing if I were to test your sample now, it would be off the charts." Dunne paused. "You know what I'm talking about, don't you?"

Matthew sighed, then nodded. "Yes. I've been . . . *feeling* things. It started as soon as we set foot on this planet. Something's familiar about it. I don't know why. It's like this sense of déjà vu. Then we met *them*, and I could somehow understand Kiva. Then the whole thing with the blood . . ."

Matthew lifted a hand in the air, then let it drop back to the table.

"It's been getting stronger?" Dunne asked.

Matthew nodded. "Yes. I don't know how to control it. How to do anything with it. But yes. It's been getting stronger. Kiva says the Ancestors favor me."

Dunne lifted a hand and massaged the back of her neck, her

head cocked to the side. "That's an interesting way to put it. And it reminds me of a thought I had earlier. A theory. Now, this is *really* speculative, so take it with a grain of salt, but—"

"Go ahead," Matthew interrupted. "Tell me your theory."

"Well, the way the Ancestors communicate with each other? These messages passed from one to the next? It almost reminds me of synapses firing, of neural pathways."

Matthew didn't say anything right away, even though he knew immediately what Dunne was driving at.

"Like a brain," he said.

Dunne nodded. "Yes. Like a brain. Individually, the Ancestors are just drones, self-replicating nanites programmed to do one thing mindlessly. But together? Communicating? We could be talking about a sentience here, an intelligence, a *mind* with thoughts and desires and a will of its own. And we're all embedded in it. The planet, the grass, the Vagri, us, this ship. We're all inside the mind of the Ancestors."

Matthew's skin tingled. The air seemed alive with energy. He thought of the story Kiva had told him—of the coming of the Ancestors to Gle'ah in a streak of white light coming down from the stars.

"It sounds almost . . . religious," Matthew said. "I know you're talking about science. But it sounds to me like you're talking about a god."

Dunne shrugged. "Maybe I am," she said. "If so, the question now becomes—what does this god want with you?"

57

kiva

That night Kiva slept without dreaming, and woke before dawn.

She walked to the doorway of her hut and looked out over the Sisters' encampment and the village beyond. After the events of the past two days, she knew that she should call a meeting to speak to the Sisters and the villagers. She'd been so busy dealing with Matthew and the Strangers that she barely had time to think about her own people. She could sense that the Vagri were afraid, uncertain about what the future might hold—they'd need a word from their Vagra soon.

But Kiva didn't feel like she could face them. Now, before the Great Mother rose over the horizon, the village was silent. Soon, though, everyone would wake up, and the thoughts and worries and emotions of each of the villagers would begin to echo in Kiva's mind, buzz in her veins. She couldn't take it. Not yet.

I want to see Matthew.

Kiva surprised herself with the thought. She didn't *need* to see Matthew because the Ancestors wanted her to; she didn't *have* to see him because it was her duty as Vagra to deal with the Strangers. There was no real reason for her to see Matthew today.

But she ached to see him nonetheless—for no reason other than that she *wanted* to.

She began to walk toward the edge of the village, moving quickly and quietly so as not to wake anyone.

At her back, the dark sky began to glow at the horizon.

matthew

Matthew woke late that morning, and found himself alone once again in the sleeping quarters of the *Corvus*. Sam hadn't returned in the night—but now Dunne was gone as well.

In the airlock, Matthew found that the speeder was gone. The gun case was still locked, but there was a note on top of it, written in a looping cursive script.

Gone out. Be back soon.
       —Dunne

Matthew squinted at the note. Why would Dunne leave? Maybe she was looking for Sam, Matthew thought.

He hit the button next to the airlock door and stepped out onto the grass, yawning and stretching his arms into the air.

In the distance, he spotted a figure moving toward the ship. Squinting, he moved further into the plain.

It was Kiva.

Matthew's mouth pulled into a smile.

"What are you doing here?" he asked when Kiva came close.

Kiva reared back, feigning hurt. "What, you don't want me here? I'm offended!"

Matthew laughed, relieved that the chill he'd felt between them the day before seemed to have thawed this morning. "No, it's not that. I was just . . . surprised to see you."

Kiva looked over his shoulder to the *Corvus*. "I wanted to see inside your ship. I've shown you our village and the inside of my hut—I hoped you'd return the favor."

Matthew's stomach fluttered as he turned back to the open airlock. The prospect of letting Kiva into the *Corvus* felt wrong somehow, like he was disobeying some command—what would Mission Control back on Earth think if they knew?

Matthew shook his head to himself. He was being silly. He didn't care what Mission Control thought. He and Dunne had been hiding plenty from them already. Plus, Kiva was right—she'd taken a much bigger risk by letting him come into her village. The least he could do was show her around inside their ship.

"All right," Matthew said. "After you."

He waved his hand toward the airlock door, and Kiva walked inside. Matthew came in behind her and hit the button to close the door. Kiva jumped with fright and looked back at the door as it closed.

"Sorry," Matthew said. "I didn't mean to startle you. You don't need to be afraid."

Kiva looked around the airlock, awed. She put her hand against one of the walls, running her palm over the smooth surface. "It's amazing. How did you make it?"

Matthew grinned. "I didn't—I could barely make a bird feeder in woodshop class. Other people made it. Scientists. Engineers."

The airlock finished decontaminating the air, and the door to the inside corridor hissed open.

"It's impossible," Kiva said, running her hands along the doorway, trying to find where the sliding door had disappeared to.

Matthew chuckled. "Funny—when I visited the village, I was thinking the same thing about you. The things the Ancestors can do through you seem pretty impossible too."

58

kiva

The ship was unlike anything she'd ever seen. It was all hard, gleaming surfaces, straight lines, sharp corners. So unlike the planet of Gle'ah, where nothing was hard, and nothing was straight—where the plains swelled and dipped and the grasses bent this way and that with the wind.

They went through a hallway and came into a big room with a long, gleaming table in the middle. The table was covered in strange, foreign-looking instruments.

"What's this?" Kiva asked.

"The lab," Matthew said. "This is where we analyzed the blood samples that we got from you yesterday."

Kiva picked up a flat piece of glass. There was a picture on the glass, like the pictures artists from the village sometimes drew in the dirt or on the walls of the huts. Except that this picture was moving—a thousand tiny black dots, vibrating this way and that. Kiva felt Matthew holding his breath while she held the moving picture in her hands. She set it back on the table and he breathed again.

Kiva moved into another room with sleeping berths set into the walls. "And this?"

"Sleeping quarters," Matthew said.

Kiva raised her eyebrows. "Which one is yours?"

Matthew nodded up. "Top bunk."

Kiva kept walking. She went back through the laboratory and craned her neck around a corner to see a small room at the back of the ship. It was dark inside.

"What's that?" she asked.

"Oh, that . . . that's nothing."

Kiva looked at Matthew and set her jaw. "Show me."

Matthew sighed and walked in ahead of her. He flipped a switch, and a dim light came on, revealing three long, narrow platforms, each with a clear box on top of it.

"What is this room?" Kiva asked.

"This is where . . . ," Matthew began, then paused. "It's where we stayed during our journey."

"How long was your journey?

"One hundred years . . . I mean, about one hundred seasons."

Kiva gasped. "One hundred seasons in this little room!"

Then she paused, closed her mouth, and studied the smooth skin of Matthew's face. What he was telling her didn't make sense.

"But you're so young," she said. "I thought you said you were my age."

"I am," Matthew said. "It doesn't work that way. It's like . . . How can I explain this?"

Matthew looked down at his feet. Kiva waited.

"We slept in here for most of the journey," he said. "Dunne,

Sam, and I. We were . . . we were frozen. In ice. You have ice on Gle'ah?"

Kiva nodded.

"The ice kept us from getting older. You see? So when we arrived here at Gle'ah, we woke up—"

"The same age as you were when you left," Kiva cut in, finishing Matthew's sentence for him.

Matthew nodded, and Kiva returned her gaze to the clear box where Matthew had spent the last one hundred seasons—frozen, unaging.

"But if you spent one hundred seasons flying from Earth to Gle'ah," Kiva said slowly, thinking as she spoke, "then life on your planet went on without you. While you were frozen, time just kept going."

She looked up at Matthew. His eyes were buried in a flinch, but Kiva could see that they were glistening. He didn't say anything.

"Why did you come here?" Kiva asked.

Matthew turned away and coughed. "I told you," he said, unable to hide the quaver in his voice even though he spoke loudly into the small room. "Our mission is to find a new—"

"That's not what I mean," Kiva said. "I mean, why did *you* come here? There are people back home, aren't there? People you care about? People who love you? Why would you leave them behind?"

Matthew breathed out. "My mother," he said. "She was sick, and we didn't have the money to get her better."

"Money?" Kiva repeated.

"It's like, it's a thing that you have, a sort of made-up thing, and you trade it for other things. But we didn't have enough to buy a cure for my mother, and there was pay for anyone who agreed to go on this mission, so—"

"You mean there was a cure for your mother's sickness, but you couldn't get it for her because you didn't have enough of this made-up thing? This is the way things work on your planet? Why don't people put a stop to it?"

"I know it must sound horrible to you," Matthew said. "And it is horrible, really, when you sit down and think about it. But I guess most people never really think about it. When it's all you've ever known, you kind of get used—"

His voice caught in his throat and he stopped talking for a moment.

"Anyway, I had to do it. My mom, she's done so much for me. I had to at least try. For her."

Kiva nodded slowly. "I understand. I understand what it is to give your life over to other people. To make it into something else to please them."

"Is that what being Vagra feels like? Giving your life to the Vagri? Making it into something else to please them?"

"Sometimes. When I'm in the village, I can hear their voices all the time. I've learned to tune them out and really listen to only one voice at a time—but they're always there, chattering away inside my head." Kiva paused, breathed out through her nose, and swallowed. "All their hopes, all their fears. Their expectations. They want me to be so much—so much more than I am. I can't be the leader they want me to be."

Kiva felt Matthew's hand on her arm, and she jerked her gaze up with surprise to look at him. Matthew flinched, took his hand away, and took a step back, his expression chastened. Something inside Kiva wilted—he'd only startled her. She hadn't meant for him to stop touching her. That wasn't what she'd meant to happen at all.

"You seem like a good leader to me," Matthew said. "If I were one of the Vagri, you'd be exactly the kind of Vagra I'd want."

Kiva smiled.

Matthew looked once again at the empty cryochambers and gritted his teeth.

"Come on," he said. "Let's get out of here. I can't stand this place."

59

matthew

Matthew walked back through the *Corvus* toward the airlock, Kiva following close behind. Together, they went out onto the grass and kept walking. Their steps took them far into the plain, into a shapeless, unmarked place where neither the *Corvus* nor Kiva's village were visible—and where it seemed, for a moment, that they might be the only two people alive in the entire universe.

Matthew fell a little behind Kiva and let himself watch the way her hips moved languidly back and forth beneath her dress. Then he glanced at her hands swinging at her sides and wondered what would happen if he were to walk up beside her and lace his fingers together with hers.

He shook his head and pushed the thought out of his mind.

"Say something," Matthew said after a few more steps.

Kiva glanced back with a smile. "You don't like the silence?"

Matthew shook his head. "It's not that. I just like hearing your voice more."

Kiva took her lower lip between her teeth as she thought.

"Let's do this," she said. "You ask me a question. One question. Then I'll ask you a question. Then you ask another question, and so on. But we have to be completely honest. We have to tell the whole truth, without leaving anything out."

"Okay," Matthew said. "Um, let's see. Here's one: why does this place seem so familiar to me? Why do you seem so familiar?"

"That's two questions. You're already cheating."

Matthew laughed. "Humor me anyway."

Kiva squinted and studied Matthew. The smile left her face. "You still don't remember?"

"Remember what?"

Kiva walked a few steps without answering. She nodded toward the horizon, in the direction of the village.

"Over those hills," she said. "Near the village, there's a spot just beyond the rise. It's a little . . . a bump in the plain. A bump with a tiny cleft in it, where a person can lie down and feel like the ground is cradling them. Like Gle'ah is holding you in the palm of its hand. That's where we met for the first time."

Matthew looked toward the horizon, then back at Kiva, uncomprehending.

"I loved that spot when I was younger," Kiva continued. "I used to go there at nightfall and nestle myself right in the little crevice. Then I'd look up and wait for the sky to go dark, for the moons and stars to come out. And it was on one of those nights that I had my first vision. When I first saw you and your shipmates, and knew that you were coming to this planet."

"I was in your first vision?"

Kiva shook her head. "I didn't know it was you. Not at first. I didn't understand the vision fully. I needed the Ancestors to tell me more."

"And did they?"

"They took a while, but yes. It was only a few days ago. I was lying there, in the same spot, and I dreamed that you came over the horizon." She nodded into the distance. "You came over the hill and saw me. You looked right into my eyes."

Matthew shook his head to himself. "But that was just a vision. A dream. Something in your mind. You don't actually think—"

Kiva snapped her head toward Matthew, hurt and anger painted clearly across her face. He took a step back, shrinking from the accusation in her eyes.

"Kiva, I'm sorry, I—"

"You were there," Kiva said. "You can't remember, and that's okay. But you were there. You were in the dream with me. That's why Gle'ah seems so familiar to you. That's why I seem so familiar to you. Because we've met before. The Ancestors wanted us to. They wanted us to be connected. All that time, ever since my first vision. All that time, they were preparing me to meet you."

"Okay." Matthew put his hands out and grabbed hold of Kiva's arms just below her shoulders. "I'm sorry I can't remember. But I believe you."

Kiva glanced away. Matthew bent to look straight into her eyes.

"Hey," he said. "Look at me. I believe you, okay?"

Kiva returned Matthew's gaze for a moment, then looked away

again. She shrugged Matthew's hands off her arms and walked a few steps, her back turned.

"Ask me a question," Matthew said.

"What?"

"Ask me a question. It's your turn."

Kiva was silent a moment. "I want to know what you thought when you first saw me. The first time you remember, anyway. What was the first thing that went through your mind?"

"You know what I thought."

Kiva's jaw stiffened. She held her neck straight, her head angled up toward him, and her chin pointed out into the air between them. "I want to hear you say it."

"I thought you were beautiful."

"And now? What do you think now?"

Matthew forced his mouth into a smirk. "Now you're cheating."

"I don't care. Answer me anyway. What do you think of me now?"

Matthew tried to swallow. His mouth and throat felt dry.

"I still think you're beautiful," he croaked.

"That's all?"

Matthew shook his head. "No. That's not all."

"What, then?"

"Just give me a *second*," Matthew snapped, his voice suddenly hoarse.

Kiva's mouth closed with a click. She waited.

Matthew looked off to the side as he searched his mind for the right words to describe how he felt about Kiva. He realized that his hands were trembling and tried to still them by wringing them together, massaging the palm of one hand between the fingers and thumb of the other. After a long silence, he spoke.

"It's just . . . *strange*, you know? I mean, you're different from anyone I've ever met. You've lived your whole life on a completely different planet. The things I don't know about you could stretch from here to the other end of the galaxy. But when I look at you . . ." Matthew's voice caught in his chest, but he forced himself to go on. "When I look at you, and talk to you, it doesn't feel *foreign*. It doesn't feel *alien*."

"What does it feel like?" Kiva asked, her voice barely a whisper on the still air.

Matthew pressed his lips together and raised his shoulders in a helpless shrug. "It feels like home."

As he spoke, Matthew couldn't bring himself to look directly at Kiva's face. He was afraid of what he'd see there. Once, back home, he'd told a girl at school that he had feelings for her and a look of disappointment or pity had flashed across her face. He didn't think he could bear to see that look from Kiva.

But finally, after a long, awkward silence, he dragged his eyes up to look at her. She returned his gaze without blinking or looking away, and Matthew knew at once that she felt the same way he did. A wave of joy and relief tingled over the entire surface of his skin. But it didn't last long. Because even though Matthew could tell by the way Kiva looked at him that she returned his feelings, he also saw a deep sadness written plainly across her face—and he knew immediately what that look meant.

It meant that for them, things would never be that simple.

Even love—if that's what it was—wouldn't be enough. Not by a long shot.

"Kiva, I—," he began, taking a step toward her, but she stopped him from saying more by putting a hand on his cheek.

"Don't," she said, shaking her head. "Not yet."

"But it's all so complicated—the Vagri, the Ancestors, my mission. I don't know what—"

"Stop," she said. "Let's enjoy this moment, okay? Let's make it last. The rest can wait."

Matthew was silent. He swallowed loudly. Then he nodded. He felt empty and helpless, both better and worse than he did before—as if by speaking he'd poured every bit of himself out onto the ground, like water from a glass.

"Ask me another question," Kiva said. "It's your turn."

Matthew licked his lips. His mind moved quickly. His heart was beating wildly in his chest.

"Okay," he said. "Here's my question. Have you ever been kissed?"

"What?" Kiva said, turning her head to the side and trying to hide the deep gray blush that rose to her cheeks with a hand that darted up to tuck her hair behind her ears.

"You learned that you were going to be Vagra when you were thirteen, right? And I imagine you didn't have much time for boys after that, surrounded by all those women in the center of the village."

"It's a silly question," she said. "I'm not going to answer."

Matthew put on a shocked look, his mouth opening in feigned outrage. "But you said we had to be honest! That we had to tell each other the whole truth, without leaving anything out. That's what you said."

Kiva narrowed her eyes at him. "I know what I said. But that's not what you're really asking."

"Isn't it?"

"No. You don't want to know if I've ever been kissed before. You want to know if you can kiss me now."

Matthew's stomach fluttered, but he forced himself to smile. "Well?"

Kiva shrugged. "There's only one way to find out."

Matthew closed the distance between them in one stride and, in a single movement, slid an arm around Kiva's waist while he lifted his other hand to the nape of her neck, lacing his fingers in her hair and setting his thumb lightly against the line of her jaw. He closed his eyes and pressed his lips against hers.

They kissed tentatively at first. Kiva's mouth was shut tight, but Matthew opened his slightly, inviting her to do the same. When he felt her lips begin to part, felt her begin to press her body against his, a thrill rippled through his body like an electric current, and for a moment he thought of what Dunne had told him about the Ancestors—about photon energy transfer, about neural pathways, about synapses firing.

Then Kiva opened her lips wider and darted her tongue between his teeth, and every last thought of the Ancestors fled his mind until all he could think about was Kiva, Kiva, Kiva—about the taste of her mouth, about the weight of her body pressed against his, and about the way her warm flesh felt under his hands.

60

kyne

Kiva.

What does she think she's doing?

She left. I saw her. We all saw her.

Sneaking away like a thief. Sneaking away to—what? To see that boy?

Kiva and the Stranger.

I can't allow myself to think these things. She's the Vagra.

But I just don't trust her.

Kyne. We should have listened to Kyne. Maybe it's not too late.

I wish we'd . . . Kyne all along . . . she knew . . .

The voices began to break up in Kyne's mind. She clamped her eyes shut and concentrated, reached for the thoughts of the Sisters, willed them to be whole in her head once more.

. . . Kyne knew . . . isn't ready . . . that Stranger boy . . . threat . . .

Kyne sighed and let her eyes come open. It was no use. The voices were gone.

The maiora was wearing off.

She glanced at the small square table next to her bed, where a leather pouch sat. She reached inside and pulled out a small ball of maiora. She rolled the cottony substance back and forth between her thumb and first two fingers. Her tongue was wedged between her lips, anticipating the bitter taste of the stuff—but she didn't put it in her mouth. Instead, she put the ball back in the leather pouch with the rest of the maiora, then put her hands on her thighs and stood up.

She'd been using maiora for only a few days—but already, Kyne feared that she was unable to stop. She'd gotten some when she visited the Forsaken camp with Po. After she left Xendr Chathe's hut she'd snuck to the den at the edge of camp and stole a couple fistfuls of the stuff, unnoticed by the maiora-eaters lying senseless on the floor.

Kyne had turned up her nose then at the Forsaken men who couldn't stop taking maiora, so obsessed with the stuff that they'd obviously gone days without washing—but now, as she strode through her hut and made her way toward the door, she realized that she'd become just like them. When she first took the maiora, she told herself that she'd only use it occasionally, to hear the thoughts of the Sisters and see what visions the substance might give her. All she wanted was to gather enough information to know if there was any chance for her to restart her rebellion, if there was still any discontent with Kiva among the Vagri and the Sisters. Once she knew that, she told herself, she'd be done with maiora.

Now, Kyne knew that it wasn't quite so simple. The feeling of being on maiora was similar to the feeling of communing with the Ancestors, of receiving a vision or hearing another person's thoughts—except more intense. The problem was that when the maiora was humming through her veins, Kyne could sense only fragments: disconnected words and phrases from the minds of the Sisters, bits and pieces of visions. As the visions subsided, it was hard to shake the feeling that she'd been *so close*, the feeling that if she took just a little bit more, then the thing that seemed to be trying to break through at the edges of her perception would finally become clear.

Kyne stood at the doorway and pulled aside the cloth. As she cast her eyes over the Sisters' camp, all she saw were more huts. The camp seemed almost devoid of life. Kyne wasn't the only one who'd scarcely left her hut since the Strangers had come. Most of the Sisters were inside, hunkering down in their isolated dwellings as if preparing for a storm.

The village was quiet. But it wasn't peaceful.

Something was building.

Kyne opened her eyes again. She'd heard enough of the Sisters' thoughts while on the maiora to know: her rebellion wasn't over. Not by a long shot. There was discontent in the village. It could be exploited.

But it wasn't enough. She needed more. She needed something on Kiva—something she could use to turn the village against her once and for all.

Kyne returned to her bed. She reached her hand inside the leather pouch and pulled out the small, feathery ball of maiora once more. She held it between her fingers for a moment, thinking. Then she reached inside again and grabbed more—a small fistful, more than three times the amount she'd ever taken at a single time.

She took a fast, quivering breath through her mouth. Licked her lips. Then put the whole fistful of maiora into her mouth. It melted at once on her tongue.

Kyne's vision blurred. Her skin went numb. The world surrounding her seemed to shrink to a single point of light, like the flame of a lamp burning in a dark room. Then even that single light collapsed in on itself and became a kind of black hole, a portal that sucked Kyne in with a force she couldn't resist—and as Kyne's consciousness hurtled through the portal faster than the speed of thought, images flashed before her eyes.

A barren, dust-swept planet, suspended in blackness.

Creatures who looked just like the Strangers—except there were thousands of them. Thousands upon thousands—millions, billions.

Lined up under a merciless sky, the creatures waited to enter the belly of a massive stone bird.

The vision pulled back to reveal a hundred more birds just like it, with Strangers streaming into every one.

So many—how could there be so many? And all of them coming to Gle'ah.

Then the vision shifted again, and Kyne saw waving grasses.

Gle'ah.

Po, her twin brother, loosed an arrow from its bow, and it struck Matthew in the chest.

Kiva, kneeling over Matthew's body, smearing her blood over the wound.

Kiva and Matthew, alone, walking together across the plain. Their lips moved, but Kyne couldn't hear what they were saying.

And then.

Matthew slipped a hand around Kiva's waist, cradled her neck with the other. Leaned in.

And kissed her.

Kiva standing limp in his arms at first, then reaching her own arms around Matthew, pulling him deeper into the kiss.

Kyne came out of the vision with a gasp. She snapped her head back and forth, half-expecting to see apparitions from the vision standing in the room with her—but no. She was alone.

Kyne stood, her whole body trembling. The remnants of the maiora still thundered in her veins, and she paced in circles around the room, unable to let her body be still. She ran a hand through her hair: it was greasy to the touch. She stopped and looked down at herself, seeing the toll that a day and a half eating one clump of maiora after another had wrought: her dress was streaked with grime, and her skin glistened with sweat. She lifted an arm and sniffed cautiously at her armpit.

Oof.

She had to get cleaned up before she went to the Sisters. She had to look completely collected, completely put together—when she spoke to the Sisters, there could be no doubt that the accusations she was making against Kiva were true.

Her eyes drifted once more to the table next to her bed, to the leather pouch that still held enough maiora to last her for the rest of the day and into the dead of night.

But no. Kyne had had enough. The vision she'd had while under the influence of maiora was gone, but it didn't matter—she could remember every image.

The Strangers, greater in number than the blades of grass on the prairie, escaping their planet to come to Gle'ah.

Kiva, healing Matthew when she could have let him die.

Matthew kissing Kiva. And Kiva kissing him back.

That was enough for Kyne to work with. That was more than enough.

61

kiva

The wind had picked up, and as Kiva walked back to the village, the long grass licked at her ankles and her dress whipped off to the side, pulling so hard at her body that it seemed as though the fabric might lift her off the ground and carry her away.

Kiva was dizzy. Her head felt as though it was floating above her neck, disconnected from the motions of her arms and legs. Her body seemed some foreign thing. She hardly knew herself. Her own actions were confusing to her, her thoughts a jumbled cacophony.

Why had she allowed Matthew to kiss her? And why had she kissed him back?

Even now, she didn't know. Romance was forbidden to the Vagra—she was the mother of all her people, and couldn't allow her allegiances to the Vagri to be clouded by love for any single person. For Kiva to kiss *anyone* would be viewed as a betrayal by the Sisters.

And the fact that she'd fallen for a Stranger, well—that could only make things worse.

Kiva clenched her fists at her side. It wasn't fair! For everyone else but her, things were so simple—if Thruss or Rehal wanted to be with a boy, and that boy wanted them back, then they could be together. But for Kiva, the Vagra, nothing could ever be that easy. Everywhere she went, she heard the voices echoing in her head: the voices of the Ancestors, the voices of the Sisters, the voices of all the Vagri. She'd heard them for so long that by now, she could no longer recognize the sound of her own voice, her own thoughts.

Kiva's mind wandered to the possibility that she'd kissed Matthew not because she wanted to, but out of some ulterior motive. After they'd broken off their kiss and disentangled from one another, Kiva had told Matthew that he would face a choice, that soon he'd be forced to side either with the Vagri or with his own people. So, had she kissed him to control him? To bring him over to her side? To give him something to think about as he made his decision?

Was it possible that even when she broke the taboos of her people by kissing Matthew, the Ancestors were controlling that, too? That even her *sins* weren't her own?

Kiva shook her head. As soon as she allowed herself to think it, that she'd kissed Matthew to manipulate him, or because she was controlled by the Ancestors, she knew it wasn't true.

No. She'd kissed Matthew because she wanted to. Because finally, after so many seasons of thinking about everyone but herself, she'd found something that *she* wanted. A desire that was hers and hers alone.

For so long, she'd felt lost—her own voice drowned beneath the cacophony that echoed in her head. But in Matthew, somehow, she'd found herself again.

The Sisters could be damned if they didn't understand that. The Ancestors too. The last Vagra had been torn apart by the struggle to please everyone but herself. Kiva didn't want to make that same mistake.

As she grew closer to the village, though, a sense of unease grew within Kiva's chest. On the plain, between the village and Matthew's ship, things were so much simpler. There, the two of them could be free of the crushing expectations of both their people and just be themselves—Kiva and Matthew instead of the Vagra and the Stranger. But when she returned to the village and he went back to his ship, things would start getting complicated again.

She came close to the edge of the village and saw her old favorite spot, the small clefted swell where she'd first seen her vision of the Strangers, the place where she'd first met Matthew in a dream—even if he couldn't remember it. Her steps slowed. She looked down at the spot, then up at the looming rise. The village lay beyond.

Whatever waited for her there among the crowded huts, among the crush of people, each with their own desires, resentments, and schemes—she wasn't ready to face it.

She knelt in the grass and nestled into the cleft. She looked up for a moment at the slowly fading light of early evening. In her mind she could hear the background chatter of the Vagri and the

Sisters. She pushed them away.

Then, Kiva closed her eyes and thought of Matthew—of the warm strength of his hands gripping her by the waist and the nape of her neck, and the soft press of his lips against hers.

62

matthew

Matthew walked back to the Corvus in a better mood than he'd been in for months—or decades, depending on how he looked at it.

For so long now, hope was something he'd lived without. His mother's cancer, being chosen for the Exo Project, the likelihood that he'd die on a planet light-years away from his own, and the certainty that even if he lived, he'd never see his family or his friends again.

But now, this.

Matthew lifted his fingers lightly to his lips. They felt swollen, bruised a bright red from the way Kiva had pressed hers against them. Matthew smiled. Of all the things he'd imagined he might find on planet H-240, the most he'd hoped for was water, breathable air, and a temperate climate that wouldn't kill him the moment he took off his helmet. He never expected to find life on the surface. He never expected the Vagri.

And he certainly never expected Kiva.

Matthew's smile gradually pulled straight and turned into a

frown as his mind moved again to what Kiva had told him before they'd parted. The kiss they'd shared on the plain was wonderful, but it didn't mark the end of their troubles. Not by a long shot.

"You have a choice," Kiva had said. "And whatever you choose, the future of my planet depends on it. The future of my people, and yours. And our future."

Matthew had been silent after that, but he knew what she was saying. She was saying that no matter how she felt about him, no matter the way her body had gone soft under his touch and melted into his as they pressed their lips together just moments earlier, there were some things that the two of them could not overcome. Some things that she could not forgive.

Now, walking back, Matthew felt certain that he knew the choice he had to make.

He had to decide if he would tell Earth that Gle'ah was a habitable planet or not. He had to decide between the Vagri and the human race.

But did he really have to choose? What if the Vagri and the humans could learn to live in peace?

Even as he thought it, he began shaking his head to himself. No. The thought that his people and Kiva's could live together on the planet was naive at best, and dangerously ignorant at worst. Matthew himself had admitted to Kiva that his people destroyed everything they touched. And it was true. How else to explain what had happened to Earth? Animal species driven to extinction, the atmosphere ruined beyond repair, the land bled dry of everything that humans could consume or sell for profit.

Matthew glanced out over the landscape of Gle'ah and wondered what it might look like five, ten, or twenty years hence if the human race resettled its billions to this place. In his mind's eye, he saw small settlements crop up here and there, growing slowly upward and outward as they changed into massive, ugly, filthy cities that stretched from one horizon to the next. He saw massive machines digging the grasses away, bulldozing smooth the gentle swell of the hills. Quarries reaching down into Gle'ah, mines and oil rigs and factories spewing contaminants into the air.

His people didn't deserve this planet. They'd destroy it, just as they'd destroyed Earth. Even the Ancestors, an alien intelligence that existed only to protect life, wouldn't survive—some businessman would find a way to capture them, package them, and sell them to the highest bidder.

Humans were a disease. A cancer.

Matthew's steps grew quicker as he became more sure of his decision. When he really thought about it, it was obvious. He couldn't allow Earth to resettle on Gle'ah. The human race had had its chance in the great evolutionary struggle to survive. Now, it was up to Matthew to make sure the Vagri had theirs.

When Matthew returned to the *Corvus*, he saw the speeder hovering riderless just outside the airlock.

Dunne was back.

He went inside the ship and found her in the lab.

"Matthew," she said, lifting her head. "I'm glad you're back."

"Where were you this morning?"

"Before you woke up, I had a visitor."

Matthew's brow lifted in surprise. "Oh? Who?"

"It was that boy. Po. The one who almost killed you. He came not long after you left."

"And what did he want?"

"It was hard to tell. Without you and Kiva here to translate, we had to communicate with hand gestures. But I gathered that he wanted me to come with him."

"And where did you go?"

"He took me to another village. It was all men. He seems to be part of some warrior culture, separate from the Vagri."

Matthew nodded. "Kiva told me about them. She said that they'd been banished from the village. The Vagri only use them when they need to, as mercenaries."

"Yes, that's what I gathered. But that's not the most interesting thing. Look at this."

Dunne reached out her hand, and Matthew came forward to see what she was holding. It was a downy, whitish substance that reminded Matthew of cotton.

"What is that?"

Dunne shook her head. "I wasn't sure at first. But they're using it as a kind of drug. Eating it, smoking it."

"Po told you all this with hand gestures?"

Dunne smiled. "Yes. It was difficult. Almost like a game of charades. But I didn't have to guess too hard. While I was in the village, practically half the people were high on it. I could see exactly what was going on. I also heard what they call it: *maiora*."

"Maiora," Matthew repeated, puzzled. Just when they thought

they'd figured out this planet, it revealed new mysteries. "Did you analyze it?"

"I did. It's the Ancestors. The same nanite we saw earlier. But arranged together into a crystalline form."

Matthew worked the ball of maiora back and forth in his hand, rubbing the white substance between his fingers and thumb. "Like snow," he offered.

"Yes. Like snow. And when they eat it, or smoke it, it lets the Ancestors loose in their body, and—"

"Let me guess. Hallucinations? Visions? Telepathic communication?"

"Well, Po and I didn't get that far. Telepathy would've been a hard one for our little game of charades. But that's my guess, yes. And there was something else. Before I left." Dunne squinted, her eyes growing cloudy.

"What? What is it?"

"Something Po was trying to tell me. I didn't quite get it. I was trying to ask him where the maiora came from. In response, he waved his hands off toward the horizon."

"That seems clear enough," Matthew said.

"I suppose. But it was what he did next that was so puzzling. I still don't know what he was trying to convey with his hand motions. But it seemed like he was describing structures. Buildings, or ruins, maybe. I don't know." Dunne shook her head and trailed off. "Anyway, I came back here to analyze the maiora. Maybe we can take out the speeder later to find what Po was talking about. What about you? I forgot to ask you what you talked to Kiva about yesterday. Did you get anywhere with her?"

Ears burning, Matthew turned away and glanced at Dunne out of the corner of his eye, checking her expression. There didn't seem to be any double meaning in her words. She simply wanted to know if he'd discovered anything new about Kiva or the Vagri.

"Nothing new to report," he said finally, then cleared his throat as he tried to change the subject. "I've been thinking, though. About what we talked about this morning. About what we're going to do about Earth."

Matthew took a long breath. Dunne looked up and waited.

"Yes?" she asked.

"Here's what I think . . . ," Matthew began, but at that moment the quantum transceiver squawked on a table in the corner of the room.

"Corvus," came Alison's voice on the other end. "Corvus, this is Control. Come in, Corvus."

Dunne nodded toward the transceiver. "You'd better get that, I suppose."

Matthew walked to pick it up. He pressed the button on the side and lifted it to his mouth.

"Copy, Control. This is Corvus."

"This is Matthew, right? Matthew Tilson speaking?"

"Yes, Alison. Same as always."

A pause. "Well, Matthew, we've got someone here who wants to speak to you."

Before Matthew could say anything, another voice came on the line.

"Matthew? Matthew, are you there?"

He recognized the voice immediately.

Matthew's heart slowed. His blood turned to ice in his veins. His hand clutched the transceiver in a grip so tight that the skin on his knuckles turned white. His thumb trembled as he pressed again on the button to speak.

"Mom?"

63

Matthew's stomach clenched. His vision went spotty and he began to feel lightheaded. He staggered back against the wall and sank to the floor, then put a hand to his forehead, the other still clutching at the quantum transceiver.

"Mom, is that really you?"

"Yes, it's really me." Through the buzzing and crackling of the transceiver, Matthew's mother's voice was exactly as he remembered it—low and sonorous, strong, but now with a slight quaver, making her sound as though she was going to burst into tears at any moment.

"Are you okay?" she asked.

"I'm fine, Mom. You don't need to worry about me. Tell me about you. What's going on over there?"

There was a long pause.

"I don't know, Matthew. I woke up not that long ago, and they brought me to this room with all these men and . . . and told me that I needed to talk to you. I thought maybe something was wrong, something at school. But then they said no, they said that you weren't in school anymore, that you'd signed up to . . . to fly across the galaxy? Matthew, is that true?"

"It's true, Mom," Matthew said. "But I did it for you, for the money, so you could wake up and get a cure for your cancer."

She let out a shuddering sound, and Matthew understood that she was crying.

"I never asked for that!" she sobbed. "When you said I should go into cryostasis, I said yes because you and your sister wanted it—but I never wanted this. I never wanted you to ruin your life for—"

The line went silent.

"Mom!" Matthew shouted. "What are you doing to her? Put her back on, you hear me? If you hurt her, I swear to God I'll—"

"Matthew," came the sound of another voice through the transceiver. This one was familiar, too.

"Soph?" Matthew shook his head, letting out a kind of desperate laugh. Beads of cool sweat formed on his forehead.

"Yeah, it's me." Sophie said. She, too, sounded exactly as Matthew remembered her. In the hundred years he'd been gone, she hadn't aged a day.

"Soph, what the hell is going on?"

"They froze me," Sophie said. "Right after you. They froze me and just kept me . . . kept me on file, until you landed."

"But what about the money?"

"There was never any money, Matthew," Sophie answered dully. "It was all a lie."

Matthew lifted his head and looked up at Dunne, who'd come around the table to listen to what was going on. Her face had gone ashen.

"What are you talking about?" Matthew asked.

"I'm telling you, they lied to us. If there ever *was* money, I never saw any of it."

The wrenching pain Matthew felt in his gut began to turn into something else. His eyes narrowed. He gripped the transceiver even tighter, until he thought he might crush it flat in his grip.

"The day you left for the Core to start your mission," Sophie said, "some guy came to the house. He said that he needed my ident to transfer the funds for Mom's treatment. But then when I held out my arm for scanning, he grabbed me and injected me with something. Next thing I know, I'm waking up in this strange place, they're telling me one hundred years have passed, and that I need to talk to you."

Matthew didn't say anything. He simply sat, stunned.

"Matthew, you have to listen to me. Are you listening?"

Matthew waited a moment before pressing the button on the transceiver. "I'm here."

"Look, things are bad over here. I don't know everything. But it seems we're in some kind of space station, orbiting Earth. Something's happened on the surface. Something bad. It's worse here than when you left. I don't know . . ."

Matthew waited. When it seemed that Sophie wasn't going to finish her thought, he asked, "What is it?"

"I don't know how much longer we can survive."

The transceiver crackled and buzzed. Matthew heard a rustling

356

as it moved from one hand to the next. A new voice came across the speaker. It was Alison.

"Matthew."

Matthew looked off to the side, pressing the back of his hand against his mouth as he felt his eyes begin to water. He shook his head.

"I can't believe this," he said. "You betrayed me."

"It wasn't my idea, Matthew. I . . . I didn't know."

"Don't say my name," he said, his voice sounding weak and pleading in his ears in spite of his efforts to project his anger across the light-years. "You don't get to say my name. Not after this."

"I'm sorry. Really, I am. You have to believe me. But you also need to listen, now more than ever. Look, things on Earth are bad. After you left, resources really started to get scarce. Not just oil and gas—basic stuff like water and crops. And about a year ago, the storms started. Huge sandstorms, over the entire face of the Earth. OmniCore crumbled. Billions died. The survivors had to go underground to stay alive. Communications are spotty, but we know they're down there."

Alison's voice cut off. There was a moment of silence, then the transceiver crackled and a new voice came on. A man.

"Matthew, this is Charles Keane," the voice said. "You know me, Matthew. I spoke to you on the day that you went into the freeze. I went into the freeze the same day. Do you know why I did that? Because I believed in you, Matthew. I believed in the mission. I believed that one of you would find a place for the human race to live."

Matthew tried his best to breathe slowly. He could feel his heartbeat in his temples.

"But my mother. My sister . . ."

"We had to do it, Matthew," Keane said. "The Exo Project was perfectly designed, but it had one flaw: after we sent people across the galaxy, how could we be sure that they'd fulfill their mission properly? So far away, traveling for so many years, you might forget about the human race. Lose perspective. That's why we had to keep your family alive. So you'd be invested in what was happening over here. The human race is surviving, Matthew—just barely, but we're surviving. And waiting. Waiting for something that could give us hope. Waiting for you."

Matthew didn't speak. He didn't know what to say.

"I understand that you're angry, Matthew," Keane said. "And I would be, too. But your mother and sister—they can survive. You can see them again. If the planet you're on is the one we've been waiting for, you can go back into cryostasis. They'll go into stasis, too. And when they arrive on the planet—when we *all* arrive—you can pick up exactly where you left off. You understand?"

Matthew pressed his lips together and breathed through his nose, trying to calm himself. "I understand."

"Good. Now can you put Dunne on? We've got someone who wants to talk to her as well."

Matthew looked up at Dunne. Her mouth came open and she lifted a hand to cover it, as if to stifle a sob—but Matthew could barely see her. His vision had gone blurry; there was a ringing in his ears. In shock, he set the transceiver clattering on the floor and dragged himself to his feet. Dunne crouched to pick it up and began speaking into it, but Matthew didn't hear what she was saying. He left her behind and staggered to the door.

Stumbling, Matthew made his way through the corridors of the *Corvus* and came out into the airlock. His breath came quick and panicked as he waited for the door to open, then he rushed out into the open air of Gle'ah. On the grass, he crouched and put his hands on his knees as a wave of nausea overtook him. He felt as though he might vomit. But the moment passed. Panting, he spat a single glob of foamy white spittle onto the ground, then pushed himself up to his feet. There was a rustle of footsteps behind him. He turned to see Dunne, her face streaked with tears.

"They've got one of your people, too?" Matthew asked.

Dunne nodded. "My grandson." Her voice was a thin croak, and Matthew understood at once that she had been weeping in the ship.

"How old is he?"

"Seven. Only seven." Dunne dropped her gaze and blinked the last of her tears into the grass. "He should have lived a full life. That money was supposed to be for him."

"What are we going to do now?" Matthew asked.

She pointed to the horizon. "I'm going," she said. "I'm going to the place Po told me about. The place where the maiora came from. I'm going to figure out what's going on here, once and for all. If we're going to bring Earth to this place, then I at least want to understand what it is we're destroying."

She turned back toward the airlock, probably to retrieve the speeder to go search for the maiora—but Matthew didn't follow her.

Instead, he stepped forward, further into the plain. His steps were slow at first, hesitant, but the farther he went—the farther he got from the ship, from the transceiver, from the voices of his mother and his sister and the manipulations of Charles Keane—the faster his steps took him. He didn't think about where he was headed. It was as though his feet had aims of their own. Soon he realized: he was walking toward the village.

Toward Kiva.

When he drew near to the village, when he knew that the crest of the next swell would bring him within sight of the clustered huts—Matthew broke into a sprint. He flew. He'd never run so quickly before. His legs churned beneath him, muscles burning, toes kicking up behind him with each step. He felt as though he was barely touching the ground.

And then, in the distance, at the foot of the hill that led to the village beyond: a figure. Distant, small, but unmistakably distinct from the sameness of the landscape.

It was Kiva. She lay in a cleft place beneath a small hillock, her eyes closed.

Matthew came to a halt a dozen paces away from her. He was panting.

On the ground, her eyes snapped open, and she sat up, her hand propped on the ground behind her. For a moment, they simply looked at each other.

Matthew gasped as the memory came surging back into his body.

Of course. This was the place. This was where they had met.

"You remember now, don't you?" Kiva asked. "You remember the dream."

Matthew didn't answer at first.

"Yes," he said finally, once he'd caught his breath. "I remember."

360

64

kiva

Kiva looked at Matthew's face and felt his mind across the space between them. She knew at once that something had happened. Something was wrong.

"So," she said, bending her knees toward her chest and grasping the backs of her thighs. "Your choice has come at last."

Matthew moved a few steps forward, his face gripped with pain. "Kiva, I—"

"And we're going to be enemies, after all?" Kiva asked—though it wasn't really a question. She knew. Somehow, she knew.

Matthew walked all the way forward and sank to his knees right in front of her. "It's my mother, and my sister, they—"

"Don't," Kiva interrupted again. "You don't have to explain."

Matthew's face took on a pleading look as he moved beside her. "It will be a while before they get here. One hundred years—one hundred seasons. Unless they've found a way to travel faster. Either way, I'll have to go back into cryostasis while I wait for them to arrive. But at least you'll have time to prepare the Vagri, for when my people arrive. And maybe when they get here and

I wake up, I'll be able to convince them to leave the Vagri alone. Let your people have their own little patch of land where they can live in peace. You'll be older then, or even dead—I'll still try. I owe you that much."

Kiva closed her eyes as Matthew went on talking. She wished he'd stop. Just a day ago he'd admitted that his people destroyed everything they touched—that they'd destroy her people and their way of life if they came to live on Gle'ah. Whether that happened tomorrow or a hundred seasons from now scarcely mattered.

But at the moment, Kiva was barely thinking of her people. All she cared about was that Matthew had chosen, and that he hadn't chosen her. Hadn't chosen them. He was ready to throw away everything they had together. Everything they might have been.

The more Matthew talked, the further and further away their moment of delicious freedom on the plain seemed to recede. Their stolen kiss, so far from the pressures of her people, and his. It seemed to have happened so long ago now, in a completely different world. Kiva wished they could go back to that world.

And so, finally, when Matthew would not stop talking, Kiva turned toward him, put a hand against his chest as she leaned into his body, and stopped his mouth with a kiss.

This time it was Matthew who was hesitant, his lips stiff against his teeth as Kiva pressed her mouth into his. Slowly, his mouth softened, then parted slightly, his breath coming more quickly in his nostrils.

Emboldened, Kiva took her hand away from Matthew's chest and stole it down under his shirt as she leaned further into him. Beneath the tight fabric, Kiva ran her hand up to his chest, then trailed her fingers back down again, to the tangle of black hairs just below his navel. Matthew's breath caught in his chest and he put his hand on hers, stopping it from descending any further—but not, Kiva noted, pushing it away from his body.

"What are you doing?" Matthew whispered.

"Pretending," Kiva said. "Pretending that I'm not the Vagra, and you're not a Stranger. Pretending that none of this is happening."

Matthew shook his head. "But it's not that simple."

"I don't care," Kiva said. "I've been alone ever since I had my first vision, right on this spot. It took me away from my family, from my friends. No one understood me, understood what I was going through. Then you came and I thought maybe it didn't have to be that way. That maybe I didn't have to be alone in this world."

"But it doesn't have to—"

Kiva wrested her hand away from Matthew's stomach and set her finger on his mouth. "Just let me talk. I need to say this. And you need to listen."

Matthew was still for a moment. He nodded.

"What you said about it feeling like home when you look at me—I feel that way too, okay? But it doesn't matter. It doesn't matter how we feel. Whatever happened out there between you and me, it ends right here, right now. When we leave this spot, you'll go back to your ship and do whatever you have to do, and I'll go back to my village and do whatever I have to do. And it will be over. So can't we just pretend, for a second, that it isn't happening? Can't we just be in this moment, before it all falls apart?"

Kiva stopped and waited for Matthew to answer, but he didn't say anything. Instead, he moved through the few inches of space that separated them and kissed her—softly, tenderly, his mouth half-open and tasting sweet on Kiva's tongue.

Kiva put her hand on his chest again and pushed him down until his back touched the ground. Then she threw her leg over his waist and straddled him, her knees settling gently into the web of grass on either side of his body, her dress creeping up on her thighs. She crossed her arms to reach down for the hem. Then she pulled the dress over her head and cast it aside in a single movement.

Matthew's hands rested on her hips and his breath caught in his chest as his eyes drank her in. For a slow moment they stayed like that, just looking at each other. Kiva saw a hesitation flicker across Matthew's face.

"What's wrong?"

"Do you really want this?" Matthew asked. "Do you really want *me*?"

Kiva frowned. "Yes. Don't you?"

"Of course!" There was a laugh in Matthew's voice, and he sat up and wrapped his arms around Kiva, buried his head against her chest. The air was cool, but his skin felt hot to the touch, almost feverish. "More than anything."

Kiva tilted her head back and closed her eyes as she felt Matthew's mouth move against her breasts. She reached down, fumbling for his shirt. Matthew raised his arms as she pulled the shirt off and threw it to the side.

Together, they fell back to the ground. Holding herself up on her forearms, Kiva kissed Matthew fiercely, pressing her tongue deep into his mouth. Matthew ran his hands softly down her back.

She let out a soft moan. When Matthew's hands reached her hips, he pulled her close and rolled her over onto her back.

For a few moments, they simply looked into each other's eyes. Kiva brushed Matthew's cheek with the back of her hand.

"Did you know this was going to happen?" Matthew asked. "Was this something you saw in one of your visions?"

She shook her head. "No."

"And yet here we are."

Kiva smiled. "Yes. Here we are."

She darted her head forward to seize Matthew's lower lip softly between her teeth, then sank back to the ground, pulling him with her.

They didn't talk anymore after that.

65

po

As Po walked to the village, the Great Mother began to sink low in the sky behind his back, throwing his shadow out in front of him. He watched the silhouette stride out ahead. He followed it, feeling for a moment—though he knew better—that the shadow was a sort of companion. No matter how quickly he ran, he'd never get ahead of it, never leave it behind. His shadow would be with him always.

Before he'd left the Forsaken camp, Xendr Chathe had called him into his dwelling.

"Kyne will require an answer," he'd said. "We must respond to her offer of alliance."

Po nodded.

"The woman, the Stranger," Xendr said. "The Vagra told you to bring her here?"

"Yes. Dunne. She has tools that can help us understand the maiora."

"Good," Xendr said firmly. "Perhaps the Vagra is right. Perhaps these Strangers can be useful to us."

"And Kyne's offer?"

Xendr raised his head to Po. "Tell her we reject her offer of alliance. Then go to the Vagra and tell her what Kyne offered to us. She deserves to know that she has a traitor in her midst."

Now, as Po walked on, he allowed his steps to slow as he thought about what would happen to him next. By rejecting Kyne's offer, Xendr was passing up the chance to move back to the village—but Po was determined to return to the village soon, one way or another. All Po had ever wanted since he was young was to have his own hut, to be chosen by one of the Sisters as a mate, and to raise children with her. As a boy, he'd dreamed that it might be Kiva who'd choose him to father her children—and he'd held on to that dream, stupidly, even after Kyne had used it to manipulate him into joining the Forsaken.

But he and Kiva could never be together. She was the Vagra, and now that Kyne's plot to overthrow her had failed, she'd always be Vagra.

Po knew this. But there was a part of him, still, that couldn't accept it, that still dreamed of Kiva's face at night, that still heard her voice, that still imagined what it would feel like to touch her and feel the warmth of her body pressed against his.

Then there was what she'd told him yesterday. Her words still echoed in Po's ears.

Po, when this is over . . .

I want you to come back to the village. Build a hut and plant a garden. Find a mate. Have babies. Have a life.

Kiva hadn't been talking about herself, Po knew that. But implicit in her words, Po thought, was the suggestion that if things had been different, if Kiva weren't Vagra . . .

Something moved at the top of Po's peripheral vision, and he flicked his eyes up, following the long line of his ever-growing shadow toward the horizon, where—

Kiva and Matthew. They lay together some distance outside the village, beyond the bottom of the rise, nestled together in the cleft of a small bump in the flatness of the plain. They were . . .

No. She couldn't. She wouldn't.

Po crouched down, fearing to be seen. He reached a hand off to one side and clutched at the tops of the grass as if for balance. His fingers ground the dry blades together in his palm. Anger surged through his body.

Could it really be her?

Po squinted and saw, unmistakably, Kiva's face over Matthew's pale shoulder, her eyes closed and her expression twisted into a look that could have been pleasure and could have been pain.

Po glanced off to the side and yanked at the grass that he had clenched in his right hand. The roots came out of the ground with a tearing sound. He cast the grass to the side. Then he crept away, keeping low, only standing once he'd come down the other side of the hill and was certain that Matthew and Kiva wouldn't see him.

Then he froze.

Another of the Strangers was standing before him. The other boy, the boy with the gun—*Sam*, they called him.

Po's fingers twitched at his side; he didn't have his weapon. Then he saw that Sam didn't have a weapon, either.

The boy's eyes flashed with anger all the same, and Po clenched his fists, preparing for a fight.

But Sam didn't run at him. Didn't attack. Instead, he flicked his gaze over Po's shoulder to the low hill that separated them from Kiva and Matthew—and Po understood at once that Sam had seen what he'd seen.

Sam spoke, said something that Po couldn't understand, then he opened his mouth wide and let loose a dark, mirthless laugh that made Po's blood turn to ice. Po backed away, fearful of what Sam might do. But he only turned and left, shaking his head and muttering to himself.

Po hurried back to the Forsaken camp. Now the Great Mother was in front of him, his shadow following rather than leading him. He couldn't see it, but he knew that if he turned around, it would be there.

In the camp, he made straight for Xendr Chathe's hut.

"Back so soon? What did the Vagra say?"

Po shook his head. "I didn't speak with her."

"No? What about Kyne?"

"I didn't talk to her either. Something happened."

Xendr's face darkened. He waited for Po to go on.

"Kiva. The Vagra. I saw her in the field just outside the village. She was with that Stranger boy—the one they call Matthew. They were . . . they were mating."

Xendr's hand tightened into a fist. He was silent, but Po could see his jaw working—tightening and loosening, tightening and loosening.

"You're sure?" Xendr asked.

"Yes. I'm sure."

Xendr blinked, looked down. "A Stranger," he muttered to

himself. "It's one thing to make peace with them, another to . . ."

His head snapped up and he gave Po a piercing stare.

"You understand what this means," he said.

"Yes," Po said. "My sister was right. Kiva's loyalties aren't with the Vagri anymore. She's unfit to be Vagra. We have to side with Kyne."

Xendr nodded and waved Po away. "Go. Gather the Forsaken. I want ten of the best fighters in the camp. Tell them what's happening. Tell them we leave at nightfall."

66

matthew

They dressed in silence afterwards, not meeting each other's eyes. Matthew pulled his shirt over his head and then stole a glance at Kiva as he pushed his arms through the sleeves. Fully dressed, she'd turned her back to him and was running her hands through her hair, pulling out tangles and bits of grass that had lodged between the strands.

After she was done, she stood and walked away, leaving Matthew behind on the ground.

"Wait!" he shouted after her, then scrambled to his feet to follow. "What are you doing? Where are you going?"

She kept on walking without answering. Matthew grabbed her by the shoulders and pulled her around to face him. She tried to pull away, her shoulders rising protectively toward her ears as if his touch were causing her pain.

"Just let me go," she said quietly, not looking at him. "Let me go. Please."

"What's going on? Just a minute ago, you—"

"Don't," she said, then loosened her shoulders and looked up

371

at him. Her eyes were wide and wounded, and Matthew bit at his lower lip, realizing for the first time the depth of the betrayal he was about to commit. Kiva would never forgive him. After he returned to the *Corvus* and called Earth to tell the truth at last, things between them would never be the same.

"Don't make this harder than it has to be," Kiva said. "Go back to your ship. Do what you need to do. This was . . ." Her gaze drifted down to the spot where they'd been lying together just a few moments earlier.

"This was what?" Matthew prodded.

Kiva smiled, but there was pain in her eyes. "We were just pretending, remember?" Her voice trembled. "Pretending that I wasn't the Vagra, pretending that you weren't a Stranger."

Matthew's jaw tightened. "I wasn't pretending anything. And neither were you. I know you weren't. Why can't we be together, the way we *really* are—no pretending?"

Kiva shook her head. "It's not that simple—you know it's not. You told me the same thing yesterday. I have my people, and you have yours. I have my responsibilities as Vagra, and you have your mission. You've made your choice. Now let me make mine. Let me go."

Matthew released Kiva's arm. She turned and hiked up the rise. Matthew stood and watched her as she disappeared over the other side, into the village, then stayed there a few minutes more, half-hoping that she'd come back and he'd get one more look at her.

After a while, he turned away from the rise and pointed his steps toward the *Corvus*.

Halfway between the village and the ship, the roar of an

engine cut the air. Matthew lifted his head. A few seconds later, Dunne came rocketing over the far hill on the speeder. She cut the thrusters and the speeder slowed. It came to a halt not far from Matthew. Dunne swung her leg over and dropped to the ground.

"I was just walking back to the ship," Matthew said. "I'm going to call Mission Control. I'm going to tell them—"

"I found something," Dunne cut in, as breathless as if she'd been running across the plain to intercept him. "You have to come see."

"But what about Earth?" Matthew protested. "They have my mother and sister. Your grandson."

Dunne shook her head. "They can wait. This is important. I need your help."

Matthew glanced at the speeder. The levitation couplings on the underside of the speeder glowed blue as the thrusters at the back cooled, giving off a thin stream of smoke into the evening air.

"Okay," he said, looking back at Dunne. "Let's go."

Dunne leapt back on the speeder and Matthew straddled the seat behind her.

"Hold on," she said, and Matthew put his hands on her waist just in time, a split second before she fired the thrusters and sent them rocketing toward the sunset.

kiva

Regret flooded over Kiva as soon as she came over the top of the rise and began descending into the village. At the bottom of the hill, she paused and looked back, thought about running over to the other side to see Matthew one more time.

But no. She continued toward the hut at the edge of the village where she'd grown up, and shook her head to herself. Best to keep moving. What was done was done. She forced her steps forward and picked her way slowly through the cluster of huts toward the center of the village.

Back on the plain, a fierce anger had risen up inside her as she'd gotten dressed, bubbling up into her throat from her stomach like bile. It wasn't Matthew she was angry at, not really. What was happening wasn't his fault. But he was the only person there, the only possible object to absorb her fury at the unfairness of it all. What they had together was real. But now, before it really started, it had to end.

Kiva thought about her options as she walked through the village. She could do what Kyne had been arguing for all along— go to the Forsaken and have them kill Matthew and the other Strangers before they called their people to Gle'ah. She'd have to move quickly; Matthew would probably bring the humans to Gle'ah as soon as he got back to his ship. But she couldn't bring herself to do it. She couldn't have him killed—not after everything they'd shared.

Her only other choice was to tell the truth, then spend the rest of her life preparing the Vagri for the day when the humans brought their millions, their billions, to Gle'ah. The humans had already destroyed one planet, but perhaps with Kiva's leadership, the Vagri could guide them toward a new way of living—a way of living in peace and harmony with the land, guided by the Ancestors.

It would be difficult—perhaps even impossible. If Kiva had learned anything, it was that violence, fighting, and conflict were always the easier choices when two peoples collided. If tensions erupted between her people and Matthew's, the Vagri would almost certainly be destroyed.

But Kiva didn't see that she had any other choice.

She had to call the Sisters together and tell them the truth about what was happening. That was the first step.

In the Sisters' camp, Kiva went to Rehal's hut. Pausing for a moment just outside the door, she heard her friend's voice, pitched at a volume that was unusual for the quiet girl.

". . . can't betray her! I won't! We must stay loyal to—"

"Loyal to who?" Kiva asked, walking inside.

Rehal's head snapped up. Thruss was inside the tent with her.

"Vagra," Rehal said. "I'm sorry, I didn't hear you there. I thought you were still with . . ." She paused, swallowed, and started again. "I thought you were still gone."

"I'm back now," Kiva said, looking from Rehal's face to Thruss's, which was flushed deep gray. "And it seems that something has been happening while I was away."

"The village is quiet," Thruss said. "Quieter than normal. You can see for yourself. People are afraid to leave their homes. When you brought the Forsaken and the Strangers here, it . . . it disturbed them. There have been rumblings."

"About me?" Kiva asked, then went on without waiting for Thruss or Rehal to answer. "Kyne's rebellion isn't over, then."

"Forgive us, Vagra," Rehal said. "We're sorry to be the ones to tell you, it's just that you've been so busy with the Strangers, and the Forsaken, and that boy, that—"

"Enough," Kiva said. "I'm not busy with the Strangers now, am I? With the Forsaken? The boy—do you see him here?" Kiva made a show of looking around the hut.

"Go," she said. "Both of you. Gather the Sisters. Tell them that I wish to speak with them. Tell them we meet at nightfall."

67

matthew

Matthew gripped his hands tight around Dunne's waist. His legs were clamped on the sides of the speeder so hard that his muscles began to ache. They hurtled across the plain at over one hundred miles an hour, moving gently up and down with the swell of the hills passing beneath them, the tips of the grass below whipping by mere inches from Matthew's toes.

They traveled for an hour without seeing anything but prairie, and Matthew began to wonder if that was all Gle'ah was—a dull but haunting sameness in every direction. Then, after an hour more, something else rose up in the distance, a single black point thrusting up into the air from the sea of grass. At first, Matthew thought it was just a tree. But as they grew closer, it rose still higher into the sky, and he realized it was no tree—it was too thin, too straight, too tall.

It was a spire.

Soon, other spires began to rise up around it, poking through the horizon one by one like needles through the underside of a balloon. Matthew drew in his breath as the whole city came into view.

It was a city unlike any Matthew had ever seen. Jutting into the air out of the flat landscape, it looked like a medieval metropolis. Limited in its growth by the outer wall that encircled it, the city looked to have grown upward rather than outward, the buildings culminating in circular turrets that loomed ever higher as Matthew and Dunne drew closer. The sun was setting behind the city in a blaze of brilliant red, illuminating a tangled web of flying buttresses and narrow walkways linking the soaring towers and spires thousands of feet above the ground.

Matthew and Dunne slowed as they drew near to the wall. Dunne circled the city until they came to an opening: a thick wooden gate that had been smashed to splinters.

"Does anyone live here?" Matthew asked.

She shook her head. "If they do, I haven't seen them. The city's abandoned. It's crumbling. It looks as though it's been standing here for hundreds of years. Maybe even thousands."

The speeder came to a halt outside the gate and Dunne swung her leg over the side. Matthew followed her through the opening in the wall.

They stepped onto a cobblestone street shaded by the looming buildings around them. Their footsteps tapped on the stones and echoed off the walls. Matthew paused and craned his neck as Dunne walked forward. He placed his hand on the outer wall of one of the buildings. Each one looked to be made of the same material, a light-colored stone that shone gold even in the fading sunlight.

"Come on," Dunne said. "Let's go before it gets dark."

Dunne moved so quickly through the streets that Matthew had a hard time keeping up with her. He followed her at a half run, but several times she slipped around the next corner so far ahead of him that he feared she'd be gone when he rounded the corner himself. The city was intricate, a dizzying tangle of streets and alleyways and open squares where stone fountains stood dry and crumbling to dust.

Soon, after they'd walked for about twenty minutes, Matthew noticed a change in the buildings and cobblestones. They were covered in a delicate white down that clung to every surface like mold. It began to bind to the bottom of Matthew's shoes. He crouched and reached his hand to the ground. He pulled together a small clump and worked it back and forth between his fingers.

"Maiora," Matthew said.

Dunne nodded. "Let's keep going. It's just up ahead."

She turned and walked around another corner before Matthew could ask where she was taking him, what was up ahead. He pushed himself out of his crouch and jogged after her. Around the corner, his steps ground to a halt.

Dunne stood before a square opening that had been cut into the street, right up against the edge of a building. There were steps leading down into the ground, under the building. On either side of the hole were flat, rusted pieces of metal—doors, by the look of them, though they were just pieces of scrap now, torn from their hinges.

"It's a bunker," Dunne said.

At the mouth of the bunker, the maiora was especially thick, clustered on the ground more than an inch deep. Dunne stepped over it and set her foot on the first stair, then descended inside. Matthew followed.

They came into a narrow corridor where there was so much maiora clinging to the walls that they had to hunch their shoulders to keep it from catching on their clothes. After a dozen paces the corridor opened into a small room with a metal door hanging off its hinges. This room was also clustered with maiora, but underneath the white substance Matthew could see a long, thin object sitting on the floor. He crouched and brushed the maiora away. It came off easily, and before long Matthew's palm was resting on smooth, rounded metal. The object was a thin, cold cylinder that came to a point at one end. At the other end were the circular openings of three thrusters. A small console panel with a blank screen and a half dozen small buttons was on the side.

"What is it?" Matthew asked.

"What does it look like?"

"A weapon," Matthew said. "A missile."

Dunne nodded. "Look at the other side."

Matthew looked and saw that the smooth metal of the missile had ruptured at a seam. The maiora was especially thick at the place where it had ruptured.

"It's broken. Is this where the maiora is coming from?" Matthew said.

"It seems so. Look. There are more."

Dunne nodded toward the wall, where under the layers of maiora, Matthew could see the shapes of more missiles stacked nearly to the ceiling.

They kept walking. At the end of the corridor stood a reinforced door.

"This is what I wanted to show you," Dunne said. She pressed a button next to the door and it came open with a hiss.

They went through the door into a long room that looked like a laboratory. In the middle of the room, a rectangular metal table was covered with beakers, flasks, burners, scales, and complex instruments that Matthew didn't recognize or know the purpose of, instruments constructed in odd, angular shapes and covered with smooth, insect-like exoskeletons. To the left of the table was a bank of displays and controls. On the far side of the room were the remains of a small living quarters: another table, a small chair, a few cupboards, and the frame of a cot, the fabric in the middle gone to tatters. The room wasn't covered in maiora, but everything was coated in a thick layer of dust.

Matthew wandered among the instruments in the laboratory while Dunne moved straight for the bank of displays. She pressed a series of buttons, and a recording came on one of the screens. The recording showed a man with the same gray skin as Kiva and her people. He was old, his face sunken and haggard. He sat in a chair and spoke into the camera. Over his shoulder were the same table and laboratory instruments Matthew now stood among.

"What is this?" Matthew asked.

Dunne turned. "What I wanted to show you."

Matthew listened to the recording for a few more seconds. "But I can't understand anything."

"You need to try. This may hold the key to everything."

Matthew shook his head. "Look, I can only understand Kiva.

No one else."

"I know that. But something's happened to you since you've been here. Maybe whatever—or whoever—chose you to be the one to communicate with Kiva also wants you to understand this. Maybe the Ancestors have some purpose for you here."

Matthew sighed as the man on the screen went on speaking in his alien language. "It doesn't work that way. I can't control the Ancestors."

"All I'm asking is for you to try."

Matthew came around the table and replaced Dunne in front of the display. He stared at it, looking directly into the man's eyes on the screen, and willed the alien words he spoke to turn into sense. The foreign sounds were a jumble in his head. But then, amidst the sounds, Matthew heard a couple words he recognized.

"*. . . death . . . Gle'ah . . . confession . . .*"

Matthew stepped back and tried to breathe slowly, fearing somehow that if he pushed, if he tried too hard, understanding would slip away. Gradually, the words in the recording clicked into meaning in Matthew's ears.

"*. . . Ilia's conquest seemed as though it would never end . . .*"

"I understand it," Matthew said softly, then louder, turning to Dunne: "I understand it!"

"*. . . happened centuries ago, before I was born. By the time I was a boy . . .*"

"Can you start it over?" Matthew asked.

Dunne pressed a few more buttons. The screen went blank, then lit up again as the recording started at the beginning.

Once again, the man's face appeared on the screen. He looked into the camera for a few silent seconds, then spoke.

"First entry, dated the seventh day of the fourth month of the season P.I. 3748. My name is Soran Thantos. I am a scientist of the city-state of Ilia, recording from my laboratory under the city. I have enough food and water for two months. After it is gone, I will die. Outside . . ."

Soran Thantos paused and looked off to the side. He put his tongue between his lips, and seemed to hold back tears.

"Outside is only death."

68

soran thantos

. . . I am recording because . . . well, I don't really know why I'm recording. Soon, all life on the planet Gle'ah will be gone, and there will be no one left to hear my voice. No one to hear my confession.

Perhaps that's it—I'm confessing. It's as good a reason as any, I suppose.

If you're listening to this, then life has found a way to thrive on this planet again, so please regard what I'm about to tell you as a cautionary tale.

Ilia is—*was*, I suppose—the most powerful city-state on Gle'ah. I learned of Ilia's glorious history when I was just a boy, forced in school to memorize the names of my city's heroes and the dates of their military victories. Over the centuries, Ilia's generals extended the city's empire over more than half the surface of the planet, conquering smaller cities and villages and forcing them to pay tribute in exchange for protection.

Ilia's conquest seemed as though it would never end—until our armies reached the foot of the mountains on the other side of Gle'ah. There, we encountered the Bakarai, mountain-dwellers who rebuffed Ilia's conquest by luring Ilian legions into the foothills and then ambushing them from higher ground.

All this happened centuries ago, before I was born. By the time I was a boy, the stories of Ilian glory were already lies, foolish propaganda that no one believed anymore. Everyone knew the truth—we were losing the war. Our armies had retreated into the plains, and the Bakarai armies—amassed in secret in underground cities dug out of the heart of the mountains—had begun to advance and take land that once belonged to us. With every step backward, our armies shrank; and with every step forward, the Bakarai numbers grew, as the farmers and villagers and city-dwellers who'd once paid Ilia tribute took up arms against us.

By the time I was a grown man and a respected scientist in the city, the Bakarai armies had grown so large that our defeat was certain. Our generals estimated that it would only be a few seasons more before the Bakarai circled our city and launched an assault against our walls. One day, Chancellor Ekto came to me and asked if I might quit my research into new medicines and cures for illness to work instead on a weapon that would rebuff our enemies.

I agreed. But now, there isn't a day that goes by that I don't regret my decision. It would have been better for Ilia to be crushed to rubble, better for my nieces and nephews to be murdered before my very eyes. To let that happen—that would have been the difficult choice. The *courageous* choice. But I took the coward's path.

As soon as I designed the weapon, I knew my mistake. I knew that what I had created would mean the end of all life on Gle'ah.

The weapon was a pulse beam—a wave of radiation that would rush outward from Ilia's outer wall and wash over the entire surface of the planet, gaining power with each life it took, each cell it destroyed, until every person, animal, and plant on Gle'ah was dead. Only the Ilians inside the city walls would survive.

But survive for what, with the rest of the planet dead?

I begged Ekto not to use the weapon, but on the night when the Bakarai finally came to our walls, shouting as they brandished their glowing light spears and fire swords in the air, the Ilians panicked and begged their Chancellor to do something. In a moment of weakness, he set off the pulse.

Now, our enemies are gone. But so are our crops. Ilia has descended into chaos as the citizens scramble for what few resources remain. They will starve soon—if the deadly radiation my weapon put into our air and water supply doesn't kill them first.

Billions of lives lost, all because of me. I should kill myself. If I were a braver man, I would. But I fear what awaits me on the other side of death—what hell the gods have waiting for me.

Enough confession for one night.

. . .

Second entry, dated the eleventh day of the fourth month of the season P.I. 3748.

It's morning. Last night I had a strange dream. I was walking outside, beyond the walls of Ilia in the wasted world I've created. Alongside me, hordes of people were staggering back and forth, stumbling toward death, their mouths crying out for water and their skin covered with sores. Only I seemed unaffected by the radiation in the air.

Then, in the distance, a cloud rose up from the dust of the ground and billowed toward us. Soon it surrounded us, and as the dust buffeted the people around me, I watched as the sores on their bodies healed and they suddenly became well again.

Just a dream. A silly dream. But now I keep thinking about putting something in the air—a cloud of something to offset the radiation and bring healing to those who are dying.

Maybe this could be my penance.

Maybe.

· · ·

Third entry, dated the twenty-first day of the fourth month of the season P.I. 3748.

You're probably wondering what P.I. means. Among my people, it stands for peace. The glorious era of Ilian peace.

It's a cruel joke now, utterly meaningless—if it ever meant anything. Today I went above ground and saw just how meaningless it is. I wore a suit to protect myself from the radiation, and brought a gun to protect myself from the people who remain.

The city is chaos. The streets are full of dead bodies. The stench of death is overpowering. Those who still live will be dead very soon. They stagger back and forth, barely seeing the world around them. They're blind to everything except their own pain, the agonizing effects of radiation sickness eating their bodies from the inside out.

While I was on the surface, I passed an old woman. She was sitting on the ground with her back to the outer wall of a tall building, weeping and asking me in a quiet voice for some water. I stopped and crouched to look into her eyes. There were hundreds of others just like her—but she reminded me of my own mother, and I wanted to help her. Her skin was covered in sores. I gave her some uncontaminated water from my canteen. Half of it dribbled down her chin, but she managed to swallow some. She begged me to help her and reached her hands toward me. I stood and backed away, left her pleading there on the ground.

Not everyone is so sick. Others are stronger. The radiation hasn't affected them too badly yet. They use their strength to take from those who are still weak, roving around in gangs that loot and kill. I have to be careful not to be seen when I come back down to my underground laboratory. If they see that I am here, they will break in and kill me.

Next time I venture out, I must be more careful.

. . .

Fourth entry, dated the twenty-seventh day of the fourth month of the season P.I. 3748.

I've done it. My research from before the war, my life's work—the search for the elixir of life, a cure for death and disease—is complete.

I went to the surface again today, with a small syringe of my creation. Careful not to be seen by the gangs, I went back to the old woman. She was still alive. Her pain must have been incredible.

I crouched in front of her and gave her a drink of water. She barely opened her eyes. Then I took her by the wrist, peeled back her sleeve, and injected my elixir into the crook of her arm. Before my eyes, in a matter of seconds, the sores on her skin healed and she opened her eyes.

She stared at me and began babbling crazily. I barely understood what she was saying. Her eyes were wild, clouded. It was almost like she wasn't seeing me—like my elixir was giving her some hallucination, some vision.

I backed away from her. She stood and grabbed at my suit. Her voice got even louder. Fearing that the gangs would hear her and come to kill us both, I tried to silence her, to calm her down, but it was no use. She went on babbling, louder and louder. Hearing footsteps echoing in the streets behind us, I fumbled with my gun and fired. The blast blew a hole in her chest, but her body stayed on its feet for a few nauseating seconds. Then she fell to her knees and crumpled to the ground.

I ran back here as quickly as I could. I hope no one followed me. A couple times I thought I heard footsteps on the cobblestones behind me. But every time I looked back, there was no one. I think I'm safe.

But I can't stop thinking about that old woman. The things that she was saying. They keep coming back to me. She seemed to know me, somehow—"It's *you*," that's what she said, "the one who destroyed everything!"

How could she have known that? Perhaps the elixir I've created does more than just heal—perhaps it brings powers of heightened perception as well.

The important thing is that my elixir worked. Now I just need to find a way to spread it across the planet, to vaporize the healing particles so they can spread and heal Gle'ah.

. . .

Fifth entry, dated the seventh day of the fifth month of the season
P.I. 3748.

I'm going to die.

The gangs on the surface have discovered my hiding place.
They know I'm here. They're attacking my door with a battering
ram, and once they come in, they'll almost certainly kill me.

It doesn't matter. I've taken steps to make sure that my creation
will get out into the world.

Before I designed the pulse beam, I invented a powerful
missile that could fly through the air and kill enemies far away. The
Chancellor ultimately rejected it as not being powerful enough
to defeat the Bakarai, so I kept on with my research. But I still
have prototypes of the missile stocked here in the lab, as well as
a prototype of the launching mechanism. I've laced each of the
missiles with my healing elixir. From here, I'll launch the missiles
into the air one by one, all over Gle'ah. When they land, the
explosion will vaporize the elixir and send the healing particles
into the air, where they will replicate themselves. From there, what
happens next is in the hands of the gods.

I've loaded one of the rockets into the launch chamber. I'll
launch it right after I sign off here. This will be my last recording.

I hope that this helps to undo some of the damage I've done.
I hope . . . I hope that the gods will forgive me for the death I've
brought upon this planet.

69

matthew

On the screen, Soran Thantos reached toward the control panel and pressed a series of buttons. The recording flickered, then ended. The screen went black.

Matthew turned to Dunne, who'd been listening to his halting translations as the recording played.

"I can't believe it," Dunne said. "All this. The radiation, the Ancestors, the Vagra. All because of one man."

Matthew nodded, his vision sliding out of focus as he tumbled headlong into his own thoughts.

"You know . . . ," he said absently, then trailed off.

"What?" Dunne asked.

"Something Kiva told me," Matthew said. "A story."

"A story?"

Matthew nodded. "Yes. It was sort of a . . . a creation myth, I guess. A story that explained how the Ancestors and the Vagri came to be."

"Tell me," Dunne said.

Matthew sighed and scratched softly at his cheek with one hand, trying to remember what Kiva had told him.

"Well, it began with chaos," he said. "That's what Kiva told me. That in the beginning there was chaos, and there was death in the air."

"That's what Gle'ah must have been like after the weapon went off," Dunne said. "Chaos. And the radiation in the air was killing everyone."

"Then she said there were these two people," Matthew went on. "First Mother and First Father. And First Mother wanted to have a family, but she couldn't because she was barren. Because of the radiation, I guess."

"Yes," Dunne said. "That could be one of the effects, yes."

"But then they saw a bright light in the air. And it hit the ground exactly where the Vagri village is now. And when First Mother went to check it out, suddenly she was healed. She could hear voices, and she could have children—and those children became the Vagri."

"That's where Soran Thantos's missile must have hit," Dunne offered. "And they must live in the blast site. In the crater made by the explosion. The place where the Ancestors are strongest."

"But what about everyone else?" Matthew asked. "When the Ancestors spread across the planet, they must have healed everyone else, too. Not just First Mother and First Father."

"True," Dunne said. "But I'm sure most people were dead by then. And society had completely collapsed, so even with the Ancestors, probably not everyone could figure out how to survive. Some of them would have become raiders, thieves—cannibals, even, to stay alive. I imagine the Vagri had to repel a lot of attacks, in those early days."

"Which is probably why they formed that warrior band. Even with the Ancestors, even though the society they made was peaceful, they still needed someone to protect them."

"Yes," Dunne said. "You know, there are probably more tribes on other parts of the planet, cultures that adapted to the Ancestors in different ways. The Vagri might not be aware of them, but I'm sure they're out there."

"So, how long ago do you think all this happened?" Matthew asked.

"Hard to say. The radiation from Soran Thantos's weapon will linger for a while. Could've been a hundred years ago, could've been a thousand. But based on the fact that the Forsaken haven't disbanded yet, there were probably still enemies around not that long ago. And judging by the size of the Vagri village, I'd guess at least five hundred years. That's enough time for the Vagri to grow to the size they are now—and for the other survivors in the area to band together into their own tribes and either get killed by the Forsaken, or retreat to their own part of the planet where they could be alone, like the Vagri."

"Five hundred years," Matthew marveled. "And they only just discovered the maiora now? Why?"

Dunne tilted her head back, toward the corridor they'd come from. "The door to that room with the weapons looked like it had been freshly torn off its hinges. The Forsaken don't have any more enemies to fight. Maybe they've started exploring places they used to ignore. Maybe they've just gotten bored."

"All those missiles," Matthew muttered, half to Dunne, half to himself.

"What about them?" Dunne asked.

"I don't know. It's just, Soran Thantos only got to launch the one. That we know of. But the rest are just sitting there, loaded up with the Ancestors. All that life, all that healing. Just waiting to be let loose."

Dunne put her hand on his shoulder. He looked back at her.

"Let's get out of here," she said. "It must be getting dark by now. Besides, I don't like this place."

She paused and looked around the room, then met Matthew's eyes again. She shook her head, less a deliberate movement than a shudder. "Too many ghosts."

.   .   .

They ran silently through the streets, their feet padding lightly on the cobblestones as the sun set at their backs. The shadows of the buildings grew long, and as they hurried together toward the outer gate, Matthew felt that they were running to beat the sun— that somehow, if they were still inside Ilia when night fell, they'd become part of the city, the two of them numbered among its voiceless, forgotten dead. A shudder trembled through Matthew's neck, and he ran faster.

They reached the speeder just as night came on. The sun sank below the horizon, and the stars began to blink on in the sky. As they climbed on the speeder and rocketed away from the city, the moons of Gle'ah lit their way, their glow falling silver on the gently rolling hills.

Holding tight to Dunne's back, Matthew looked out over the plain. It had looked so beautiful before. But something about it had changed, now that Matthew knew about what had happened there centuries before, knew about the billions of lives that had been snuffed out in a single instant. Gle'ah was still beautiful—but now there was a harshness to its beauty. An indifference.

He and Dunne and Sam, Kiva, his mother and sister, the Vagri, the humans back home—they were all so small. So insignificant. Gle'ah didn't care whether they lived or died. Neither did Earth. The universe would go on being beautiful and harsh in equal measure long after every living thing in it had died away—long after there was no one left to lament its harshness, no one left to appreciate its beauty.

Matthew buried his head against Dunne's back and cried quietly. He shed only a few tears into the fabric of her suit, but even that was enough. Those few paltry tears seemed to contain something that had been building up inside him for a long time.

They arrived back at the Corvus and left the speeder hovering just outside the airlock.

"What happens now?" Matthew said as he climbed off the speeder and set his feet on the grass. "We have to tell Earth the truth, right?"

"I don't know," Dunne said. "On that recording, Soran Thantos said we should take his story as a cautionary tale. Do you really think the human race is ready to learn from the history of the Ilians? From its own history, for that matter? Or will we just make the same mistakes in a new place?"

"We'll probably screw up this planet just as bad as we did the old one," Matthew said. "But the Exo Project has my mother and sister. Your grandson. Don't you want them to live? If they stay on Earth, they'll die. The whole human race will go extinct."

"The Ilians faced extinction too," Dunne answered. "They destroyed their planet, just like we did. But life found a way to go on. Maybe the same can happen on Earth. Besides, Soran said that to let his own family die instead of destroying the planet would've been the courageous choice. Maybe that's true now, too. Maybe calling the human race here and saving the ones we love is the cowardly thing to do."

Matthew gritted his teeth. "You have an answer for everything."

Dunne sighed. "Come on, let's talk about it inside."

Matthew nodded after a moment, and they walked together to the airlock. Matthew stepped inside, then Dunne.

"Matthew," Dunne said over his shoulder. It was just a single word, but the shock in her voice was palpable.

"What is it?"

"The gun locker. Look."

The locker stood open. The metal lid was bent and scuffed. On the floor next to it sat a rock the size of Matthew's head.

Matthew ran to the locker and went to his knees next to it.

The guns were gone. All of them. The locker was completely empty.

"Oh my God."

"What is it?" Dunne asked.

"Sam." Matthew whirled around. "We have to stop him."

70

sam

"Don't think of them as people. Think of them as targets."

Sam muttered under his breath as he strode across the prairie with a small arsenal strapped to his body: half a dozen grenades hanging from his waist, an automatic rifle slung from his shoulder, and the ion shotgun cradled in his hands. He flexed and unflexed his hands on the stock of the shotgun, then pictured the Vagri village with its gray-skinned occupants ambling unarmed from hut to hut—the men, the children, and above all the women.

"They're not people. They're targets."

The air was still. Sam's words resonated small but clear on the open plain. And yet, when the words came from his mouth and reached his ears, it wasn't his own voice he heard.

It was his father's.

.   .   .

Sam's father had been the one to raise him. They lived together in a decaying house in the forest. His father feared the city, feared the

OmniCore government—and so they hadn't left, not even after the sun grew hot in the sky and the forest withered around them. Instead, his father blacked out the windows and made radiation suits for them out of old scraps of cloth and rubber tubes and pieces of plastic from the barn. They survived on canned food Sam's father had been stockpiling since before Sam was born. And during the long days they spent trapped together in the cramped house, Sam's father taught him.

Taught Sam about the city: "It's an evil place, Sam. Full of greed and depravity. It's a monster that eats men whole."

Taught Sam about the government: "OmniCore turns citizens into slaves. It's a bunch of tyrants. And the tree of liberty must be watered by the blood of tyrants."

Taught Sam about people of other races: "Birds of a feather flock together. Stay with your own kind, Sam. Remember that."

And taught Sam about women: "Don't be ensnared by their beauty, son. They're evil at heart. A whorish woman brings a man to ruin."

Sam's father seemed to have a saying for everything—and when he delivered them, he was usually sitting at their kitchen table, pointing at Sam with his other three fingers wrapped around a whiskey bottle. On the table next to him sat a black leather book. Sam had the idea that much of what his father said came from the book, but he couldn't be sure, because his father never opened it, never read from it.

Sam once asked his father where his mother was, and his father had an answer for that too: "Ran off to the city with another man. But good riddance. Better to live in the wilderness than with a nagging wife. You remember that, Sam. When some woman tries to bewitch you—and they will, they always will—you remember it was your daddy who raised you, your mother who abandoned you. Don't you ever forget it."

One day, Sam's father also taught him how to shoot a gun. Packed Sam up in one of their homemade radiation suits and brought him to the barn, where he put a target on the far wall and a rifle in Sam's hands.

"They'll come for me one day, Sam. That's why you need to learn how to shoot. Because they're coming for me—and when they do, we'll need to protect ourselves."

Sam looked at the rifle in his hands and swallowed. He liked shooting at the target, but he couldn't imagine shooting at a person.

"Don't think of them as people," his father said, as if reading his mind. "Think of them as targets."

Sam's father had been right—one day men from the government did come for him. But they came at night, bursting into the house while both Sam and his father were asleep, and Sam couldn't get to his gun in time. They'd dragged Sam away screaming and crying; the last he saw of his father, he was being marched to a prisoner transport with his hands cuffed behind his back.

Sam was eight at the time.

"Your father did something bad, something against the law," the social worker said. "He got mixed up with some dangerous people, some anti-OmniCore terrorists. Do you know what that means?"

Sam nodded. The social worker was a woman; the skin around her eyes was soft, wrinkled.

"He's going to go to jail for a while. And you're going to live with a nice family."

Sam nodded again, but in his heart he hated the social worker. She was lying. His father wasn't bad. *She* was bad.

Sam visited his father in prison over the years. Each time he saw him, the old man seemed to grow weaker, smaller. And with every visit, Sam's anger grew—anger at the world that had broken a man he'd once thought unbreakable, the man who'd taught him everything he knew about the world.

Then, one day, his father had a request.

"The Exo Project," he said. "You should volunteer."

Sam was confused. "You hate the government. Why would you want me to help them now?"

"The reward."

Sam squinted. "One million units? What are you going to do with that in this place?"

"They've got a special reward for people with family in prison," his father answered. "The winners get a pardon, for anyone they choose. You could get me out of this place if you won. You don't want me to die locked up, do you?"

And then he'd started crying. It was a horrible thing, seeing your own father cry.

Sam had agreed.

.   .   .

He hadn't wanted to come. But he'd done it for his father. And now he was here.

This horrible planet, ruled over by women who saw visions,

and healed with their black blood, and kept the men as their slaves.

The others were blinded. They couldn't see what was in front of them. Dunne thought she could figure everything out with her tests, and her theories, and her pointless bustling around the laboratory. And Matthew . . .

Matthew had been enchanted. Sam had seen them together. Him and the witch. She was clouding his judgment. Blinding him to everything but his own desire.

It was up to Sam. Only he could save them.

They'd see. They'd all see. Soon, they'd know that he and his father had been right all along.

"They're not people. They're targets. They're not people. They're targets. Not people. Targets."

Sam tightened his grip on the shotgun and walked a little faster.

po

Po waited for nightfall in queasy anticipation. He stood just outside his tent, clenching and unclenching his hand around the handle of his spear, staring intently at the door to Xendr Chathe's hut.

Waiting. He hated waiting. He'd been waiting his whole life, it seemed—waiting to grow up, waiting to make his own life, waiting for Kiva to notice him the way he noticed her. Waiting for things that never came.

Now, when he closed his eyes, he saw them. Kiva and Matthew. Together. He couldn't get the image out of his mind.

He was tired of waiting. Tired of thinking. He wanted to move, to lose himself in action. He wanted to destroy something, to channel the pain that he felt and give it to someone else, to make the world hurt as he hurt.

Mostly, he wanted to finish what he'd started when he shot Matthew in the chest with an arrow. He wanted to put a spear in Matthew's gut and watch as the life bled out of his body. He wanted to look into Matthew's eyes and see the exact moment when he died.

Finally, the sun set. A few minutes later, Xendr Chathe came out of his hut, an animal skin draped over his shoulders, a spear in one hand. He looked at Po across the camp and nodded.

Po stood and quickly found the eyes of the nine other Forsaken men he'd recruited, huddled nearby around a campfire.

"Let's go," he said.

Together, they fell in step behind Xendr and made their way across the plains.

71

kiva

"Sisters!" Kiva shouted, then paused to look back and forth at the crowd that had gathered outside her hut. After she was sure that everyone was listening, she went on.

"I have spoken with the Strangers, and I have discovered why they journeyed across the stars to come to our planet. They are looking for a new home. Their planet is no longer a place that will sustain them. So they've sent their scouts ahead to see if Gle'ah would be a good place for their people to live."

"But Gle'ah is our planet," came a voice off to Kiva's side. Kiva turned. It was Kyne.

"The Strangers can't be allowed to live here," Kyne continued. "They must be stopped. We must kill their scouts before they can call their people."

Kiva clenched her teeth. Kyne certainly didn't waste any time. Kiva had expected Kyne to challenge her, she just didn't expect her to do it so soon. No matter. Now was as good a time as any to deal with her.

"You need to get out of the village more, Kyne," Kiva said, forcing a confident, dismissive smile. "Perhaps you've forgotten how big Gle'ah is. There's enough room on this planet for both of us—the Vagri *and* the Strangers."

Kyne sneered. "Is that what they told you? You're a fool if you believe that. The Strangers outnumber us. They're more numerous than the blades of grass on the prairie, and when they come there will be enough of them to fill a thousand villages like ours, and a thousand thousand after that. They've ruined their planet. And they'll ruin this one too."

A murmur of agreement rippled through the crowd. Kiva felt herself losing the Sisters to Kyne. Her arguments were difficult to respond to—especially since, as far as Kiva knew, everything Kyne said might be true. Even so, Kiva couldn't let Kyne take control. She couldn't let the Vagri kill Matthew.

Kiva put on the most contemptuous face she could muster and made sure the Sisters saw it, made sure they saw how little she thought of what Kyne was saying.

"You seem to know a lot about the Strangers," Kiva said. "Where did you learn all this?"

"The Ancestors told me," Kyne said.

Kiva shook her head. "Come on, Kyne, no one believes that lie anymore."

"I have a way of communicating with the Ancestors," Kyne insisted. "The Forsaken showed it to me."

Kyne turned and spoke directly to the Sisters.

"They call it maiora. They found it in a place beyond the plain, where it grows so plentiful that there is enough for every woman here. When you eat it, it gives you the power to communicate directly with the Ancestors. With the maiora and the cooperation of the Forsaken, we no longer need the Vagra. Now we all can have her power."

Kiva felt the Sisters' temptation at what Kyne offered, felt them gravitate toward Kyne's vision of the future.

"Sisters, the maiora is dangerous," Kiva said, trying to keep her rising panic from coming through in her voice. "Kyne isn't communicating with the Ancestors. She's hallucinating. What she offers you isn't power, but slavery. Slavery to the maiora and slavery to the Forsaken, who control it."

"No," Kyne said simply and softly—and the moment she heard this single, simple word, Kiva knew that she was in trouble. She knew that there'd be no recovering from what Kyne said next.

"Sisters, the Ancestors have shown me many things today through the maiora," Kyne said, moving in front of Kiva and speaking directly to the crowd. "I know things that the Vagra has chosen to hide from you. I know, for instance, that she had the opportunity to let one of the Strangers die, but she saved him instead."

There was a rumble of disapproval in the crowd.

"I know that she performed the healing ritual on one of them after my brother, Po, put an arrow in his chest."

The rumble grew louder.

Kyne turned to look at Kiva. "And I know that she has mated with one of them. With the boy who came to her hut yesterday."

405

Kiva held her breath. A shocked silence had fallen over the crowd. She closed her eyes and waited for the Sisters to erupt in cries of outrage.

But the cries never came.

What Kiva heard instead was the sound of a weapon firing, and agonized screaming coming from the edge of the village.

72

matthew

Matthew pushed the speeder across the plain as fast as it would go, praying that they would intercept Sam before he reached the village.

But they didn't. They were too late.

Matthew stopped the speeder at the top of the rise. Below, the village was in chaos. The bodies of a dozen Vagri men and children littered the ground near the edge of the village, some lying alone, others slumped atop each other, their limbs and necks bent at unnatural angles. One hut had burned to the ground; two more were ablaze.

"Where is he?" Matthew said. "Where's Sam?"

Dunne, seated behind him on the speeder with one arm wrapped around his waist, reached the other over his shoulder and pointed.

"There."

Matthew squinted and saw Sam. At the moment Matthew spotted him, he was throwing a grenade into a hut. Then he ran away, clutching his shotgun in his hands, scanning the village for a new target as exploding fire billowed through the door behind him.

"Go," Matthew said to Dunne. "Help the wounded. I'm going to stop Sam."

Dunne stepped off the speeder, clutching her medical kit under her arm. "How? You don't have a weapon."

"I don't know. I'll think of something."

He squeezed the throttle and zoomed down into the village.

kiva

Kiva ran toward the screams against a stream of Vagri men and children fleeing in the other direction.

If she'd had time to think about what she was doing, she might have asked herself why she was running *toward* a danger everyone else was running *away* from—but she didn't. The only thought in her mind as she darted between the huts was that her people were dying and she had to stop it.

Then she saw him. Sam stood in a small clearing, a triangle of open space made by three huts built close together. His gun was nestled firmly against his shoulder, roving this way and that as he searched for something to kill.

Kiva saw a flicker in Sam's eye and knew at once that he had spotted her. Her feet halted in the dirt at the edge of the clearing. The gun swiveled through the air to point directly at her. Time seemed to slow. Kiva looked down the eye of the shotgun's barrel; above it, Sam's eyes glinted with a mad, hateful glee.

Kiva knew she should run, but she couldn't. Her body wouldn't move.

Then, out of nowhere, an object rocketed through the air and slammed into Sam. It happened so quickly that Kiva could barely understand what her eyes were seeing, but in the blur she could make out the sight of Matthew straddling the object, which hovered above the ground.

The object struck Sam at the waist and bent him sideways. Then Sam's body snapped straight again and he flew to the ground. His gun slipped from his fingers and soared through the air. It landed between two huts as Sam writhed in the dirt in the middle of the clearing.

He didn't stay down for long. Sam pushed himself up from the ground and swung another gun from where it hung on his shoulder into his waiting hands.

Kiva dove behind the nearest hut just as Sam pointed the gun in her direction. The gun made a loud rattling sound; flecks of dirt sprayed her ankles as she dove through the air. She tumbled onto the ground and leaned against the rough wall of the hut, panting.

She inched around the base of the hut, searching for Sam. He was still standing in the clearing, the black gun trained toward the hut where she was hiding. He didn't see her—but if he came any closer, he would.

Kiva scurried back behind the hut, and as she did, something else caught her eye, motion just at the edge of her field of vision. She looked across the base of the clearing toward the other hut and saw Quint hiding there, waving her arms to get Kiva's attention.

Kiva met her sister's gaze and held her finger to her lips. Quint nodded frantically toward the ground between them. Kiva looked and spotted the gun Sam had dropped, lying in the dirt. Then she looked back at Quint, who was eyeing the gun feverishly.

Kiva shook her head and mouthed the word *no*. Sam was standing right there, waiting to shoot at anything that moved. If Quint went for the gun, he'd kill her—but Kiva might be fast enough to dodge his fire. If she could get a running start, roll to the ground as she grabbed the gun, and dive behind the hut where Quint was hiding before Sam had the time to line up his shot, then maybe . . .

matthew

Running into Sam had saved Kiva for the moment—but the collision had also sent Matthew flying off the speeder, rolling over the ground as the speeder crashed into a hut. Now, his ankle felt as though it were sprained, his ribs as though they'd been broken.

But he couldn't give up. Sam certainly wouldn't.

Matthew limped toward the triangular clearing, where Sam was stalking toward one of the huts, the automatic rifle in his hands.

"Sam," Matthew said as he came into the clearing.

Sam wheeled around and pointed the gun at him.

"I don't want to kill you, Matthew. I don't want to fight you and them at the same time."

"You don't have to fight anyone. Put the gun down."

410

Sam shook his head. "I'm done listening to you. You and Dunne. You've fallen under their spell. Her spell. I'm the only one who still cares about the mission."

"Really?" Matthew asked. "Is that what this is about? The mission? Is that why these people need to die?"

"It is," Sam said, his voice dull and dead. "It's the only way to break the spell. To break their hold on you. The only thing I don't know yet is whether you're too far gone. Whether you're going to need to die with them."

Sam lifted the gun a little higher, his grip tightening around the stock, his finger pulling lightly against the trigger. Matthew saw all this, saw the tension building in Sam's body, and felt certain that he was going to die.

Matthew held his hands out. "Look, I understand you're upset. But there's a better way. Just put the gun down and we can talk about a better way."

An arrow came whizzing through the air and pierced the ground between them. Sam lifted his eyes from the gunsight with a look of bewilderment just as another arrow flew through the air and pierced his arm at the shoulder. He bellowed in pain.

Matthew turned to see who had shot the arrows.

The Forsaken were thundering down the hill.

Matthew ran and dove behind a hut for cover as a volley of arrows rained down into the clearing. He huddled next to the wall and turned back to the clearing, praying that Sam had been killed by the Forsaken's assault.

But all the arrows had missed. Sam was still standing.

He seemed to be invincible.

Sam pulled the arrow from his arm and cast it aside as if it were nothing but a splinter. Then he raised the automatic to his shoulder once more and began laying down rifle fire on the hillside, his shoulder juddering against the butt of the gun as it rattled with each shot.

The *rat-tat-tat-tat* of the gun thundered in Matthew's ears.

73

kiva

The Forsaken didn't stand a chance.

Kiva saw it all from her hiding place—saw the Forsaken thunder down the hill toward Sam and Matthew, saw Matthew go for cover as Sam was shot by an arrow, then saw Sam turn and effortlessly mow down the Forsaken men on the hill.

Sam sprayed the hill indiscriminately, not even bothering to aim. One by one, the Forsaken fell, their spears and arrows dropping impotent at their sides.

Kiva had never seen anything like it. Who could stand a chance against weapons like these?

Kiva's eyes darted toward the gun lying on the ground between her and Quint, then back toward Sam.

His back was turned. Now was her chance.

She ran for the gun and picked it up off the ground, then pointed it at Sam's back. On the hill beyond the clearing, the Forsaken who hadn't gone down were falling back or scattering into the village. Soon, Sam's attention—and his gun—would turn back to Matthew or to her, looking for a new target. She had to act before it was too late.

Kiva aimed and fired.

The weapon screamed in her arms. It reared into the air and the back of the gun slammed into her chest. She flew backward, her spine crashing against the ground and her head tumbling back and hitting the dirt. She twisted in pain, her limbs sprawling, her vision swimming as she looked up at the stars. For a moment, she couldn't take a breath.

Kiva gasped, pushed herself up, and looked into the clearing.

She'd missed. The shot hadn't even grazed Sam—it had only alerted him to her presence.

Now, he towered over her and pointed his gun.

Kiva closed her eyes and waited to die.

matthew

"No!" Matthew screamed as Sam turned to aim the rifle at Kiva.

He ran toward Sam. His ankle throbbed with every step, but he pushed himself forward through the pain. He launched himself through the air and slammed into Sam's back, wrapping his arms around his chest and trying to hit the rifle away as they crashed together to the ground.

The ribs he'd broken when he was thrown from the speeder blazed red in his chest. The agony began in his torso and spread through his body, twisting his limbs as he rolled in the dirt. He ground his teeth together, willing the pain away—willing his body to move.

Matthew pressed his fists against the ground to push himself up. And then, all at once, Sam was on top of him, pressing him back to the ground, squeezing the air from his lungs.

"You shouldn't have done that," Sam said dully.

Matthew looked up into Sam's eyes. They were completely empty. There was no rage in them, no anger. Not even hatred.

Sam's eyes were simply dead.

Sam punched Matthew's chest twice, once with each fist. The pain of his broken ribs shot through Matthew's body like an electrical current, tensing all his muscles at once. His neck arched. He looked past Sam's face and into the sky. Tears pooled in his eyes, but he didn't scream. He couldn't. He had no energy left to scream.

Matthew felt his arms being pinned back under Sam's knees. Then he felt Sam's dry fingers curl around his neck and squeeze tight around his windpipe.

His vision went dim.

kiva

Sam had his hands around Matthew's neck. Matthew's face was turning red; his mouth came open and shut as he tried to take a gulp of air.

Kiva stood and picked up the gun again. Quint came out of her hiding place and started walking toward her.

Kiva shook her head. "Stay back."

Every part of Kiva was trembling. Matthew was dying. Sam was killing him right before her eyes.

But even though every cell in her body bled panic and screamed for her to hurry, she took her time. She breathed slowly through her nose, trying to still her quivering arms. She carefully lifted the gun and pressed the back of it hard against her shoulder, as she'd seen Sam do.

And then, so quickly and so quietly that Sam didn't have time to react, she walked into the clearing, put the gun to his back, and squeezed with her finger.

The gun roared. Kiva kept her feet.

And Sam slumped to the ground.

matthew

Matthew gulped air, his aching lungs filling with oxygen. His hazy vision began to clear. Things had gone dark there for a minute, but now the world was taking shape again around him. The sensations of his body returned one by one. Even the pain in his chest was a comforting sensation. He welcomed the pain, embraced it as if it were an old friend he hadn't seen in ages.

The pain meant he was still alive.

Gradually, he became aware of his surroundings. Sam was no longer on top of him. Matthew glanced over and saw Sam's body lying a few feet away—facedown, a pool of blood growing in the dirt around him.

Matthew turned over onto his hands and knees and vomited onto the ground.

"Shhh," came a whisper next to him. "It's okay. You're here."

He felt a hand resting warm on his back, rubbing softly back and forth. He looked away from Sam's body and saw Kiva kneeling next to him, the ion shotgun resting on her knees.

"What . . ." He sat back onto his heels and looked to Kiva with rising panic.

"It's fine," she said, putting her hand to Matthew's cheek and giving him a comforting smile. "It's not your blood. It's Sam's."

Matthew looked again at the gun across Kiva's knees, and Sam's bloody corpse on the ground nearby, and understanding washed over him. The air came out of his lungs in a rush.

"You saved me," he said. "That's the second time you saved me."

"No." Kiva ran her thumb lightly along the line of Matthew's cheekbone. "We saved each other."

Matthew let out a sound that was half laugh, half sob. Kiva's words burrowed under his skin and grew there, broadened and deepened inside him until they seemed to contain all the truth in the universe.

We saved each other.

"Kiva, I . . . ," Matthew began, not quite knowing what it was he wanted to say but feeling the need to say something anyway, to give voice to all the ways Kiva had saved him.

"I know," Kiva said, her voice thick in her throat. "Okay? I know."

Matthew's chin began to tremble. "I'm sorry. I almost threw it all away. I was so stupid."

Kiva shook her head. "Come on. You think you can stand?"

Matthew swallowed, collected himself, and nodded silently.

Kiva helped him to his feet. Matthew clutched at her hand even after he found his balance.

Then he heard the sound of footsteps behind him.

He turned to see Po coming around the hut at the top of the triangle, a spear held overhand above his shoulder.

74

kiva

Po threw the spear at almost the exact moment he came into view. Kiva had no time to raise the gun to her shoulder and fire.

Her next reaction was one of instinct. She didn't think. She just moved.

"Down!" she shouted.

She grabbed Matthew by the shoulder and pulled him with her as she crouched low to the ground. They ducked quickly enough, but only barely—Kiva felt the spear whiz by above her in a rush of air that rustled the hair at the top of her head.

As she crouched, she turned—and as she turned she saw that Quint had come out of her hiding spot behind the hut and was right in the path of the hurtling spear.

"NO!"

The spear caught Quint square in the middle of her chest with a sickening thud. Her feet flew out from under her as she fell backward. She didn't move.

Kiva ran toward Quint with a scream that felt as though it

was being ripped from her body. She knelt down and reached her hands toward her sister, but couldn't bring herself to touch her. Her hands hovered inches from Quint's body, her fingers splayed and quivering—as though by laying her hands on Quint or the spear she might make things worse than they already were. Quint's eyes were wide and glassy, her mouth hanging open as if in dull shock at what had happened to her.

For a moment, Kiva's mind couldn't fathom what she was seeing. This couldn't be happening. Lying before her, Quint's body seemed a foreign thing—it couldn't *really* be her sister lying dead in front of her eyes, could it? There must be some mistake.

She closed her eyes, ground the heels of both hands against them, then opened them again. Nothing had changed. The scene was still the same. Quint was still on the ground with a spear through her chest.

Kiva seized the shaft of the spear with both hands and pulled at it, trying to yank it from Quint's chest. At first, the girl's body came a few inches off the ground with the rising spear, then fell back as the blade slid free of her flesh. After the spear had come out of her body, Quint's black blood flowed fresh in the wound—so much blood. Panic bloomed in Kiva's stomach as she saw the blood pool in the hole in her sister's chest.

Frantically, Kiva turned the spear around and, holding it awkwardly near the tip, began slashing at her own hand with the blade.

"What are you doing?" Matthew asked from behind her.

Kiva ignored him and went on stabbing at the palm of her hand. When her blood began to run, she balled her hand into a fist above Quint's body and watched as the blood dropped on the gaping wound. She searched Quint's eyes for some sign of recognition, some sign of life as the Ancestors swarmed into the wound and brought healing to her sister's young body—but Quint's eyes only gazed lifelessly at the sky, catching the glint of the moons.

Kiva needed more blood. She turned the spear on herself again, now slashing indiscriminately at her hand, her fingers, her wrist.

"Don't!" Matthew shouted. He went to his knees beside her and grabbed at her hands. "You're hurting yourself."

Matthew's hands clamped around her wrists.

"No!" Kiva yelled, and tried to yank her hands free of his grip.

But Matthew was too strong. When she knew she couldn't overpower him, she let her arms go limp. The spear fell from her fingers. Matthew grabbed it, threw it away, to where she couldn't reach it, and seized her by the shoulders.

"It's too late," he said, turning her to face him. "She's gone."

Kiva let out a single dry sob as Matthew pulled her body toward his and squeezed her tight. Her back was stiff, resisting Matthew's embrace—but after a few seconds she let her body soften and go limp.

She closed her eyes and wept. The sobs shook her body like convulsions, like a seizure—she'd never cried so hard in her entire life. Matthew just went on holding her. Tears slipped between her eyelids and ran down her cheek to her chin, then dropped onto Matthew's shoulder.

Soon, Kiva's eyes opened again. Still slumped in Matthew's arms, she looked over his shoulder into the clearing. Her vision was wobbly as the tears cleared from her eyes—then it became clear, and she saw them.

Po. He was still, rooted to the spot where he stood.

And Kyne. She stood at the edge of the clearing, her face filled with shock at the scene she'd come upon, one hand lifted to her open mouth.

"You!" Kiva said, her anguish turning instantly into a fury that filled her whole body.

She pushed Matthew away and stood. She walked into the clearing, knelt to pick up the gun, then went toward Po and pressed the end against his chest.

Po made no move to run or push the gun away from his body. His face showed a despair that was even deeper, perhaps, than Kiva's own.

Behind Po, another Forsaken man walked into the clearing. His shoulders were covered by an animal skin, and he held a spear in one hand. As he surveyed the scene in the clearing, his jaw hardened, his eyes taking on a steely look.

He met Kiva's gaze, and though she'd never met him before, she knew immediately that she was looking at Xendr Chathe. He nodded at her.

"Do it," he said. "Take your vengeance. I won't stop you. This is not why we came here—to kill little girls. This is not our way."

Kiva looked back to Po's face and willed him to meet her gaze. She wanted to look into his eyes before she killed him.

But he wouldn't look at her. Po wouldn't meet her eyes— instead, he looked over her shoulder at Quint's dead body. As Kiva looked into Po's eyes looking glassily beyond her own, she knew that this image would be with him for the rest of his pitiful life: the image of the little girl he'd killed, a gaping hole in her chest from where he'd pierced her body with a spear.

Kiva tried to feel again the rage that had coursed through her body only moments before. But she couldn't. It was bleeding away, replaced by something else.

"Go on," Kyne said from the edge of the clearing. "Kill him. Get it over with."

Kiva loosened her grip on the shotgun and let it fall to the ground.

"No," she said. "Too many have died today."

She turned and walked away from Po and Kyne and Xendr, back toward Matthew and Quint's body.

"We will punish him," Xendr's voice said from behind her. "We will see that you have justice."

Kiva turned back and shook her head at Xendr. "No justice can come of this," she said. "Death is too good for him. The real punishment would be to let him live."

Xendr didn't say anything to that, but Kyne walked into the clearing and stepped between Po and Kiva.

"This is your fault, you know," Kyne said. "Yours and that boy's." She nodded past Kiva toward Matthew. "If it weren't for what you did, none of this would have happened."

"No," Kiva said, "it's not. It's his fault." She nodded at Sam's bloody corpse on the ground, then toward Po. "And his."

She looked at Kyne for a few moments, daring her to contradict her.

"And yours," Kiva said. "This is your fault too. With your

scheming, and your plotting. Dreaming up ways to undermine me, to make war with the Strangers. When all *we* did was try to imagine another way."

Kyne's lip curled. "Even so," she said, "you can no longer live in this village. You can no longer be Vagra. Take your dead. Take your Stranger, if you want. We'll let you go in peace. We owe you that much. But you must go."

"But this is my home," Kiva said. "These are my people."

Kyne shook her head. "Not anymore. Not after this."

75

matthew

"We're leaving," Kiva said when she came back toward Matthew—toward Quint's dead body.

"What?" Matthew asked.

"We're leaving," Kiva said again. "They're banishing me. I can't live here anymore."

"Why? You didn't do anything wrong."

"It doesn't matter. It just—it doesn't matter."

Matthew put his lips together and swallowed. A sick feeling washed over his body. Why should Kiva be punished for what Sam and Po had done?

But Kiva herself seemed calm, emotionless—empty, even. Her face was dazed; her eyes, as she looked at him, were distant and detached.

"Okay," Matthew said. "Do you want to get anything before we go? Anything you want to take with you?"

"No," Kiva said firmly, shaking her head. "Only her."

She nodded toward her sister's corpse.

Just then, Dunne walked into the clearing with her medical kit tucked under her arm.

"Most of the wounded were beyond saving," Dunne said, "but I managed to patch up a few—"

Dunne stopped talking when her eyes fell on the carnage in the clearing: on Quint's body, and Sam's.

Matthew explained to her what had happened. Together, they gathered up Sam's guns, then went to retrieve the speeder from where Matthew had crashed it. They managed to get it hovering again—but its thrusters wouldn't fire. Matthew cradled Quint's body onto the seat, and they pushed it to the edge of the village.

They walked back to the Corvus like that, Matthew pushing Quint's body on the hovering speeder, Kiva and Dunne walking behind. When they reached the ship, Matthew went inside, got the transceiver, and brought it back out to Dunne and Kiva.

"What are you going to do?" Dunne asked.

Matthew didn't answer. He pushed the button on the side and spoke into the transceiver.

"Come in, Control," he said. "This is Corvus."

"Copy, Corvus. We read you loud and clear. What's your report?"

"Sam's dead. He was killed by . . ." Matthew paused and looked at Dunne and Kiva, thinking of all the damage that had been done as a result of three humans landing on Gle'ah—all the violence, all the death, all the pain and grief. How much more damage could a thousand, a million, a billion humans do?

"The radiation killed him," Matthew said at last.

The transceiver was silent for a few moments before crackling back into life.

"Roger, *Corvus*," Alison said. "Are you telling us that H-240 is a negative planetary match?"

"That's right, Control."

"And what about you and Dunne?"

"We're sick too. We don't have much longer. We're going to take the suicide pills. This will be our last communication."

There was no response.

"Tell our families . . . ," Matthew began, meeting Dunne's gaze as he spoke. "My mother and my sister. Dunne's grandson. Tell them we're sorry. Tell them we wish we could've found a place where we all could've been together again. More than anything. But it just wasn't meant to be."

Dunne nodded slowly.

"We'll tell them, Matthew," Alison said. "I promise. I'm sorry it had to end this way. Good luck and Godsp—"

Matthew put the transceiver on the ground and stomped it under his boot until he felt it smash to bits. Every time he brought his foot down he felt a ripping pain inside himself, as if the transceiver were a part of his body. He thought of his mother, of his sister—he'd never see them again, never hear their voices.

After what had happened in the village, after what Sam had done, smashing the transceiver felt like the right thing to do. But it still hurt.

When Matthew raised his head, his eyes were blurry with tears. He blinked them away and saw Kiva.

She faced away from him, standing on the crest of a small hill and looking into the far distance. She'd stayed quiet since leaving the village; on the walk to the *Corvus* she'd trailed behind Matthew and Dunne, looking at her feet as she trudged through the grass. She seemed to have retreated inside herself—and looking at her now, Matthew wondered if the real Kiva would ever come back out. If perhaps part of her had died with her sister in the village.

He walked up behind her and gingerly put a hand on her shoulder.

"Kiva?" he said.

She turned.

"Are you—are you going to be all right?"

"We have to go," Kiva said as if she hadn't heard Matthew's question. She pointed to the horizon—away from the village, away from the *Corvus*, away even from the place where the Forsaken camp and the city of Ilia lay.

Matthew looked to where she was pointing. The grass stretched out as far as he could see.

"Where?" he asked.

"I don't know," Kiva answered. "I'll know when we get there."

Something in her voice told Matthew not to question her any further.

. . .

They walked through the night and into the morning, and as they trudged through the grass—Matthew and Dunne on either side of the speeder while Kiva strode out ahead—the sick feeling that had come over Matthew in the village got worse and worse. He glanced down at the body of the dead girl on the speeder, her spine balanced on the seat as her arms hung limply to either side.

It should have been me.

The thought came from nowhere, but he felt immediately that it must be right. It should be *his* dead body on that speeder. If it weren't for him—if Kiva hadn't saved him—then maybe Quint would still be alive. If only they'd never come to Gle'ah—

"Matthew," Kiva said a few steps in front of him.

Matthew raised his eyes. Kiva looked back.

"Come up here," she said. "Come walk with me."

Matthew looked at Dunne. She nodded at him across the speeder—she could push it on her own for a while. Matthew ran forward and drew up beside Kiva.

"What is it?" he asked.

"You can't let yourself think that," she said.

"Think what?"

"That it was your fault."

Matthew sighed and looked ahead.

"But it is my fault," he said. "If I'd never come here, then Quint would still be alive. You'd still be Vagra."

Matthew felt Kiva slip her hand into his. Her fingers laced between his, she tugged at his arm, pulled him back to her. He turned his head.

"But if you'd never come, I'd never have met you," she said.

Matthew felt as though something in his chest were breaking.

"Is that enough, though?" he asked. "Enough to make up for everything else?"

"I don't know," Kiva said, and smiled the saddest smile Matthew had ever seen. "It will have to be enough. We'll have to make it enough."

They walked on in silence for a few more steps, then came to

429

the top of a hill—and Kiva stopped and said, "We're here."

Matthew looked down. They'd come to a long, low place in the prairie, bordered at one end by the hill they stood on and at the other end by a gentle ridge. At the edge of the ridge was a single jagged tree reaching up into the sky—leafless and dry.

Kiva reached out her arm and pointed at the tree.

"There," she said.

"There what?" Matthew asked.

"There is where we're going to bury Quint."

76

kiva

Matthew dug the grave at the foot of the tree while Kiva and Dunne looked on. Then he and Dunne laid Quint's body in the hole and covered her with dirt.

They were on their knees, patting the soil smooth, when Kiva heard the rustling in the grass at the bottom of the hill.

"Who's there?" she shouted, fear fluttering in her chest.

But when the grasses at the bottom of the hill parted, it was only Grath and Liana who came through and walked up toward the tree at the top of the ridge.

Kiva breathed out. "What are you doing here?" she asked.

Liana stepped forward. "We tracked you across the plain all night," she said. "We couldn't stay in the village. Not after what happened. Not after—"

Liana abruptly stopped talking as her eyes looked over Kiva's shoulder to the freshly turned soil of Quint's grave.

"Is that . . . ?"

Kiva nodded, then stepped aside as Liana walked toward the grave. Her mother sank to her knees beneath the jagged branches of the tree, then reached forward and put her hand flat on the dirt. Kiva couldn't see her face, and Liana didn't make any sound—but her shoulders quaked, and Kiva knew at once that she was crying.

Grath walked up behind Liana and put a hand over her shoulder, draping his fingers across the soft of her throat. Liana reached up and clasped his hand in both of hers, then leaned back into him.

Kiva had been numb since leaving the village—but now, watching her parents weep over her sister's grave, her tears began to flow again.

The pain of losing Quint would hurt for a long time. It might never stop hurting.

Grath turned. "Vagra, will you say the words?"

Kiva shook her head. "I'm not the Vagra anymore. I'm Kiva again. Just Kiva."

"Even so," Grath said. "Someone should speak."

Kiva's eyes came closed for a long moment, then opened again. She bowed her head.

"Every death contains within it the seeds of a rebirth," she began, squinting as the light of the Great Mother began to crest over the prairie. "Every end is a beginning."

. . .

After, they drifted apart—Dunne wandered off through the hills, as Grath and Liana walked down into the valley. Matthew paced slowly away from the tree, skirting the ridge, then sat on the ground, his arms resting on his bent legs as he looked down into the valley.

Kiva walked up behind him, the grasses rustling underneath her feet.

Matthew half-turned but didn't say anything.

"May I?" Kiva asked.

"Of course," Matthew said.

Kiva sat beside him and studied his face. He looked intently in front of him, his eyes fixed on the empty prairie as if some apparition, some vision, were appearing to him there.

"What do you see?" Kiva asked.

"Hmm?" Matthew asked, coming out of his daydream. "Oh. Nothing."

"Tell me," Kiva said.

Matthew let out a sigh.

"I was just thinking about what you were saying over your sister's grave. What was it?"

"*Every death contains within it the seeds of a rebirth,*" Kiva recited. "*Every end is a beginning.*"

Matthew nodded. "Yeah, that's it. Do you really believe that? Do you think it's true?"

Kiva looked out and shrugged. "I don't know. I hope it is."

"Me too," Matthew said. "I was also thinking about that story you told me, about First Mother and First Father."

Kiva squinted. "Yeah? What about it?"

"Well," Matthew began, angling his eyes into the space between them, "they made a life out of chaos, didn't they? Out of death. Together, they started something new."

Kiva didn't say anything.

"And I'm thinking—well, maybe we can do that too. Start something new. Our own village. Our own tribe. One where things are different."

Kiva looked down into the valley where Grath and Liana wandered shoulder to shoulder, speaking softly to one another—and immediately she felt the rightness of what Matthew was saying.

She was sad, still, about what had been, and afraid of what might come—but Kiva was hopeful, too: hopeful that this place might be better than the places that she and Matthew had left behind.

She looped her arm through Matthew's elbow and pulled him close. She set her head on his shoulder and looked out with him on the vast, empty plains of Gle'ah.

"Yes," she said softly. "Yes, I think that's exactly what we'll do."

PART 6

THE FLIGHT
OF THE
CORVUS

77

kiva

She woke that morning before the dawn.

Normally Kiva was a late sleeper, Matthew an early riser—and in the months since they'd begun sharing a bed, Matthew had learned how to get up in the morning and slip out of their hut without waking her.

But on this particular day, as Matthew rose quietly from the bed, Kiva was already awake, lying on her side with her face toward the wall. She closed her eyes and listened to Matthew's movements as he slipped his clothes on in the darkness and splashed his cheeks with tepid water from the clay bowl in the corner. When the sound of splashing water had stopped, Kiva turned over onto her other side and watched him mop his face with a dry cloth, then sat up when he walked to the doorway.

"You aren't even going to say good-bye?"

Matthew looked back toward the bed.

"I thought you were asleep," he said. "I didn't want to wake you."

"You didn't," Kiva answered. "My back hurts."

Kiva stretched forward, wincing into the pain. Then she sighed and set her hands on the shelf made by the curve of her pregnant belly, her body aching and swollen with the weight of the life that grew inside it.

Matthew crossed the hut and, still standing, leaned over the bed, propping himself up with one hand while he hooked a finger under Kiva's chin with the other.

"I'm sorry your back hurts," he said.

He gave her a long, slow kiss. Kiva closed her eyes, then tucked her lower lip between her teeth as Matthew rested his forehead against hers.

"You're going to the ship?" she asked.

"Yes."

Kiva opened her eyes and put her hands on Matthew's cheeks, tilting his head to look directly into his eyes.

"Be careful," she said.

Matthew nodded. "I will."

He went to the door, then paused again with his hand on the frame. "I'll be back soon."

Then he was gone.

matthew

The sun hadn't crested the horizon yet, but its glow was already beginning to warm the dark edge of the sky as Matthew walked quickly through the camp toward Dunne's hut.

She was waiting for him just outside her door.

"You're up early," Matthew said.

"Couldn't sleep," she said. "Today's the day, right?"

Matthew nodded. "It is. Everything's ready."

"You want company?"

Matthew shook his head. "No. This is something I need to do alone."

"Take the shotgun."

Matthew grimaced. "I don't want to."

"Well, I'm going to insist, and you need to respect your elders," Dunne said.

Matthew laughed and nodded his assent.

He grabbed the ion shotgun from where it leaned against the outer wall of Dunne's hut, then climbed on the speeder. He and Dunne had managed to fix the damage done during the battle with Sam, but the speeder had never been quite the same. Now the steering was, in Dunne's word, persnickety, and the thrusters couldn't push the speeder as fast as it had gone before. Still, it was the best and quickest way to travel across the plains of Gle'ah.

Matthew hit the throttle and shot out across the grass. He leaned left, then right, feeling the way the speeder responded to his shifting weight. Then he glanced at the navigation display under his nose and corrected course, pointing the vehicle's nose toward the Corvus.

kiva

Kiva lay in bed for a while after Matthew left, but when the Great Mother rose and began to curl her golden tendrils across the floor, Kiva rose and padded to the door.

She leaned against the doorframe and surveyed the small village before her. There were only a handful of huts scattered here and there, but more were built with each passing month, as more and more Vagri left the old village to join the new settlement.

Grath and Liana had been among the first to settle in the valley. They'd never gone back to the old village; instead, they built a new hut in the valley shortly after Kiva told them that she and Matthew had decided to stay there. Thruss and Rehal joined them some time after that, along with half a dozen other young Sisters and young men—ones who hadn't yet chosen mates or borne children. They came bearing news of how bad life in the village had become. Kyne's promise of a community made equal by the maiora hadn't come to pass—if anything, power and influence were even more concentrated among a lucky few. Kyne was technically the new Vagra. But she was just a figurehead, Thruss said. Xendr Chathe was the one who really ruled. He had weapons, he commanded the Forsaken—and he also knew how to find the maiora, which had become a kind of currency among the Vagri.

In the new village Kiva and Matthew had founded, life was different—and, for the time being, better. From the doorway, Kiva looked to Dunne's hut at the edge of the village. Nearby, most of the villagers were busy tending a vegetable garden. Grath bent over the dirt with his hoe, then paused and pointed as he gave some instructions to Liana and Rehal, who were working a few rows over.

Kiva smiled. Though they all worked the soil now—women and men toiling side by side, with no official leaders—Grath was effectively in charge of the garden. Perhaps, one day, he'd teach the new children of the village to bring life out of the dirt as well.

Kiva walked through the village. She ambled slowly past the garden, smiling and nodding to the workers as she went by. Beyond Dunne's hut, at the foot of the ridge marking the unofficial border of their new village, Kiva paused for a moment, ambling around the bottom of the hill with her eyes on the ground. Soon, she paused and crouched, picked up a rock the size of her fist. She stood and weighed the rock in her hand for a moment. Then she began to hike up the ridge to the tree, the place where they'd buried Quint's body.

The tree, dead when they'd first arrived, had begun to bloom. Tiny white flowers and a smattering of red leaves quivered in the wind at the tips of the jagged branches. Below, Kiva stepped into the tree's paltry shade and looked at the place where her sister's body lay.

There was a small pile of rocks on the grave, a cairn heaped to Kiva's knees. Each morning since they'd buried Quint, Kiva had returned to this place with a rock in her hands to mark the spot. She'd built the cairn day by day, stone by stone. And now, she leaned forward and placed the rock she'd picked from the bottom of the hill on the top of the pile. The capstone.

Kiva knelt and put her hand on the cairn. She closed her eyes. Sighed deeply.

And thought of the dead.

78

matthew

Matthew moved quickly when he reached the *Corvus*, wanting to finish what he'd come to do and leave again as soon as possible. Though Kyne and Xendr Chathe hadn't technically claimed any of the prairie as their territory, Matthew felt as though he was treading on contested ground whenever he neared the ship. The *Corvus* wasn't far from the old village, and he didn't know what would happen if he encountered one of the Forsaken out on patrol.

He opened the airlock and went inside, making straight for the control room. He sat in front of the computer and with a few taps at the keys brought the system online and called up the navigational program that he and Dunne had written.

The two of them had been coming here together every few days, experimenting with the ship's various systems and trying to figure out how they could program it to fly back to Earth. For a long time, they didn't get anywhere, but then they found some ship manuals on the computer's hard drive—though even then, Matthew couldn't understand most of what he was reading, especially when it came to the complex physics of the lightspeed drive. But Dunne, though she protested ignorance, was a quick study, and she'd soon devised a way to send the *Corvus* home.

Matthew knelt and checked the wires connecting the computer to the missile on the floor. It was one of Soran Thantos's, taken from his laboratory bunker under the streets of Ilia. Though Dunne and Matthew couldn't decipher the missile's controls, understanding its detonation mechanism was easy enough once they'd cracked open the casing and taken a look inside. Then they'd managed to rig the warhead to explode when the *Corvus* entered Earth's atmosphere and the computer initiated the landing sequence—spreading the Ancestors across the sky. If there was any life left on Earth when they arrived, the Ancestors would help it to live and thrive and grow into something new.

Something better.

Matthew moved back to the computer. His forefinger paused above the control panel. His heart thundered in his chest. He pressed a button and started the program.

"Initiating takeoff in two minutes," a computerized female voice echoed throughout the ship.

Matthew walked from the control room to the airlock, then stepped outside and closed the door behind him. He ran clear of the *Corvus* and turned back to watch from beside the speeder.

The thrusters fired. Smoke billowed out from the base of the *Corvus*. The sound was deafening. The grass surrounding the ship burst into flames. Soon, the ship lifted off the ground and accelerated into the sky with a ground-shaking roar.

Matthew lifted his arm to block the sun from his eyes as he watched the *Corvus* shrink to a dot in the sky. For a moment, it disappeared entirely. Then, there was a bright flash of thunderless lightning as the lightspeed drive fired.

Matthew breathed a sigh.

He'd done his part. The rest was up to the Ancestors.

He climbed on the speeder and pointed it home.

kiva

Kiva lay on the hill below her sister's cairn, her fingers laced behind her head as she gazed up at the sky.

She listened.

This was how it had all started. Lying in the grass and listening.

Kiva was no longer the Vagra, but she still had the power of the Ancestors. She could still sense the minds of others. She could still feel their emotions and hear their thoughts.

But she hadn't had a vision for a long time. She had no sense of what the future might hold. Perhaps not even the Ancestors knew.

She and Matthew talked about the future often, worried deep into the night about what might be waiting for them and their new people.

Would the Vagri and the Forsaken allow them to live in peace? Or would those who lived in the old village come to regard the new settlement as a threat?

And Earth—did they believe Matthew when he said that they shouldn't come to Gle'ah? Would they stay away, or were they planning a new expedition even now?

Kiva couldn't say.

She took her hands out from behind her head and set them on

her belly, thinking of the life—half-Vagri, half-human—growing inside her.

She'd name the baby Quint. That much Kiva could say with certainty: that whether her child, the firstborn of a new world, was a boy or a girl, she'd name it after the one who'd died so that world could be born.

The rest was unknowable.

Kiva sat up and looked toward the horizon, waiting for Matthew to return.

It wouldn't be long now.

acknowledgments

Thank you to . . .

Mary Colgan, my wonderful editor, for seeing the potential in this story and knowing exactly what had to be done to realize it,

John Rudolph, my agent, for being a tireless advocate for this book and for me throughout the process,

Jaime Zollars for her beautiful cover illustration, and Barbara Grzeslo for the fine book design,

Kerry McManus, Toni Willis, Sue Cole, and all the good people at Boyds Mills Press who touched this book in some way,

Christian Dahlager, Alison Nowak, Jenny Lock, Larina Alton, Eric Jensen, and Christopher Zumski Finke for being so generous with their time and insight as they read early versions of this story,

My teachers throughout the years, but especially James C. Schaap, for mentoring me and providing words of encouragement exactly when I needed to hear them, and Luanne Goslinga, for urging me, when I was a high school freshman, to name aloud my dream of writing a novel someday,

My parents, Jim and Sue DeYoung, for reading to me when I was young,

And to Sarah, of course, for being my toughest critic, my biggest fan, and my partner in life and love and parenthood.

447